NEW YORK TIMES BESTSELLING
AUTHOR OF *THE IRON DUKE*

MELJEAN BROOK

D0016958

Heart of Steel

A NOVEL OF THE IRON SEAS

**BERKLEY
SENSATION**

$7.99 U.S.
$8.99 CAN

ISBN 978-0-425-25104-1

5 0 7 9 9

EAN

Heart of Steel

"More charming and funnier and less angsty . . . than *The Iron Duke,* but the world-building is just as rich, the characters [are] incredibly vibrant, and the love story [is] just as amazing."

—*Dear Author*

"Immense fun and a wonderful read."   —*Fangs for the Fantasy*

"This outstanding steampunk series combines dangerous women, adventurous men, endless action, and scintillating romance. Lovers of this genre really can't do better than to pick up one of these tales."   —*All About Romance*

"Brook is of a rare breed of authors. Each book is better than the last. Her novels are filled with intrigue, adventure, and steamy romance. *Heart of Steel* is the perfect blend of all three."

—*Book Binge*

The Iron Duke

"I loved it! As far as I'm concerned, with *The Iron Duke*, Meljean Brook has brilliantly defined the new genre of steampunk romance. From now on, everyone will compare other writers in the genre to her."

—Jayne Ann Krentz, *New York Times* bestselling author

"A stunning blend of steampunk setting and poignant romance—smart, sexy, breathtaking, and downright addicting. I'm ready for the next book or anything else Meljean Brook writes."

—Ilona Andrews, *New York Times* bestselling author

"Engrossing steampunk adventure . . . a complex, gripping read."

—*Publishers Weekly* (starred review)

"With adept writing and a flair for creating believable worlds, Brook's first in the Iron Seas series showcases her masterful storytelling."   —*Booklist*

continued . . .

"A high seas/airborne adventure that's filled with zombies, pirates, and deadly betrayal. Along with the pulse-pounding adventure, there's plenty of serious sizzle for readers to enjoy."

—*RT Book Reviews* (4½ stars)

"I absolutely loved this book . . . Everything from characters to world was done with care and precision . . . Any current fan of Ms. Brooks has to read this one and those who aren't fans should. Steampunk has never been written so well."

—*Night Owl Reviews*

Demon Forged

"Dark, rich, and sexy, every page makes me beg for more!"

—Gena Showalter, *New York Times* bestselling author

"Another fantastic book in a beautifully written series. [It] has all the elements I love in Meljean's books—strong, gorgeously drawn characters, a world so real I totally believe it, and the punch of powerful emotion."

—Nalini Singh, *New York Times* bestselling author

"A dark, gripping read . . . The characters are brilliant, and the breathtaking romance, vivid setting, and darkly delicious adventure will immerse readers in this spellbinding world until the satisfying conclusion."

—*RT Book Reviews*

Demon Bound

"An excellent entry in a great series . . . Another winner as the multifaceted Guardian saga continues to expand in complexity while remaining entertaining . . . As complex and beautifully done as always."

—*Book Binge*

"Be prepared for more surprises and more revelations . . . Brook continues to deliver surprising characters, relationships, paranormal elements, and plot twists—the only thing that won't surprise you is your *total* inability to put this book down."

—*Alpha Heroes*

"Raises the bar on paranormal romance for sheer thrills, drama, and world-building, and hands-down cements Brook's place at the top of her field."

—*Romance Junkies*

Demon Night

"Meljean is now officially one of my favorite authors. And this book's hero? . . . I just went weak at the knees. And the love scenes—wow, just wow."

—Nalini Singh, *New York Times* bestselling author

"This is the book for paranormal lovers. It is a phenomenal book by an author who knows how to give her readers exactly what they want . . . a story that is dangerous, sexy, scary, and smart. *Demon Night* delivers all that and more . . . [It] is the epitome of what a paranormal romance should be! I didn't want to put it down."

—*Romance Reader at Heart*

"Poignant and compelling with lots of action, and it's very sensual. You'll fall in love with Charlie, and Ethan will cause your thermometer to blow its top. An excellent plot, wonderful dialogue . . . Don't miss reading it or any of Meljean Brook's other novels in this series."

—*Fresh Fiction*

"An intense romance that will leave you breathless . . . I was drawn in from the first page."

—*Romance Junkies*

Heart of Steel

MELJEAN BROOK

BERKLEY SENSATION, NEW YORK

THE BERKLEY PUBLISHING GROUP
Published by the Penguin Group
Penguin Group (USA) Inc.
375 Hudson Street, New York, New York 10014, USA

Penguin Group (Canada), 90 Eglinton Avenue East, Suite 700, Toronto, Ontario M4P 2Y3, Canada
(a division of Pearson Penguin Canada Inc.) • Penguin Books Ltd., 80 Strand, London WC2R 0RL,
England • Penguin Group Ireland, 25 St. Stephen's Green, Dublin 2, Ireland (a division of Penguin
Books Ltd.) • Penguin Group (Australia), 250 Camberwell Road, Camberwell, Victoria 3124, Australia
(a division of Pearson Australia Group Pty. Ltd.) • Penguin Books India Pvt. Ltd., 11 Community
Centre, Panchsheel Park, New Delhi—110 017, India • Penguin Group (NZ), 67 Apollo Drive,
Rosedale, Auckland 0632, New Zealand (a division of Pearson New Zealand Ltd.) • Penguin Books
(South Africa) (Pty.) Ltd., 24 Sturdee Avenue, Rosebank, Johannesburg 2196, South Africa

Penguin Books Ltd., Registered Offices: 80 Strand, London WC2R 0RL, England

This is a work of fiction. Names, characters, places, and incidents either are the product of the author's
imagination or are used fictitiously, and any resemblance to actual persons, living or dead, business
establishments, events, or locales is entirely coincidental. The publisher does not have any control over
and does not assume any responsibility for author or third-party websites or their content.

HEART OF STEEL

A Berkley Sensation Book / published by arrangement with the author

PUBLISHING HISTORY
Berkley Sensation trade paperback edition / November 2011
Berkley Sensation mass-market edition / July 2012

Copyright © 2011 by Melissa Khan.
"Tethered" by Meljean Brook © 2012 by Melissa Khan.
Excerpt from *Riveted* by Meljean Brook copyright © 2012 by Melissa Khan.
Cover photos by Claudio Marinesco.
Cover design by Rita Frangie.
Interior text design by Kristin del Rosario.

ISBN: 978-0-425-25104-1

BERKLEY SENSATION®
Berkley Sensation Books are published by The Berkley Publishing Group,
a division of Penguin Group (USA) Inc.,
375 Hudson Street, New York, New York 10014.
BERKLEY SENSATION® is a registered trademark of Penguin Group (USA) Inc.
The "B" design is a trademark of Penguin Group (USA) Inc.

PRINTED IN THE UNITED STATES OF AMERICA

10 9 8 7 6 5 4 3 2 1

ALWAYS LEARNING   **PEARSON**

Archimedes Fox and the Last Adventure

London, England
May 23

O! brilliant Zenobia,

It is time to brush up on your knowledge of Venice, for I have determined that it will be the site of my next adventure. As a practical man of good sense and judgment, I am well aware that it might be my last adventure (as all of them might have been) so please forgo the warnings, lamentations over daft brothers, insults to my intellect, and etc. in your reply. The moment after I post this letter I will be en route to Bath, where I am boarding the first available passenger flight to the New World and the University in Wien, where I will waltz through their lovely map archives. Please pray that the airship does not combust over the Atlantic, that I do not have to share a cabin with a minister or one of those absurdists who believes he can discern a man's character by studying the shape of his skull, and that we are not beset upon by pirates or mercenaries—unless that mercenary is she who freed us from patriarchal tyranny, because I would like to finally express our gratitude. I should do it while wearing my yellow waistcoat. Do you think she would fall immediately in love with me, or would I need to charm her for a full hour?

I have delivered your manuscript to The Lamplighter Gazette *and enclosed their bank check. You ought to begin asking them to pay in livre; English money is worth nothing, and will not be until they are better recovered from the Horde occupation.*

I am off! Yours,
Archimedes

P.S. You should title it Archimedes Fox and the Ravenous Cadavers of Venice.

Fladstrand, Upper Peninsula, Denmark
June 7

My dearest brother,

When you meet our favorite mercenary, I recommend wearing
only *your yellow waistcoat—her hysterical laughter will*
afford you another thirty seconds of life before she recovers
her wits and runs you through.

   I will not stab you, but my *hysterical laughter began at the*
word rational *and continued on for a good hour after finishing*
your letter. Do you not remember that you considered Venice
before? Not long after poor Bilson ran off, and you still fever-
ish and vomiting from an assassin's poison. Venice! *you*
cried. Marco Polo was imprisoned there after he returned
from the Mongol territories along the Silk Road, and in prison
he penned his mad writings about the machines of war the
Horde were creating! *And then,* Leonardo! While the Horde's
war machines were held back at the Hapsburg Wall, the great
men of Europe convened in Venice, and da Vinci was among
them, inventing weapons to hold back the Horde! Surely there
must be something left in the city!

   How is it that you are as stupid now, in your full senses, as
you were half out of your mind with sickness? Must I remind
you that when the zombie infection came across the Hapsburg
Wall and it was discovered that the creatures would not cross
water, almost everyone in that region fled to Venice? Must I
also remind you that blowing the bridges did not save them—
and that once the infection reached the city, only the few who
made it to a boat escaped? There is not a building or a foot of
dry land in Venice that a zombie does not stand upon, and
they are more numerous there than anywhere else in Europe.
Only a few years ago, even you *in all of your dim-witted, thick-*
skulled rationality deemed it too dangerous.

   No, I cannot believe that you've forgotten. So although you
do not mention it, your Awful Dilemma must have raised its
ugly head again. You must be desperate indeed. You also had
planned to go to the Ivory Market, not to the New World after
London. Did an assassin find you? It is the only explanation

I can find for such a foolish move, even from you. Does he know the name you travel under now? Should I be looking out my window for a sign of the Horde's elite guard?

Lovingly,
Zenobia

P.S. I intend to call it Archimedes Fox and the Idiotic Impossible Quest. *Anyway, there is no point. A survey by Bishop Mendi reported that most of the buildings along the canals were all underwater, as were the streets, and that zombies filled every inch of dry land. Overgrown with moss and vines, nothing on paper could possibly have survived. It is a fool's errand, brother.*

Wien, Ludwig Principality, Johannesland
June 27

Z—

Regarding the Awful Dilemma: So far, he has sent only bumbling fools to kill me. You know that he has much better at his disposal, who will not give any sign of their coming. I cannot return his goods, but returning their value may appease him—and I'm far more likely to find such a treasure in a city that I haven't already picked over, and that wasn't emptied while its population fled to the New World.

Tomorrow I am bound for Copenhagen. A man claims that he's developed a breathing device for underwater that doesn't take two to operate. If I keep to the canals, I will avoid the zombies.

What airship captain dared to take Bishop Mendi to Venice? My only worry was finding someone to take me directly to the city, because they must fly too close to Horde outposts and the occupied territories across the sea. Now you say someone did?

Archimedes

P.S. It will be Archimedes Fox and the Astonishing Discovery.

Fladstrand
July 3

Idiot,

By now you will have looked up the scientific article and know that Mendi was aboard Lady Corsair. *Do not do the same, brother. You will never reach Venice. If you are lucky, she will only hang you naked and upside down from her bow like she did that Castilian comte—but more likely, she will open you from gut to gullet like she did Bloody Bartholomew, then feed your dismembered limbs to megalodons.*

Zenobia

P.S. Archimedes Fox and the Merciless Mercenary.

Copenhagen
July 19

O! doubting Zenobia,

How will she know who I am? Like you, I resemble our departed Mother, and no one suspects anything of Archimedes Fox, Adventurer. Even if I do see someone I knew, I no longer wear a beard and have dropped two stone since my last run to Horde territory.

I have purchased the underwater breathing device, along with a glider contraption that converts into a waterproof satchel to carry any letters or writings, so that it is useful after I leave the airship rather than dead weight. I have already jumped from a balloon and the glider maneuvers perfectly. You can see for yourself when I visit next week. You will not be able to resist taking a jump.

He has also repaired my grapnel and spring-loaded ma-

chetes at my wrists. I am ready to flee from zombies—though I much prefer it when you write me fighting them.

Yours,
Archimedes

P.S. Archimedes Fox and His Brilliant Acquisitions.

Chatham, England
September 6

Zenobia—

Quickly, for Lady Corsair *is about to depart, and I must hand this letter over to the porter before the captain fires the engines.*

The Iron Duke is aboard. I have been recognized and exposed by that damned pirate, but I still live. I wore my yellow waistcoat. I'm certain that our favorite mercenary rather fancied me before she threatened to slit my throat. She relented when I reminded her that she would lose out on the price of my passage—and I am certain that she also recalled that she will receive a quarter of my salvage, if any.

I have learned her name: Yasmeen. She's as magnificent as I'd hoped, and I'm tempted to write poetry celebrating her green eyes, tight breeches, and sharp blades. If she gives me the least bit of encouragement, I will fall in love.

If I do not return, you should make an arrangement with her to provide stories for new adventures. I am certain that she would agree, as long as she receives a percentage of your royalties—and as long as those royalties don't come in English pounds. She is a mercenary, not a fool.

Completely wrecked and ridiculous,
Archimedes

P.S. Do not begin scheming yet! I shall return, of course. I will be three weeks in Venice, add on a few days for the flight;

*you should expect a letter this time next month, and my visit
a few days after—unless I have found something worth taking
to auction. If I have, I will head directly to the Ivory Market,
but I will send a letter regardless, including every detail of the
encounter between* Archimedes Fox and the Captivating Captain Cutthroat.

Venice
October 8

Zenobia,

*You are expecting a letter this week, but I am only now writing
it. I've little hope that you will be able to read the words when
you eventually receive it; the ink bleeds on the damp paper
even as I stroke my pen. Everything in Venice is damp, grown
over with mold and ivy.*

*It has taken me almost seven days to travel half a mile,
though when I first arrived, I was traveling the same distance
through the canals in an hour. The breathing apparatus works
perfectly. The food pack that the inventor in Copenhagen
promised was watertight began leaking swamp water within
a day, however, and my supplies rotted within a week—even
my gunpowder is soaked and my pistols are useless. I dare not
risk the same leaks in my satchel. I have made an Astonishing
Discovery, one that will solve my Awful Dilemma. Yet it will
be all for naught if my discovery becomes wet.*

*If I were a practical man of good sense and judgment, I
would abandon the treasure and make an attempt to recover
it later, or take the risk that the satchel would remain watertight. But we both know that if I do not pay off this debt soon,
I will not have another chance. I have killed too many of his
assassins. Soon, he will send one that I cannot possibly defeat.*

*So I am on foot, traveling from deteriorating roof to dete-
riorating roof. Fifteen minutes ago, it began raining, and I've
taken shelter in one of the upper chambers of a palazzo.
Water has flooded the ground levels, and so the zombies are
trapped in the building—God knows how long they have been*

*trapped here, three hundred years perhaps—and I have pro-
vided them their first entertainment in as long. I can hear
them mobbing the door. But I am in luck. Unlike most of the
houses, the wood has not rotted, and the interior walls still
stand. I will try to take a rest while it rains, but I fear sleeping
too long.*

I am late returning to the airship. By some miracle, Lady
Corsair *still waits for me. I can see her white balloon from
my window, hovering over the rusted ruins of the great basilica, exactly where I asked her captain to meet me a week ago.
Was it only my waistcoat, is it the remainder of my payment,
or does she have tender feelings for me? If it is not that, I
must make certain that she eventually comes to care for me.
I have had much time to think, and I have heard that extreme
hunger clears the mind. I have seen that she respects the
Iron Duke—a man who Gives Orders—and so to win her
heart, perhaps I will affect the same attitude when I next
see her.*

*That must be soon. I cannot hold out hope that she will
wait much longer.*

*The airship is only a mile away. I have searched for a boat
or a gondola, but every one of them must have been taken
centuries ago when people fled the zombie infection, or has
sunk. I think that the chamber door might serve as a raft,
however—keeping me dry while I paddle through the canal,
where the aviators will certainly see me. I will only have to
remove the hinges and throw it over the balcony into the
canal. If it floats, I will lower myself on top of it. When I
remove the hinges, however, I will have no protection—and I
do not know how many zombies are in the palazzo.*

*Night approaches, and the light grows dim. I would con-
tinue, but my spark lighter is also damp. Rusted iron hinges
and a valiant fight await. What an adventure that will be,
Geraldine—and I trust that you will write a fine ending for me.*

*With love and affection, always,
Wolfram*

P.S. *You will never read this, of course, because I will prevail,* *and paddle my door to the airship, where I will take charge and give orders. Once there, I will discard this letter and write another. Do not despair, sister! Soon, you will hold in your hands the adventures of* Archimedes Fox and the Mysterious Lady Corsair.

Chapter 1

Yasmeen hadn't had any reason to fly her airship into the small Danish township of Fladstrand before, but her reputation had obviously preceded her. All along the Scandinavian coast, rum dives served as a town's only line of defense against mercenaries and pirates—and as soon as the sky paled and *Lady Corsair* became visible on the eastern horizon, lights began appearing in the windows of the public houses alongside the docks. The taverns were opening early, hoping to make a few extra deniers before midday . . . and the good citizens of Fladstrand were probably praying that her crew wouldn't venture beyond the docks and into the town itself.

Unfortunately for them, *Lady Corsair*'s crew wasn't in Fladstrand to drink. Nor were they here to cause trouble, but Yasmeen wasn't inclined to let the town know that. Let them tremble for a while. It did her reputation good.

Dawn had completely faded from the sky by the time *Lady Corsair* breached the mouth of the harbor. Standing behind the windbreak on the quarterdeck, Yasmeen aimed her spyglass at the skyrunners tethered over the docks. She recognized each airship—all of them served as passenger ferries between the Danish islands to the east and Sweden to the north. Several heavy-bottomed cargo ships floated in the middle of the icy harbor, their canvas sails furled and their wooden hulls rocking with each swell. Though she knew the skyrunners, Yasmeen couldn't identify every ship in the water. Most of Fladstrand fished or farmed—two activities unrelated to the sort of business Yasmeen conducted. Whatever cargo the ships carried probably fermented or flopped, and she had no interest in either until they reached her mug or her plate.

When *Lady Corsair*'s long shadow passed over the flat,

sandy shoreline and the first rows of houses overlooking the sea, Yasmeen ordered the engines cut. Their huffing and vibrations gave way to the flap of the airship's unfurling sails and the cawing protests of seabirds. Below, the narrow cobblestone streets lay almost empty. A steamcart puttered along beside an ass-drawn wagon loaded with wooden barrels, but most of the good people of Fladstrand scrambled back to their homes as soon as they spotted *Lady Corsair* in the skies above them— hiding behind locked doors and shuttered windows, hoping that whatever business Yasmeen had wouldn't involve them.

They were in luck. Today, Yasmeen only sought one woman: Zenobia Fox, author of several popular stories that Yasmeen had read to pieces, and sister to a charming antiquities salvager whose adventures Zenobia based her stories on . . . a man whom Yasmeen had recently killed.

Yasmeen had also killed their father and taken over his airship, renaming her *Lady Corsair*. That had happened some time ago, however, and no one would consider Emmerich Gunther-Baptiste *charming*, including his daughter. Yasmeen had seen Zenobia Fox once before, though the girl had been called Geraldine Gunther-Baptiste then. As one of the mercenary crew aboard Gunther-Baptiste's skyrunner, Yasmeen had watched an awkward girl with mousy-brown braids wave farewell to her father from the docks. Zenobia had been standing next to her pale and worn-looking mother.

Neither she nor her mother had appeared sorry to see him go.

Would Zenobia be sorry that her brother was dead? Yasmeen didn't know, but it promised to be an entertaining encounter. She hadn't looked forward to meeting someone this much since Archimedes Fox had first boarded *Lady Corsair*—and before she'd learned that he was really Wolfram Gunther-Baptiste. Hopefully, her acquaintance with his sister wouldn't end the same way.

A familiar grunt came from Yasmeen's left. *Lady Corsair*'s quartermaster stood at the port rail, consulting a hand-drawn map before casting a derisive look over the town.

Yasmeen tucked her scarf beneath her chin so the heavy wool wouldn't muffle her voice. "Is there a problem, Monsieur Rousseau?"

Rousseau pushed his striped scarf away from his mouth, exposing a short black beard. With gloved hands, he gestured to the rows of houses, each one identical to the next in all but color. "Only that they are exactly the same, Captain. But it is not a problem. It is simply an irritant."

Yasmeen nodded. She didn't doubt Rousseau could find the house. Though hopeless with a sword or gun, her quartermaster could interpret the most rudimentary of maps as if they'd been drawn by skilled cartographers. That ability, combined with his expressive grunts and eyebrows that could wordlessly discipline or praise the aviators—and a booming voice for when nothing but words would do—made him the most valuable member of Yasmeen's crew. A significant number of jobs that Yasmeen took in Europe required *Lady Corsair* to navigate through half-remembered terrain and landmarks. Historical maps of the continent were easy to come by, but matching their details to the overgrown ruins that existed now demanded another skill entirely—that of reading the story of the Horde's centuries-long occupation.

Though not ruins, Fladstrand's identical rows of houses told another tale, one that Yasmeen had seen repeated along the Scandinavian coastlines.

In one of her adventures, Zenobia Fox had written that the worth of any society could be judged by measuring the length of time it took for dissenters to go from the street to the noose. Zenobia might have based that statement on the history of her adopted Danish home; a few centuries ago, that time hadn't been long at all. Soon after the Horde's war machines had broken through the Hapsburg Wall, they'd deliberately created a zombie infection that had outpaced their armies, and the steady trickle of refugees from eastern Europe had opened into a flood. Those who had the means bought passage aboard a ship to the New World, but those without money or connections migrated north, pushing farther and farther up the Jutland Peninsula until they crowded the northern tip. Some fled across the sea to Norway and Sweden, while others bargained for passage to the Danish islands. Those refugees who were left built rows of shacks, and waited for the Horde and the zombies to come.

Neither had. The Horde hadn't pressed farther north than

the Limfjord, a shallow sound that cut across the tip of Jutland, separating it from the rest of the peninsula and creating an island of the area. The same stretch of water stopped most of the zombies; walls built near the sound stopped the rest. Poverty and unrest had plagued the crowded refugees, and the noose had seen frequent use, but the region slowly recovered. Rows of shacks became rows of houses. Now quiet and stable, many of the settlements attracted families from England, recently freed from Horde occupation, and from the New World. Zenobia Fox and her brother had made up one of those families.

"We are coming over her home now, Captain." Rousseau's announcement emerged in frozen puffs. "How long do you intend to visit with her?"

How long would it take to say that Archimedes had discovered a valuable artifact before Yasmeen had killed him, and then pay the woman off? With luck, Zenobia Fox would send Yasmeen on her way in a fit of self-righteous fury—though it might be more entertaining if she tried to send Yasmeen off with a gun. In both scenarios, Yasmeen would hold on to all of the money, which suited her perfectly.

"Not long," she predicted. "Lower the ladder."

Rousseau relayed the order and within moments, the crew unrolled the rope ladder over *Lady Corsair*'s side. Yasmeen glanced down. Zenobia's orange, three-level home sat between two identical houses painted a pale yellow. Unlike many of the houses in Fladstrand, the levels hadn't been split into three separate flats. The slate roof was in good repair, the trim around the windows fresh. Lace curtains prevented Yasmeen from looking into the rooms. Wrought-iron flower boxes filled with frosted-over soil projected from beneath each windowsill.

Large and well-tended, the house provided ample room for one woman. Yasmeen supposed that much space was the best someone could hope for when living in a town—but she couldn't have tolerated being anchored to one place. Why would Zenobia Fox? She had based her adventures on her brother's travels, but why not travel herself? Yasmeen couldn't understand it. Perhaps money had been a factor—although by the look of her home, Zenobia didn't lack funds.

No matter. After Yasmeen paid her off, Zenobia wouldn't need to base her stories on Archimedes' adventures. She could go as she pleased—or not—and it wouldn't be any concern of Yasmeen's.

As this was a social visit, she removed the guns usually tucked into her wide crimson belt. At the beginning of the month, she'd traded her short aviator's jacket for a long winter overcoat. The two pistols concealed in her deep pockets provided enough protection, and were backed up by the daggers tucked into the tops of her boots, easily reachable at mid-thigh. She checked her hair, making certain that her blue kerchief covered the tips of her tufted ears. If necessary, she could use her braids to do the same, but the kerchief was more distinctive. There would be no doubt exactly who had dropped in on Zenobia Fox today.

The ladder swayed when Yasmeen hopped over the rail and let the first rung catch her weight. Normally she'd have slid down quickly and landed with an acrobatic flourish, but her woolen gloves didn't slide over the rope well—and Yasmeen didn't know how long she would be waiting on the doorstep. Cold, stiff fingers made drawing a knife or pulling a trigger difficult, and she wouldn't risk them for the sake of a flip or two.

The neighbors might have appreciated it, though. All along the street, curtains twitched. When Yasmeen pounded the brass knocker on Zenobia's front door, many became bold enough to show their faces at the windows—probably thanking the heavens that she hadn't knocked at their doors.

No one peeked through the curtains at Zenobia's house. The door opened, revealing a pretty blond woman in a pale blue dress. Though a rope ladder swung behind Yasmeen and a skyrunner hovered over the street, the woman didn't glance up.

A dull-witted maid, Yasmeen guessed. Or a poor, dull-witted relation. Yasmeen knew very little about current fashion, but even she could see that although the dress was constructed of good materials and sewn well, the garment sagged in the bodice and the hem piled on the floor.

The woman must have recognized Yasmeen as a foreigner, however. A thick Germanic accent gutted her French, the common trader's language. "May I help you?"

"I need to speak with Miss Zenobia Fox." Yasmeen smoothed the Arabic from her own accent, hoping to avoid an absurd comedy of misunderstandings on the doorstep. "Is she at home?"

The woman's eyebrows lifted in a regal arch. "I am she."

This wasn't a maid? How unexpected. Despite the large house and obvious money, Zenobia Fox opened her own door?

Yasmeen liked surprises; they made everything so much more interesting. She'd never have guessed that the tall, awkward girl with mousy-brown braids would have bloomed into this delicate blond thing.

She'd never have guessed that her first impression of the woman who penned clever and exciting tales would be "dull-witted."

Archimedes certainly hadn't been. Quick with a laugh or clever response, he'd perfectly fit Yasmeen's image of *Archimedes Fox, Adventurer.* She could see nothing of Archimedes in this woman—not in the soft shape of her face or the blue of her eyes, and certainly not in her manner.

Blond eyebrows arched ever higher. "And you are . . . ?"

"I am *Lady Corsair*'s captain." Kerchief over the hair, indecently snug trousers, a skyrunner that had once belonged to Zenobia's father floating over her house—was this woman completely blind? "Your brother recently traveled on my airship."

"Oh. How can I help you?"

How can I help you? Disbelieving, Yasmeen stared at the woman. Could an aviator's daughter be this sheltered? What else could it mean when the captain of a vessel appeared on her doorstep? Every time that Yasmeen had knocked on a door belonging to one of her crew members' families, the understanding had been immediate. Sometimes it had been accompanied by denial, grief, or anger—but they all knew what it meant when Yasmeen arrived.

Perhaps because Archimedes had been a passenger rather than her crew, Zenobia didn't expect it. But the woman should have made the connection by now.

"I have unfortunate news regarding your brother, Miss Fox."

The "unfortunate news" must have clued her in. Zenobia blinked, her hand flying to her chest. "Archimedes?"

At a time like this, she called him "Archimedes"—not Wolfram, the name she'd have known him by for most of her life? Either they'd completely adopted their new identities, or this was an act.

If it was an act, this encounter was already turning out better than Yasmeen had anticipated. "Perhaps we can speak inside, Miss Fox."

With an uncertain smile, the other woman stepped back. "Yes, of course."

Zenobia led the way into a parlor, her too-long skirts dragging on the wooden floor. A writing desk sat by the window, stacked with blank papers. No clickity transcriber's ball was in sight, and no ink stained Zenobia's fingers. Obviously she hadn't been busy penning the next Archimedes Fox adventure.

A shelf over the fireplace held several baubles, some worn by age, others encrusted with dirt—a silver snuff box, a lady's miniature portrait, a gold tooth. All items that Archimedes had collected during his salvaging runs in Europe, Yasmeen realized. All items that he'd picked from the ruins but hadn't sold. Why keep these?

Her gaze returned to the lady in the miniature. Soft brown hair, warm eyes, a plain dress. The description seemed familiar, though Yasmeen knew she hadn't seen this portrait before. No, it was a description from *Archimedes Fox and the Specter of Notre Dame*. In the story, he'd found a similar miniature clutched in a skeleton's fingers, and the mystery surrounding the woman's identity had led the adventurer to a treasure hidden beneath the ruined cathedral.

How odd that she'd never realized that fictional miniature had a real-life counterpart. That she'd never imagined him digging it out of the muck somewhere and bringing it to his sister. That he'd once held it, as she did now.

The stupid man. Yasmeen lied often, and so she didn't care that he'd lied about his identity when he'd arranged for passage on her airship. It *did* matter that she'd allowed Emmerich Gunther-Baptiste's son aboard her airship without knowing who he really was. A threat had sneaked onto *Lady Corsair* right beneath her nose.

She couldn't forgive him for that. Too often, she led her crew into dangerous territory, and they would only be loyal to a strong captain. A captain they could trust. She'd invested years making certain that her crew could trust her, and rewarded their loyalty with piles of money. There wasn't enough gold in the world to convince a crew to follow a fool, and Archimedes Fox had come close to turning her into one when he'd boarded her ship. She'd only been saved because he'd openly thanked her for killing his father, negating his potential threat. He'd become a joke, instead.

And later, when he *had* threatened her in front of the crew, she'd gotten rid of him . . . maybe.

Yasmeen turned to Zenobia, who stood quietly in the center of the parlor, tears trailing over her pink cheeks.

"So Archimedes . . . is dead?" she whispered.

Funny how that terrible accent came and went. "As dead as Genghis Khan," Yasmeen confirmed. "Unfortunate, as I said. He was a handsome bastard."

"Oh, my brother!" Zenobia buried her face in her hands.

Yasmeen let her sob for a minute. "Do you want to know how he died?"

Zenobia lifted her head, sniffling into a lace handkerchief, her blue eyes bright with more tears. "Well, yes, I suppose—"

"I killed him. I dropped him from my airship into a pack of flesh-eating zombies."

The other woman had nothing to say to that. She stared at Yasmeen, her fingers twisting in the handkerchief.

"He tried to take control of my ship. You understand." Yasmeen flopped onto a sofa and hooked her leg over the arm. Zenobia's face reddened and she averted her gaze. Not accustomed to seeing a woman in trousers, apparently. "He hasn't come around for a visit, has he?"

"A visit?" Her head came back around, eyes wide. "But—"

"I tossed him into a canal. Venice is still full of them, did you know?"

Zenobia shook her head.

"Well, some are more swamp than canal, but they are still there—and zombies don't go into the water. We both know that Archimedes has escaped more dire situations than that, at least according to his adventures. You've read your brother's stories, Miss Fox, haven't you?"

"Of . . . course."

"He mentions the canals in *Archimedes Fox and the Mermaid of Venice*."

"Oh, yes. I'd forgotten."

There was no Mermaid of Venice adventure, yet the woman who'd supposedly written it didn't even realize she'd been caught in her lie. Pitiful.

But the question remained: Did that mean Zenobia wasn't the author after all, or was this not Zenobia? Yasmeen suspected the latter.

"So he might be alive?" Zenobia ventured.

"He still had most of his equipment and weapons. But if he hasn't contacted you after two months now . . . he must be dead, I'm sorry to say." Yasmeen meant it, but she wasn't sorry for the next. "And so he is the second man in your family I've killed."

Surprise and dismay flashed across her expression. "Yes, of course. My . . ."

She trailed off into a sob. Oh, that was good cover.

"Father." Yasmeen helped her along.

"Yes, my father. After he . . . did something terrible, too."

That was good, too. Smart not to suggest that the armed mercenary sitting in the room had been at fault.

Obviously this woman had no idea who she'd targeted by taking Zenobia Fox's place. If asked, she'd probably say that her father's surname had been Fox, as well. She wouldn't know that Emmerich Gunther-Baptiste had once tried to roast a mutineer alive. Yasmeen hadn't had any love for the mutineer—but she'd shot him in the head anyway, to put him out of his misery. She'd shot Gunther-Baptiste when he'd ordered the other mercenaries to put her on the roasting spit in the mutineer's place. When Yasmeen realized that she'd attained a beauty of an airship in the process, she'd shot every other crew member who tried to take it from her.

After a while, they'd stopped trying and began taking orders, instead.

"Did he do something terrible? I've killed so many people,

I forget what my reasons were." A lie, but Yasmeen wasn't the only one telling them. Now it was time to find out this woman's reasons. With a belabored sigh, she climbed to her feet. "That's all I've come to say. A few of Archimedes' belongings are still in my ship. Would you like to have them, or should I distribute them among my crew?"

"Oh, yes. That's fine." For a moment, the blond seemed distracted and uncertain. Then her shoulders squared, and she said, "My brother hired you to take him to Venice, and was searching for a specific item. Did he find it . . . before he died?"

Ah, so that's what it was. Yasmeen had spoken to three art dealers about locating a buyer for the sketch Archimedes Fox had found in Venice. A flying machine drawn by the great inventor Leonardo da Vinci, the sketch was valuable beyond measure.

She'd demanded that the dealers be discreet in their inquiries. Not even Yasmeen's crew knew what she'd locked away in her cabin. But obviously, someone had talked.

"It was a fake," Yasmeen lied.

No uncertainty weakened Zenobia's expression now. "I'd still like to have it. As a memento."

Yasmeen nodded. "If you'll show me out, I'll retrieve it for you now." She followed the woman from the parlor and into the hallway. "Will you hold the rope ladder for me? It's so unsteady."

"Of course." All smiles, Zenobia reached the front door.

Yasmeen didn't give her a chance to open it. Slapping her gloved hand over the blond's mouth, she kicked the woman's knees out from beneath her. Yasmeen slammed her against the floor and shoved her knife against the woman's throat.

Quietly, she hissed, "Where is Zenobia Fox?"

The woman struggled for breath. "I am Zen—"

A press of the blade cut off the woman's lie. Yasmeen smiled, and the woman's skin paled.

Her smile frequently had that effect.

"The dress doesn't fit you. You've tried to take Zenobia's place but you've no idea who you're pretending to be. Where is she?" When the woman's lips pressed together in an unmistakable response, Yasmeen let her blade taste blood. The woman whimpered. "I imagine that you're working with someone. You didn't think of this yourself. Is he waiting upstairs?"

The woman's eyelids flickered. Answer enough.

"I can kill you now and ask him instead," Yasmeen said.

That made her willing to talk. Her lips parted. Yasmeen didn't allow her enough air to make a sound.

"Is Zenobia in the house? Nod once if yes."

Nod.

"Is she alive?"

Nod.

Good. Yasmeen might not kill this woman now. She eased back just enough to let the woman respond. "Where did you hear about the sketch?"

"Port Fallow," she whispered. "Everyone knew that Fox boarded your airship in Chatham. We realized he must have found the sketch on his last salvaging run."

Yasmeen had only spoken to one art dealer in Port Fallow: Franz Kessler. Damn his loose tongue. She'd make certain he wouldn't talk out of turn again—especially if this had been his idea. This woman certainly hadn't the wits to connect the sketch to Zenobia.

"You and the one upstairs. Was this his plan?"

Yasmeen interpreted her hesitation as a yes—and that this woman was afraid of him. She'd chosen the wrong person to fear.

"What airship did you fly in on?"

"*Windrunner.* Last night."

A passenger ship. "Who's upstairs?"

"Peter Mattson."

Miracle Mattson, the weapons smuggler. A worthy occupation, in Yasmeen's opinion, but Miracle Mattson sullied the profession. He always recruited partners to assist him with the job, but as soon as the cargo was secure, the partners conveniently disappeared. Mattson usually claimed an attack by Horde forces or zombies had killed them, yet every time, he miraculously survived.

No doubt that if this woman had secured the sketch for him, she'd have disappeared soon, too.

"Did he hire you just for this job?"

"Yes. I'm grateful. I've been out of work for almost a full season."

A full season of what? This woman's soft hands had never seen any kind of labor. Only one possibility occurred to her.

"Are you an *actor*?"

The blond nodded. "And dancer. But the company replaced us all with automatons."

If this woman's performance was an example, Yasmeen suspected that the automatons displayed more talent. "All right. Call Mattson down."

"Why?"

"Because I'll make you a better deal than he will." Yasmeen wouldn't kill her, anyway. Probably. "And because if I go upstairs holding a knife to your throat, he might do something stupid to Miss Fox."

"Oh." Her eyes widened. "How do I call him?"

God save her from idiots. "I'll let you up. You'll open and close the door as if you've just come in from outside, and yell, 'I've got it! Come see!' You'll be very excited."

"And then?"

"I'll do the rest." She waited for the woman to nod, then hauled her up. "Now."

Yasmeen had to give the actress credit; even with a knife at her throat, she played her part perfectly. Mattson must have realized that something was amiss, however. No answer came from upstairs. Perhaps he'd taken a look out the window and saw that Yasmeen had never climbed back up to the airship. She didn't think he'd heard their whispers. When noise finally came from above, the walls and ceiling muffled Mattson's low voice.

"*Get up.*" A thud followed the rough order, the sound of a body falling onto the floor, then the slow shuffle of feet and the heavy, regular tread of boots. "*Stay quiet. Don't try anything stupid.*"

Ah, Mattson. Always predictable. Of course he wouldn't come down alone and risk his neck. He was bringing Zenobia with him, probably with a gun at her head—and he likely intended to offer the woman's life in exchange for the sketch. Yasmeen couldn't imagine why he thought it would work. Did she look that foolish? After she handed over the sketch, nothing would stop him from shooting them all.

No, Mattson was the only fool here. Knife still at the actress's throat, Yasmeen dragged her into the parlor. She stopped with her back to the window, the actress in front of her and facing the parlor entry—an escape in one direction, a shield in the other. If Mattson began firing, Yasmeen preferred that the bullets didn't hit her first, and the actress's body hid the gun Yasmeen tucked into the sash at her waist. No need to draw it yet. Her blade would do until she tired of talking.

As if suddenly realizing what her position meant, the actress emitted a desperate squeak. Yasmeen hissed a warning in her ear, and the woman fell silent, trembling.

The tread of boots reached the stairs. Slowly, they came into view, Zenobia's pale bare feet and Mattson's shining black boots. Her hands had been bound at the wrists. He must have surprised Zenobia while she slept. Rags knotted her brown hair, and she wore a sturdy white sleeping gown. A wide strip of torn linen served as a gag, stretched tight between dry lips and tied behind her head. Her eyes were the same shade as Archimedes'—emerald, rather than the yellowish-green of Yasmeen's—and bright with anger and fear.

Zenobia's gaze locked on Yasmeen's, but aside from a quick glance at the woman's face and at the revolver that Mattson held to the side of her throat, Yasmeen didn't bother to pay her any attention. Mattson served as the greater threat here, and Yasmeen wasn't a fool to be taken unawares while making cow-eyes at a writer whose work she adored.

Though Zenobia was a tall woman, Mattson's height left him completely exposed from chin to crown. Idiot. He ought to have been crouching, but perhaps he considered any sort of cower an affront to his dignity. Sporting a neatly trimmed blond mustache and wearing a pressed jacket and trousers, he stood straight as any soldier, but Yasmeen had never known any soldier who took offense as easily as Peter Mattson. The sun reddened his skin rather than tanned it, so that he always appeared flushed with anger—as he often was, anyway. Belligerent the moment anyone questioned his character and big enough to pose a challenge, he'd become a favorite amongst the regulars at the Port Fallow taverns who found their entertainment by picking fights.

He stopped just at the entrance to the parlor, standing in the foyer and with Zenobia filling the door frame. He'd have a direct line to the front door—so he also kept a shield and an escape. The fool. If Mattson didn't want to be shot, he shouldn't have come down the stairs with his gun already drawn.

Pale blue eyes met hers. "Lady Corsair."

Captain Corsair. Her airship was a lady, but Yasmeen certainly wasn't. She didn't bother to correct him, however. Everyone called her by the wrong name. No surprise he did, too.

"Mr. Mattson," she said. "I believe you are here to make an exchange. Your woman for mine, perhaps?"

"I want the sketch."

Of course he did—and of course he'd never get it. But as a woman of business, she was curious as to what he'd offer. "In exchange for what?"

"Nothing."

"So generous, yet I'm not tempted to accept."

"You should be. Give the sketch to me now, and my associates might let you live. I'll tell them you cooperated."

Yasmeen couldn't have that. "And ruin my reputation? I don't think so, Mr. Mattson—especially since *you* usually kill your associates. I doubt I'll have much to fear from them."

"You have no idea who you're up against." His gaze left Yasmeen and fell to the knife at the actress's throat. His lips curled. "Do you think I care whether she dies? Go on, slit her—"

The crack of Yasmeen's pistol cut off the rest. Mattson's brains splattered against the foyer wall. His body dropped, gun clattering against the wood floor—and luckily, not discharging on impact.

Eyes wide, Zenobia lifted her bound hands and touched the blood sprayed across her cheek and temple. She startled from her stupor and almost tripped over Mattson's boots when the actress suddenly shrieked, ducking and covering her ears. A bit late for that—though if she kept screaming, Yasmeen might shoot her just to shut her up.

She tucked the weapon back into her sash and crossed the room to nudge Mattson's thigh with her toe. Dead. Yasmeen knew many people who seemed to function well without brains, but her bullet had definitely done this one in. Blood pooled beneath his head.

"A hell of a mess," Yasmeen said, and slipped her blade between Zenobia's wrists, slicing through the ties. She did the same to the woman's gag. "If you need to vomit, I suggest you do it on him. There's less to clean up."

"Thank you," Zenobia rasped. The corners of her mouth were raw. "But I don't need to."

Then she glanced down at Mattson's face, bent over, and did.

Chapter 2

Yasmeen found the maids tied hand to foot on the floor in a bedroom upstairs. She cut through the ropes, accepted their thank-yous, and when Zenobia rushed into the room a moment later, left them to do their weeping and dressing.

She retreated downstairs, where the actress had finally stopped screaming. Yasmeen led her outside and signaled to Rousseau. He sent down two aviators to escort the woman up to the airship while Yasmeen returned to the parlor. Her cabin girl, Ginger, brought Yasmeen's favorite mint tea down from *Lady Corsair*, and relayed that Rousseau had locked the actress in the stateroom. Good enough for now. Yasmeen would let Zenobia decide what to do with her.

When Zenobia came downstairs, she stopped and studied Mattson's body for a long moment. Jaw set, she stepped over him and poured herself a cup before sitting on the chair opposite Yasmeen.

"You've come to tell me that Wolfram is dead," she said.

"Yes." Yasmeen studied the other woman's expression. She saw resignation. Sadness. But no sudden grief. "You aren't surprised."

"I was supposed to receive word from him two months ago. By the third week, I had to accept that a letter wasn't coming. So I have had some time to accustom myself to the idea that he wasn't returning." She sipped her tea before leveling a direct stare at Yasmeen. "Wolfram isn't part of your crew. So why have you really come?"

"He was on my ship. He wasn't my crew, but he was my responsibility," she said, marveling at the other woman's composure. How was it that Yasmeen didn't feel as steady as his sister looked? She slipped her fingers into her pocket, producing her cigarillo case and lighter. "Do you mind if I . . . ?"

"Yes," Zenobia said bluntly. "It reeks."

"If you smoke one, too, you won't notice it as much." Yasmeen smiled when the other woman only fixed a baleful look on the proffered cigarillo. She slid it back into the silver case. "I have his belongings and his purse—minus the five livre he owed to me for his passage."

Five livre was a large sum of money, but Zenobia didn't blink. "I'll take them. And the da Vinci sketch?"

"You'd be a fool to keep it in your possession."

"As aptly demonstrated today."

Though dryly stated, Yasmeen could see that the other woman knew it was the truth. "Mattson will only be the first."

"Yes." Zenobia took another sip before coming to a decision. "Sell it, then."

Exultation burst through Yasmeen's veins. She contained it, and merely nodded. "I will."

A tiny smile curved the woman's mouth. "I understand that on dangerous flights, the airship captain receives twenty-five percent of the salvage."

Yasmeen met Zenobia's steady gaze. "For this job, I'll take fifty percent."

Zenobia studied her, as if weighing the chances of coming to a different agreement. Finally, she took another sip and said, "I suppose fifty percent of an absurd fortune is still a ridiculous amount of money."

Clever woman. *This* was the Zenobia that Yasmeen had expected to find. She wasn't disappointed. "I'll see that you receive your half when the sale is finalized."

"Thank you." She hesitated, and some of the hardness of negotiation dropped from her expression, revealing a hint of vulnerability. "I heard a little bit of what you said about the zombies, Captain. Is it true that you deliberately threw him into a canal?"

Yasmeen shook her head. "It was the middle of the night. I couldn't know where he landed."

Lies. Her eyes saw well enough in the dark. She'd watched him splash into the canal. She'd known that with luck and brains, he'd survive—and her crew wouldn't think she'd gone soft.

But even for Archimedes Fox, his chances of survival were slim. She wouldn't give this woman any more false hope than she offered herself.

"I see." Zenobia's fingers tightened on her cup. "If, on your travels, you see him with the other zombies . . ."

"I'll shoot him," Yasmeen promised.

"Thank you." The vulnerability left her face, replaced by sudden amusement. "Speaking of your travels, Captain . . . you've tossed the source of my stories overboard."

Yasmeen looked pointedly at Zenobia's fingers. Unlike the actress's, ink stained their tips. "You're writing."

"Only letters."

"You won't need the income when I've sold the sketch."

"You misunderstand me." Zenobia set her cup on the table and leaned forward. "I don't need the income now. I write because I enjoy it. Will you leave your airship when you've received your portion of the money?"

"No." When she left her lady for the last time, it would only be because her dead body had been dragged away.

"It is the same with me for writing. I won't stop, not voluntarily. But I do need inspiration for the stories. With the basis for Archimedes gone, I'll have to create another character. Perhaps a woman this time." She sat back, her gaze narrowed on Yasmeen's face. "What about . . . *The Adventures of Lady Lynx?*"

Yasmeen laughed. Zenobia didn't.

"You're not joking?"

The other woman shook her head. "You live a life of adventure and meet with many different people, particularly the villainous sort."

Yasmeen *was* the villainous sort. "Yes, but—"

"I'll write them. You receive twenty-five percent of royalties."

The sudden need for a cigarillo almost overwhelmed her. A drink, a hit of opium. Anything to calm her jumping nerves. Was she going to agree to this?

Yes. Of course she was. Even without royalties, she would have.

But still, no need to be stupid about it.

"Fifty percent of royalties," Yasmeen countered. "Paid quarterly in French currency or gold."

"Twenty-five percent. You send me reports of where you go, who you see, what you eat. I need to know how long it takes you to fly to each location. I want your impressions of your crew, your passengers, and everyone you meet."

Impossible. "I won't share everything."

"I won't name them. I only seek authenticity, not a reproduction of the truth."

"I *won't* share everything," Yasmeen repeated.

For a moment, Zenobia looked as if she'd try to negotiate that, too. Then she shrugged. "Of course you can't. But let us begin with your background. Thirteen years ago, you joined my father's crew. After you killed him—well done, by the way—you sold *Lady Corsair*'s services as a mercenary in the French and Liberé war, where you worked both sides, depending upon who paid the most. You earned the reputation of being willing to do anything for money. But what happened before that? Where were you before my father's ship?"

In a very pretty cage. But did she want to share that? Yasmeen shook her head. "As far as I'm concerned, my life started when I boarded *Lady Corsair*. Make up what you like about what came before."

"All right. A mysterious past will only make Lady Lynx more fascinating," she mused. "I could deliver the background in bits, like crumbs."

"Whatever you like." Yasmeen stood. "I'll send the other reports to you regularly."

Zenobia's expression sharpened as she rose. "Where are you heading after you leave Fladstrand? Do you have a job now?"

"No. We'll spend the day traveling to Port Fallow. Mattson was only here because an art dealer talked about the sketch. I need to have a conversation with him."

Then she'd fly to England, and ask the Iron Duke to hold the sketch safe at his London fortress until she found a buyer. If word of the sketch had begun to spread, she couldn't risk carrying it with her any longer.

Zenobia glanced at Mattson's body. "A man has been killed in my house, and I suppose I must explain it. Will you come with me to speak with the magistrate? This time of morning, he's always at the Rose & Thorn taking his breakfast. You can give him your account and I'll buy drinks for your crew afterward."

And let word spread that Yasmeen had run to the authorities after Miracle Mattson had threatened her? That she'd answered to a magistrate? Not a chance.

"He'll believe that I shot Mattson without my word on it," she told Zenobia. "But if you like, I'll have the actress taken to him. She's on my lady now, and we can fly her wherever you wish—whether to the Rose & Thorn or to a mob of zombies in Paris."

Zenobia smiled. "The magistrate will do, thank you. May I come with you? For research."

Yasmeen didn't care. She nodded, then waited outside while the other woman retrieved her coat. The frigid air shivered through her. Lighting a cigarillo, she let the smoke warm her lungs and ease the tiny shakes.

A few neighbors had ventured outside, gaping up at *Lady Corsair*. When Zenobia finally emerged, she waved to them and called a good morning, and Yasmeen couldn't decide whether surprise or relief added such volume to the "Good morning!"s they called to her in return. Feeling the cold down to her toes, she started for the rope ladder.

"Captain Corsair?" When Yasmeen turned, Zenobia avoided her gaze. She seemed to find the act of pulling on her gloves either fascinating, or extraordinarily difficult. "I thought we might walk rather than fly."

"I thought you might want to have a look at my lady. For authenticity." And because the boilers kept the cabins heated and the deck beneath her feet warm.

"I've seen her." She shot a glance upward. "When she was my father's."

Damn it. Yasmeen wouldn't ask what had happened. She'd seen enough of Emmerich Gunther-Baptiste's cruelties to guess.

"We walk, then."

She signaled for Rousseau to follow overhead, then started for the taverns along the bay. Zenobia's boot soles clipped across the cobblestones as she matched Yasmeen's long stride. So loud. Yasmeen's soft leather boots weren't as warm, but at least they were quiet—and didn't announce her approach from hundreds of yards away.

"I can't remember if I've thanked you for saving us." Zenobia's cheeks had already flushed with cold. "That was quite the crack shot. I never saw you draw your weapon or aim."

That was the point. "If Mattson had seen it, you'd be dead."

"Are you infected, then? I have heard the bugs make a person stronger and quicker."

Infected with Horde nanoagents, the millions of tiny machines that lived in her body like industrious little ants. Though Yasmeen's nanoagents weren't exactly like the two strains Zenobia was probably familiar with—the "bugs" used by the Horde to control large populations, or the ones that infected the zombies—Yasmeen didn't bother to explain the difference. The woman had only asked if they'd made her fast and strong—and they had.

"Yes," she said.

"Mattson must not have been, then."

Oh, he had been. His bruises had always healed too quickly after each tavern brawl for him to have been anything but infected. But Yasmeen only nodded. "He was slower," she said.

"Are you originally from one of the occupied territories, then?" Zenobia asked. "Or did you take a blood transfusion and infect yourself later?"

"Is this a search for a crumb?"

"For your background? Yes."

"Surely you've already picked up a few."

"Yes, but they tell me little. Your accent, for instance. Perhaps you were born in the occupied territories of northern Africa or farther east. Perhaps you came from one of the tribes who fled to the southern American continent when the Horde moved across the Arabian Peninsula."

Only her accent was of note? Was Zenobia trying to be delicate? Or, considering the woman's hatred toward her father, perhaps she simply didn't want to echo him. "And my complexion?"

"Tells me nothing. In the New World alone, I cannot name a city that you couldn't have hailed from. Who does not have family that is native or African, or some mix of both in their blood?"

Spoken like a true Liberé supporter. "As your father often pointed out, your family doesn't."

"Yes, well. Even that means little as far as discerning your origin by complexion. Without the sun, Wolfram is as pale as I, yet after a summer spent diving along the Gold Coast, he returned as dark as you. How many of your own crew are, too?—and how many are from the New World?"

Most of them. "So I could be from anywhere. Your options are open. You cannot make a story out of that to please your readers?"

"Of course, but it does not satisfy *my* curiosity." She huffed out a breath. "At least tell me how you became such a crack shot. Did you learn before you joined my father's crew? Of course you did, since you shot him in the head, too. You must be from the New World, then—perhaps along the frontier borders, or in the disputed territories. I cannot imagine anywhere in the Horde empire that they would teach a young girl to fire a gun."

"Can't you? I imagine they'd have reason to in the walled cities. If a zombie came over the barrier, a girl's ability to shoot it in the head might be her—and the city's—only chance of surviving."

"That is true enough. But I didn't realize the Horde armed the citizens in the occupied cities. They didn't in England."

"They don't. But they should." Amused by Zenobia's second exasperated huff, Yasmeen smiled and blew a stream of smoke through her teeth. "I think every woman should be armed, including writers in quiet little townships like Fladstrand."

The woman's color deepened. "I have a weapon. But I don't sleep with it."

"I do." Yasmeen kept so many weapons in her bed that her friend Scarsdale had once called it an orgy.

"And I am grateful that you were so well prepared. I'll admit that I despaired when I thought you only had a blade."

"I never *only* have a blade—but the only weapon I bring to a conversation is a knife. A gun means the talking is over."

"Oh. Oh! I must make Lady Lynx say that." Without a break in her stride, Zenobia tore off her right glove with her teeth before digging out a paper and pencil from her pocket. She scribbled the line as she walked.

Inspiration was to be taken so directly? Yasmeen slowed to accommodate the other woman's preoccupation, wondering if

she'd often done the same when walking with Archimedes . . .
who was charming and fun, much like the character Zenobia
had created. Yasmeen had assumed it also reflected the sister,
but Zenobia seemed far more sober and practical than her
brother had been.

"How much of Archimedes came from Wolfram, and how
much was you?"

Zenobia tucked her notes away. "All Wolfram. It was easy,
though, because I know him well. Lady Lynx will likely have
more of me in her."

Because she didn't know Yasmeen as well. Fair enough.
"And so she'll be French? Prussian?"

"Oh, no. English again, probably, just as I made Archimedes."

She'd already decided? "Then why the interrogation about
my background?"

"My own curiosity, as I said—and to build a better character. But the English bit, it's the audience, you understand. The
New World is fascinated with the Horde occupation and those
who've lived under their heel, and the English like to see
themselves as heroes—and I sell more copies all around."

Which meant more money for Yasmeen, too. The mention
of heroes worried her, however. She'd carefully cultivated her
reputation to protect her lady and her crew; she wouldn't see
it destroyed with a stroke of a pen. "They won't know she is
me, will they?"

"No. They'll assume it is based on that lady detective, the
one every newssheet from London has been writing about. She
was your passenger once, I believe?"

Ah, Mina Wentworth. Yes, the detective had spent some
time on *Lady Corsair*. Yasmeen liked her, even though the
woman had been idiot enough to go soft for a man—especially a man like the Iron Duke. He captained a ship well, and
was one of the few people Yasmeen would trust at the helm of
her lady, but in pursuit of the detective he was as dense and as
possessive as any man who ever lived.

Yasmeen nodded. "She'll do."

"Perhaps I will give Lady Lynx a background connected to
the Horde rebellion—I could use some of Wolfram's old letters to establish that, and the stories would be of her current

adventures." She paused, as if considering that, before continuing. "Yes, that will work very well. Were you ever part of the rebellion, Captain?"

More crumbs? This trail would lead Zenobia all the way to Constantinople—what little remained of it after the Horde had crushed the rebellion there.

"I've never been a part of it," she said truthfully. "But I've had business dealings with the rebels. I'll share the details with you in my letters."

"Thank you. If there is anything that you think she *shouldn't* be, Captain Corsair, I would appreciate you telling me now. I can't promise that you'll like what I write, but I prefer not to be . . . inaccurate."

Or to offend her, Yasmeen guessed. She appreciated that. "Don't let her be an idiot, always threatening someone with a gun. Only let her draw it if she intends to use it."

Zenobia blushed again. "Unlike Archimedes Fox?"

In her stories. "Yes. You *have* to assume that someone will try to kill you while you're deciding whether or not to shoot them. So by the time the gun comes out, that decision should have been made."

"I see." Her notes were in her hand again, but Zenobia didn't add to them. "Is that what Wolfram did—wave his gun around?"

"Yes."

Her eyes closed. "Idiot."

So Yasmeen had often said, but his sister should know the rest of it. "Stupid, yes. But also exhausted. He returned a week late, and Venice wouldn't have given him time to rest or eat." A month spent in the ruined city with too many zombies and too few hiding places. "When he climbed up to the airship, he ordered my crew to set a heading for the Ivory Market. I refused and told him to sleep it off before making demands. That's when he drew his gun and—"

She broke off. Zenobia was shaking her head, a look of disbelief on her face. "You *waited* for him?"

Yasmeen had. Blissed on opium and wondering why the hell she was still floating over a rotten city. But she'd known. She'd read through each damn story of his, each impossible escape, and she'd known he'd make it out of Venice, too. So she'd waited. And when he'd finally returned to her ship, she'd had to toss him back—believing he might still make it.

But after he'd tried to take her ship, she wouldn't wait for him again.

"I waited," she finally answered. "He still owed me half of his fee."

Zenobia studied her expression before slowly nodding. "I see."

Yasmeen didn't know what the woman thought she saw—and didn't care, either. She was more interested in the reason Archimedes had been late. "He couldn't have known I'd wait," she said. "And the sketch wouldn't have been worth anything to him if he died there."

Zenobia's chin tilted up at an unmistakable angle, a combination of defiance and pride—as if she felt the need to defend her brother. "Perhaps he was late for the same reason you stayed: money."

Yes, Yasmeen believed that. If she had followed Archimedes' orders and flown directly to the Ivory Market, he could have quickly sold the sketch. Which suggested that he'd risked his life because if he'd left Venice without the sketch, he'd have been dead anyway.

He'd owed someone, and whoever it was intended to collect. Few debts would need a da Vinci sketch to cover them, though. Even small salvaged items like those Archimedes usually collected sold high at auction. Of the baubles in Zenobia's parlor, the miniature alone would purchase a luxury steamcoach.

"Does he really owe so much?"

"Yes."

"So you changed your names and went into hiding." Not that Archimedes Fox had done a good job of hiding, traipsing all over the world as he did.

"Yes." Zenobia's sigh seemed to hang in the air. They'd almost reached the Rose & Thorn before she spoke again. "Is there anything else? For Lady Lynx," she added, when Yasmeen raised a brow.

"Yes." The walk here had reminded her of one rule that she'd been fortunate to have learned before Archimedes Fox had boarded her airship. "Don't let her go soft for a man."

Zenobia stopped, looking dismayed. "A romance adds excitement."

"With a man who tries to take over everything? Who wants to be master of her ship, or wants the crew to acknowledge that she's his little woman?" Yasmeen sneered. God, but she imagined it all too easily. "What man can tolerate *his* woman holding a position superior to him?"

Zenobia apparently couldn't name one. She grimaced and pulled out her notes. "Not even a mysterious man in the background? More interest from the readers means more money."

Yasmeen wasn't always for sale, and in this matter, the promise of extra royalties couldn't sway her. "Don't let her go soft. Give her a heart of steel."

"A heart of steel," Zenobia repeated, scribbling. She looked up. "But . . . why?"

Why? Shaking her head, Yasmeen signaled for the rope ladder, which would take her back to her lady. Zenobia had begun that morning tied up and gagged, then had a gun shoved against her throat and her body used as a shield—and yet she had to ask *Why?*

The answer was obvious. "Because there's no other way to survive."

Yasmeen flew into Port Fallow from the east, high enough that the Horde's combines were visible in the distance. After their war machines had driven the European population away and the zombies had infected those remaining, the Horde had used the Continent as their breadbasket. They'd dug mines and stripped the forests. Machines performed most of the work—and what the machines couldn't do was done by Horde workers living in enormous walled outposts scattered across Europe. Soldiers within those compounds protected the laborers from zombies and crushed any New Worlder's attempt to reclaim the land.

But thirty years before, Port Fallow had been established as a small hideaway for pirates and smugglers on the ruins of Amsterdam, and had boomed into a small city when the Horde hadn't bothered to crush it. Either they hadn't considered the city a threat or they hadn't been able to afford the effort. Yasmeen suspected it was the latter.

Two generations ago, a plague had decimated the Horde population, including those living in the walled compounds. A rebellion within the Horde had been gaining in popularity for years, and after the plague, had increased in strength from one end of the empire to the other. Now, the Horde was simply holding on to what they still had, not reclaiming what they'd lost—whether that loss was a small piece of land like Port Fallow or the entire British isle. No doubt that in the coming years, more pieces would fight their way out from under Horde control.

Just as well. A five-hundred-year reign was long enough for any empire. Yasmeen would be glad to see them gone. But then, she'd be glad to see a lot of people gone—and currently, Franz Kessler was at the top of her list.

It wouldn't be difficult to find him. Port Fallow contained three distinct sections between the harbor and the city wall, arranged in increasing semicircles and divided by old Amsterdam's canals: the docks and warehouses between the harbor and the first canal, with the necessary taverns, inns, and bawdyrooms; the large residences between the first and second canals, where the established "families" of Port Fallow made their homes; and beyond the second and third canals, the small flats and shacks where everyone else lived. Kessler's home lay in the second, wealthy ring of residences, and he sometimes ventured into the first ring—but he'd never run toward the shacks, and only an idiot would try to climb the wall. Few zombies stumbled up to Fladstrand, but not so here. The plains beyond the town teemed with the ravenous creatures, and gunmen continually monitored the city's high walls. Kessler couldn't run that way. The harbor offered the only possibility for escape, but Yasmeen wasn't concerned. Though dozens of boats and airships were anchored at Port Fallow, not a single one could outrun *Lady Corsair*.

And of those ships, only one made her glad to see it: *Vesuvius*. Mad Machen's blackwood pirate ship had been anchored apart from the others, floating in the harbor near the south dock. Yasmeen ordered *Lady Corsair* to be tethered nearby. She leaned over the airship's railing, hoping to see Mad Machen on his decks. A giant of a man, he was always easy to spot—but he wasn't in sight. She caught the attention of his quartermaster, instead, which suited her just as well. Yasmeen liked Obadiah Barker almost as much as she liked his captain.

With a few signals, she arranged to meet with him and descended into the madness of Port Fallow's busy dockside. Men loaded lorries that waited with idling engines and rattling frames. Small carts puttered by, the drivers ceaselessly honking a warning to move out of their way, and rickshaws weaved between the foot traffic. A messenger on an autogyro landed lightly beside a stack of crates, huffing from the exertion of spinning the rotor pedals. Travelers waiting for their boarding calls huddled together around their baggage, while sailors and urchins watched them for a drop in their guard and an opportunity to snatch a purse or a trunk. Food peddlers rolled squeaky wagons, shouting their prices and wares.

Yasmeen lit a cigarillo to combat the ever-present stink of fish and oil, and waited for Barker to row in from *Vesuvius*. His launch cut through the yellow scum that foamed on the water and clung to the dock posts.

Disgusting, but at least the scum kept the megalodons away. In many harbors in the North Sea, a sailor couldn't risk manning such a small boat—barely more than a mouthful to the giant sharks.

His black hair contained beneath a woolen cap, Barker tied off the launch and leapt onto the dock, approaching her with a wide grin. "Captain Corsair! Just the woman I'd hoped to see. You owe me a drink."

Possibly. Yasmeen made so many bets with him, she couldn't keep track. "Why?"

"You said that if I ever lost a finger, I'd cry like a baby. But I didn't. I cried like a *man*."

Yasmeen frowned and glanced at his hands. Obligingly, he pulled off his left glove, revealing a shining, mechanical pinky finger. The brown skin around the prosthetic had a reddish hue to it. Still healing.

She met his eyes again. "How?"

"Slavers, two days out. I caught a bullet." He paused, and his quick smile appeared. "Literally."

"And the slavers?"

"Dead."

Of course they were. Mad Machen wouldn't have returned to port otherwise. He'd have chased them down.

She looked at the prosthetic again. Embedded in his flesh, the shape of it was all but indistinguishable from a real pinky, the knuckle joints smooth—and, as Barker demonstrated by wiggling his fingers—perfectly functional. Incredible work.

"Your ship's blacksmith is skilled." So skilled that Yasmeen would have lured her away from *Vesuvius* if the idiot girl hadn't been soft on Mad Machen.

"She's brilliant," Barker said. He replaced the glove and glanced up at *Lady Corsair*. "None of your aviators have come down. Is this just a stopover?"

"Yes." Even if it hadn't been, she wouldn't leave the airship unmanned while the sketch was aboard. "I'm only here long enough to have a word with someone. We'll fly out in the morning."

"A word with someone?" Barker had known her long enough to guess exactly what that meant. "Would you like me to come along?"

She didn't need the help, but she wouldn't mind the company. "If you like."

"I would. I'll fetch a cab. Where to?"

His brows lifted when she told him their destination, but he didn't say anything until they'd climbed into the small steamcoach.

He had to raise his voice over the noise of the engine. "Why Kessler?"

"He talked when he wasn't supposed to."

"Is anyone dead?"

"Miracle Mattson. Kessler gave information to him."

Barker's frown said that he was having the same thought Yasmeen had: Men like Kessler and Mattson didn't usually do business together. Though plenty of art was smuggled into the New World, it wasn't something Mattson ever handled. If Kessler needed weapons, yes. Not a sketch.

The coach slowed over the bridge across the first canal, crowded with laborers passing from the third rings to the docks. Three ladies wearing narrow lace ruffs around their

necks and dresses of embroidered linen over corsets and crin-
olines stood at the other end, as if waiting for the bridge to
clear of rabble before they crossed it. Yasmeen watched them,
amused. Five years ago, the residents of the second circle had
tried building bridges that were only for their use. That
arrangement hadn't lasted beyond the first week.

By the time the bridge was out of Yasmeen's sight, the
ladies still hadn't crossed it. She looked forward again. Kessler's home lay around the next corner.

"Do you want me to go in with you?" Barker asked.

"Just wait in the cab. I doubt I'll be long."

"What do you plan to do?"

The same that she'd done to Mattson. "Make certain he
won't talk again."

The cab rounded the corner and slowed. Yasmeen frowned,
rising from the bench for a better look. Wagons and carts
blocked the street ahead, each one loaded with furniture and
clothes. Men and women worked in pairs and small teams,
hauling items from Kessler's house.

Barker whistled between his teeth. "I don't think he's talking now."

Barker was right, damn it. The households in Port Fallow
operated in the same way as a pirate ship. When the head of
the business household died, the household's members voted
in a new leader who took over the family. But Kessler's business was in knowing people, and keeping those names to himself. No one could carry on in his profession, and his blood
family had no claim—and so everyone who worked for him,
from his clerk to his scullery maid, would split his possessions
and sell them for what they could.

Seething, Yasmeen leaned out of the coach and snagged
the first person who passed by. "What happened to Kessler?"

The woman, staggering under the weight of a ceramic vase,
kept it short. "Maid found him in bed. Throat slit. No one
knows who."

He'd probably flapped his lips about someone else's business. Yasmeen let the woman go.

"So we turn around, then?" the driver called back.

If he could. Carts, wagons, and people were in motion all
around them, crowding the narrow street. Several more had

already parked at their rear. A steamcart in front of them honked, and earned a shouted curse in response. Beside them, a wagon piled high with mattresses lurched ahead, giving them more visibility but nowhere to move.

The cart that took its place didn't block Yasmeen's view. Her gaze swept the walkway across the street—and froze on one figure. *Oh, hell.* Her muscles tensed, ready to fight . . . or flee.

Dressed in a simple black robe, the woman stood facing Kessler's house. Unlike everyone else, she wasn't in hurried motion. She watched the activity with her hands demurely folded at her stomach and her head slightly bowed. Gray threaded her long brown hair. She'd plaited two sections in the front, drawing them back . . . hiding the tips of her ears.

As if sensing Yasmeen's gaze, she looked away from Kessler's home. Her stillness didn't change; only her eyes moved.

Yasmeen had been taught to stand like that—to hold herself silent and watchful, her weight perfectly balanced, her hands clasped. She'd been taught duty and honor. She'd been taught to fight . . . but not like this woman did. Yasmeen knew that under the woman's robes was a body more metal than flesh. Designed to protect. Designed to kill.

It was difficult not to appreciate the deadly beauty of it—and hard not to pity her. Yasmeen couldn't see the chains of honor, loyalty, and duty that bound the woman, but she knew they were there.

And she knew with a single look that the woman pitied her in return. That she saw Yasmeen as a woman adrift and without purpose—a victim of those who'd failed to properly train and care for her.

Yasmeen lowered her gaze first; not out of cowardice, but a message that she wouldn't interfere with the woman's business here—and she certainly wasn't stupid enough to challenge her.

Next to Yasmeen, Barker eyed the woman with a different sort of appreciation. Of course he did. She'd been designed to provoke that response.

"Don't try," Yasmeen warned him.

"She's a little older, but I like the mature—"

"She's *gan tsetseg*, one of the elite guard who serves the Horde royalty and the favored governors."

Barker didn't hide his surprise—or his doubt. He studied

the woman again, as if trying to see beneath the demure posture and discover what had earned the elite guard their terrifying reputation.

He wouldn't see it. The elite guard earned that reputation when they dropped that modest posture, not when they wore it.

He shook his head. "She's not Horde."

"She's not a Mongol," Yasmeen corrected. The Horde weren't a single race. In five hundred years, their seed and the empire had spread too far for every member of the Horde to be Mongols. Only royalty and the officials from the heart of the empire were still relatively unmixed, but since they provided the face of the Horde to New Worlders and the occupied territories, the assumption that everyone in the empire were Mongols had been carried along with it. "Just as not every man and woman of African descent born on the southern American continent is a Liberé spy . . . or a cart-puller."

His face tightened. "Cart-puller?"

"I am saying that you are *not*. You cannot even hear it without being ready to go to war again?"

"Because you haven't been called one," he said, before adding, "I wasn't a spy."

Yasmeen snorted her response.

He grinned and glanced over at the woman again. "Why is she here? No one in Port Fallow is Horde royalty."

"Then she's here to kill someone, or to take them back to her *khanate*." Obviously not Yasmeen, or she'd already be dead. Instead, she was forgotten. The woman was watching the house again . . . waiting. "Whatever her purpose, don't get in her way."

"All right." Barker leaned forward and tapped on the cab driver's shoulder before dropping a few deniers into his palm. "Shall we walk? By the time we return to the docks, I'll be ready for that drink."

Yasmeen would be ready for three.

Yasmeen drank three, but not quickly. Barker took his leave after finishing the one she owed him, but Yasmeen stayed on, nursing hers until they were warm. Some nights in a tavern were meant for drinking, and others were meant for listening. Fortunately, nothing she heard suggested that word of the sketch had gone beyond Mattson and Kessler. She turned down one job—a run to the Ivory Market along the Gold Coast of Africa. Lucrative, but he hadn't been willing to wait until she returned from England, and she wasn't inviting anyone onto her airship before the sketch was in the Iron Duke's fortress.

She hadn't always been able to turn down jobs. Now she had enough money that she could be choosy. Even without the fortune that would come after selling the sketch, she could retire in luxury at any time—as could her entire crew.

She never would.

Midnight had come and gone when Yasmeen decided she'd heard enough. She emerged from the dim tavern into the dark and paused to light a cigarillo, studying the boardwalk along the docks. It was just as busy at night as during the day, but the crowd was comprised of more drunks. Some slumped against the buildings or slept beside crates. Groups of sailors laughed and pounded their chests at the aviators—some of them women, Yasmeen noted, and not one of them alone. The shopgirls and lamplighters walked in pairs, and most of the whores did, too.

Yasmeen sighed. Undoubtedly, she'd soon be teaching some drunken buck a lesson about making assumptions when women walked alone.

She started toward the south dock, picking out *Lady Corsair*'s sleek silhouette over the harbor. Familiar pride filled her chest. God, her lady was such a beauty—one of the finest skyrunners ever made, and she'd been Yasmeen's for almost thirteen years now. She knew captains who didn't last a month—some who weren't generous toward their crew or not strict enough to control them. Some were too careful to make any money or too careless to live through a job.

She'd made money, and she'd lived through hundreds of jobs during the French war with the Liberé: scouting, privateering, moving weapons or personnel through enemy territory, destroying a specified target. Both the French and the Liberé officers sneered when she'd claimed that her only loyalties were to her crew and the gold, but they used her when they didn't have anyone good enough or fast enough to do what she could.

Then the war had ended—fizzled out, with the Liberé possessing the most territory and thereby considered the victor. All of the same animosities still simmered, but there wasn't enough gold left in the treasuries to pay for more fighting. So Yasmeen had left the New World, returned back across the Atlantic, and carved out her niche by taking almost any job for the right money.

Lately, that meant ferrying passengers over Horde territory in Europe and Africa—a route that most airships-for-hire would never take. Sometimes she acted as a courier, or she partnered with *Vesuvius* when Mad Machen carried cargo that needed airship support, fighting off anyone who tried to steal it from them.

A routine life, but still an exciting one—and the only kind of settling down that she would ever do.

Yasmeen flicked away her cigarillo, smiling at her own fancy. *Routines, excitement, and a particular version of settling down.* She'd have to record that thought and send it to Zenobia—along with an account of the little excitement that was about to take place.

Someone was following her.

A man had been trailing her since she'd left the tavern. Not some drunken idiot stumbling into a woman walking alone, but someone who'd deliberately picked her out—and if he'd seen her in the tavern, he must know who she was.

But he must not be interested in killing her. Anyone could have shot her from this distance. Instead, he tried to move in closer, using the shadows for cover. He needed lessons in stalking. Her pursuer paused when she did, and though he tried for stealth by tiptoeing, his attempts only made him more obvious. Of course, he couldn't know that Yasmeen was at her best during the night—and that she had more in common with the cats slinking through the alleys than the lumbering ape that had obviously birthed him.

She'd only taken a few more steps when he finally found his balls and called her name.

"Captain Corsair!"

The voice was young and quivering with bravado. He'd either taken a bet at the tavern or was going to ask for a position on her ship. Amused, Yasmeen faced him. A dark-haired boy wearing an aviator's goggles and short jacket stood quivering in the middle of the—

Pain stabbed the back of her leg. Even as she whipped around, her thigh went numb. An opium dart. *Oh, fuck.* She ripped it out, too late. Pumped with this amount, her mind was already spinning. Hallucinating. A drunkard rose from a pile of rags, wearing the gaunt face of a dead man.

No, not a drunkard. A handsome liar.

Archimedes Fox.

Yasmeen fumbled for her guns. Her fingers were enormous. He moved fast—or she was slow. Within a blink, he caught her hands, restrained her with barely any effort.

She'd kill him for that.

"Again?" he asked, so smooth and amused. "You'll have to try harder."

The bastard. She hadn't tried at all. And though she tried now, she sagged against him, instead—and for a brief moment, wondered if she'd fallen against a zombie. Each of his ribs felt distinct beneath her hands.

But zombies didn't swing women up into their arms. And they didn't talk.

"My sister sends her regards," he said against her cheek. "And I want my sketch."

"I'd have let you have it." She couldn't keep her eyes open. Her words slurred. "You just had to ask."

"Liar," he said softly. "You'd never have given it back."

Ah, well. He was right about that. But he might have been able to talk her down to forty percent. She began to make the offer, but couldn't form the words.

Blissful darkness swirled in and carried her away.

Chapter 3

Perhaps drugging the woman he intended to fall in love with wasn't the accepted method of kindling a passionate romance, yet Archimedes considered it the most sensible way to proceed. If Captain Corsair had killed him immediately, their relationship would have been just as tumultuous as he could have hoped, but much too short.

As it was, she'd hung on to consciousness longer than he'd expected. Infected with nanoagents, she should have dropped when the opium dart hit her, but she'd managed to reach for her guns. Another second or two, and she could have shot him. Death had galloped close. His heart still pounded from how near it had come.

All in all, a good start.

With a grin, he looked to Sven, whose wary gaze had locked on the captain's face as if he expected her to wake at any moment. "You'd be wise to return to Fladstrand tonight."

The young aviator nodded. "Any message for your sister?"

"Confirm that I received her express. I'll reply to her letter within a few days."

"I'll tell her." He pulled on the woolen cap that would keep his ears from freezing in the open seat of his skipper balloon. "I don't envy you when she wakes up."

Archimedes doubted that. Any boy who built his own flyer and regularly raced it around the North Sea had a taste for danger. Even if that taste wasn't as well-developed as Archimedes', any man who held this woman should be envied, no matter what she did upon waking.

Which might be sooner than he'd anticipated. The long muscles of her back flexed against his forearm as she stirred, turning her cheek away from his shoulder. A line formed between her dark brows. Even unconscious, she was aware that something was wrong. Perhaps dreaming of gutting him—except she'd probably be smiling, if that was the case.

He'd have liked to see her delectable lips curve when she opened her eyes, but he'd work for her smiles later. For now, he needed the sketch, and he'd risk her anger to recover it.

He wouldn't risk her reputation. A few of the drunks stumbling along the walk or rutting between the crates might have heard her name called or seen her fall into his arms, but they probably hadn't glimpsed the dart—and most of them probably wouldn't remember tomorrow, anyway. Those who did would assume she'd taken a man for a night's sport. When he carried her to the room he'd rented, however, Archimedes had to be more careful. There'd be others about in the boarding-house, and not all of them would be sloshing stupid with rum. Captain Corsair might forgive him for the opium dart, but wouldn't forgive a rumor that she'd been taken to his bed, unconscious and completely at his mercy.

Her long coat concealed her distinctive tall boots and black breeches, but the blue kerchief might as well have been a signal flag. He tugged at the silk tails tangled in her braids until the kerchief slipped from her head, then lifted her higher against his chest. Her face tipped back toward his shoulder, obscuring her angular features. The dark and a quick step should prevent anyone from realizing exactly who he held.

A damn quick step. He started into it as she stirred again— his heart still pounding, but feather-light against his ribs.

He'd known that she'd be in his arms one day. And he wasn't the least bit surprised that he hadn't gone about it in the usual way.

In the garret that served as his room, Archimedes changed out of the drunkard's rags and turned to find Captain Corsair awake and regarding him with narrowed eyes. His fingers stilled on the buckles of his emerald waistcoat.

She hadn't stirred again on the way to his room, hadn't made a single noise after he'd laid her on the narrow bed. Now she stared at him, her gaze a whetted blade. No confusion or uncertainty clouded her eyes. Only the thin ring of green around her dilated pupils told him that she was still blissed on opium.

"Captain," he greeted her. Unwilling to take his attention from her again, he left his boots lying on the floor and finished buckling his waistcoat. The emerald silk matched his eyes, and he was certain she'd notice. By the time he'd taken the two short steps to the side of the bed, he was certain she'd noticed everything—particularly the contraption locked around her left wrist and the pile of weapons on the bureau.

He glanced toward the knives and pistols. "How does your airship fly with you aboard? You've tucked enough steel and iron into your pockets to weigh down Father Calvin the Blowhard."

She smiled, and the curve of a soft mouth never seemed to have so many sharp edges. Archimedes knew that if he'd been a sensible man, he'd have run to the nearest priest—blowhard or not—fallen to his knees, and prayed that she wouldn't come after him. He'd heard of men who'd boldly hunted boilerworms across the Australian deserts freezing in terror at the sight of Captain Corsair's smile, but the shiver it gave Archimedes had nothing to do with fear.

Instead, he thrilled to the realization he hadn't had to work very hard for her smile after all.

As there was room on the mattress next to her hip, he sat. Her smile vanished. He suspected that if he'd run his fingers the length of her thigh, tension would have hardened her muscles to stone.

But although he wasn't always a sensible man, Archimedes didn't touch her. He *hadn't* touched her beyond the brisk, necessary search for weapons. And though it had killed him, he hadn't even touched her warm skin during that brief exploration, not even when he'd spotted the small key on the silver chain around her waist. Some actions crossed a boundary into unforgivable. Captain Corsair was uncharted territory, but he didn't think he'd crossed the line yet.

No need to mention that he'd sniffed her hair while searching through the thick strands for pins that she could use to stab him. *Tobacco and coconut.* He'd never smell either again without remembering the silken plaits that weaved the intricate crown, usually hidden beneath her kerchief. Without wondering whether she braided them herself, arms lifted like a dancer's and her neck arched.

And absolutely no need to mention the short black tufts at the tips of her ears. She'd purposely concealed them under her braids and kerchief, and he suspected that admitting the inadvertent discovery would leave her feeling as violated as shoving his hand between her legs.

She could keep her secrets. One day, when he nibbled on her ears, perhaps she'd reveal them.

"No doubt I missed a few weapons," he told her. "You've likely tucked some away in places that no man would search—at least, no man who intended to live."

Her eyes narrowed farther, but her gaze turned inward, as if searching out the truth of his statement. When she focused on him again, he saw anger and irritation, but nothing like his sister's description of the biting cold that had come over the captain's face before she'd shot Miracle Mattson.

If she hadn't believed that he'd kept her clothes on and his hands to himself, Archimedes knew he'd already be dead.

"Do you intend to live, Mr. Fox?" Blissed, her accent was strong, but she didn't slur the words.

"I always intend to live, Captain."

"You have a stupid way of going about it."

He grinned. "Not too stupid, as I'm still alive. Would I have been if I hadn't dosed you with the opium? You'd have seen me rise up out of those crates, assumed I was a threat, and shot me."

"I wouldn't have considered you a threat if you hadn't ambushed me."

True. "But it wouldn't have been as exciting."

This time, her smile didn't show the edge of her teeth, but he wasn't fool enough to consider himself safe. "Are you threatening me now, Mr. Fox?"

Until he'd turned around and found her watching him, Archimedes had considered it. The threat would have been simple: If she didn't turn the sketch over to him, he'd invite half of Port Fallow up to see her on his bed, wearing a slave bracelet. He wouldn't have made good on the threat, of course. No one else would ever see her like this. But the moment Archimedes had met her eyes, he'd realized that she'd never forgive him for simply speaking that threat.

Threatening her life was another matter entirely.

"Of course I am." He gestured to the room's single window, which offered a moonlit view of her airship hovering over the water. "You're going to invite me up to *Lady Corsair* and hand over the da Vinci."

"Or . . . ?"

His gaze flicked to the bracelet. Constructed of copper, the segmented casing concealed the delicate clockworks and springs inside, as well as a dozen small needles that pierced skin and injected a deadly dose of poison. A terrible device, it had been outlawed in most of the New World—and in Port Fallow, was ridiculously easy to obtain. The bracelet could only be removed if the segments were rotated in the correct order; the wrong sequence activated the springs, injecting the poison.

Of course, a bracelet that could be worn without fear wasn't enough—a slave could run away and live, as long as he took care not to twist the segments. Something had to guarantee the property would come back.

She sat up, running her fingers over the hairline joints in the copper casing. "Did you set the timer?"

"For one hour."

"These contraptions are notoriously unreliable."

"So am I." He rose, ducking his head beneath the steeply sloped roof. "The bracelet flatters you. I wouldn't bother to take these precautions with anyone else, but I know very well how quick you are."

After boarding her airship in Venice, he'd stood with his back to the rope ladder, pulled out his gun—useless though it was, the gunpowder soaked through—and aimed it at her. A moment later, Captain Corsair simply hadn't been standing in that spot anymore. She hadn't been anywhere on the deck. He'd barely had time to draw a breath before she'd come up behind him—*up the outside hull of her ship*—and dragged him over the gunwale.

Her lips pursed. "So the bracelet is your revenge, then."

"Revenge because you threw me off your ship?" Did she think he blamed her for that? Surprised, he shook his head. Someone would have to wrong him before he'd ever take revenge. "You were justified. No, that bracelet is only to make certain that you don't throw me off it again before you give me the sketch."

"I might still—and I'll make certain to drop you to the ground rather than the water this time."

"Ah!" Elation lifted through him. He braced his hands against the sloping roof and leaned in close. "I knew you spared me. Shall I tell you what I thought as you dangled me over the mob of zombies?"

"Return the favor and spare me whatever idiot thought it was."

"No, not idiotic." He waited until she looked up from the bracelet and met his eyes. "I thought, *Finally, the mysterious and beautiful Captain Corsair is holding me in her arms.* And I swore that you would again."

Her brows rose. "And what part of that *isn't* idiotic?"

"You'll see. I have a collection of fine waistcoats and a handsome face." He stepped back to let her take in the full effect of both, and her smile spread to the edge of a laugh. Perfect. "You've already proven susceptible to them, and refrained from killing me at least twice: when you discovered who my father was after I first boarded your airship, and again when you threw me from it. I'm certain that means we're destined to be together."

"That it does, but only until our business concludes—and I still want fifty percent."

If Archimedes could, he'd have given it to her. "You'll only get the standard twenty-five."

"I prefer your sister's offer."

"Mine isn't negotiable."

"Isn't it?"

"No."

She regarded him for a long moment before shrugging. "I suppose twenty-five percent is still a goodly sum," she said. "Can you give me any assurance that I'll receive it after the auction?"

"Do you trust my word?"

"No." Despite her smile, her eyes were hard as polished agates. "I'll take you to the Ivory Market on my lady."

"Can you give me any assurance that I'll reach the market alive?"

"Do you trust my word?"

He grinned. "No."

"Then we don't—"

"I'll see that you get your share," he said. "Because if you don't, I know you'll find me—and I'm tired of being chased down for money. So I'll find you instead."

"You won't need to find me. I'll meet you at the market."

Of course she would. He expected to see *Lady Corsair* riding the tailwind of his hired airship from the moment they flew out of Port Fallow. *The Swan*'s captain would probably arrive in Africa with a few new gray hairs, but with Yasmeen as an escort, no doubt it would be the safest route he'd ever flown.

"Then I'll buy you a drink when I see you there," he promised before warning her, "I'll begin courting you then, too."

Her laugh was soft and low. With a movement that seemed to exist between a lazy stretch and an acrobatic flip, she swung her legs off the mattress and rose from the bed. Ah, God. Had she any idea how watching her affected him? Graceful, lithe, strong—and deadly. Her every step seemed to contain a threat. Unhurried, she crossed the small room toward the bureau topped with pistols and knives, and despite the bracelet she wore, every moment he expected to feel her foot smashing in his skull, her fingers crushing his throat.

She only retrieved a silver case from the pile of weapons and slipped a cigarillo between her lips. He reached for the spark lighter before she did, and the captain had no objection when he came close enough to hold the flame to the cigarillo's tip. She regarded him over his clasped hands. When the tip glowed orange, he stepped back and lit his own.

The captain looked pointedly at his cigarillo. "You court your sister's wrath. You're a brave man."

Not that brave. "I don't smoke them near her. Only with you."

"Why is that?"

"They're expensive, and although a bulging purse in my pants might appeal to you, it also attracts the wrong sort of attention."

"So they boast that you're wealthy?" Her eyes were bright with amusement or opium. Perhaps both. "But not rich enough, if you need the sketch so badly."

"True," he said. "But that will change after I sell it."

If he had any money left over after he settled his debt, that was. He felt her assessing stare as he sank into the chair and began pulling on his boots.

Her expression thoughtful, she tapped ash into her palm. "If you sell it quickly at auction in the Ivory Market, you won't receive as much from the sale as you could from a private collector. You probably won't even receive as much as the sketch is worth—and my twenty-five percent won't amount to as much as it could be."

"It won't, but I don't have the luxury of time."

"I propose a deal, then. I'll hold on to the sketch—or we can ask a third party whom we both trust to keep it for us."

Who did a woman like Yasmeen trust? "Is there such a person?"

"The Iron Duke."

Archimedes laughed. Almost ten years ago, when the Iron Duke had only been known as the pirate captain Rhys Trahaearn and Archimedes had still been smuggling weapons as Wolfram Gunther-Baptiste, he'd provided Trahaearn with enough explosives to destroy the Horde's controlling tower in London. After Archimedes delivered the bombs to *Marco's Terror*, however, Trahaearn hadn't trusted him enough to sail with them—and into the ocean he'd gone.

"He threw me over the side of his ship, too."

"Yet you aren't destined to court *him*?"

He flattened his hand over his heart, fluttered his lashes. "Alas, the sight of his face does not make me catch my breath."

"And Scarsdale?"

"Your lover?" Or friend. During the journey to Venice they'd all shared dinner in her cabin, and Archimedes hadn't been able to determine exactly what the relationship between the mercenary captain and the Earl of Scarsdale was. But whatever the nature of it, Scarsdale posed no threat. The man was terrified of heights, and Captain Corsair would never abandon her airship.

"Yes." She turned to the bureau and began sheathing knives, tucking away pistols. "You get along well with him."

"But do I trust him to hold the sketch? He might use it to tempt you into running away with him and making you his countess."

She snorted, a half-laugh that emerged on a puff of smoke.

That response was good enough for Archimedes. "But suppose I did trust them. What would you propose?"

"Take the cash I have aboard my lady. If that isn't enough, I'll withdraw the money I keep in trust for the aviators' families. You pay off your debt, and we sell the sketch at our leisure . . . each receiving fifty percent."

A fine proposal, but with one flaw. "You have ten thousand livre?"

Her ragged gasp cut off mid-inhalation. She choked, coughing on smoke and astonishment. She pounded her fist against her chest, stared at him with wide, watering eyes.

"Ten *thousand*?"

"Yes."

"By the lady's shining teeth," she breathed. "Little wonder you changed your name. Altogether, I only have a fifth of that."

A significant fortune by any standard, but still not enough. Archimedes stood and stomped his feet more snugly into the tall leather boots, ignoring the shouted curse from the room below.

"We need to be aboard your airship before the hour is up," he reminded her.

He half-expected her to kill him now, but she only shook her head, muttered, "Ten thousand," and started for the door. On the stairs, she tied the kerchief over her hair, but waited until they were outside before speaking again.

"How the hell did you stack up ten thousand in debt?"

"I lost a shipment."

"One shipment worth that?"

"Yes." He tossed the stub of his cigarillo into the water sloshing against the dock. "My supplier was unhappy."

"If you'd lost ten thousand of mine, I'd have killed you for it, too."

But she wouldn't kill him for a sketch worth more? He didn't ask, though. No need to encourage her. "Zenobia told me what you did to Mattson. Thank you for that."

"You can thank me with fifty percent." She arched her brow at him when he laughed. "No? Don't give me your gratitude, then. It was never for her. Mattson tried to cheat me with an actress. Did he believe I'd be so stupid and not see through it?"

"The actress tried to cheat you, too. She's still alive."

"And she was as much of a threat to me as you are: none. Unless, of course, you manage to make a fool of me. She didn't."

But he had. Archimedes fought the sinking sensation in his gut. "How many men have ever managed to make a fool of you?"

She offered her hard-edged smile and glanced down at the bracelet. "The better question is: How many are still alive?"

"One," he guessed.

"And if you'd like to keep it that way, Mr. Fox, make certain not to do it again." She smoothed her woolen cuff down her wrist, hiding the bracelet. "If you even *suggest* to my crew that you've threatened your way aboard my lady, I'll rip out your spine."

He could see she meant it. God. "That's unbearably arousing."

She swept a considering look the length of his body, pausing once. Her gaze lifted to his again. "Your purse is bulging, Mr. Fox. Tuck it away before you board."

There wasn't any room in his breeches to tuck it, but a walk to the end of the docks and the breeze carrying the harbor's stench into his face did the trick. Yasmeen stopped beside *Lady Corsair*'s steel tethering cable and gave it three hard strikes with the flat of a blade. Above, a woman's head popped over the side, her pale blond hair washed in gold by the light of the deck lanterns. Ms. Pegg, Archimedes remembered from the journey to Venice. After the captain had taken her knife from his throat and allowed him on board, Pegg had shown him to his cabin, shaking her head all the way as if he'd been headed to the gallows rather than a finely appointed stateroom.

Silently, Yasmeen held up her fist. Pegg nodded and disappeared. A loud *clank* sounded. A moment later, the cargo platform unfolded from the side of the wooden ship and lowered on rattling chains. When it reached a few feet above the docks, the captain leapt to the metal platform and struck one of the chains. It jolted to a halt, and Archimedes climbed up before it reversed direction. She looked him over, cool amusement settling into her expression.

Ah. So his presence would be played as a joke in front of her crew. That suited Archimedes. If no one took him seri-

ously, no one would consider him a threat—and they'd ask
fewer questions when he left.

The platform rose, and the loud continuous clink of the
chains being winched into the windlass prevented any further
conversation until the platform clanged into place against
the rail.

Yasmeen hopped to the deck. "Thank you, Ms. Pegg."

Pegg's hand remained frozen on the windlass's lever, her
eyes wide and fixed on Archimedes' face. After a sharp look
from the captain, the aviator managed to stammer a reply. Yasmeen nodded briskly and started for the quarterdeck. Archimedes followed, aware of the nudges and whispers moving from
aviator to aviator, the surprise and the disbelief. Several crossed
themselves—they must have been Castilian, Lusitanian, or
hedging their bets.

And amusement was exactly the right way to play his
return from the dead, Archimedes realized. It was as if the
captain had never expected any other outcome after she'd
thrown him from the ship.

Rousseau waited amidships, near the ladder that led to the
lower decks. The quartermaster had been with *Lady Corsair*
since the war, but whether he'd fought for the French or Liberé,
Archimedes hadn't been able to guess. Aside from the lift of
impressive black brows, the man didn't comment on his mirac-
ulous reappearance.

Formally, he stepped to the side as Yasmeen approached,
deferring to her lead. "Your ship, Captain," he said.

"Thank you, Mr. Rousseau." She crushed out her cigarillo.
"You remember Mr. Fox, of course, and how our last meeting
concluded with me dropping him into a canal to see whether
he could swim."

The quartermaster's mouth twitched. "Yes, Captain."

"It turns out that he can. So I've lost that bet, and now I'll
feature in his newest adventure."

"As a villain, of course," Archimedes said. No need to tar-
nish her reputation.

"Of course, sir." Rousseau looked him over. "How far did
you have to swim?"

"Only to the door I'd been using as a raft. From there,
I rowed to sea."

Rousseau nodded. "A boat picked you up?"

"Yes." And a boat in the Adriatic meant either smugglers or Horde fishermen. "But if I tell you about it now, you won't have reason to buy copies of the serial adventure."

The amusement in Yasmeen's eyes warmed to something genuine. She continued on to the ladder. "Mr. Rousseau, please inform Ginger that I'll be in my cabin. I won't need dinner, but she can bring mine for Mr. Fox."

"Right away, Captain." Rousseau turned toward the bank of copper pipes that ran throughout the ship and allowed the aviators to communicate between decks.

Archimedes followed Yasmeen down the ladder and into a dimly lit passageway. Ropes and gliders hung from bulkheads. At the end of the corridor, the captain's quarters occupied almost a full third of the deck, with the passenger cabins directly below. Narrow doors along the passageway led to locked storerooms and berths for the senior crew members.

A sturdy, dark-haired girl of twelve or thirteen in a cobalt tunic and loose trousers emerged from a small cabin near the entrance to the captain's quarters. Archimedes had a glimpse of bunks filled with two more girls before she slid the door closed. The girl turned to the side to let them pass, standing tall with her shoulders pressed against the wooden bulkhead.

"Only one dinner, Captain?"

"Yes, Ginger." She hauled off her long coat and handed it over to the girl. "Tea for me."

As soon as they were past, the girl took off at a run, her bare feet slapping the boards. Though Archimedes wasn't hungry, he wouldn't refuse food from *Lady Corsair*'s galley. Fragrant and delicious, the dinner he'd taken here had rivaled any other meal that he'd ever eaten. The same couldn't be said of the fare on many airships.

Still, he had to wonder about the offer. "Should I check for poison?"

"I can fit my fist between your stomach and the buckles of your waistcoat, Mr. Fox. How long were you at sea?"

Long enough. The whole ordeal had stripped every pound of extra weight from his body and then some. But if his appearance made her imagine putting her hands under his clothes, it was worth the hunger he'd suffered. "As I'm still alive, it obviously wasn't *too* long."

"And what sort of boat rescued you?" She glanced back at him. "As you are still alive, it obviously wasn't a smuggler's."

"No, but I'll ask Zenobia to tell it that way."

"And what would be the true route?"

"A fisherman's boat to Pflaum. From there, I decided between walking north along the top of the Hapsburg Wall, or taking a grain barge to Cairo."

"Zombies or a city full of Horde soldiers," she said. "What did you choose?"

"In summer, I'd have chosen the wall. Winter, the only choice is Cairo." Where there hadn't been nearly as many soldiers as he'd expected; they'd been replaced by rumors—the most popular that they'd been ordered east to defend the heart of the empire. "From there, I boarded an airship to the Ivory Market, and then a ship to Port Fallow."

"All without your purse?"

"I stowed away and stole what I needed to. And I still had my guns."

"You threatened your way aboard? That didn't work so well the last time."

Archimedes disagreed. She'd thrown him overboard but he'd ended up on her lady again, so it had worked perfectly well. He didn't mind taking a roundabout way. "I traded the guns. Horde rebels are always looking for weapons."

"That they are, though the rebels are also difficult to find." Yasmeen lifted her cabin's door latch and led the way inside. "Interesting that you knew where to look for them."

He bowed before stepping through the entrance. "I have many talents, Captain."

With a roll of her eyes, she shook her head and crossed her quarters toward the writing desk bolted to the starboard bulkhead. He watched the pull of her tight breeches across her luscious bottom before glancing around her quarters—the same quarters his father had once occupied. Gone were the shelves of leather-bound books, the unforgivably firm bunk, the straight-backed chairs, and the solemn table as simply made as the sparse fare that had topped it. Emmerich Gunther-

Baptiste had been a lean, hard man, and his cabin had been the same.

Though also lean and hard, Yasmeen had filled her quarters with softness and color. His boots sank into thickly woven rugs. Bright silk cushions surrounded a low mahogany table; carved grapevines and leaves created an intricate pattern in the wood. In the recessed berth, red curtains formed a tent over her mattress, which appeared to be little more than an enormous pillow. The cabin's two portholes had been enlarged to let in more light, and between them hung a large metal cage. Inside, two lovebirds flitted and chirped.

Yasmeen sank to her heels beside the desk, where a steel strongbox squatted on wide feet—though not quite like any strongbox he'd seen before. Shaped like a fat egg standing on end, the smooth casing possessed no hinges, and he couldn't determine the location of a lid or a door. Curious, he joined her.

She didn't attempt to conceal the movement of her fingers across its face. This close, he could see the thin seams joining the steel, but he still couldn't make out the pattern of a door. She rotated one section clockwise. At the front of the strongbox, a steel panel the size of his palm lifted a few inches, parallel to the casing. Not much room. Archimedes had to lay his cheek against the strongbox to peer beneath the panel to see the twelve flat metal dials, each resembling the face of a clock, and each of them blank except for a faint, raised dot.

"Based on the al-Jazari locks," she said, sliding her hand under the panel. "But with improvements."

A combination lock, like the slave bracelet. "You can't see the dials."

"No." She grinned. "And neither can you."

No numbers to memorize, just the position of the dots—and she had to do it blind. "And if you mistake the sequence?"

"Then I'll need to ask my blacksmith to make me a new hand. But not this time."

She sat back. A series of hollow clangs sounded from deep within, like knocks from inside a tomb. The rounded top slowly unscrewed, widening the gap in the midline seam and revealing the six inches of steel that formed the housing. Christ. When closed, a firebomb could hit it and wouldn't do any more damage than a few scratches and a smear of smoke.

The top finished spinning. With another hollow *thump*, the belly of the strongbox opened like a drawbridge, pivoting on an interior steel rod. Coin bags were stacked neatly inside. She reached in, withdrew a leather portfolio cover, and held it out to him.

"Your sketch, Mr. Fox."

She'd transferred the sketch from his protective satchel to this? Dear God. He hadn't trusted the satchel to be watertight, but he also hadn't exposed the paper to air and moisture again. Had it been damaged? Heart pounding, he untied the strings and lifted the cover. Two plates of tempered Rupert glass shielded the delicate paper, yellowed with age. Ink had faded to brown, but the elegant lines of the glider and the distinctive backward handwriting were unmistakably da Vinci's.

Or rather, an incredibly well-rendered copy of his work. He closed the portfolio. "Where's the original?"

She bristled. "The *what*?"

"I don't traipse through zombie-infested cities to be fooled by a fake, Captain." He tossed the portfolio back into her strongbox. "You should sell that. Scholars will be clamoring for a look at the sketch, and a replica will be as close to it as most of them will ever get."

Her hand dropped to the knife at her thigh. "Mr. Fox—"

"I wondered why you agreed to hand it over so easily. It's a clever ruse. Had someone held a knife to your throat, you could have given them the fake and they wouldn't have known the difference. I do."

Silence reigned for a moment. Even the lovebirds quieted, as if aware of the tension. Finally, Yasmeen relented and shook her head.

"Very well." Her smile held no apology as she rose to her feet. "You understand I had to try."

He'd have been disappointed if she hadn't. A da Vinci sketch falling into the hands of someone unprepared to protect it would only end in tragedy.

Ducking his head, he looked into the strongbox. "Is it hidden in here?"

"Feel around inside and find out."

Even without the wicked edge of her voice to serve as a warning, he wouldn't have. "Does it close on a timer, too?"

"Yes."

Clever and useful—his favorite sort of device. Curious, he looked up at her. "What would you have done if I'd left with the forgery?"

"Laughed. Then I'd have sold it for no less than fifteen thousand, and kept a portion."

Only a portion? Yet she said it so easily that he believed that had truly been her plan. "And what of the rest?"

"I'd have given you your ten thousand." Her cool smile appeared again in response to his surprise. "If I possess five thousand livre, Mr. Fox, then adding another ten thousand means nothing. It is like having two hundred puddings. It doesn't matter if I give away half, because it's impossible to eat the hundred that remain, anyway."

A scratch at the door prevented his reply. He stood as Ginger rushed in. She wound through the cushions scattered around the table and set down a covered tray. As she straightened, her gaze darted from the open strongbox to Yasmeen's face.

"Will there be anything else, Captain?"

"No. I'm to be left alone until I call for you." When the door closed behind the girl, Yasmeen glanced at him. "She'll be upset when she hears that the forgery didn't fool you. But if scholars will buy copies, she won't be too disappointed."

"*She* created that?" Incredible. "Where did you find her?"

"Oyapock." She named the Liberé capital on the coast of the southern American continent. "But to hear the rest, you'll have to buy the first Lady Lynx serial adventure."

Archimedes almost laughed, but the same instinct that often saved him from stumbling into a room full of zombies stopped the sound in his throat. If he'd taken the forgery, she'd claimed her response would have been laughter, too. But she wasn't laughing. Instead, she regarded him with the same cool amusement that she'd used with her crew—the amusement that said everything was happening exactly as she'd anticipated. And it was, in one way: When he sold the sketch, she'd still be receiving a ridiculous fortune. Perhaps not five thousand, but even two thousand was the equivalent of having more puddings than could ever be eaten.

Apparently the money wasn't the issue at all. If he'd taken the forgery, she wouldn't have laughed because she'd gotten away with the fortune—she'd have laughed because she'd gotten away with the sketch . . . and made a fool of *him*. Instead, he'd thwarted her at every turn.

He was treading close to the unforgivable, he realized. His captain possessed a heart of steel, but he'd managed to wound her pride.

God help him when that bracelet came off.

"Zenobia still intends to write those," he told her. "All of England loves Mina Wentworth. They want more adventures featuring women hunting kraken on airships, and my sister is nothing but practical. *I* am the romantic."

"The fool."

"I'm a man of sense and restraint." To prove it, he walked to the table and lifted the silver dome from the plate. God, a man could weep. Cubes of seasoned lamb on skewers lay atop fluffy yellow rice. The scent of saffron and garlic wafted upward on a cloud of steam. Archimedes prayed he'd be alive long enough to eat a few bites. For now, he only plucked a swollen purple grape from the cluster beside the plate. He turned to Yasmeen and approached her with slow steps. "My sense tells me that I could derive no greater pleasure than to feed you grapes and lick the sweet juice from your lips. A rational man needs only to take one look at your delicate fingers to know that heaven could be found in the scratches across his back, and then to wake you the next morning with a kiss to your mouth . . . and then I'd kiss you everywhere else."

She watched him come, heat burning through the cold amusement. "This is sense?"

"*And* restraint. Because I also know that if I tried to kiss you now, you'd kill me." Stopping an arm's length away, he popped the grape into his mouth, and triumphed when she laughed. "Don't pretend that I'm the only fool in these quarters, Captain. My father's cabin spat in the face of love and companionship. Yours invites it in. And he certainly didn't keep a pair of lovebirds."

"This cabin merely invites my own comfort. The birds remind me of the difference between caged and free—and that cage might free me, one day." She tilted her head and studied his features, her gaze caressing his face like the flat side of a razor. "Do you love me, Archimedes?"

He couldn't have mistaken the calculation in her eyes. If he loved her, she was already deciding how to use that emotion against him. God, what a woman. Never accepting defeat, and using any means necessary to win.

When he *did* fall in love with her, he'd fall painfully hard. It would be as inevitable as death . . . but he hadn't yet dug his grave.

"Not yet," he said. "I'll need encouragement first."

"Encouragement from me?" She laughed when he nodded. "Then we're both safe—and you should be relieved. Two men have said they loved me. You've probably heard stories of what happened to them."

He had. One gutted, the other stripped naked and hung from her ship, his ass bared to his own city when she'd flown into the Castilian port. "Loving you would be worth it."

Her laugh seemed to catch on a bitter note. Perhaps some man had said those words to her before?

Perhaps they hadn't.

Unfortunately, he didn't have time to prove that he meant it. "Our hour is almost past. I need the sketch."

"I don't have it aboard—"

"Use the key around your waist." He regretted the hardening in her eyes, but it couldn't be helped. "These were my father's quarters—and my sister reminded me of the hideaway behind the wardrobe."

Archimedes preferred to forget the hideaway behind the wardrobe. Their father had used it to hide them away whenever they'd spoken out of turn—or simply spoken.

"Goddammit." She turned toward the wardrobe with a growl of frustration. Her fingers dipped beneath the sash at her waist, withdrew the silver key. "You and your sister. Wily foxes, the both of you. You chose your name well."

"It was a toss between that and the equally apt 'Archimedes Stallion.' But Zenobia won."

"Yet she still calls you Wolfram."

"To her, Archimedes Fox is a character, or a disguise I wear."

"And you? Do you still think of yourself as Wolfram?"

"Only when I've done something foolish or I'm about to die."

"And who are you now?"

"The man who plans to fall in love with you."

"Wolfram, then."

"No," he said, and the gravity in his voice must have surprised her. She paused, looked back at him. "With you, I am always Archimedes."

Her lips parted, but she didn't immediately respond—perhaps she couldn't decide *how* to respond. Her gaze searched his features for a long moment.

"Archimedes Fox," she mused. The corners of her mouth tilted gently. "With balls of iron and a silver tongue. I admire both in a man."

His heart almost stopped. Then it began to race, his body tensing—his instincts screaming at him to flee. Captain Corsair would never soften so easily. He was in trouble.

"You're dangerously close to encouragement," he warned her.

"I forgot to mention your thick head."

She reached beneath the wardrobe, pulled on some hidden lever, and stepped back. The large cabinet swung open like a door, revealing the small keyhole in the bulkhead behind it.

"My father always had to shove the wardrobe aside." And then shove it back into place until he was ready to let them out.

"And the scratches in the boards gave away the location," she said. "So I improved it. I can move the wardrobe from inside the hideaway, too, so that no one can trap me within."

Archimedes couldn't respond.

"There were scratches inside, too." She didn't glance back at him as she inserted the key. "All around the lock and in a few places on the walls. Tally marks, as if counting off days. And the name *Geraldine*, written beneath a bawdy little poem."

Their father had beaten her for that. "She's always been a writer."

"And what have you always been?"

"Lucky."

"So it would seem. You are not still in there, after all."

"Oh, he always let us out in time for the sermon on Sunday. In truth, that was crueler than leaving us inside."

"After hearing a few of those sermons, I have to agree." She opened the panels and stepped inside the shadowed closet. For a moment, Archimedes wondered whether to worry that she'd stowed weapons inside—but of course she had. And it hardly mattered, because she'd been armed the entire time.

When she emerged, he immediately recognized the converted glider in her hands. *His* glider, transformed into a reinforced satchel that he'd designed to carry delicate paper artifacts. "You didn't open it?"

"Of course not. Only a look through the glass as we left Venice, and again when Ginger created the forgery. I have not even smoked in my quarters since I've had it aboard."

Oh, his captain was simply amazing. "I could kiss you."

"I'll bare my ass for your lips later."

He laughed and took the contraption, not bothering to hide the shaking of his hands—excitement and relief, a powerful combination. He flicked open the satchel's cover and the familiar pain lodged near his heart, the incredible sensation of beholding something beyond price, beyond beauty. How could she *not* kill him for this?

Intending to ask her, he glanced up, but the words caught in his throat, his voice arrested by her expression. Lips softly parted and eyes bright, her face echoed his emotions as she looked at the sketch, but with something more: *longing*. Then she blinked, and the familiar hardness appeared. Her gaze met his.

"Why?" he asked hoarsely.

Though he'd only managed to speak part of the question, she understood him perfectly.

"For the same reason you don't seek revenge. Just as throwing you overboard was completely justified by your stupid attempt to take my ship, so is your desire to reclaim this sketch. It *is* yours—and I've been a thief, but I prefer to steal only when necessary. And then there is this." She rolled her sleeve back over the bracelet. "Remove it now, please."

"Of course." He set the glider contraption aside. Her fingers were warm and callused, the skin of her inner wrist smooth, her nails strong and curved like claws. He rotated the first copper segment. "You'll follow me to the Ivory Market?"

"Yes. And when our business is settled, perhaps we'll make time for something more."

Her voice was low, throaty. His heart began to pound. Carefully, he turned the next segment. A brief touch against the side of his neck almost made him jump.

The fingers of her right hand slid along his jaw. Her slow smile exposed sharp teeth. "Careful, Mr. Fox. I'd hate to be poisoned."

Sweat dampened his heated skin. His blood raced. "Only one more segment."

Her hand drifted across his shoulder, down his left arm. He twisted the copper once . . . then again. The bracelet clicked.

Yasmeen stiffened. Anger and disbelief flashed over her expression, followed by terror. "You fucking bast—"

Her eyes rolled back. He caught her when she dropped.

"Opium," he said urgently against her ear, hoping she was still conscious enough to understand. "Not poison. Never poison for you."

Her head lolled forward, her muscles went lax. Copper glinted as an object fell from her right hand and thunked against the boards.

Archimedes stared at it in astonishment. Another slave bracelet—larger than the one still around her wrist. *Good God*. When had she palmed it? Only a few seconds ago, she'd been running her fingers over his skin.

He'd known he was in trouble. He hadn't realized just how close she'd come to turning the tables on him.

Thankfully, the opium had acted more quickly this time. He'd expected to dive into the hideaway until the drug had taken her down, but apparently even Captain Corsair didn't have much resistance against a second dose. Was it too much? *No.* Her breathing and pulse were both strong. She simply needed to sleep it off. He glanced at the bed but immediately recognized the folly of it. She might forgive him the trickery, but she wouldn't if any of her crew came in and saw her drugged in bed, fully dressed.

She also wouldn't forgive him if he stripped her naked.

Damn it all. He looked to the hideaway—and hoped she could forgive him this, too.

He didn't risk the food, no matter how tempting. And if, during the ride down to the docks on the cargo platform, he entertained the fantasy of wearing only a slave bracelet in

Yasmeen's bed and feeding her tender morsels on command, at least none of the crew could discern his thoughts.

That probably wasn't what *she'd* had in mind for him. Ah, well. She'd be after him soon enough, and he looked forward to the chase.

With the satchel strapped to his back, he hopped off the platform to the dock. Though the night was in the wee hours, there were still a few handfuls of sailors and aviators about, most of them staggering. The only person not in motion was a robed figure at the west end of the docks—

Oh, Christ save him. Archimedes almost stumbled over his own feet when his heart burst into a rapid pace and his gut urged him to run, then forced himself to continue walking as if nothing were amiss.

Cold sweat gathered along his spine. A man with a taste for danger, he embraced the sweet excitement and challenge of it, but even standing a hundred yards from that woman was nothing like the delicious thrill of being next to Yasmeen. With the captain, there always existed the hope of success.

If the woman at the end of the docks spotted him, there would be no hope at all.

Archimedes walked almost forty yards before casually turning toward the wooden crates stacked along the boarded walk. They'd hid him well before, and they could do the same now. He hunkered down next to a sailor passed out and his clothes soaked in urine—if he was lucky, his own.

Breathing through his mouth, Archimedes forced a crate forward a few inches and created a narrow opening through which he could watch the woman. Judging by the angle of her body, she didn't appear to be looking his way, though he couldn't be certain. From this distance, he couldn't even be certain that she was Temür Agha's assassin—but the rebel's personal guard had stood exactly as this woman did now: quiet and watchful, as if nothing escaped her notice.

Hopefully, Archimedes had.

Minutes passed. The awkward crouch cramped the muscles in his thighs, but he'd sat through worse for longer. The woman didn't move. What was she looking at? Perhaps the harbor itself, studying the boats and airships. He glanced back at *Lady Corsair*. Like the other airships, her balloon shone like a pearl in the moonlight, and the deck lamps emitted a soft glow.

Or perhaps the woman was simply watching the aerial acrobats.

He saw them now, swooping their gliders around *The Grecian Queen*. Two of the four broke their arrow formation and spiraled upward, before dipping back around the *Queen* in a long, looping dive. Late for practice, but some of the troupes that traveled the North Sea guarded new maneuvers as carefully as state secrets, to build anticipation for their shows.

As skilled as they were, these acrobats would be nothing compared to some of the spectacles the woman saw in Temür Agha's court.

He looked toward the west end of the docks. She wasn't there. His heart seized, but he didn't dare poke his head up over the crates. He waited, stiff with tension. Footsteps approached on the boards. Not the assassin. He wouldn't hear her.

A sailor swaggered into view, with a satisfied puff to his chest that told Archimedes he'd spent time in the bawdyhouse or a serving girl's bed.

Archimedes cleared his throat as the sailor passed. "Do you see a woman in a black *djellaba*? A Musulman's robe," he clarified when the sailor simply looked at him.

Recognition lit the man's eyes. "I saw her. A pretty little raven. She turned onto the north dock."

Away from them. Thank God. Archimedes tossed the sailor a gold sous and took off at a run.

That silver-tongued bastard.

Blissed and spinning, Yasmeen kicked out four times before her foot connected with the wardrobe lever. She felt like total shit: cotton-mouthed, feverish as hell, her lungs aching. She didn't trust her legs to stand. Opium had never affected her like this before—and it wasn't the first time she'd taken two darts in less than an hour. But her head wouldn't clear. Her eyes burned. She smelled smoke.

Smoke?

"Captain?"

The voice echoed in her head. Yasmeen struggled to her knees, fell against the hideaway doors. They slid open, vomiting her onto the cabin floor. The pattern on the rug beneath her cheek blurred. The edges of her vision narrowed, darkened.

"Captain! You have to come!"

Strong hands grabbed her wrists. Wool burned across her back, and Yasmeen recognized Ginger, blood dripping from a gash on her forehead, cheeks wet with tears.

Dragging her toward the door . . . because there'd been smoke.

Oh, Lady. No.

Viciously, Yasmeen bit her own tongue. Blood flooded her mouth. Clarity flooded her mind. She pushed her feet under her. Ginger hauled her up.

"I'm up." And steady enough. "To the bell, girl. Wake the crew!"

The girl shook her head, more tears spilling. Her tunic was soaked in blood, Yasmeen realized. Too much to only come from the cut on her head. "They're dead, Captain. They're all dead."

"What? How?" Had the boiler exploded? Without waiting for an answer, she raced for the corridor. Her feet slipped just outside her cabin door. Her hands slapped against the bulkhead, and she caught herself before—

Oh, God. Sarah. Thema. The two girls lay in the passageway, throats slit.

Yasmeen stared, horror and disbelief filling her stomach with bile. Behind her, Ginger's chest heaved on a wretched sob.

Hardening herself against the sight, the sound, Yasmeen drew her pistols. "Who did it?"

"I didn't see. I ran to your quarters. They hit me coming through."

They. Yasmeen stopped breathing and listened. No steps. No sounds but a deep crackling. "Are they still here?"

"I don't think so. I closed the ladders to the lower decks, Captain, and cut off the air. But she's burning down below."

Burning. The word slashed across Yasmeen's heart, but she forced herself not to feel it. "Take a glider, Ginger. Go to *Vesuvius.* Tell Mad Machen everything you know."

"But—"

Yasmeen turned, looked at the girl.

Ginger's mouth snapped closed, and she nodded. "Yes, Captain."

By the time the girl unhooked the glider from the bulkhead, Yasmeen had searched the remaining cabins on the deck. Not one of her aviators had been caught in bed. Though some were in their smallclothes, each had daggers in their hands or guns at their sides.

They were all dead.

The iron covers over the hatchways to the lower decks blazed hot as a stove. She'd have risked a burn to save her crew, but she didn't dare open them. The rush of air would blow any fire into a conflagration and kill anyone left alive. The only hope for *Lady Corsair's* crew was to drown her.

She met Ginger at the ladder leading topside. Yasmeen climbed to the weather deck first, but it was impossible to shield the girl from the carnage. Steeling herself, Yasmeen moved carefully through the bodies to the tether line anchoring the airship to the dock. She hauled back the capstan's lever. Her lady gave a great shudder as the machine began to wind the tether cable, dragging her down to the water.

Ginger came up out of the hatchway and unfolded the glider. "Are you coming, Captain?"

Yasmeen didn't know. "Go, Ginger. Now."

The girl ran for the side and jumped. A heated updraft lifted her, and the glider wobbled, but she quickly gained control.

One made it off alive, then. It could never be enough.

Yasmeen turned back to her crew. Anger and desolation followed her around the deck. Pegg, blond hair matted with blood. Pegg the Mister, his staring eyes fixed in his wife's direction. Bebé Laverne, who'd once saved the entire crew with a derringer she'd hidden between her ample ass cheeks. Rousseau.

Oh, sweet lady, Rousseau. She knelt beside him, closed his eyes, smoothed her fingers over his wonderful, bushy brows. If only she'd been here to fight beside him.

His stomach had been opened. All of the aviators had been killed with blades—quietly and quickly. As soon as her crew had become aware of the danger, they'd been able to reach their weapons, but most hadn't had time to use them.

Whoever had done this, Yasmeen would do the same to them—but she wouldn't promise quiet or quick.

The sound of grinding metal stopped her heart. *No.* Yasmeen raced to the capstan. The tether line vibrated with tension. The air around her wavered with heat. Gritting her teeth, she braced her feet against the deck, threw her weight against the capstan's steel spokes, adding her strength to the machine's.

It wouldn't matter. She knew it wouldn't. The capstan was strong enough to pull the airship down, but not when a fire was heating the hydrogen in the balloon's envelope, expanding the gas. The capstan couldn't become any stronger—but her lady would become lighter and lighter. Eventually the tether line would snap.

But more likely, her lady would explode first.

Already stretched tight as a drum, the balloon appeared ready to burst at the seams. It would only take a tiny leak, enough air to fill a sigh.

Or a scream. Yasmeen let hers loose, pushing against the spoke with all her might, her muscles shaking with effort. It didn't move.

Her lady shuddered again. Yasmeen's feet skidded out from beneath her. Her knees crashed into the deck. Spikes of pain shot up her thighs.

The deep rumble from below became a roar.

Yasmeen's throat closed, and she listened to the sound of fire tearing through the lower decks. Her lady's belly had burned through. Perhaps only a small hole in the hull, but now air was rushing in . . . and there was no hope of saving her now.

A spark landed near her knee. Another. Yasmeen forced herself to her feet. Fire climbed the ropes toward the envelope. Not much time—and there was one thing left to save.

She dropped down through the hatchway into a corridor of smoke and flame. The door to her quarters was burning. She slammed through.

The steel strongbox was closed. That was all she'd needed to know—but she couldn't return the way she'd come. Flames rolled across the ceiling of her cabin.

Left alone since they'd wound down during Archimedes' visit, the mechanical lovebirds were still quiet. She ripped the bottom of the cage away, fitted it into the starboard porthole, twisted until the escape mechanism engaged. Glass shattered and wood shredded as the porthole rotated open, doubling in size. With another twist, she could create a standing autogyro from the two portholes, but she had no time, and the turbulence from the fire would likely tip it over, throwing her into the spinning blades. Better to dive into the harbor, and swim for the docks.

Yasmeen hauled herself up to the porthole's steel ring—and paused to look back once, like a sentimental fool.

The moment she turned away, her lady exploded.

If not for his sister, Archimedes would have abandoned everything at the boardinghouse and kept running. But there were letters in his belongings that connected Zenobia to him, the directions to her home written clearly—and Temür Agha's guard wasn't anything like the bumbling assassins he'd sent before.

Everything he needed fit into a single sack. He lay the converted glider on the bed and scribbled a letter to his sister. They'd already determined the safest location if she needed to flee. As soon as he was able—*if* he was able—he'd contact her there.

With luck, he'd be able to board *The Swan* tonight and convince the captain to leave immediately. After selling the sketch at the Ivory Market, he'd sail to Morocco and satisfy his debt with Temür.

With enough luck, that would be the end of this, and the rebel would call off his assassin.

Archimedes extinguished the lamp and moved to the window, his gaze searching the docks below. He didn't see the woman, but there were too many shadows to be certain.

He looked to the harbor. *The Swan*'s deck lamps were lit. Probably best to run to the airship now rather than to wait—and if *The Swan* had an early start, Yasmeen's anger might have cooled by the time she caught up to him.

Perhaps she was already looking. *Lady Corsair*'s decks were ablaze with light, as if she'd woken the entire crew and planned to—

No. His heart skidded to a stop. Not ablaze with light. Just ablaze . . . and he'd left Yasmeen drugged and hidden in a closet.

Dear God.

The explosion came in a great flare of light. Archimedes shouted, shielding his eyes. The window cracked. The walls shuddered. And then he was flying down the stairs, onto the docks, joined by men, women, all running, half of them still pulling on their clothes. Even in Port Fallow, an airship catching fire was a disaster that brought help, not the vultures. On the water, ships unfurled their canvas sails, moving away from the burning, floating debris that had once been the finest sky-runner on the seven seas. Above, airship engines started, huffing great bellows of steam, dropping their tethers and fleeing the heat and sparks.

Pieces of burning envelope fluttered through the air like confetti. The south dock was ablaze. Archimedes raced down the flaming boards, eyes watering from the intensity of the heat and smoke and *he'd left her drugged and helpless.*

"Yasmeen!" He shouted over the noise of the engines and cries for help, but the sound was lost beneath the roar of the burning ship. Desperately, he searched the glowing water. *"Yasmeen!"*

The end of the dock collapsed. Hands gripped Archimedes' shoulders in an unbreakable hold, yanked him backward, then dragged him when he struggled. He froze when a burning timber crashed into the boards where he'd been standing. He looked back, recognized the giant man.

"Eben Machen?" His voice was hoarse from screaming her name.

The mad pirate's fingers hardened painfully on his shoulders. "Wolfram Gunther-Baptiste."

"Yes." A fool, about to die, but he still had hope. This man was a friend to her. "Yasmeen. Oh, God. She was—Did she survive? *Did you see her?*"

Hope vanished when Mad Machen shook his head. Archimedes couldn't mistake the despair in the pirate's eyes when he looked at the burning ship. It quickly hardened into a mad resolve. He let go of Archimedes' shoulders, slapped his arm.

"We'll haul out the boats and search the water. We'll find her."

*   *   *

They didn't find her. They found bodies, so many bodies—all burned beyond recognition but for scraps of cloth, prosthetic limbs, a few gold teeth. No one that fit Yasmeen's size and shape.

The ship was still burning when it sank beneath the surface. Archimedes dove again and again into the water, trying to fight his way inside before it sank too deep. He tried past the rising of the sun, until his hands shook and his teeth chattered, and Mad Machen threatened to break his neck rather than let him go down again. He attempted to drink the coffee they brought him, but vomited it back up when he imagined her at the bottom of the harbor, still trapped in the hideaway.

A boiler explosion, everyone said. It happened all the time.

And every time it was repeated, Captain Machen got a mad look in his eyes. Only after the man finally called him Archimedes did he realize what the pirate had been thinking when they'd met on the docks: Wolfram Gunther-Baptiste provided weapons and explosives.

But Archimedes Fox hadn't done this.

He'd killed Yasmeen, though. The knowledge crushed every other thought, every other care. He didn't remember making his way back to the boardinghouse, or climbing the stairs to his room, but his legs were still trembling from the effort when he opened the door.

The *unlocked* door.

He stared at the empty bed. The glider contraption was gone. They hadn't taken anything else, but that was enough. Too much. He dropped his head to his hands, slid to the floor.

And knew his luck had finally run out.

Chapter 4

Eventually, Archimedes crawled to the bed. Fever set in. For three days, he tossed in his sheets, and woke shivering in clothes drenched with sweat. When the boardinghouse matron came round, he discovered that during his delirium, he'd somehow had sense enough to post the letter to Zenobia. As arranged, she didn't reply. He didn't send another message telling her the sketch had been taken. When he could manage the stairs without tumbling down, he took a meal and a pint at the nearest tavern. Around him, everyone spoke of where they'd been when *Lady Corsair*'s boiler had blown; no one mentioned a da Vinci sketch or a satchel that could convert into a glider. The next day, he chose another tavern, bought a meal and several pints, drinking as he listened to the talk around him. By the next week, he rarely bothered with the meals. He drank and listened, and then drank more.

Two months after *Lady Corsair* had burned, Archimedes woke with a pounding in his head and a knife at his throat.

A low voice purred in his ear. "What will you call this adventure? *Archimedes Fox and the Drunkard's Filthy Stench*?"

Yasmeen? Archimedes opened his eyes to a coal-dark room, not daring to hope. Dreams of her had come before. He'd always woken, cold and shaking, his face wet—but it wasn't wet now, and he wasn't shaking. A weight pushed on his chest until he could hardly breathe. Was she sitting on him?

"You're heavier than you look, Captain," he said on a wheeze.

She hissed. Pain bit his neck with the edge of her blade. Ah, sweet bliss. Not dreaming at all.

And she was alive.

Without any air to laugh, Archimedes grinned as elation

poured through him. It didn't matter if she killed him now. Focusing on the feel of her, he realized that she'd straddled his chest, her knees and shins pinning his shoulders and upper arms to the mattress—but he could bend his elbows. He could lift his hands. He could reach her waist. She stiffened when his fingers slid over her hips.

Solid. Real. Warm.

He felt the trickle of blood down his throat. Her breath skimmed over his jaw. Her hair tickled his face. Was she close enough to kiss him?

Oh, God. Please.

Her voice was soft. "Tell me the truth and I'll make it quick: Did you set fire to my ship?"

What the hell? *No.*

But he could only mouth the word—and it was too dark for her to see. Goddammit. He shoved his hands beneath her ass. As if prodded, she jolted forward, her weight shifting long enough for him to breathe.

Long enough for him to bite out, "I *never* would!"

"So you already said." She settled back down, trapping his hands, but this time allowing him room for shallow inhalations. "I can see, you idiot. Why would I ask if I couldn't?"

"Why say you'd make it quick if you wouldn't?"

Her dark laugh filled the room. "That's true enough. I'd have flayed you alive."

Why say it—and why ask? Suspicion crawled into his mind. "Is there someone who needs to be flayed?"

"Yes. It wasn't a boiler explosion." A sharp claw scraped down his jaw. "And you don't have my twenty-five percent, do you? Do you even have the sketch?"

Could she see the flush of his skin? He wasn't often ashamed or embarrassed, but admitting that someone had stolen the sketch was pure humiliation. "I've been searching for it."

"At the bottom of a pint?"

"I've found treasures in odder locations." He'd found one sitting on his chest.

"Who took it?"

"I wish to God I knew. But if the idiot thief didn't use the sketch for privy paper, he'll try to sell it. So I'll hear word of it soon."

"Find me when you do. Good-bye, Mr. Fox."

Her weight lifted suddenly, and he sat up, blindly trying to follow her. His searching hands caught her thigh before she could move away, and he snaked his arms around her hips. Her fingers fisted in his hair, but she didn't rip his head off.

"Yasmeen. I'm sorry for the hideaway. And I'm so very, very—" He cut himself off, recognizing the swelling through his chest, the choking grief that would come, now overwhelmed by incredible joy. He finished in a rough voice, "*Very* moved by your survival."

He released her. She didn't let go of his hair. "Because of you, Mr. Fox, I couldn't protect my crew. Instead of fighting when my lady was boarded, I was lying in that closet."

God. Archimedes closed his eyes.

Pain tore through his scalp as she yanked his head back, forcing him to look up at her. "But I also suspect that if I hadn't been in that damn hideaway, I'd be dead, and no one would be left to avenge them."

He would have. If he'd known, he'd have hunted them to the ends of the earth.

If he'd known . . . and now he knew.

Determination filled him. "Who are they?"

"I don't know. Yet."

Abruptly, she let him go. A spark lighter scraped. The flickering glow illuminated her face. She drew on the cigarillo, the tip burning orange. He stared at her, all but overwhelmed again by the beautiful angles of her cheekbones, the point of her chin, the fullness of her lips.

Icy amusement curled her mouth as her gaze ran from his head to his toes. "Did you have company?"

He looked down at himself. Naked. Ah, yes. It had been snowing when he'd stumbled home. He'd slipped into a garbage heap, and the matron hadn't allowed the stink to enter her house. Walking up three flights of stairs without a stitch of clothing obviously hadn't offended her, however. She'd watched him the entire way.

Lying back, he folded his arms behind his head and offered Yasmeen a more flattering view. "My only companions have been my dreams of you."

She snorted and turned for the door. Terror ripped through

to his bones. No, he couldn't lose her this quickly again. He reared up out of bed, but stopped in surprise when she said, "Zenobia sends her greetings from London. You ought to let her know that you're not dead."

Greetings from—"What? When?"

Yasmeen grinned over her shoulder. "Take a bath, Mr. Fox. Then come find me at dawn. Perhaps I can think of a use for a man with balls of iron and a silver tongue."

He *was* dreaming. "Find you where?"

"If you can't figure that out, you're of no use to me after all."

By the time the door closed behind her, leaving him in the dark again, he'd already figured it out. *Vesuvius* had sailed into Port Fallow that evening. He'd find her on Mad Machen's ship. But that was the easy one—because if an exploding boiler hadn't destroyed *Lady Corsair,* then who the hell had attacked her? He'd need to figure that out, too . . . but the *why* was all too obvious.

They'd been looking for the sketch.

Yasmeen's knees always ached in the mornings now, as if during the short hours of sleep, her body returned to the three weeks she'd spent in bed, healing her shattered legs. Upon every waking, she stared up at the deckhead over her narrow berth, thinking that she ought to have just let Mad Machen cut them off after his men dragged her out of the water. His blacksmith could have given her better legs. Stronger. Faster. Impervious to pain. Maybe with a few concealed weapons that let her shoot bullets from her toes.

And perhaps Yasmeen would take to wearing a robe and demurely folding her hands, too.

Gritting her teeth, she pushed down the worsted wool blanket and swung her legs around. A film of ice covered the water in the washbowl. She shivered through her quick bath, and dressed in the new clothes that felt as stiff as her body. They'd wear in, eventually. Within a half hour, her damn knees would loosen up, too.

Rubbing warmth into her hands, she paced her tiny cabin, listening to *Vesuvius*'s crew go about their duties on the deck above. When the ship's bell rang the hour and she could walk without shuffling like an old woman, she joined Barker and Jannsen, the ship's surgeon, in the wardroom for breakfast.

Jannsen looked up from his book when she entered, and watched her over his reading spectacles as she crossed to her chair and sat. "You look well."

"I slept well."

"Did you use the sleeping draught?"

"No." She preferred to smoke her opium—and she preferred to wake up aching rather than to wake up needing more. She knew better than to take a draught every evening; too many people went straight from a surgeon's tender care to the bowels of an opium den. She glanced at Barker and narrowed her eyes. "Why the fool's grin?"

"You owe me a drink. Tenner saw you leave the ship."

Ah, her midnight excursion. When they'd been sailing out of London, she'd bet the quartermaster that she could slip away from *Vesuvius* without being noticed. Last night, she hadn't even tried to be furtive; she'd asked Tenner to help her lower a dinghy to the water.

But she'd pay up, simply because of how good it had felt to be out and about again—almost as good as it had felt to straddle a naked Archimedes Fox's chest. She hadn't expected to take such pleasure in meeting with him. Even now, she couldn't fathom how the anger that she'd carefully nurtured for months had been disarmed. Perhaps it had been his unabashed joy upon seeing her alive, and his earnest apology for his part in it. Perhaps it had been the dangerous stillness that had overtaken him when he'd determined to avenge her crew. Perhaps it had been the rough shadow on his jaw, the laughter in his emerald eyes, his easy grin.

Perhaps it was the fire that spread through her veins, kindled by every ridiculous word he said. If he hadn't smelled like a bilgewater trout, she'd have stayed a bit longer and burned it out. No reason not to. They'd played a short game of chase through obstacles of his identity and the sketch, but Yasmeen wasn't playing anymore. She had a single purpose now: to find the pig bastards who'd attacked her lady. It would take time and money, but she'd happily spend both.

Outside the wardroom's porthole, the sky was dark, with

only a faint lightening in the eastern sky. Work would begin soon. If today's salvage expedition went well, she'd have reason to celebrate. There were worse ways to go about it than riding the sheets on a handsome man with a lean body and a silver tongue.

Not *many* worse ways, but still tempting enough to try it out once or twice.

Because the thought of that silver tongue made her feel generous, she said, "After I have my strongbox, I'll buy you a drink *and* a pound of Guajaca coffee."

Barker's eyelids became heavy, as if his latest ladylove had just whispered into his ear. A weak version of the brew was a sailor's staple, but as Barker often rapturously described it, the difference between the strong Guajaca blend and the drink aboard *Vesuvius* was akin to the difference between cream and whey.

Yasmeen rarely drank either, though the beans had once lined her strongbox with gold. To her mind, coffee was simply proof that civilization still existed in the New World after the Europeans and Africans had fled the Horde, whose khans and generals had believed that everyone beyond the Ural Mountains was a soulless barbarian. Yasmeen wasn't inclined to agree with that belief, except for when she drank the barbaric piss that New Worlders called tea. But coffee was *supposed* to taste like barbaric piss, and the French and Liberé had fought a war over the ownership and taxing of it.

War and taxes. The Horde and the New World were separated by oceans, but in Yasmeen's experience, all civilizations were the same in essentials.

But because she was feeling generous, she wouldn't disrupt their quiet breakfast by saying so.

Dawn had filled the clouded sky with a faint light when Yasmeen emerged onto the weather deck. The chill wind slapped her face. She folded her heavy collar up, tugged her woolen scarf in place over her nose and mouth. *Vesuvius* had anchored near the north dock. Her gaze searched the busy boardwalk, the dinghies cutting across the water, the rowboats-for-hire.

A flash of bright color near a tinker's cart caught her attention—a tall man wearing lime-green breeches. Though he faced away from her and a hat concealed his hair, that couldn't be anyone but Archimedes.

So he'd come.

She reached for her silver cigarillo case. Tucked into her belt, it had been one of the few things that had survived the explosion and her fall into the harbor. Her gloves made her fingers thick, and she fumbled the catch before sliding it open. Only a few cigarillos remained inside. No matter. When Ivy Blacksmith retrieved the strongbox from beneath the water, she'd buy more.

The cigarillo calmed her jumping nerves. On the docks, Archimedes weaved through the carts and coaches, passing the boats-for-hire. Was he light on coins? If the sketch had been stolen, maybe his purse had been, too.

But, no. He stopped by a messenger in an autogyro, and a coin passed between them. Perhaps sending the message that he couldn't join her?

Footsteps approached across the boards. Yasmeen recognized Ivy's quick stride and turned to greet the blacksmith. Her copper hair tucked beneath a wool cap and her freckled cheeks red from the cold, the woman usually wore a smile that was sweet to behold.

But now she was grinning, all but vibrating with excitement. "It's ready as soon as you are. We only need to sail closer to the south dock before we launch."

Yasmeen glanced around the decks. Though she had no doubt that Ivy's submersible had been brilliantly designed and perfectly constructed, the diving machine hadn't been tested before. If the blacksmith went into the water and anything were to happen to her, Mad Machen would likely go truly mad, and strangle Yasmeen for not stopping her. But if he were here from the outset, he'd only blame himself.

"Where's Captain Machen?"

Ivy's grin became a laugh. "There." With a hand made of mechanical flesh, she pointed to an old herring buss floating nearby, its sails furled. "It's Big Thom's salvage ship. Eben's borrowing his diving suit so that he can keep an eye on me while I'm down there."

Madness. The whole point of the submersible was that it would be safer than a suit, but Eben had a reputation to uphold. A feared pirate couldn't also be a softhearted sap who desperately loved a sweet blacksmith, so he'd worry about her below the water, where there wouldn't be any witnesses to it—and probably claim that he only wanted to prevent Ivy from using the submersible to escape him.

Still, those dive suits were a death trap. Love made idiots of everyone. "A gold sous says that you end up rescuing him," she said.

"I'd be a fool to bet against that." Ivy's gray, ungloved fingers curled over the edge of the gunwale as she leaned forward, eyes widening. "Is that man attacking the messenger?"

Yasmeen looked to the docks, where the autogyro was hovering above the boards, the young messenger's legs spinning full tilt, the long blades a blur overhead. Beneath it, Archimedes had hold of the horizontal steel bar that served as the bottom of the boy's seat frame. He began to run, pushing the autogyro to the edge of the dock, the unbuckled sides of his overcoat flapping open like wings and revealing an orange waistcoat.

"Oh, blue heavens!" Ivy cried out as man and autogyro dropped from the dock, wobbling wildly. His boots splashed in the water before the machine leveled out and began to gain altitude. Archimedes whooped, and his familiar deep laughter carried across the harbor.

Yasmeen had to laugh, too. He just couldn't take the easy route, could he?

The worried furrows in the blacksmith's brow smoothed, and she watched them approach *Vesuvius* with an expression that seemed at once distracted and intensely focused. "With this much wind, I wouldn't ever climb on one of those. But do you see how his weight stabilizes it? It's because he's so low. I'd have to figure out a way to land despite some heavy object hanging below—or design them not to land at all. For an airship, perhaps. And with that much weight, two to spin. That boy is sweating already. And by the blessed stars, those breeches are something else."

"So is Archimedes Fox," Yasmeen said.

"The adventurer?" Ivy glanced at Yasmeen for confirmation. After a moment of disbelief, her eyes softened and she looked to the man hanging beneath the autogyro again. "In London, the girls in our house who knew their letters would read his stories aloud to the rest of us. We'd pool our pennies when a new copy of the *Gazette* was printed, though sometimes it meant going without a supper. It was worth it, though. No matter how terrible the danger, he always escaped. *Always.* Even when it seemed impossible." She smiled with the memory. "We listened to them so often, I knew chapters by heart."

So did Yasmeen. Perhaps that was why she'd found it so difficult to hold on to her anger—not because of his lean body or charming grin, but because in a sense, Archimedes Fox had been one of her closest companions for almost a decade.

And now, he made her laugh when she had little reason to.

"I heard he was someone else," Ivy said quietly.

Of course she had. Mad Machen wouldn't have known any better, not immediately. "It's funny, the things you hear on these seas. About ten years ago, I heard a story about a weapons smuggler who was betrayed by the Lusitanian mercenary he'd hired to carry his cargo from Reval to Copenhagen. Santos Silva was the mercenary's name—have you ever heard of him?"

"No."

"That's because Silva and his men put a gun on the smuggler, and promised to leave him alive if he handed over the crate of weapons. Of course they wouldn't have, so the smuggler dove behind the crate for cover and shot all of Silva's men except for two seamen and the cook—he's the one I heard the story from. But a smuggler who can kill eight men and then sail their bodies across the Baltic Sea so that his remaining associates will know better than to betray him doesn't sound like the sort of man who'd laugh his way across a harbor beneath an autogyro, does he?"

"No, he doesn't," Ivy agreed, smiling. "That sort of man sounds like Archimedes Fox."

Clever girl. "So he does."

Flying near enough now that Yasmeen could see the buckles of his waistcoat and the diamond pattern in the orange brocade, Archimedes called out, "Permission to board, Captain?"

"It's not my ship!" she called back. "You'll have to wait for your welcome!"

"Wait? Well, that's a fine way to ruin my entrance!"

Grinning, he tilted his head back and said something to the messenger above him. Their direction veered slightly, carrying Archimedes to *Vesuvius*'s tall poop deck, where the autogyro's blades were less likely to catch on the rigging.

"I have to talk to him for a bit," she told the blacksmith. "Then I'll bring him over to meet you. He'll probably try to persuade you to take him under."

"Not today, not until I've tested her. But give me ten minutes to polish her guts, and I'll let him crawl around inside."

"He's charming," Yasmeen warned her.

"Yes, but I can't try to escape Mad Machen with a passenger in my boat, can I?"

"If you escape with my strongbox, I'll quarter you."

Ivy heaved a great, theatrical sigh. "And now fear for my life forces me to come back."

Yasmeen shook her head. She'd once paid the girl a fortune to leave Eben alone; Ivy had used the money to set up a blacksmith's shop on *Vesuvius* instead. But Yasmeen supposed that it had worked out in the end: Ivy had also used a portion of that fortune to build the submersible for her, and it hadn't cost Yasmeen a bit.

The autogyro flew up over the stern, blades whirring. Lines of sand provided traction on the icy boards as Yasmeen made her way aft, where Archimedes landed lightly on the deck, his face flushed with exertion and laughter. Around them, *Vesuvius*'s crew gave him a hearty cheer, and he bowed, sweeping lower when he caught sight of Yasmeen.

"Not their captain, but *my* captain," he said.

"I wouldn't have you. Within a day, you'd be strapped to a whipping post for disregarding my orders."

"That's true enough," he said, straightening. Heat flared in his emerald eyes as he looked her over, and Yasmeen stiffened. Oh, he'd ruin everything. From his silver tongue would come a suggestion of *where* she could whip him and order him about, the crew would hear it, and then she'd have to string him up naked from the side of Mad Machen's ship.

His gaze caught on her face. Relief slipped through her when he said, "I have followed one of your orders, however."

So he had. He'd bathed—and shaved, though he hadn't needed to exert himself to that degree. She liked a rough jaw.

"And here I am, at your disposal," he continued. "What do you require?"

She turned toward the stairs and gestured for him to follow. "Only a conversation, Mr. Fox. And I hope to soon have a gift for you."

Ivy Blacksmith hadn't yet named her submersible, but Yasmeen had heard the crew members call it *The Copper Prick*. Yasmeen could see a faint resemblance in the cylindrical body and the rounded head, but she thought the name was wishful thinking on their part—the width of the capsule was as tall as a man, and in length was three times a man's height. From there, the resemblance in shape ended. The tail tapered off into a propeller set over a pair of flat rudders, and she'd never encountered a prick with a raised bump on the shaft similar to Ivy's glass observation dome in the capsule's hatch.

Perhaps she was more selective in her pricks than Mad Machen's crew.

She led Archimedes amidships and stopped near the port rail, where they could watch the activity around the copper submersible without standing in the crew's way—and where they could speak in relative privacy.

"Is this my gift?" He gestured to the submersible. "I already have my own, you realize."

God's truth, men were all the same. But he also appeared suitably impressed by the machine—as any man ought to be. "Your gift is the copy of your sketch, if all goes well. Depending upon the sort of person you'll have to steal the original back from, you'd be wise to put distance between you before she has a chance to realize it's missing."

His gaze snapped to hers. *"She?"*

He knew, Yasmeen saw immediately. His expression resembled that of a man who faced an oncoming battalion of war machines, with a mob of zombies closing in from behind. For all of his frivolity, for all of his charm, this man was also deeply aware of the dangers the world threw at them.

"I can't be certain," Yasmeen said. And it seemed strange that the elite guard would steal such an item—they didn't steal anything, unless it were necessary. But who could say what another person considered necessary? "But Miracle Mattson learned about the sketch from Franz Kessler. You've heard what happened to him?"

"His throat slit. That wasn't you? In her express, Zenobia said you were coming to speak with him."

"I didn't arrive in Port Fallow until after it happened. But a woman was there, watching the house. I had no reason to think she knew anything of the sketch at the time—not until I heard from one of Mad Machen's men that you were hiding in a crate, and paid him a sous to look for a woman in a robe. Were you truly hiding?"

"Wouldn't you?"

"If I thought I was her target. So you knew what she was. How?" Not many New Worlders recognized a *gan tsetseg* woman.

"I've seen Temür Agha's guard."

Temür Agha. Fifteen years ago, the general had crushed the rebellion in Constantinople by razing the city to the ground. Of royal blood, cunning and ruthless, his name inspired terror across the empire—including the ruling houses in Xanadu. Even the Khan hadn't dared an assassination, and instead had named him the governor of the Moroccan occupied territories, sending Temür to the farthest edge of the empire.

Even that meant risking an insult: officials and *dargas* were assigned to the territories outside of Asia as a punishment, not reward. Temür hadn't retaliated, but from the beginning of his governorship, rumors had been swirling that he was amassing great power in Morocco and would soon try to march across the empire. Ten years had passed, and he hadn't yet—but Yasmeen wouldn't place bets against it happening, eventually.

She didn't care one way or another. In the meantime, she avoided Morocco as much as possible. Archimedes apparently hadn't had the sense to, and the idea that he'd hidden from the woman amused Yasmeen; obviously, someone had explained what the elite guards were capable of, but hadn't mentioned that they weren't rabid murderers who gutted everyone who passed them. Only loyalty and duty were more sacred to the guard than self-control and compassion. If the woman had found him huddling near a crate, she'd have probably given him a blanket or a coin.

Unless Archimedes had reason to think the woman had targeted him.

Yasmeen froze with her cigarillo halfway to her lips. "Your debt," she said. "Is it to Temür Agha?"

"Yes."

Her stomach rolled into a hard knot. "And that woman was his guard?"

"I don't know. I didn't see her clearly. I didn't want to take the risk."

Only an idiot would. "I saw her clearly. What did Temür Agha's guard look like?"

"Long black hair, braided here." His fingers met at the center of his forehead and dragged back over his ears. "Beautiful. Skin like teak on her face, but gray hands."

Yasmeen pursed her lips. He'd just described half of the elite guard after the women had been altered with mechanical flesh. "Anything helpful? Was she tall? Full-lipped, thin-nosed, curly-haired, round-faced? Did her features give any hint of her ancestry? Did you hear her speak?"

"Straight hair. She didn't speak. She was as tall as that blacksmith." He indicated Ivy. "A Turk, perhaps. Or Hindustani."

A better description, but it was still impossible to be certain. "Perhaps the woman I saw was Temür's guard, then. But as two months have passed and you aren't dead, I suspect not."

Yasmeen *hoped* not. If she discovered that the woman had boarded her lady, Yasmeen wouldn't be able to avenge her crew alone; she'd need to hire a group of mercenaries and assassins. If the woman was Temür Agha's guard, however, it hardly mattered whether Yasmeen went by herself or with a small army; either would turn into a suicide mission.

"Franz Kessler and her presence on the docks might be a coincidence," Archimedes said softly. "But not likely. If Kessler had told her of the sketch, she might have guessed it was aboard *Lady Corsair*. Were all of your crew killed before the explosion?"

Yasmeen nodded. He'd put it together exactly as she had. "They barely had time to draw their weapons."

"That sounds like the elite guard. What I've heard they can do."

"What they *can* do, yes." But not what they *would* do—and that was where Yasmeen became uncertain again. "But if she was only after the sketch, she could have stolen it without killing anyone, and without anyone aboard seeing her."

"And if she couldn't open your strongbox?"

Would she rage through the airship, taking out her frustration on the crew? Yasmeen didn't think so. But perhaps the woman hadn't been alone. Though Ginger had never seen who'd attacked her, she'd had an impression of "they." Yet at such a moment, in the dark, one quick person could have seemed like many.

Yasmeen simply didn't know. "Whatever happened, when she didn't find the sketch, she might have realized that you'd had it when you left my lady."

"*If* she saw me," Archimedes said.

"She saw you."

"But—"

"She saw you." Suddenly amused, Yasmeen caught his gaze. He'd managed to surprise her by hiding beside a crate in a pile of rags, but he wouldn't have escaped the attention of that woman. "Even if we're wrong and she was only strolling along the docks for her own pleasure, she saw you."

His eyes searched her face. "How do you know so much about them?"

"Don't be dense, Mr. Fox. And don't tell your sister, either. I'm waiting until her curiosity about my background is on the verge of killing her—and then I'll negotiate a better royalty in exchange for each new crumb." She appreciated the deep laugh that served as his response, the squint of his eyes as it shook through him. "Was seeing this woman your reason for sending Zenobia to London?"

His laugh faded. "Yes."

"To the Iron Duke, no less. I thought you didn't trust him?"

"I wouldn't trust him to protect *me*. But who's more capable of protecting her?"

Yasmeen could only think of a few names, but none who

had incurred the same sort of debt to Archimedes that Rhys Trahaearn had. The Iron Duke had thrown him from his pirate ship, but Wolfram Gunther-Baptiste *had* boarded that ship in good faith and fulfilled the job asked of him. Trahaearn considered anyone who served his ship under his protection—which meant providing help when needed. When Archimedes asked for something of this nature, there was no question that the Iron Duke would do it.

But Archimedes probably didn't understand that—most likely, he'd just rolled the dice.

"And if the Iron Duke is reluctant, who more likely to talk him into it than Scarsdale?"

He grinned. "Did he need to?"

"No. But you're right. How could Scarsdale resist the author of the Archimedes Fox adventures? He and your sister have been inseparable since she arrived." And because she couldn't resist, either, "Perhaps Zenobia will soon be a countess."

Archimedes' grin fixed to his face, and he gave his head a hard shake, as if to clear it. "Eh?"

She flicked her cigarillo over the side of the ship. "She's a practical woman. It'd be a good fit—and perfect timing. He's searching for a wife. Duty calls, and he needs the heir and spare."

He stared at her, as if trying to read the truth from her face. Yasmeen smiled, showing her teeth. An expression of relief slipped over his features, then worry, then relief again. Finally, he said, "I can't decide if you're serious. I think I ought to write her."

"Perhaps you should," Yasmeen agreed.

The wind picked up, chopping the harbor's surface into rough waves, but making for a quick sail to the south docks. Mad Machen ordered the anchor dropped near the site where her lady had crashed into the water and returned to the main deck, where Big Thom ran a test of the dive suit's air pump, checking the flow through the long, coiled tube. The hand-cranked device forced air to circulate through the water-proofed leather hose and into the diver's brass helmet—which meant the diver relied on someone else simply to *breathe*.

Madness. Even the tiny enclosed space in Ivy's submersible would be preferable, and Yasmeen wouldn't take money to dive underwater in *that*.

No doubt Archimedes would do it for free. Yasmeen looked starboard, where a hoist suspended the submersible over *Vesuvius*'s side, copper skin gleaming in the dull sunlight. From inside the capsule, Archimedes' exclamations of awe and questions to Ivy had echoed hollowly through the open hatch for the past twenty minutes, but his voice had smoothed out now, hints of flattery and teasing slipping through.

Trying to charm her into taking him down, no doubt. Good luck to him.

She made her way across the deck toward Mad Machen, who was holding the full-length canvas suit at arm's length, a frown darkening his scarred face.

"How does a man get into this blasted thing?"

"There's a double-flap fastening in the back," Yasmeen said, but his question sparked a note of alarm in her head. "You've done this before, haven't you?"

"I've dived before. This looks to be a hell of a lot easier. You don't even have to hold your breath."

Yasmeen looked to Big Thom, who rose from his crouch next to the air pump, shaking his head. The man lived up to his name, with broad shoulders made wider by the pneumatic braces across his back and chest. Combined with his steel prosthetic arms, the apparatus gave him tremendous hauling power—and during the Horde's occupation in England, he'd hauled fish. He ran a salvaging boat now, though by the looks of it, he hadn't been hauling up much treasure.

"No," Big Thom said. "It's not easier. When you told me you'd dived, I thought you understood that. But you're not going down. Not in my suit."

Big balls, too. Not many men would say "no" so baldly to Mad Machen's face.

Quiet fell over the main deck. The crew wasn't used to hearing that word said to him, either.

"She's not going down alone. Not on this first run."

"That's your business," Big Thom said, as if he didn't see the pulse throbbing in Mad Machen's temples and the tension whitening the pirate's knuckles and lips. "Unless you've practiced swimming with the brass guards over that canvas, weighing you down, you aren't any good to her anyway—and I'll probably be hauling up your dead body."

"Then I won't use the guards."

Ivy's voice called from starboard, "And lose your *other* leg to a shark?"

Yasmeen glanced over her shoulder, where the blacksmith was climbing out of the submersible's hatch, her eyebrows drawn and mouth tight. She leapt to the deck, followed by Archimedes.

"There's more than that," Big Thom added. "You've got to know to keep your hose from kinking. You've got to know how fast you can come up. Give me a few hours and I'll find a diver who can go down with her. You can't."

"I can," Archimedes said.

Yasmeen huffed out a laugh. Of course he could. And was idiot enough to offer.

Mad Machen's wild gaze landed on her face. Ah, soft-hearted Eben. She'd have blamed love for this, but he'd already been a bit mad before he'd met Ivy.

She shrugged. "He made it through the Underwater Perils of Porto."

The pirate looked to Archimedes. "You go down, then. If she doesn't come back up, I'll kill you."

That wouldn't do at all. Yasmeen said, "But before he kills you, make sure to hook that hoist chain to my strongbox."

Archimedes grinned. "I'll do that."

He shrugged out of his coat, Mad Machen handed the canvas suit to her as he crossed the deck to meet Ivy—and that quickly, Yasmeen became an idiot's valet. Facing her, only a foot away, Archimedes held her gaze while he shed his waistcoat.

"Will you fear for me, Captain?"

"No. You have a fool's luck."

"It does seem to be returning." He sat back against a tackle chest and hauled off his boots. "Perhaps because you came back to me. My favorite mercenary."

That nonsense didn't even warrant a response. He stepped into the diving suit and she fastened the back, checking the edges for a watertight seal. The water would be cold. Wet and cold could be disastrous.

"I think Big Thom's half in love with her," Archimedes said. "I probably ought to warn him about Mad Machen."

Yasmeen looked around his shoulder to where Mad Machen and Ivy stood with the salvager. The blacksmith was showing him the submersible's air pump, which operated in the same way as the diving suit's pump, but was cranked by a windup mechanism instead of by hand. Big Thom did appear stricken with longing, yet not by Ivy herself.

"It's her *arms*, you idiot." When the Horde grafted tools onto the laborers in the occupied territories, it cared about function, not appearance. The skeletal prosthetics beneath the salvager's heavy coat sleeves and gloves probably looked more like thin steel bones than limbs. "He's likely never seen mechanical flesh before."

"And couldn't afford it even if he had?"

"Yes." The only person outside of Xanadu who could manipulate the nanoagents necessary to create mechanical flesh was the Blacksmith in London, but his work didn't come cheap. And though Big Thom could buy a pair of arms on credit, few people risked owing a debt that large to the Blacksmith—especially if they couldn't be certain of making every payment. She gestured to the quartermaster, standing near the main mast. "Barker will be paying off his leg for a decade."

Archimedes whistled softly. "That's a heavy weight."

"Not as heavy as ten thousand livre."

"That only weighs as much as a stolen da Vinci sketch." He smiled faintly when she snorted, his gaze on Ivy and Big Thom again. "What of the other sort? Your Pegg had a foot that looked like a foot, even if it was metal. One of your gunners had arms of the same type. I forgot his name."

Yasmeen ignored the ache in her throat, the sudden tightness around her lungs. "Mr. Pessinger," she supplied. "That was Ivy's work, too."

"Ah. Why am I not surprised? I thought they were mechanical flesh until Pegg let me have a closer look. But her prosthetic was an actual machine, not metal made flesh and shaped by the nanoagents. I've never seen such intricate gearwork and hydraulics before. Incredible."

"Yes."

She couldn't keep the thickness out of her voice. Archimedes' head swung round, his gaze sharpening. Avoiding his eyes, she handed him the first of the brass guards that buckled around his lower leg—he could put these on himself.

"Won't you go down with us?" he asked softly.

"To see my lady broken and to pick at her shattered bones?" She'd do better stabbing herself through the heart. "No, thank you, Mr. Fox. I'll leave the traipsing through ruins to you."

His eyes searched her face for a long moment before he nodded and stooped to fasten the guards at his lower legs and thighs. She buckled more plates over his chest, back, and arms, until he resembled an invading crusader from the centuries before the Horde's invasions.

She hefted the domed helmet over his head and fastened the bolts, then tapped the round glass plate over his face. "You ought to have had one of these in Venice! I couldn't have lifted you to toss you over!"

His muffled laugh fogged the small window. She smiled in response, and his splayed, awkward walk across the boards continued to improve her mood. Big Thom verified the air flow in the domed helmet. The crew rolled back the net stretched across the gangway so that he wouldn't have to climb over the side of the ship.

He dropped into the water a few minutes later, followed by the submersible. Mad Machen stood at *Vesuvius*'s starboard bulwark, his fingers clenched on the gunwale as the capsule sank beneath the surface. Yasmeen paced the decks and smoked the last of the cigarillos in her case.

Eleven hundred livre sat at the bottom of the harbor. That money was a skyrunner, swift and sleek. A full complement of arms and cannons. A seasoned crew, supplies. She'd buy mercenaries, information, loyalty. If necessary, she'd purchase a war and bring it to the doorstep of those who'd dared to hurt those under her protection.

They'd pay. Oh, how they'd pay.

A shout hailed from starboard. Heart pounding, Yasmeen ran to the side. The water alongside the ship seemed to boil, and the submersible suddenly emerged through the roiling surface—with Archimedes riding astride the large capsule.

Hoots of laughter and lewd shouts joined the cheers of the crew, and this time Yasmeen was inclined to agree with them: The man did have enormous balls.

Mad Machen ordered his men to the hoist. Below, Ivy threw her hatch open and poked her head out. Her gaze locked with the pirate's before she searched out Yasmeen's.

Her grin almost split her pale cheeks. "We got it!"

They had it, but forever seemed to pass before she *saw* it. The submersible's cable winch had to be wound by hand, and even after Big Thom replaced the straining crew, the going was slow. Brought in too fast on a rocking ship and swinging cable, the strongbox could smash like a cannonball against the hull.

Yasmeen distracted herself by helping Archimedes out of his suit, and shouted for coffee and a blanket when she saw the chattering of his teeth, discovered the icy cold of his hands. When she rubbed his fingers between her own, a man had never seemed so pleased with himself.

But, hell—she was pleased with him, too. She was pleased with the whole damn world.

The strongbox finally lifted out of the water, the casing dull but undamaged. Archimedes stood beside her, a wool blanket clutched over his shoulders, as Big Thom carefully brought the strongbox around over the side and lowered it to the deck. Yasmeen sank to her heels in front of it.

"Captain Corsair!" Ivy called her name before she could touch the casing. "That's one of the Blacksmith's, yes? A blind-dial combination?"

"Yes." No doubt the girl had constructed a few when she'd worked in the Blacksmith's shop. "Why?"

Ivy crouched beside her. "They're strong, but sometimes the dial mechanisms are knocked out of alignment if they're hit hard. That explosion shattered your legs. A force like that might have been enough."

Enough to change the combination? "So what do you propose?"

"I'll open it for you."

Unease flittered through her. "*You* can open my strongbox."

Could the *gan tsetseg*?

The blacksmith wiggled her gray fingers. "I can touch your skin and feel your nanoagents moving. Sensing the tumblers falling into place . . ." She trailed off, as if unable to think of a comparison to anything as easy. "It'll be safer for you."

And Yasmeen preferred not to spend her first coins on a prosthetic hand. She gestured for Ivy to proceed. The girl did so quickly, and if Yasmeen jumped a little when the steel panel snapped closed on Ivy's wrist, she wasn't alone. But the mechanical flesh was unharmed, and a moment later, Ivy smiled and sat back. The top unscrewed and the belly opened.

An empty belly. No sacks of gold coins. No leather portfolio.

"Oh!" Ivy said. Her brow furrowed. "But I thought—I . . . *Oh.*"

"Yasmeen," Archimedes said quietly.

Her hands shook. She reached for a cigarillo, then remembered she didn't have any more. Her stomach formed a sick, aching knot.

I have nothing.

Not even a way to avenge her crew. Panic began to build, shortening her breath. She fought it back, fought the terror.

This was what a heart of steel was for—and she'd crawled out of *nothing* before.

"I'm sorry, Mr. Fox. I don't seem to have your forgery, after all." She rose to her feet, ignoring him when he repeated her name. "Thank you, Ivy, for all of your help. Mr. Barker? I believe I owe you a drink. I'd like to pay up now."

While she still could.

Chapter 5

Of all the rough taverns near the docks, the Charging Bull was arguably the worst of the lot. Archimedes didn't expect to find Yasmeen there, but after a tour through half of Port Fallow's rum dives, he realized that was *exactly* where to find her. There was no counting the number of tales he'd heard about Captain Corsair in a tavern brawl, tearing through the other patrons like paper. Not so many stories lately, but the captain had been gutted by that empty strongbox. If she was looking to take out that pain on someone, there was no better place to look than the Charging Bull.

Approaching the entrance, he thought the brawl had already started. A crowd shouted encouragement inside—chanting *Henri! Henri! Henri!* above the noise of the musicians. A glass shattered against the floor as he walked in, followed by the crash of a chair and two swearing sailors. The scent of stale sweat and tobacco filled the air. Every table was occupied, all looking to the middle of the room, where a boy of about fourteen lay on a table with his trousers around his ankles. A woman straddled his narrow hips, her bodice down and skirt up. A crowd of aviators chanted in time with the whore's bouncing breasts. Someone had paid to make the boy a man, apparently.

Automaton musicians dressed in French navy uniforms played a jolly tune on the harpsichord and violin. No live musician would play here; too many had been knifed through the ribs for an off-key tune or in simple drunken bad temper. Archimedes found Yasmeen sitting at a table in the back corner, watching the boy's deflowering with a mildly amused expression. Her seat was situated in the only relatively quiet part of the tavern, given that those around her sat askew to their tables, hunched over their drinks as if they didn't dare turn their backs on her but also weren't going to risk looking her in the eyes.

A half-finished pint waited in front of her, a smaller glass empty beside it. Her brows lifted when she saw him, and she pushed out a chair with the toe of her boot. An invitation. More than he'd hoped for, but as she didn't immediately speak, Archimedes wouldn't assume that conversation was included with it. He ordered a round for them both when the barmaid appeared, sweating from the heat of the room.

From the center of the tavern came a chorus of cheers. Only the boy's feet were visible, his toes spreading wide, ankles stiff, and legs jerking as he orgasmed. Yasmeen picked up her pint, raised it with the rest of the room. Her gaze met his.

"To young love," she said.

Archimedes grinned. "May it always be so innocent."

"And as lucrative for at least one partner." She downed the pint in a few swallows. The table shivered as she slammed the glass back down. "What brings you to the Bull, Mr. Fox? Looking for sport on a table?"

"Looking for you."

Her knuckles rapped the tabletop. "Then climb on up."

Another invitation? And one that he could imagine, all too easily: wood at his back, and Yasmeen riding him. His hands filled with her soft breasts. Her claws digging into his shoulders. Wet heat surrounding his prick, taking him deep. Archimedes shifted in his seat, his body hardening. Not tonight. By God, he wanted to—but he'd wait until he *needed* to.

Yasmeen leaned forward, looking intently into his face. He could have distilled a potent liqueur from her breath. Too drunk for any sport, though he wouldn't have known just watching her, listening to her. The woman could hold her drink.

He wasn't a bit surprised by that fact.

"I believe I've done the impossible and rendered you speechless." She sat back. "I don't like it. I never thought to choose between your iron balls and your silver tongue."

"They're both at your disposal."

"That's much better. Ah, so is this." She accepted a foaming pint from the barmaid. "Thank you, Mr. Fox. Now, then. What brings you here?"

"You brought me here. I remembered tales of Captain Corsair and tavern brawls."

She laughed into her glass, lowered it. "You've heard those?"

"After you shot my father, I listened for any news of you." He lifted his drink to her. "I ought to have bought you one thirteen years ago."

In truth, he ought to have just killed the old man himself, but he'd still had some vision of proving him wrong. Now, he knew: If a job needed doing, then best just to get it done.

"I was glad to oblige. I've never had ambition of being roasted alive."

"So you had ambition of being bloodied and drunk in tavern brawls. Such honorable pursuits, Captain."

"Quite honorable." As if to prove it, she took another drink. Her tongue swiped the foam from her upper lip, and she used the tip of her middle finger to catch the bit left at the corners of her mouth. "I'd made a name for myself in the New World, but I couldn't get a job in Port Fallow. I offered to go into England—this was still when the Horde's tower was up, controlling everyone infected by the right nanoagents, and no one else dared to fly in. I lowered my rates to a pittance. But the only offer I got was from a sailor, for that sort of work."

With a lift of her chin, she indicated the woman who'd just climbed off the boy and was sidling up between twin brothers.

"The offer came with a grab to my tits, so I broke his arms. Then his mates decided to show me that I was nothing but a whore." Brimming with amusement, her gaze met his again. "I was the only one left standing—and afterward, I picked up a job from someone who'd seen the fight. So I fought until I made a name for myself again. I suppose that was around the same time you were making a name for yourself, too."

A new name. "Mine came later. About six months after you gutted Bloody Bartholomew."

"Ah, Bart." Eyes narrowing, she reached into her red sash and withdrew her cigarillo case. "You had a partner, too, didn't you? Besson, Barson—"

"Bilson."

"Yes. And he's dead?"

"So the story goes."

"I see—" She broke off, frowned. The expression disappeared in a blink. Without opening the silver case, she slipped it back into her sash. "In truth, he ran from Temür Agha."

"Yes. He stayed for a while. After the first assassin came, though . . ." Archimedes shook his head. "Last I heard, he took an airship to the heart of the northern American continent and leased a farm from one of the native confederacies."

"You never thought of doing the same?"

"Staying in one place? I'd be better off dead."

She nodded. "And so it is with me, too. I also feared that without an airship, I'd have more trouble. But you get around well enough without one."

"I'm an outstanding example," he said.

"Oh, yes. Only two months after the Iron Duke threw you off the *Terror* near England, you were making an enemy of Temür Agha in Morocco. Getting around quite well, and making an outstanding example, indeed."

Her eyes shone with laughter, another invitation to join in, and he did easily. A crash near the bar silenced them both, their hands dropping to their weapons. Only the twins, wrestling over who'd be the first to have a go. He turned again to Yasmeen, who was watching the fight, her fingers tapping against her glass.

"I would bet on one, but there is not even a scar for difference."

If she bet on one, Archimedes would put a coin on the other. "We could call them the red shirt and the blue."

"If they end this fight without the both of them losing their shirts, it's not worth the wager." She looked to him. "And what did you think of Ivy's submersible?"

"Astonishingly brilliant." He'd seen submersibles before, but none so nimble. "Did she build it for you?"

With her drink to her lips, she nodded.

And that was perhaps even more astonishing. "How is it that you are friends with Mad Machen, Scarsdale, and the Iron Duke?" The *Terror*'s surgeon, navigator, and captain. "As you said, you'd barely made a name for yourself here by the time Trahaearn blew up the Horde's tower in London. Yet you seem to know a good number of men who were aboard his ship."

"You've heard that story, too."

"No." He was certain.

"Yes. You just haven't heard all of it." She angled toward him in her chair, hooking her arm over the back. "It was Bart. So dangerous and handsome. Older, with silver at his temples and scars in all the right places, and tales of when he'd sailed his own mercenary ship. I was twenty years old, and couldn't have fallen faster if I'd jumped from my lady."

"In love with him." Not so innocent, but still young.

"Oh, yes. That wasn't all, of course. He knew Europe, knew the locations of the Horde outposts. He taught me well and took only a reasonable percentage. Soon enough, I let him move into my cabin. I got pregnant." Her eyes glittered. "I told him."

She reached for her sash again. Archimedes pulled out his cigarillo case first, flipping it open. She selected one, holding it to her lips while he lit the end.

"Thank you." Her exhalation of smoke sounded like a grateful sigh. "I hadn't planned on a baby, but I liked the thought well enough. I'd raise her on my lady, free to go wherever we wished. Bart, however, decided that he'd rather just have my ship. We went to bed the night I told him, celebrating. As soon as I was asleep he stabbed me through the belly."

Christ. "So you gutted him."

"And then some. I don't often lose control, but . . ." She shrugged. "I had reason. I didn't have a surgeon aboard my lady, though. I wasn't healing well and fever was setting in. After two days, I took a risk and hailed the nearest ship."

"The *Terror*?" A hell of a risk.

"Yes. Mad Machen cut me open, sewed me up, and kept me aboard for two weeks. Afterward, when the Iron Duke asked me to scout the coast ahead for them, I did. It's still the only job I've ever done for free."

"And so your heart of steel was born."

She snorted. "No. I was still young. More wary, but not wary enough yet—and Bloody Bartholomew wasn't the only man who has wanted my ship."

And damn them all. "The comte, too?"

"No. By that time, I'd learned. But he didn't want my ship, he wanted adventure. He paid for passage to Egypt, the Hapsburg Wall, the ruins of Greece. And he was charming, handsome, rich."

"Nothing at all like me, thank God." Archimedes couldn't claim to be rich.

Her laugh was warm and low. "Not as entertaining, at least. But fun. I took him to my bed."

"Yet you strung him up?"

"He pinched my ass."

"A bedding usually involves a hell of a lot more than that." Done well, at least. "I never took you for a prude."

"He did it in front of my crew." The humor left her face. "I could have an orgy in my cabin and my crew wouldn't care. But if I allow a man to pinch my ass while I'm treading my lady's decks, there's no reason the crew couldn't, either."

A severe punishment for the offense, however—unless that offense wasn't accidental. "Did the comte know?"

"I warned him. He'd made comments before, innuendos that I told him would undermine my authority. But his pride couldn't accept that I ranked above him on my ship, that I was master and commander. He had to show my crew that I was under him, in some manner." She suddenly shifted to the side as a mug flew past her head, shattering against the wall—half the tavern had joined in with the brothers. "And that was the end of my association with the comte."

"Rich, handsome, charming. As is Scarsdale."

Sharp amusement curved her mouth. "Yes, he is. Would you like to hear that I recently spent three weeks in his bed?"

No, he wouldn't. Not out of jealousy that she'd gone to Scarsdale's bed—though he felt the swift pain of that—but the jealousy that Yasmeen had gone to Scarsdale when she'd been hurt. After hearing Ivy mention shattered legs that morning, he knew there was more to this story than she suggested.

"Recovering?" At her nod, he asked, "Do you love him?"

"Yes."

And more pain sliced near his heart. God. Was he so far along already? This was more unsettling—more terrifying—than he'd expected. "Yet you hand him over to my sister."

"If she's truly a practical woman, it would be a good match. She couldn't ask for a more dedicated companion."

Yet Scarsdale would never love Zenobia as she deserved, because he was pining for the heart of another.

But, no. The amusement in Yasmeen's eyes didn't match that of a woman who was longing for an impossible love.

"He's your friend," Archimedes realized.

Now a full smile shaped her lips. "Yes. We did try the bed once. But we were both laughing so hard by the middle that we couldn't make it to the end."

He couldn't imagine. Laughing with her, yes. Not being able to finish? What kind of man would look at her, touch her, and not be . . .

"Ah," he said. "He's a—"

Archimedes cut himself off before disaster struck.

Her brows lifted. "A what?"

He knew many words for men who swived other men, but not a single one that wouldn't insult the man she loved. "A friend."

She offered him an appreciative nod. "You're a clever man, Mr. Fox."

"I thought I was. But although I believed that I was taking clever advantage of your drunkenness to discover so much about you, I'm coming to realize that nothing you've said has been anything you didn't intend to say. And I wonder why."

She hesitated. The sounds of the brawl intruded, a nearby table collapsing beneath the weight of tussling men, but he didn't think that was why she waited. She was gathering herself.

Finally, she said, "After I swam to *Vesuvius*, I spent those first three weeks in bed. The next weeks, I spent writing letters and talking to solicitors. I had money in trust for my crew, you remember. A significant amount."

"Yes."

"I've used it often. When an eye is lost, a leg, a hand—I'll pay for the replacement or give them a retirement. A true retirement. With the amount I gave, combined with what they earned on my ship, they wouldn't need to work again. And those who died in service to my lady . . . my crew made a prince's wages, but dead, their families lived like kings. I didn't expect to pay it all out at once, however."

Twenty-five crew members and a king's sum to the families of each. "So it's all gone."

"Yes. But it shouldn't have mattered."

Because of the strongbox. God.

She must have seen the realization in his face. "Yes. And if I correctly interpreted a few things that your sister said while we were in London, I believe we are in the same situation, Mr. Fox—though yours not as dire."

It was true. "I haven't had a significant find in some time."

A laugh slipped from her. "No?"

"No. Enough for room, board, a few extras." He lifted his cigarillo case as an example, then understood why she was laughing. He *had* made a significant find. "And the sketch, of course."

"Yes, the sketch. Though now there are two sketches of interest to us: the forgery, because whoever possesses that must have taken it from my lady and killed my crew. And the original, because whoever has it stole a significant sum from us both—and stole your freedom from Temür Agha. So I'm proposing an arrangement between us."

"To find the sketches."

"Yes. You know people. I know other people. Between the both of us, we will hear word of at least one sketch. Perhaps we'll be lucky and find the original and the forgery in one person's hand." She sat back. "The arrangement I propose is to share information and retrieve the sketches together. No trickery. No slave bracelets."

"And not much money." Not that it mattered. If she hadn't proposed this, he would have.

"No. Do you find that a significant obstacle, Mr. Fox?"

"It never has been before."

Satisfaction and determination set her expression like stone. "Good. I have a few items to sell. They won't amount to much, however, so I doubt we'll be buying information. Your charm and my blades will have to do."

Fascinating. She was friend to the richest man in London, yet relied on her blade? "You won't borrow it from the Iron Duke?"

"A debt has more weight than the coin that pays it," she said. "I don't like to owe anyone. Especially friends. Why do you not borrow from your sister?"

"Oh, no. I've heard that story before: To support the needs of her wastrel brother, a sister shackles herself to a leering, dissolute rake who beats her every night and brings diseases home from a whorehouse every morning." He shook a clenched fist. "I vow I will *starve* and throw myself at my own leering rake before I subject Zenobia to that."

Laughing so hard that tears formed in her eyes, almost a minute passed before Yasmeen caught her breath. She wiped her cheeks. "You're the most absurd romantic. She'd leave you to rot first."

"That's true enough." Both statements were. "So do we have an agreement, then?"

All trace of laughter faded. "As long as we both understand: We are partners. I will not give you orders, and even if I take you to my bed, you will do nothing to undermine me or assume superiority. If you betray me, I will gut you."

If I take you to my bed. This was one of the finest moments of his life. "I understand."

"You don't have anything to add? No stipulations of your own? Warnings?"

"I've already given warning that I intend to fall in love with you."

Her gaze hardened. "The time for games is past, Mr. Fox."

"It's not a game." He matched the gravity of her tone. "Not for lack of trying, I've never been in love. I desperately want to be. And I've come to realize that you've been in my thoughts so long, you're the only one for me."

"I won't encourage you."

"It's too late for that. You encourage me with the way you blow the smoke from between your teeth when you're frustrated. You encourage me with every quick thought and irritated glance. The flick of your eyelashes, the fullness of your lips." He let his gaze slip over her features, worshiping each one. "Your sneer."

Her lips smashed together, and she seemed to fight another laugh before finally relaxing into a smile. "Very well. Fall in love with me, if you like. But don't expect me to do the same."

"I don't."

"All right, then." She leaned forward, green eyes locked on his. "Shall we seal our agreement in blood?"

"I've already promised you my heart."

"Not *our* blood." She tossed a glance to the next table, where a tangle of men beat each other senseless. At the bar, a whore had her legs locked around a sailor's thick neck and her hands over his eyes while a female aviator pummeled his stomach. The other end of the tavern was a mass of shouting and punching, tables tipping and glass breaking. "Theirs. And we'll see how well we watch each other's backs."

Archimedes grinned and shrugged out of his jacket. Far quicker than he, she was already across the room before he stood—and he took a few seconds to watch Yasmeen's very delectable back before a burly woman picked up a chair to swing at it. With a whoop, he dove in.

His head throbbed again, but not with drink—and instead of Yasmeen's knife at his throat, her arm supported his waist. She hadn't stopped laughing since pulling him up from the tavern floor and half-carrying him out to the docks. Her arms were warm and strong, and Archimedes thought that he'd let himself be coshed over the head more often.

Which might, he realized, be the sort of thought only a coshed brain would have.

Her feet slid on the icy boards. Archimedes braced his own, caught her against him, his arm hooked around her waist. *Heaven*. Swearing, she steadied herself and lifted her hand, signaling for a steamcoach idling near a cabstand. As soon as it began puttering toward them, she looked up into his face. Her fingers touched his forehead and came away with a bit of blood.

She shook her head. "I yelled a warning that she was behind you."

He'd heard, he'd looked. "She winked at me."

"Idiot," she said, with no real bite to it. "Barmaids live to smash brawlers over their heads and steal their purses. You're lucky she only got away with your waistcoat."

He sighed. "My favorite, too."

"I like the blue best."

"Then it's not such a loss, after all."

They both backed up a few steps as the rattling coach slid

to a stop next to them. Yasmeen called the direction of his boardinghouse up to the driver. *Then to the docks, where she'd row out to* Vesuvius? Archimedes didn't ask, didn't dare presume. He opened the carriage door, and though she rolled her eyes when he held out his hand, her fingers folded over his as she climbed aboard.

He'd barely seated himself before she climbed aboard *him*.

His breathing stopped. She straddled his legs, the inner muscles of her thighs taut. His hands caught her waist. The coach lurched into motion. She fell against him and he felt the press of her breasts into his chest, the play of her fingers through the back of his hair. In the dark, he couldn't see her expression, but there was no mistaking the warm purr in her voice when she said, "Perhaps we ought to seal our agreement in another way, Mr. Fox."

A devil's choice. Archimedes clenched his teeth against the answer his body demanded him to give. She was still drunk. This would just be a fuck—for her. He wanted more.

But he didn't want to reject her. Her pride was an enormous thing, and even his tongue might not be able to soothe this wound.

Her hot mouth found his neck. A tortured groan welled up from his chest, and she laughed softly. Sharp teeth grazed his jaw before her lips tugged on his earlobe.

"You hold my waist, yet you're all but holding me away," she said into his ear. "Is this a no?"

God help him. "Yes."

"A pity. You'd fall in love with me *much* faster."

No doubt. "I don't want to fall in love too quickly and miss every emotion along the way—even if it leads to frustration and pain."

"Truly?" Though unable to see her, he sensed that she was studying his expression. "You're an unusual man, Mr. Fox."

Then her weight and warmth were gone, his body left aching. A spark lighter flared in the seat opposite; he saw her face, the amused smile, and his cigarillo case—he hadn't even felt her lift it—before the light died.

"Stay with me anyway," he said. "Don't row out to *Vesuvius* this late. Sleep in my room."

"I don't *sleep* in the same bed as a man."

Of course she wouldn't. Not after Bloody Bartholomew. "I'll use the floor."

"Uncomfortable for you."

Better than fishing her body out of the harbor. "There's an empty room next to mine," he said. "Sleep there tonight, and I'll explain it to the house matron in the morning."

Her pause told him she was considering it. "All right. I'll need a room soon, anyway."

"When does *Vesuvius* sail out?"

"In a few more days."

The coach shuddered to a halt. Yasmeen didn't wait for him to open the door. Hopping out, she flicked a coin to the driver. So he *had* hurt her pride, and now she was stabbing at his— but he'd known she was a difficult woman.

That didn't make her paying for the cab sting less, especially now that he knew how little money she had. Gritting his teeth, Archimedes followed her through the boardinghouse entrance. A small lamp offered feeble light in the foyer. A boy in tweed trousers, coat, and hat slept on a bench against the wall. Probably some urchin who'd sneaked in from the cold. When Archimedes closed the door, he jerked awake and blinked owlishly.

"Stay there if you like," Archimedes told him as he passed the bench. "I won't alert the matron."

"She knows I'm here, sir." The boy rubbed his face. "Mr. Gunther-Baptiste?"

Archimedes froze. Ahead, Yasmeen turned smoothly, as if she'd never been headed in the opposite direction. Her gaze found his before she glanced past him, peering into the next room as if searching the darkened parlor for more visitors.

He faced the boy. "I am."

"A message, sir." The boy offered him a letter, the paper rolled and tied with a string rather than folded and sealed. "He told me to wait for you. He said if you couldn't come tonight, to please send a reply that you will come tomorrow morning."

Dread clutched at Archimedes' throat, but he took the message and moved closer to the lamp. The Arabic script was small, neat.

Wolfram,

An opportunity for true freedom has arisen, and your assistance would be appreciated. I will explain all when I see you. Please accept my apologies for the abrupt notice and the hasty summons. I depart from Port Fallow tomorrow.

Hassan

Archimedes glanced up at the boy. "Hail that cab again. Tell him to wait for me."

The boy darted for the door.

"Shall I come?" Yasmeen said. Her fingers rested lightly on the knives sheathed at her thighs.

"No." He wouldn't risk her. "It's only an old friend, but I don't know when I'll return. Take my room tonight; I'll take the other if I need it."

"Are you certain?" Her gaze slipped over his face as if searching out the truth.

God. He should have kissed her in the cab. But if he kissed her in desperation now, no doubt she'd follow him. "I'm certain," he said. "Sleep well, Captain."

She smiled and turned for the stairs. "Beware the barmaids, Mr. Fox."

Hopefully, that would be *all* that he had to beware.

Chapter 6

Hassan's lodgings lay beyond the first canal, in the heart of Port Fallow's wealthy ring of residences. Archimedes knew the location; when his purse had been heavier, he'd spent several nights in a suite of well-appointed rooms. But although they were larger and more comfortable than in Archimedes' current boardinghouse, they hardly befitted Temür Agha's prime counselor.

So did the lack of guards and attention that Archimedes received upon his arrival. A liveried house porter showed him inside, led him up the stairs. The door of Hassan's suite opened to the porter's quiet tapping.

Opened by Hassan himself. A grin widened his bearded cheeks. He spread his arms in welcome, the loose sleeves of his knee-length tunic billowing with the movement. A rectangular bulge beneath the linen was the only remaining evidence of the apparatus that had once been grafted to his chest, designed for labor in the Rabat salt factories. The lung tanks had allowed him to remain beneath the surface of the salinity pools while he cleaned the crystallization from the filters—and now, lent a deep metallic resonance to his every breath and word.

"Wolfram!" He came forward, clasping Archimedes' hand between his. "It is very good to see you."

A warmer greeting than Archimedes anticipated—or deserved, perhaps. Hassan couldn't have known that Archimedes had deliberately sunk the barge that carried Temür Agha's war machines rather than simply losing the shipment, but the counselor might have guessed.

"As it is to see you, Hassan," he replied. "Though unexpected."

"Yes, well—Come. Come inside. I will explain all."

Archimedes followed, disconcerted by the counselor's ebullience. Though he knew the cause of the difference—Hassan was far enough from the Horde's control tower in Rabat that the radio signal couldn't suppress his emotions—in every previous meeting, the counselor had been reserved, choosing each word thoughtfully.

Archimedes was glad for the man, though if Hassan hadn't had much time to adjust to the change, the counselor might be hoping for a swift return to Morocco. Archimedes had once experienced the tower's dampening effect, and the terrifying inability to feel what he'd *known* he ought to feel still lingered like a cancer in his mind. Yet Hassan had lived his entire life under its influence. It was possible that the strength of the man's emotions would be more frightening than the lack of them.

For now, however, Hassan only seemed filled with pleasure at seeing him.

A parlor decorated in pale blues lay to the left. Though three men—two in French naval uniforms, and another as simply dressed as Hassan—were standing around a card table with a large map spread between them, Hassan led him to a sitting room. More rolled letters lay atop a writing desk. A window looked over the tree-lined canal, the bare branches flocked with ice and snow. Hassan gestured to two armchairs flanking the open fireplace.

The counselor settled into the chair nearest the flames. "You'll forgive me. I feel the cold to my bones here. Do you see the gray?" He lifted his chin, stroked his fingers through his curly black beard. "I grow old. Has it been ten years since I saw you last?"

"Not quite nine," Archimedes said.

"Ah, yes. Yes." A faint smile touched the man's mouth. "I can still hear Temür's rage echoing through the *kasbah* when word of the barge's destruction came. Much has changed since that day. But not *enough* has changed."

And with that single statement, the counselor's reserve returned—but it wasn't completely familiar. Weariness accompanied it now, the sort that Archimedes usually saw in soldiers who'd been at war for too long, and with no end to the fighting in sight.

"What would you change?"

"We have long been under the foot of the Horde, Wolfram, and Temür has sacrificed much to lift it. But now the heel is his."

From rebel to dictator. "I'm sorry to hear that."

But not completely surprised. A man with as much power as Temür would not give it up easily, no matter his intentions at the beginning.

The man nodded once, an understated gesture that said Archimedes' sorrow was nothing to his. A deep sigh resonated from his chest. "You have always been a friend to the Horde rebels, Wolfram. I wonder now if you will be a friend to the rebels in Rabat."

"I didn't know there *were* rebels in Rabat."

"A growing number, led by Kareem al-Amazigh." He tilted his head toward the door, as if indicating the man Archimedes had seen in the parlor. "He inspires many of us and reminds our people of the old ways, but we are a people who have not fought for centuries. We need to light a fire beneath them—as was done in England, when the fall of the tower sparked the revolution and drove the Horde out."

"But you want to drive Temür out," Archimedes guessed.

"Yes. And if God wishes it, to put a new man in his place—to create a hero, as the Iron Duke became when he destroyed the tower in London."

"For this, you want my help?" Archimedes grinned. "I *do* have the looks of a hero."

"You have never been serious. It is fortunate that I know you, or I would believe you mock our struggle."

"Never that."

"Which is why I met with you alone. Kareem does not know your heart. Please consider that when you speak with him." Hassan leaned forward, holding his hands to the fire. "You provided the Iron Duke with explosives."

Was this the help that he wanted Archimedes to give? Shaking his head, Archimedes said, "I procured those through Temür. I can't find more for you, not quickly."

And his obligation to Yasmeen came first.

But Hassan made a sweeping motion, as if to return his response. "No, this is not what I hope for. We have a man to supply the weapons, but we do not have the money. This is why we turn to you."

For money? Archimedes had to laugh. "My purse is light, old friend."

"You misunderstand me. I know your life has moved away from smuggling. It is your new occupation that interests us. We will not plunder our own people, but there are treasures of value to the north, and they all belong to no one. Treasures like the da Vinci sketch you discovered."

Archimedes' heart gave a heavy thump. "Where did you hear of the sketch?"

"It is known that Temür possesses it." A frown creased the counselor's brow. "Did you not pay your debt to him?"

Did he? Christ. Did the man have the forgery or the original—or both?

He realized Hassan waited for an answer, and though it felt as if he were speaking after a blow to his stomach, he managed, "I did."

The counselor nodded. "Then you see how such treasures might help us, though you are not Kareem's first choice because of your former association with Temür. We've secured the services of another man, Vincent Ollivier, from the university in Martinique. Are you acquainted?"

He'd never heard of him. Archimedes shook his head.

"He has many maps, diaries. He has studied da Vinci's movements during the Fifty-Years' Siege of the Hapsburg Wall. He believes he can find the location of the clockwork army."

For God's sake. "He's a fraud. I can't tell you how many times I've—"

"Fraud or not, we *are* funding the expedition. I am certain that even if such a rare find eludes us, God willing, we might collect enough smaller items to pay our supplier. But Ollivier lacks practical experience, so I've persuaded Kareem that your participation is necessary . . . and that your loyalty isn't misplaced."

It wasn't. His loyalty lay with Yasmeen, but this expedition might solve several of their problems. "Will you be aboard?"

"Yes, if God wills it. Kareem leaves tomorrow for the New World, hoping to win support and allies there. I will oversee the expedition."

"Do you return to Rabat afterward?"

"That is my intention."

"Will I be able to return with you?"

"Ah, now I see." A chuckle resonated in the counselor's chest. "Your debt is paid, but you wonder if you'll be shackled the moment you step off the airship. I can promise you safe entry if God wishes you the same."

Perfect. "I'll want the same for my partner—and I'll be going as Archimedes Fox. Wolfram Gunther-Baptiste is dead."

"Of course. Are you still partnered with Bilson? I heard a rumor he was also dead, but I hoped it was not true."

"It is. Zombies took him in Paris. The woman I'm partnered with now has ten years' experience flying over Europe, however. There's no question of her skill or trustworthiness."

"If you say that, I believe you." But doubt or worry entered the man's eyes. "A woman?"

A step near the door prevented Archimedes from replying. Kareem al-Amazigh entered. Archimedes stood and took the measure of the future hero of Rabat. Tall and wiry, he gave the impression of strength without the added bulk of overindulgence. Soft brown eyes, a firm mouth, and a full beard suggested compassion and maturity—and a handsome face didn't hurt his cause.

"Mr. Gunther-Baptiste." Kareem smiled with warmth, but Archimedes could see the sharp scrutiny the man gave him, pausing briefly on his bruised jaw and rumpled clothing. "Did you win?"

"I was on my feet when I left." No need to mention that Yasmeen had supported him. "In some fights, that's as close to a win as a man can hope for."

"True words, Mr. Gunther-Baptiste. I trust Hassan has relayed our needs to you?"

"He has. I need to confirm with my partner, but I'm confident we'll be joining the expedition."

"Excellent. We've secured the airship *Ceres*. If God wills it, she leaves tomorrow at noon."

A pit formed in Archimedes' stomach. With effort, he maintained his pleasant expression. "*Ceres*? Under Captain Guillouet?"

"You know the captain? That is good. It is always best not

to begin important endeavors with surprises." With a sweep of his hand, Kareem gestured for Archimedes to precede him to the parlor. "We searched for some time before finding an airship that didn't include females on the crew. I believe that is one of the great tragedies the Horde has forced upon us all: our unmarried women pressed into labor, rather than protected and supported by their fathers and brothers."

"A great tragedy," Archimedes echoed gravely.

The resounding noise behind him might have been a groan.

Yasmeen woke, aware that she wasn't alone in the room. Hopefully it was only Archimedes. Her knees hurt too much to relish a fight with anyone else.

Her eyes immediately adjusted to the dark. Archimedes sat slumped in the chair opposite the bed, wearing a linen shirt with tails pulled free of his lime breeches, legs extended and crossed at the ankles. Even relaxed, the muscles of his calves were strongly defined. A dusting of hair covered his skin, and his feet were heavily callused. When they'd met, the sun had burnished the hair on his head with streaks of gold, but winter had darkened it. The same shade roughened his jaw.

She wanted to rub her cheek against that dark stubble. To climb into his lap and feel his body hard against hers. He'd burned like a furnace. He'd probably keep her warmer than the bed, and as long as he was that, she wouldn't care if he didn't touch her again.

For a while, anyway. She liked to be touched, loved the slow curl of sensation over her skin that followed a hand smoothing over her stomach, the flex of fingers down her spine. She trusted very few men to do it, however—and now one of them was holding back while he fell in love with her.

Foolish man. No good could come of it. Sense told her to stop him. But she suspected that if she tried, Archimedes would only be encouraged. He wasn't a man who took the easy path. No, he *sought* the more difficult ones.

Which meant there was nothing to be done. The only way to discourage him would be to make herself easy—and a woman didn't come any easier than she'd been last night.

Perhaps he heard her stifled laugh, or saw the gleam of her

grin in the dark. His head lifted. "Are you awake?" he asked softly.

She came up onto her elbow. "Awake, and wondering why you aren't in Iceland, trying to pry apart the frozen thighs of the virgin cults. They pose much more of a challenge than I do."

"If all I wanted was to fuck, yes. But I've lusted before, and that's not what I desire now." He reached for the lamp, filled the room with a soft yellow glow. She watched as his gaze slid over her. She'd slept in one of his long shirts, and the untied neckline had slipped down her arm. Unbound for the night, her hair curled over her bare shoulder. He paused only briefly on her ears before meeting her eyes again. "I also want to be certain that I'm not confusing lust with love."

Yasmeen had done that before. "Perhaps there's no difference. Or perhaps you can only know if you've satisfied one, and the other remains."

"Then I will soon be a very frustrated man." He drew a deep breath. "Also, we are married."

Yasmeen grinned. She hadn't been *that* drunk last night. "Caught by the boardinghouse matron, were you?"

"I know where a sketch is."

Her humor vanished. She jolted up to sitting. "What? Where?"

"With Temür Agha in Rabat. There is also a rumor that my debt is settled."

Oh . . . oh, fuck. She did not care for money *that* much. Vengeance was another matter. "Is it the forgery?"

"I don't know. I hope it is not. If Temür discovered that the debt was settled by a fake . . ?" He drifted into a laugh, shaking his head.

Temür would be enraged. But it wouldn't matter, because if he had the forgery Yasmeen would kill him. "We have to see it."

Archimedes nodded. "To that end, we are to join an airship expedition that will eventually take us to Rabat, and my friend Hassan will help us past the trading gates."

Ah, good. That would have been the most difficult part. Though the Horde-occupied territories traded with the New World, few merchants and officials were invited past the port gates and into the cities—and Rabat wasn't easily approached from another direction like England, which was shielded from zombies by the surrounding water and often cloudy enough to fly an airship over, unseen. Yasmeen and Archimedes could have sneaked past Rabat's heavily guarded gates, but it was far simpler to walk through.

"Hassan," she said. "Who is he?"

"One of Temür Agha's advisors. His prime counselor, though he has retired from the position, and gives quiet support to Temür's opposition. He enjoys more freedom than most in Rabat, and that retirement is how he traveled here without question—he has been taking small tours, so that his absence would be unremarkable."

Yasmeen doubted that. Any man who did not note the comings and goings of a close advisor was a fool, and Temür Agha was not. But she cared little about politics; if Hassan could grant them entry to the city, she would take it. "Who is he to you?"

"When I was smuggling, he was Temür's right hand. I often negotiated and secured weapons from him when Temür wasn't available, sent messages through him. He's a good man."

Now he made no sense. "Weapons *from* Temür Agha? I thought he was buying them from you—that you got the weapons from the rebels."

"He *is* a rebel."

"No."

"Yes," he insisted quietly.

"He burned Constantinople to the ground to destroy a rebellion. Do not tell me I am wrong; I was there. I heard the screaming as the firebombs dropped and the war machines rolled over homes. I smelled the bodies roasting and left to rot." She would *never* forget that smell. "Do not say he is a rebel."

His face dark and eyes haunted, Archimedes nodded. "You aren't wrong. But I have heard another story—though probably only bits of it. Hassan can tell you."

Perhaps he could, but it didn't matter. Rebel or not, the only thing to know was that Temür Agha was a ruthless man, not to be crossed lightly.

"So tell me about this expedition—and why we are married."

Archimedes closed his eyes. "It's aboard *Ceres*."

"*Ceres?*" Her laugh started, and she couldn't hold it back. "Guillouet will never let me aboard."

"He will, because you won't be crew, but part of the expedition."

Would money outweigh Guillouet's self-righteous loathing toward her? Oh, but that would be fascinating to see. "Then why are we married?"

"Because Kareem al-Amazigh, who is paying for the expedition, doesn't believe that unmarried women should be flying around without the protection of their brothers and fathers. So we'll be married and sharing a cabin."

She laughed again, loving the absurdity of it. Though the protection of a loved one was a noble sentiment, most of the women in Rabat didn't even know who their fathers and brothers were. In the occupied territories, the Horde's practice of taking laborers' children from their parents and raising them in a crèche erased all familial ties.

Finally able to breathe, she wiped her eyes. "So he has found religion, then? He sounds much like your father."

"Even my father hired you."

"Yes, but I wasn't a woman. I was foreign." She grinned when he tilted his head back, groaning as if in memory of his father's speeches. "But don't worry—I won't shoot Kareem al-Amazigh. Hopefully."

"He won't be aboard." He met her eyes again, and the sudden seriousness of his expression stopped her response. "I have to warn you now. Perhaps I should have spoken up when we made our agreement, but before I spoke to Hassan, I'd still hoped that the woman we saw wouldn't be Temür Agha's guard and we wouldn't have to travel to Rabat to find the sketch. It's a long story, but I was shot, and Hassan gave me a transfusion of his blood—infecting me with his nanoagents so that they could heal me."

"I see." Each occupied territory had a different tower, operating on a slightly different frequency. An infected Englishman could travel to Morocco without being affected by the signal. But a man infected by someone susceptible to the tower would be, too—even if the infection were passed on far away from the occupied territories. As soon as he traveled within the tower's range, it would affect him. "Will you be useless to me in the city?"

His skin had drawn tight, paling over his cheekbones and

jaw. "I can follow orders, carry out instructions. I can act of my free will, but there's no driving emotion, no need, no fear. I wouldn't react to danger or respond to a threat in the same way."

"So you'd lose your balls of iron and silver tongue."

"Yes."

And that terrified him, she realized. Yet he wasn't backing out of this arrangement. He still planned to help her . . . if he could.

"We will see what happens," she said. "Perhaps it will not matter at all. And as long as we are discussing possible shortcomings—"

She swung her legs over the side of the bed. The crack of her knees sounded like muffled gunshots.

"Mornings are difficult," she said. "They loosen up, but I don't know how quickly I can move before they do. If we're ever attacked, I'll probably just stay in bed and shoot whoever comes through the door."

Gaze locked on her knees, Archimedes slipped out of his chair, knelt in front of her. Fingers hovering an inch above her skin, he traced the path of the still-fading scars.

"The ones on the right leg are cleaner," she said. "Those were Jannsen's—the surgeon on Mad Machen's ship. Ivy tells me that Eben's hands were shaking a bit on the left leg, because he'd just spent most of the night in the harbor looking for me, but he wouldn't let her take over. There are about thirty screws still in the bones. Sometimes I think I should have just let Eben cut them off, but they are fine legs, aren't they?"

He looked quickly up into her face, brows drawing together as if not quite believing her wicked tone. When he saw the grin that matched it, he gave a smile of his own.

"Very fine legs. But I'm still waiting."

"Why? We're married now."

"I will not even kiss you until my heart is so full of longing that I cannot help myself. And if you initiate a kiss, I'll consider it a sign that you've fallen madly in love with me, too."

He was serious, she realized. "I'll *say* I love you in bed, if that's what you want to hear."

His brows rose. "Would you truly?"

Would she? If he came to love her, could she tell him the same? Yasmeen had no compunction about lying, but she'd been on the receiving end of such a lie before, and the knife to her belly had hurt less. She wouldn't do that to him.

"No." She shook her head. "I wouldn't."

"Thank God," he said. "Because I'm not ready for you to break my heart."

"But if you fall in love with me, I *will*."

"I know. But try not to break it in Rabat, where I wouldn't feel the anguish properly." He stood and held out his hand. "Now, then. Shall I help you loosen up? *Ceres* awaits us . . . Mrs. Fox."

"Captain Fox," she said, clenching her teeth as he pulled her to her feet and slid his arm around her waist. "And now I'm doubly glad you didn't call yourself 'Stallion.' "

"That will be your secret name for me. I hope you tell everyone."

She laughed through her first step, gritted her teeth again. But with every step, anticipation built. They'd soon be en route to the sketch.

And she was going to completely ruin Captain Guillouet's day.

Chapter 7

They found *Ceres* tethered on the main dock, spars extended and sails furled. Constructed in the fashion of a sugar sloop, a fat balloon held up her heavy-bellied ship, and two propellers flanked a tapered tail. Well made, and although not as sleek or as swift as her lady, *Ceres* would have been fine to look upon if she hadn't been decorated to advertise Guillouet's loyalties. A Huguenot cross was emblazoned across both sides of the balloon in gold and blue, shouting his allegiance to the French king.

Yasmeen hopped out of the steamcoach, and held open the carriage door while Archimedes dragged out their trunk and hefted it onto his shoulder. They didn't have to walk far, though they missed the cargo lift's current run. Four marines and their equipment were already ten feet into the air when she and Archimedes reached the loading platform. *Marsouins*, by the regimented look of them, skilled in aerial and underwater combat—and as they weren't wearing uniforms, probably turned soldiers-for-hire. If Kareem al-Amazigh had secured them for this expedition, he must be expecting Archimedes to find a significant amount of treasure. Al-Amazigh would need at least ten livre just to recoup the cost of the mercenaries.

Archimedes set the trunk by his feet. "Aside from his famous opinion that women shouldn't be serving aboard airships, what have you heard of Captain Guillouet?"

"That opinion is not just his, but famously a navy opinion," Yasmeen said.

No matter the New World nation, very few sailing ships allowed females to join their crews. Guillouet had simply carried on the tradition after he'd been decommissioned and purchased *Ceres*.

"So the makeup of his crew isn't cause for concern, then."

"Don't mistake me, Mr. Fox: I don't have much confidence in any ship that doesn't include women. It means that either the captain doesn't trust his crew to follow his rules, or he doesn't trust his own ability to keep them in line."

"Or he thinks women have no place aboard an airship."

For Guillouet, it was probably a bit of both. "I think *sailors* have no place aboard an airship—and Guillouet is still a sailor. He has no business in the air."

"Is captaining a boat so different from captaining an airship?"

"You truly ask? I'd hate to kill you on our first day of marriage." When he grinned, Yasmeen looked up at *Ceres* with a sigh. "See how he's dressed her up? Guillouet treats her like a whore, parading her around and pandering to patriotism simply to secure a few more rides and a few more coins."

"Forgive me, but—you hired out your lady for men to ride."

She turned narrowed eyes on him. "I didn't say she wasn't a whore. I said he *treats* her like one."

His brows rose. "And that makes all the difference?"

"If ever you'd been treated like a whore, you'd know it does." His lack of reply felt like a brief, angry silence. On her behalf? It was kind of him, but she was sorrier for the airship. "Guillouet was also a cousin to Rousseau."

"*Your* Rousseau?"

"Yes. They both served the French in the war—Guillouet with the navy, Rousseau with the aeronauts. When the treasuries ran low, they were among the first to go. But Guillouet still claims that the continued Liberé Obligation was justified."

"I see," Archimedes said.

Probably better than Yasmeen did. She hadn't arrived in the New World until a few years before the end of the decade-long war, which had been brewing for centuries. Every person gave a different reason for it, but almost everyone agreed that the root of the conflict lay in the sixteenth century, when the zombie infection began to spread west across Africa. The Huguenots, who'd already established settlements in the Caribbean and plantations in the southern American continent, had sent fleets of ships to the west coast of Africa on a mission of mercy. Full kingdoms were given passage across the Atlantic and resettled on Huguenot territory north of the Great Cinnamon River, their only obligation to pay for the use of the land with gold or labor.

Of the next hundred years or so, Yasmeen knew little—until the French, embroiled in a war for territory with the Catholic Lusitanians to the north, offered to release any Africans of their Obligation if they joined the French armies. Thousands went, but Castile and the native confederacies put their weight behind Lusitania, and the French gained little territory north of the Caribbean Sea. The war over, thousands of families who'd fought for the French—now calling themselves the Liberé—found few places to settle and work, and many were told they weren't fit for anything better than pulling carts. Some returned south, but many more moved north, where trade and land agreements with the native confederacies made for more factories and fields offering pay equal to skill.

Archimedes' sister had overstated when she'd claimed that every family in the New World had Liberé and native relations. Many did now, it was true. But if she'd said "neighbors," it would not have been an exaggeration at all.

In the southern American territories, still owned by the king, the Liberé name slowly spread—even among the French nobles and officials who governed the territories. Resistance began with the refusal to acknowledge the long-standing Obligation taxes, still imposed on anyone of African descent. French troops moved south, squashing rebellions as they flared up. Governors and officials were assassinated or replaced, and nobles fled. Overt resistance faded, and began to gain strength in parlors, instead. Supported by the king, churches in the French islands spoke eloquently of duty and obligation—and cart-pulling families like Rousseau's and Guillouet's spent more time in churches than in parlors. When the king promised full citizenship for those who fought for him, they both answered the call.

When the war fizzled, the French began to cut costs. In the first order, twenty thousand commissioned and warrant officers were pared away—the majority of them Liberé. Though the government claimed the decision of whom to let go had been based on officer seniority, Rousseau had said he'd finally seen the truth of where he stood with his countrymen, and would stand with them no longer. Guillouet had accepted the promised citizenship.

But now he was here, because there'd been little opportunity for him in the remaining French territories following the war.

"And what do you think?" Archimedes said.

"Of the war?" At his nod, Yasmeen laughed. Oh, but she'd started many entertaining tavern brawls this way. "I think that the French kings owned the land, and that taxes are the way of the world." When his face darkened and his mouth opened, she grinned and continued, "I also think that, for hundreds of years, it was in the Huguenots' best interests to think of the Liberé as cart-pullers, and so they justified their every action with the original obligation so that they could continue believing they were right—and continue filling their treasury."

The thunderous expression lightened. "I can still fall in love with you, then."

He would do well to wait until she was done.

"I also know that the Liberé are burning down villages and massacring natives to clear land and grow more coffee. The Lusitanians supported the Liberé in the war, but they smuggle in slaves from the Horde-occupied territories to work their mines. The Castilian queen and her court eat from plates of gold while her people starve in the streets and call for her head."

"And Johannesland?" His eyes were bright with amusement. "My mother's people are not so terrible."

"Their princes squabble among themselves, and they supported the French simply because the king is not Catholic. They are not terrible, but they are stupid, and that is almost as bad." She looked up as the cargo lift began to descend. "The French are no better or worse than all of them, because everyone serves their own interests. And that is why I prefer Port Fallow and the Ivory Market to all the rest of the world: No one pretends they are doing anything else."

"Including you . . . even though it would serve your interests to reach Rabat more quickly aboard Mad Machen's ship."

Damn him for picking at nits. Of course she'd thought of that, and rejected it. "It serves my interests *not* to have my friends killed while helping me." She gave him a smile that showed the sharp edges of her teeth. "A husband, however . . . it will be quicker than divorce."

His laugh was loud and full, and continued over the clank of the lift coming to a rest on the platform. He dragged their trunk aboard—filled primarily with his weapons and contraptions, and the warmest of their clothes. For Yasmeen, that meant *all* of her clothes, and the few heavy woolen and fur pieces she'd traded for her silver cigarillo case that morning.

She braced her feet when the lift began to rise. "Did you bring any cigarillos?"

"A few, but not many. I only smoke them with you."

Because they were so expensive. Yasmeen sighed. "I'll probably become irritable."

"Do you think I'll notice the difference?"

The look she gave him would have cowed a lesser man, but nothing of Archimedes Fox was less, including the width of his grin. She could not help but laugh, and it was still in her mouth when the lift locked into place against *Ceres'* side. Waiting to welcome them aboard, Captain Guillouet stood a few feet away, looking so much like his cousin Rousseau that pain stabbed her chest.

His gaze landed on her, and his face contorted with disbelief and anger, erasing all resemblance to his cousin. He turned to the man waiting next to him, who by description Yasmeen guessed was Hassan.

"*That* is the wife?"

Every aviator on deck turned to look. Clearly taken aback by Guillouet's tone, Hassan only nodded.

"She is not welcome on this vessel!"

Guillouet bellowed the declaration so that everyone would hear—and would know him for a fool when he was overruled on his own ship. Yasmeen barely contained her amusement; that would not go over well with the crew, either. No need to antagonize the only people who could make this trip unbearable.

Hassan looked bewildered. "Explain, Captain."

"Corsair. She calls herself Lady Corsair. It means she was a privateer—a friend to the French, you understand? But she was no friend to us."

She'd done every single job well. Yasmeen reached for her cigarillo case, but it wasn't there.

When Hassan looked to her, she said, "The French newssheets gave me the name."

"Newssheets." Guillouet spat. "Misguided fools, supported by the nobles. You took our money *and* Liberé money that rightly belonged to our king."

Already, the irritation began to set in. "Then it seems I only took French money," she said.

Understanding finally came to Hassan's face, and Yasmeen realized that he hadn't been lost, only having difficulty with the language. "A mercenary?"

"Yes," Yasmeen said.

Though there was no visible hardening of Hassan's expression, though he didn't stand any straighter or raise his voice, he suddenly gave the impression of quiet strength and authority. He looked to Guillouet. "Does her presence mean you will not take *my* money, Captain?"

The threat was clear. Guillouet's jaw tightened, the struggle visible on his face. An airship captain who stood on principles over money soon had no ship to stand on. "I will not allow her to share meals in my cabin. You cannot ask that insult of me."

"You will insult her, too?"

"It's no insult," Yasmeen said. She didn't want to eat with him, either. "The wardroom will do."

Faint apology entered Hassan's voice. "The wardroom is taken by the *marsouins*. I have already displaced several of the captain's men."

"We can eat with the crew," Archimedes suggested. "We've made the acquaintance of several, and enjoyed their company before."

They had?

"Very well, then." With a sharp nod, Guillouet pivoted on his heel, began shouting orders.

With the only threat to her diminished, Yasmeen finally looked away from Guillouet and glanced over the aviators on deck. Her gaze stopped on one large man who sported a puffy bruise over his left eye and a split lip. The red-shirted twin. She couldn't suppress her grin when the recently deflowered Henri raced toward them, offering to show them to their cabin. The boy reached for the trunk but was stopped by Archimedes.

"I've got that, young Henri," Archimedes said. "It's heavier than it appears."

The trunk wasn't at all heavy for a man infected by nano-agents, but it did look impressive when he so easily hefted it over his shoulder and turned to Hassan.

"Hassan, allow me to introduce my wife—Captain Yasmeen Fox."

He took far too much pleasure in saying that. She returned Hassan's greeting, adding in Arabic, "Thank you for handling that so well. Though I am not surprised by your diplomacy, given all that my husband has told me of your association with him."

His eyes widened slightly, and his gaze ran over her face, as if trying to place her appearance and dialect. Yasmeen wondered what his reaction would be when she removed the warm hat with the Arctic fox-fur flaps that covered her braids—and her ears.

"It is sometimes the nature of business, unfortunately," he said. "And now I see that it was wise to bring your husband on as Archimedes Fox. We will hope that Captain Guillouet doesn't realize who Wolfram was selling those weapons to."

When her brows rose, Archimedes supplied under his breath, "Primarily, the Liberé."

Yasmeen laughed, and was favored by a grin from the older man.

"It *is* very good to meet you, Captain. I hope you will come speak with me later, after you've settled—and I have had my midday rest. I am but a frail old man."

He continued smiling as he spoke, but Yasmeen couldn't miss the weariness behind the good humor. She nodded and looked to Henri, who had been waiting, listening, and clearly not understanding a word.

"Well, Henri. Show us the way, then."

Their cabin was tiny, housing two stacked bunks with barely space enough to walk beside. Brass hooks screwed into the bulkhead offered a place to hang their clothing, and their trunk slid below the bottom bunk. A washstand stood in the corner. A porthole offered just enough sunlight to see.

It was perfect.

"Top or bottom?" Archimedes said, indicating the bunks.

"Bottom." Her knees wouldn't allow anything else. "That went well with Guillouet, didn't it?"

"Very. And now it will be easy to avoid him."

"Yes." Seeing the man would be inevitable, especially on the main deck, but no one would expect them to exchange any words. "I'd like to go above before we start out."

"And see how a sailor's crew handles her?" Archimedes guessed correctly. He retrieved his fur hat and their aviator goggles. "I'll accompany you, and count the number of faults you add to Captain Guillouet's character."

"We will see if they ever equal yours." Tugging on her own hat, she stepped into the corridor and almost collided with a portly man, face long and belly ample. Receding brown hair had been combed back from his pale features, and he wore a mustache and beard in the current French fashion, with chin and jaw shaven, and whiskers sweeping to his ears like a walrus's.

Recognition hit her. "Why, it's Mr. Ollivier!"

"Lady Corsair." His eyes darted from her face to Archimedes', then down the passageway as if looking for an escape. "I didn't realize you were aboard."

"Oh, yes. With my husband, Archimedes Fox. You've heard of him?"

"Yes." Surprise brought his focus back to Archimedes, and curiosity slipped through his panic. "Yes, of course. I follow your adventures with interest, Mr. Fox."

"Of course you do," Yasmeen said. "Tell me, will you be eating at the captain's table?"

"Yes."

"Wonderful." She grinned. "I have heard we will speak to you about the expedition when our friend Hassan awakes. I look forward to seeing your maps. Until then, Mr. Ollivier!"

She had to give Archimedes credit—he waited until they were up on the main deck before asking, "What was all that?"

"I will tell you." The engines started, a familiar thrum beneath her feet. *Oh.* Her heart hitched painfully. On earth or in sky, there was no sweeter sound than a well-tended propulsion engine. "Come with me aft!" she called to Archimedes over the noise. "There's no net across her bow—we don't want to be killed by a bird!"

A few aviators heard her. Yasmeen didn't care. A captain took care of their safety, or he didn't deserve the title. She led Archimedes to the stern, where the engines spewed clouds of smoke and steam into the air.

He turned his back to the rail. "Also, because it's loud!" he shouted. "You won't be overheard!"

"Yes!" she called out and leaned closer. "Do not eat or drink anything without letting me taste it first. *Anything.* Even something from your trunk, if you keep a flask."

Suddenly serious, his green eyes met hers. "Why?"

"Ollivier's an assassin. Or he was, during the war. A Liberé sympathizer. He'd pose as an academic—in truth, he *is* an academic—and make his way into important households. He uses poisons." A cowardly way to go about it, in Yasmeen's opinion, but Ollivier considered poison a more refined method of assassination than knives or guns. "Guillouet probably doesn't know. He calls me a traitor, but Ollivier *is* a traitor."

"Do you think he would poison us, then?"

"I don't know. The war is long over, but he might fear that I'll say something—or hold it over his head. So we'll be careful."

Archimedes nodded. The engines directly below their feet were huffing hard now. With the propellers beginning to spin, even shouts were difficult to hear. She held up her goggles and gestured to the pair around his neck. When the wind started, he'd want to put them on.

The crew hauled in the canvas sails that had taken them out of the harbor. *Ceres* skimmed over the snow-covered plain south of Port Fallow, beyond the high wall, where the bodies of zombies lay piled against the base. The sugar sloop wouldn't gain as much speed as Yasmeen's skyrunner, perhaps forty-five knots at her best, but even at that speed the wind tangled her hair and the icy cold burned her face. Yasmeen pushed the goggles up to her forehead. Archimedes might wonder if her tears were from the wind or the joy of flying again—but there was no difference. She looked over at him, found him watching her through the smoked lenses of his goggles.

"Do you see how she can make you feel?" she shouted. "And if you care for her, there's nowhere she can't take you.

So it doesn't matter how she earns her money. If she can make you feel like this, you treat her like a lady."

But, oh *how* she missed hers.

Archimedes remained with her above decks for hours, watching the plains run up into the great forests. Enormous sections had been cut through them, swaths of tree stumps with seedlings growing between. Knowing that stripping the land would leave it useless to future generations, the Horde had established a regulated system of harvesting and replanting over the centuries.

Yasmeen leaned in, called over the wind. "Does it seem that we're heading toward Vienna?"

He hoped not. Nothing was there. But he couldn't confirm it; Hassan hadn't woken from his rest, after which they'd meet with Ollivier.

Shielding her eyes against the setting sun, she pointed west. In the distance, a Horde outpost rose out of the trees like a giant stone citadel.

"They are flying dangerously close," Yasmeen said. "Who is their navigator?"

He shook his head. They hadn't had a moment to talk to any of the crew, though several were on deck. Beneath the watchful eye of Captain Guillouet, they probably didn't dare. Initially, Archimedes had wondered if Yasmeen remained above decks just to piss the man off, but no—she simply couldn't bear to go below.

A large stand of old forest appeared below them. Archimedes pointed to a path cutting through it. "Is that a road?"

Yasmeen frowned. "I can't recall seeing it before. Do you have a pair of biperspic lenses?"

She wouldn't ask the captain or helmsmen for the spyglass, of course. "I do," he said. "But they're in my trunk."

A bell rang. Yasmeen's head jerked around, and she opened her mouth before snapping it closed. She caught his gaze, sighed. "It's not my ship."

He didn't need to ask how difficult this was for her. She'd remarked many times on what the crew did right and what could be improved. Other times, she simply watched with frustration tugging at her lips, her fingers twitching and reaching for her belt. If he went below for the lenses, he'd probably serve her better by bringing a cigarillo—though she'd have a difficult time keeping one lit when she wasn't behind the helm's shield on the quarterdeck. That might irritate her more than the lack of smoke.

She turned her back on the deck to look over the side, as if determined not to be interested in the goings-on. The slowing of the propellers turned her back round.

"Are we stopping?"

Yasmeen looked to him as if he might have seen something while her back was turned, but he shook his head. The aviators had suddenly become more active, and the captain gave orders from the quarterdeck, but Archimedes couldn't make out the words.

The engines quieted, blowing only steam now, venting the boilers with no propulsion. The aviators extended the spars in preparation for unfurling the sails.

"Oh, look at that." Yasmeen's amused voice brought him to the side again. She was looking over into a clearing below. "It's Jasper Evans's harvester. I can't believe he made it all the way here."

Archimedes believed it. Shaped like a combination of an armored coach and a scorpion, the machine rolled on tracks of steel plates rather than segmented legs, with giant shears in the front and shredders behind. Whether it met a forest or a mob of zombies, the harvester would tear through it . . . and must have torn through almost two hundred miles.

Five months ago, Jasper Evans had famously escaped the English navy, who had been firebombing his underground compound in Calais. He'd taken with him his ladylove, Dame Sawtooth—an airship pirate who was everything that her name suggested. Unlike the laborers in the occupied territories who had tools grafted to their bodies by the Horde, the Dame was a New Worlder who'd chosen her augmentation: a jaw full of sawblades instead of teeth.

He glanced back at the crew. Captain Guillouet had disappeared from the quarterdeck, probably gone below. Most of the aviators on deck were at the side of the ship, looking down at the harvester.

A light dusting of snow covered the machine. The round hatch at the top had been left open. Though Archimedes couldn't believe that the two fugitives would be hiding inside, Yasmeen knew them better than he. He'd heard tales of Scarsdale and Captain Corsair drinking them under the table in the Port Fallow taverns, simply for the fun of listening to Evans's soused ramblings.

"Would Evans and the Dame be in there?" he asked.

"No. But if he is, we're complete fools to be hovering over the clearing like this. Jasper is cracked but he isn't harmless." Her gaze swept the edges of the clearing. "No zombies yet."

"No. But they'll come." Archimedes nodded toward the four marines who'd climbed up to the main deck and were setting their rapid-fire guns near the bow. "Especially if they begin shooting."

Zombies were attracted to noise and movement. When Archimedes was on the ground, he couldn't always avoid moving, especially if he needed to get around. But avoiding any noise was critical to survival.

Unless he was running for his life. Then noise became optional and better than dying.

Hassan climbed out of the hatchway and onto the deck, rubbing the sleep from his face. He joined Archimedes and Yasmeen at the side and looked over. "Captain Guillouet tells me that this man and woman have a large reward on their capture, whether dead or alive."

"That's true," Archimedes said. The English navy had sent notice to almost every town on the North Sea, spurring too many unprepared excursions into zombie-infested Europe. "It's fifty livre each."

"Shall we attempt it, then? I know it is not the sort of treasure we intended to find."

Not a clockwork army, but still lucrative. He looked to Yasmeen, who was shaking her head.

"The Dame was barely alive when they escaped. She might have died during their journey, but he loves her. He wouldn't leave her body down there to rot. And leaving the hatch open . . . if he's alive, he wouldn't have. If he died inside, he wouldn't have."

"He might have left it open while he was gathering provisions." Archimedes was familiar with that tactic. "If he's chased, he doesn't have to take time to open it again."

"But that also means that he hasn't returned—so he'd be a zombie or lying dead out there somewhere." She indicated the dense forest with a sweep of her hand. "But there's also the way he left the harvester out in the open like this. It's not like him. After the navy stole the steelcoat suits from him, he guards his inventions."

Hassan nodded thoughtfully. "I agree, it sounds unlikely that either is inside. But would you be willing to take a closer look to be certain?"

Fifty or a hundred livre was a lot to pass up. "I'll go down," Archimedes said.

"Then I will, too." Yasmeen met his eyes. "At least if Dame Sawtooth's body is there, she's easy to identify."

Archimedes saw the crew moving toward the cargo lift and stopped them. "That makes too much noise. We'll take the rope ladder."

They unrolled it quickly. He glanced at Yasmeen, who was slipping off her long coat and heavy hat.

"I'll go down first," she said.

"But—"

"I'm faster. If any zombies do come, I can kill them before you do." She glanced at the marines. "Tell them to hold off shooting."

Almost faster than he could track, she went over the side. Not bothering with the rungs, she slid quickly down the ropes. Near the bottom, she flipped her legs out, spun through the air like an acrobat, and landed silently in a crouch. God, what an incredible woman. His own descent was embarrassingly slow by comparison.

He reached the ground. Snow crunched softly under his feet. The light was fading quickly, the edges of the clearing lost in shadows.

"Do you see anything?"

"No." Her voice was as quiet as his. "Let's go."

She ran toward the machine. God, she was quick and light

on her feet. She rounded the machine and paused. The oval door-sized hatch on this side was also open.

Unease slipped through him. Leaving the hatch open on top made sense—zombies didn't climb. But they could walk right through the main hatch. "Would he do *this*?"

"No." She studied the dark interior. "But I would wager anything that he's set it to blow."

"When's the last time it snowed?" He judged the snow around them. "Two, three days ago? But there's barely any on the machine, and no tracks. The wind might have cleaned it off, but either way, it hasn't been sitting long."

"He's probably hiding around here somewhere and this is his warning system." She met his eyes. "What do you think?"

"I trust my gut. If we go in there, we're dead."

Yasmeen agreed. They ran back to the ladder, climbed up. Hassan met them at the top. "You didn't go inside?"

"She's rigged to blow," Archimedes said.

One of the marines stepped forward. The leader of the group, Archimedes guessed. His boots polished to a high shine, each buckle of his jacket in a straight line, his brown beard precisely trimmed, he looked the sort that lived by details and never let imperfections pass by without correcting them—or destroying them.

"What sort of explosive? We're trained to defuse several types of devices."

"Including Jasper Evans's devices?" He looked to Hassan. "You know me well. If there's a chance to survive, there's nothing I won't try. I don't believe there's much of a chance here."

After a brief moment, Hassan nodded. "All right, then. We will let it be."

"But you didn't *see* the device, Mr. Fox?" This from Captain Guillouet. "You only *think* that it's there."

"I didn't see it," Yasmeen said. "But I know Evans well enough to say he'd rather destroy the machine than let someone else have it."

Archimedes gritted his teeth when the captain didn't acknowledge her answer with so much as a glance. Christ. She had more experience and knowledge than half the men on that deck put together.

Guillouet continued, "Mr. Hassan, if you've passed on this opportunity to collect the reward, I hope you'll forgive the small delay as I allow my crew to try?"

"Yes, but I counsel against it."

"And pass up a possible fifty livre reward?" Guillouet smiled. "If I split it equally between my men, that's two each. That's more than they make in a year. I believe they'll take that risk."

Several of the aviators nodded, eyes widening at the mention of such a sum. Yasmeen's mouth tightened.

Guillouet turned to the marine. "Mr. Bigor, please lead your men down. Be quick, before you lose the light."

"Yes, sir." Bigor jerked his head at his men, and they moved in step to the rope ladder.

Anger was one of the few emotions that Archimedes never deliberately stoked, and he was slow to rise to a temper. But it could happen, now and again.

"Mr. Bigor, a moment!" he called out. When the man paused at the side of the ship, Archimedes joined him and said, "Have you encountered many zombies before?"

The man gave a stiff nod, eyes hard. "A few."

Only a few? Archimedes wasn't surprised. The four men were skilled, no doubt, though he'd have wagered they hadn't been long on this side of the Atlantic.

A moan sounded from below, barely audible above the creak of the ship and the flap of canvas. But of course there was—Archimedes had just yelled the man's name, hadn't he? And no one had called him an idiot.

From the corner of his eye, he saw Yasmeen lean over the side and scan the tree line. Apparently she'd been listening for the moan, too.

"Then you probably know to destroy the brain, or take off the head," Archimedes said. "But there's more to know."

He drew his revolver. The other man tensed, but Archimedes was already turning away from him, looking toward the harvester. He tipped the bullets out of the chamber. Picking up one, he flung it at the machine. The bullet struck the top with a faint *ping*!

"They're fast," he said as one burst from the shadows and

raced across the clearing, hissing. With matted hair and sunken features, the zombie was too emaciated and filthy to determine gender—or perhaps all indications had been eaten or rotted off.

Many of the aviators recoiled in instinctive repulsion. Bigor didn't flinch. He raised his hand, stopping his comrade when the other marine aimed his rifle.

"They'll investigate any noise." Archimedes threw another bullet. *Ping!* The zombie was growling now, a rasping, ravenous sound. "And if they encounter a structure, they'll search for a way in."

The zombie disappeared around the side. Archimedes waited.

The explosion rocked the harvester back, flipping the shredder's tail up like a scorpion readying to strike. Metal shrieked. Smoke boiled from the top hatch.

"And that's all there is to know." Archimedes clapped the man on the back. "You can go down and look for the Dame and Evans now, Mr. Bigor, but you'd best hurry. I can already hear more of them coming."

Yasmeen wouldn't have handled that half as well. Too used to giving orders, she'd have insisted that Guillouet retract the order he'd given the marines, and probably would have ended up shooting someone—or at least throwing punches. She'd never have considered throwing bullets.

She followed Archimedes down the ladder from the main deck, and was halfway to their cabin before she realized that he was furious. He stalked into the small room, throwing his hat and coat over his bunk. Two paces brought him to the washstand. He whipped around, almost paced into her.

Taking a quick step back, she flattened her hand against his solid chest. His heart pounded. His jaw had set like stone, his emerald eyes were bright. Her breath seemed to slip away. Oh, he was magnificent when roused. She could have looked at him for hours, but she settled for the time it took to breathe again.

"You're an impressive specimen of a man, Mr. Fox," she finally said.

His gaze narrowed, fell to her lips. The pace of his heart quickened. Then he all but wrecked her when he stroked the back of his fingers down her cheek.

Pleasure streaked through her, the urge to lift into his touch and purr. She contained her shudder, remained still as he covered her hand with his, holding it to his chest. His eyes closed, and she was never more grateful for a moment alone.

She pressed the tips of her fingers to her cheek, steadied herself. He didn't even know what he'd done to her—and how rarely she felt a sweet touch that asked for absolutely nothing. Swallowing, she said, "You averted that disaster up there perfectly. Of course, Guillouet will hate you now, too."

"It can't be helped. He's a shit captain." He expelled a hard sigh. "It's not just that he's a sailor."

Perhaps not. There were many reasons that men unsuitable to be captains were put in the position. "Well, I'm beginning to believe I was wrong about why the French cut him from their ranks. It's not because of ancestry or money at all. He's a blind ass."

A smile finally lifted the corners of his handsome mouth. His eyes opened—not angry now, but not amused either. He regarded her thoughtfully. "There are few things my father said that I've ever agreed with, but one of them was: There are men who give orders, and men who take them. Captains, they often seem like they give them, but there's always a superior officer somewhere that he answers to, and an admiral that answers to a king or a parliament, who answer to their people. But a man making his living out here—or a mercenary—answers to no one. So a man fit to be captain in a war might not be fit to captain his own ship, because there's no one thinking for him anymore and telling him what to do, how to act."

Though Yasmeen didn't disagree, she couldn't help but be amused. "I remember this from a sermon. I believe your father's point was that we are all deceived about our place, and we all take orders from God."

He grinned. "I just take the bits I want to."

"And what are you, Mr. Fox?" Yasmeen knew what she was. "Do you give orders, or take them?"

"I'm the type to get the damn job done myself." He lifted her hand, pressed a warm kiss to the backs of her fingers. "Now, let's find out where this job is taking us."

Chapter 8

Featuring a private privy and wardrobe, a writing desk and a berth that was wider than a plank, Hassan's stateroom was larger than their cabin by far. A small table allowed him to eat in privacy, if he preferred—now, it was spread with a large map. Hassan settled into the table's cushioned chair, quietly sipping his tea and leaving Yasmeen and Archimedes to discuss their route with Ollivier, who didn't speak Arabic. On the desk, Ollivier had piled several books, sheaves of notes, and old maps.

The first city he pointed to made Archimedes groan. "No," he said. "Vienna is picked clean. I myself have been there seven times, a total of four months on the ground. There's simply nothing left."

Yasmeen said, "All of the men I've carried there have said the same. There's nothing to be found. It's been abandoned the longest, so it's been picked over the longest."

"I am not interested in Vienna, but just outside of it. I had opportunity to study Prince Albert the Fair's archives," Ollivier said, as if in explanation. "His many-times great-grandmother was one of the Fleeing Hapsburgs."

A member of the ruling family in Vienna and the surrounding principalities during the Horde's advancement into Europe, the Hapsburgs had fought to the bitter end—and in the New World, were as celebrated as da Vinci. But a few of the Hapsburg family had fled; they had not been looked upon kindly, and were often portrayed as villains and cowards in the theatrical plays and histories.

From beneath his notes, Ollivier brought forth a colored woodcut print protected beneath a glass plate. Faded greens and browns depicted rolling hills behind a walled city, with a river and swimming swans in the foreground. The peaked roofs of the city were all in orange and blue, and the buildings stood tall, with several ornate spires reaching into the pale sky.

"The old man was the last of his line before his demise, so I was able to acquire this woodcut from his collection, which is a faithful reproduction of a painting made by the Hapsburg grandmother."

Yasmeen looked up at Archimedes. No doubt "acquiring" meant stealing after he'd poisoned the man. Lovely.

Ollivier continued, "Her painting of the city was the latest one that I've seen created by someone actually *in* Vienna. Many others are based upon older artworks or drawn from memory. Do you see this?" He pointed to a stout stone structure in the background, almost hidden in the rolling hills. "I've never seen it in any other depiction."

Eyes narrowing, Archimedes leaned close to study the woodcut. "That's true. I haven't seen it before, either. But I also haven't seen anything like this ruin when I was in the city."

"But it is up in the hills, do you see? If the forest had grown up around it, the view might have been obstructed."

Archimedes nodded. "All right. What do you think it is?"

The assassin hauled out another map of Vienna and the surrounding area. "A possible place to build the clockwork army. Its position is perfect: near enough to the Hapsburg Wall that if the Horde were to break through, the soldiers would be readily available to stop them—but also far enough away to allow time to mount a defense."

"The Hapsburgs had da Vinci's machines on this side of the wall."

"But they were created to defend the wall and to halt the Horde's machines, not to stop troops of mounted soldiers from coming through. A clockwork army could slow them."

Though clearly doubtful of that possibility, Archimedes peered at the woodcut again, asking Ollivier about dates, verifying the history of the piece. Yasmeen only half-listened, watching him, admiring the line of his jaw, his careful study of the items Ollivier had brought. She'd never given much thought to how he'd prepared for his adventures, but he'd obviously done something similar to this: poring over old maps, reading through letters, comparing different accounts of the Horde advance and Europe's retreat.

Finally, he nodded. "Clockwork army or not, if the structure was newly built before the zombie infection came through the city, then it's worth looking for—and hopefully it was built solid enough that it's more than a pile of rubble."

Ollivier beamed. Encouraged, he selected more maps. "If we find nothing there, our next location is Brenner's Pass."

Brenner's Pass? Yasmeen shook her head. She easily found the pass on Ollivier's map. She placed her finger directly beside it. "There is a Horde outpost right here."

"And that only supports my theory. This has long been recorded as an important pass. If the Horde broke through the wall, they would have needed to come through the pass to the Italian peninsula. And we know from the letters of generals and merchants that there were supplies being sent up to the pass, along with engineers and laborers. They were building something there."

"Da Vinci's machines," Archimedes said.

"Those, too. But even if we do not find the clockwork soldiers, this location isn't picked over. We'll find something in the fortress they constructed there. And in the deep snow, the zombies won't be such a threat."

Archimedes gave him a long, unreadable look before glancing at Yasmeen. She grinned, showing him the tip of her tongue caught between her teeth. His shoulders shook in a silent laugh, and the exaggerated lift of his brows said he was astonished that she'd managed to remain silent.

Ollivier might know his way around a map, but he clearly hadn't spent any time on the ground. Although severe cold could freeze a zombie, it didn't kill them, and they were mobile again as soon as they thawed. A very cold zombie was sluggish; because of that, many people thought that if one of the creatures was surrounded by snow, it posed less of a threat. But the worst danger came from deep snow, with zombies under it, and not quite cold enough to slow them down.

"What of the outpost?" Yasmeen said. "If *Ceres* is spotted, the Horde will come and look."

"We could hike in to the fortress or drop in on gliders at

night, and arrange for pickup after a few days," Archimedes said. "As long as *Ceres* doesn't hover during the day, it won't draw attention to us."

Ollivier nodded, and seemed to breathe a sigh of relief. "From there we move around the Adriatic Sea," he said. "I've picked out a few locations to search, all based on their tactical position."

Archimedes frowned. "Tactical position for what?"

"You recall the fragment of the correspondence between da Vinci and Luca Pacioli? They were discussing Hannibal marching on Rome."

Shaking his head, Archimedes said, "Rome has been picked through like Vienna. The Church has been sending salvagers for hundreds of years."

"Oh, no—I was thinking not of Rome itself, but the strategy. The Hapsburg Wall had already been constructed. If da Vinci and the generals wanted to send an army east, they'd have to get over their own wall first. But if they go about it as Hannibal did, and come from an unexpected direction . . ." He pointed to the boot of the Italian peninsula. "Launching from here, perhaps, and attacking the Horde from the south. And they'd have kept it quiet, so that the Horde wouldn't know they were coming."

Again, Archimedes didn't appear convinced, but he nodded. "All right. It's worth a look. May I study your notes?"

Obviously pleased by the request, Ollivier nodded and began gathering his papers. "Yes, of course. Let me put them in order, and I will have them brought to you."

Arms full, he left the stateroom. Archimedes looked to Hassan. "He knows what he's about. He has unique sources. He's put the information together in unusual ways, but it's good information."

"Good. We'll be in Vienna tomorrow morning; you can start your work then, God willing." With effort, the older man stood, his heavy breath resonating deeply in his chest. "Forgive me. I'd hoped to have more opportunity to sit with you before I joined the captain for dinner, but the business with the reward has cut into that time. Perhaps tomorrow, you will take the midday meal here with me."

"We will," Archimedes said.

Hassan's gaze moved to Yasmeen, then to the kerchief over her hair. Though the tips of her ears were concealed beneath the blue silk, she had no doubt that he'd recognized what she was.

He smiled faintly. "You are a surprise to me, Captain Fox. I am tempted to throw diplomacy away and miss dinner in the captain's cabin simply so that I can discover more about you."

Miss the captain's dinner the first night aboard *Ceres*, after he'd brought an insult to the captain aboard, and allowed Archimedes to destroy a possible hundred-livre reward? "You flatter me," she said. "But you are too wise to be tempted at all."

Hassan's smile broadened. "There are times I wish I could be the fool—especially when I face a night spent soothing ruffled feathers."

"It is too late. *I* have taken the part of the fool," Archimedes said, coming around the table and sliding his hand into hers. "I have already succumbed to temptation and will spend the night basking in her presence. Come, my wife. A fine meal awaits us."

It had been some time since Yasmeen had eaten with an aviator crew, but the messes on an airship's berth deck were all the same. Long tables ran down the center of the deck. Benches on either side provided seats. Farther aft, beyond a set of paneled partitions that provided little privacy, rows of bunks lined the sides of the deck.

Silence fell when Archimedes and Yasmeen climbed down the ladder, though the aviators must have known they were coming; word of the altercation with Guillouet as they'd boarded would have swept through the crew before she and Archimedes had settled in their cabin. Eighteen men sat at the table—only the deck crew on watch was missing. She saw curiosity, irritation, a refusal to meet her eyes. All right. She wasn't sure whether each of those reactions was because she was a woman or because she was Captain Corsair, but she'd figure it out soon enough.

But whether these men considered themselves her enemy, it was always best not to make an enemy of a cook. Though the stew slopped onto her tin plate wouldn't have been fed to her crew, Yasmeen smiled and said thank you.

Archimedes walked with her to the table. She'd already told him who to sit by, if possible—the first mate had influence over the other aviators, and they'd already made his acquaintance. With his charming grin in place, Archimedes stopped beside the big man with the bruise over his eye.

"Last night, I thought you hit me so hard I saw double. Now I know it's not true."

The first mate laughed and made room on the bench. Across from him, his twin did the same. "I wish I'd known I was fighting Archimedes Fox. I'd have shined my knuckles up a bit."

Yasmeen took the seat next to him as Archimedes rounded the table. The first mate glanced at her, but though she'd taken twice as many men down in the brawl, he didn't invite her into the joke as he had Archimedes. That was all right. They didn't have to feel comfortable with her. She was here to observe and listen, not to make friends.

She picked up a powder biscuit, broke it in half, and stared. It was wormy.

The mutter came from farther down the table. "Captain thinks she's too good for us."

No, worms didn't bother her—she simply didn't understand why an airship carried infested supplies. Unlike a ship that spent weeks between ports, an airship could refill their stores easily.

She bit off a chunk, searching for any unusual flavors. The barley and salted-beef stew had already begun to congeal. The watered-down grog tasted like shit, but it was all safe to eat—and all from the same source. She met Archimedes' eyes, gave a small nod.

A thin aviator on Archimedes' right cleared his throat. "I was sorry to hear about *Lady Corsair*, Captain. A fine ship, she was. It was always a pleasure to see her fly."

"She's not a captain." This came from the other end of the table. "She has no ship, no crew, no commission. She's not a captain."

"She's my captain," Archimedes said.

Yasmeen smiled and waited for it.

"Mon capitaine?" The first mate's brother lifted his head. "On this ship, there's 'my arse' and 'my God,' but no 'my captain.' "

Cheers sounded up and down the table, the men laughing. Archimedes' brows rose. She shook her head. It wasn't mocking, and their reactions told her what she'd hoped to discover: A good portion of these men had once been sailors, but they weren't tied to the navy with bonds so tight that good-natured humor couldn't slip in between.

"You're still mine," Archimedes said, holding her gaze.

Yasmeen's lips parted. How did he do that? It was a personal, possessive claim, stated in front of a crew, but it was clearly supportive rather than undermining her.

Flustered, she looked to the thin aviator beside him, the one who'd complimented her lady. "Thank you, Mr. . . . ?"

A blush darkened his cheeks. "Leroy, ma'am."

"Thank you, Mr. Leroy. It was a pleasure to fly her."

The first mate leaned forward, stuck his hand over the table. "Vashon, here. Peter. That's Paul."

"Vashon," Archimedes repeated. "Of the Flying Vashons?"

Yasmeen's brows rose. The Vashons were a famous French aviator family whose generations of military honors and aerostat inventions had built them into a legend.

"Cousins, but they don't claim us," Peter said. "We ran into a bit of trouble when we were younger, flying off in airships that didn't belong to us."

"Vashon airships," Paul added.

"We'd probably still be welcomed in the fold if they'd been anyone else's. And if we hadn't tried to race to the Arctic Circle, deflated the balloons in an ice storm, and ended up making a boat of the ships. Have you ever seen a great white bear? Me, either. One day, though." He shook his head and continued the introductions, gesturing toward the quiet man on Yasmeen's left. "The shy one there is Cassel. He talked to a woman once—then his mother put her tit back into his mouth to shut him up. The raggedy one next to him is Simon. That bitter one next to him is Mr. Engels, our navigator's mate." He indicated the man who'd said she wasn't a captain. "He never left the war."

"There are a lot of men that haven't got out." Engels didn't glance at her. "My brother Vincent, who was killed by a fire-bomb in Bonaire after she scouted out his garrison for the Liberé. You're licking the ass of that woman, Vashon. Even the captain thought it was an insult to eat with her."

"Yet the captain thought it appropriate for me to eat with you," Yasmeen said. "Either I'm an insult he's passed on to his crew instead of bearing the burden of my presence himself, or he decided that my company is tolerable, after all. Which do you think it is, Mr. Engels?"

Engels's mouth shut. He gave a sharp nod and looked down at his plate.

He'd hate her still. That was just fine. She'd made her point. If he continued tearing her down, he'd be calling out his own captain with every word.

"I think the captain wanted to give us something more pleasant to look at than our first mate's ugly face," Paul said, and grinned when chuckles started around the table.

"That's very kind, Mr. Vashon." Yasmeen met Archimedes' eyes across the table. "I'm pleased that you find my husband as handsome as I do."

The first mate laughed outright before he settled back, gave her a thoughtful look. "Your crew had women."

"About half of them were."

"Don't you worry about fornication?"

He said the word as if he'd suffered through a few too many sermons.

"No," Yasmeen said. "They're welcome to do whatever they like, as long as it doesn't interfere with their duties or disrupt my crew's ability to work."

"But aren't women always falling pregnant? Aren't you always losing crew members?"

"It takes two to make a baby, Mr. Vashon," she said dryly. "So I let them know that if a pregnancy occurs, it won't just be the woman going. I've found it makes the both of them more willing to use sheaths."

"Sheaths?" Peter looked to his twin. "How do you suspect Guillouet would respond to that suggestion if we offered it to him?"

"Maybe as well as the other suggestions we've given him." Paul glanced at Yasmeen, then to Archimedes. His voice lowered. "Captain believes that women only serve one function, and it's not aboard a ship. But he thinks the whorehouses are just fine—and I'll say that I do, too. There's no one looking at you with big eyes in the morning."

"Whorehouses are damn fine, I agree." Peter sighed. "I'd still prefer the women and the sheaths."

Yasmeen preferred women and sheaths on a ship, too—especially when they were aboard *her* ship. The familiar ache of losing her lady started up halfway through dinner, and while she remained quiet, Archimedes entertained them all with stories of his adventures. She excused herself early, and was cleaning her guns when Archimedes came into the cabin almost an hour later, his hands empty.

"No notes?" she asked.

"Ollivier is still in the captain's cabin. It'll wait until morning." He looked her over, sitting on the bunk in her breeches and shirt. "How modest are we, Mrs. Fox?"

"Not very."

"Good."

Turning his back to her, he shrugged out of his jacket and hung it on a hook. Yasmeen tucked a pistol beneath her pillow and the other between the frame and mattress over her head. She moved to the washstand, poured water from the ewer into the bowl.

She heard Archimedes' breath catch when she stripped off her shirt. Without turning, she pushed her breeches and small pants to her ankles, kicked them to the side. The water was cold, her soap slippery. Goose pimples raised under her fingers as she began to wash. Her nipples hardened. She didn't pretend it was the cold. Knowing that he watched her was almost as pleasing as a touch.

The scent of resin filled the air with every stroke of her hand over her skin. His rough voice came from behind her. "What's that fragrance?"

"Olibanum," she said. More subtle than a flowery perfume—and to her nose, warmer and more luxurious. Too expensive for her now, the soap had been a gift from Scarsdale before leaving England. "My favorite."

"It was coconut the night I shot you with the dart."

"That was oil for my hair."

She glanced over her shoulder. Archimedes wore only his drawers, the drawstring tied at the waist, the linen stretched over an impressive erection. The glow of the lamp cast gold over the hardened muscles of his chest, the ripple of his abdomen. Watching her, his emerald eyes burned with a hot light.

By the lady, she wanted him.

How long had it been since she'd wanted a specific man? Forever, it seemed. She'd wanted the sport and pleasure of the bed. If she found someone attractive, she'd take them for one night, have a quick tussle, and leave with her need satisfied. It had little to do with wanting them, and everything to do with finding release.

But after all this time, she wanted him. Archimedes Fox.

She reached for the small towel folded beside the bowl, but stopped her hand when she heard the pad of his feet, coming closer.

"Allow me, Yasmeen," he said. "Please."

Please. She felt like saying it instead, but she only nodded. Standing behind her, he took the towel, unfolded it over his palm. The rough caress of cotton began at her shoulders, drying the length of her back in long sweeps. Yasmeen clenched her teeth, her head falling forward. She wanted him inside her—but this was even better. Though he practiced restraint, allowing himself only this, such a caress was her sweetest pleasure. Only his bare hands would have been more welcome.

The stroke of the towel slowed over the curve of her ass. Oh, sweet lady. The men she was with were rarely patient. And those who took their time still never moved beyond a squeeze of her tits, a grab of her ass.

Not that she'd have wanted them to. Those men served a purpose, but she didn't look to them for this, wouldn't trust them to touch her with such intimacy. She trusted Scarsdale, and his caress had been pleasurable—but never combined with this exquisite ache, the wetness gathering between her legs.

The rough towel slipped around her waist. He pulled her closer, her back to his chest, thin linen doing nothing to shield her from the press of his erection between her cheeks and against her lower back. His free hand flattened across her belly, the towel sweeping slowly beneath her breasts. From deep in her chest, her purr vibrated against his hand, his stomach.

His low voice reverberated against her ear. "You won't try to seduce me into bed?"

"I don't need to." Her head fell back against his shoulder. "This is just as good."

"It is," he said, and she heard his surprise. Boldly, he slipped his hand between her legs. She lifted her foot to the washstand, and he swept slowly down her thigh. "I thought it would be torture, but no."

"You would do that to yourself?"

"Yes. I'd enjoy it."

She laughed. "Come, Mr. Fox. I will do the torturing for you."

She slipped into the shirt he'd discarded—God, but she liked his smell. Many in the Horde believed a person's essence could be trapped in clothes worn so close to the skin. Yasmeen only knew that he was pleasant to look upon and delicious to her senses.

She tugged at his drawers. "Do you truly want to sleep in damp clothes?"

"No."

The hoarseness of his voice said that *this* would be torture. Pleasurable, but not as she experienced it. He untied the waist, and they slipped down his muscled legs. The defined ridge over his hips told her he still hadn't completely gained the weight he'd lost after Venice, but although he'd drunk his meals for two months, it hadn't softened him. He carried no extra flesh anywhere.

"You keep yourself strong."

"If I lie around for two months and try to run from zombies, I can't run very quickly."

"No, I imagine not." She rolled the soap between her fingers. "What did you do in Port Fallow? Not running through the streets."

"I went to the pugilist's club." Though his response came easily, his muscles were rigid, his head bent. Waiting for her.

"As your face is still handsome, you must not have fought too many men."

"They've installed the weaving machines. Trying to punch those bags of sand takes more of an effort than fighting." He closed his eyes. "It's not half the effort of holding still for this."

She smiled up at him, then moved around to his back as he'd been to her. Fingers slippery with soap and water, she slid them over his shoulders, washing in a long swathe. His muscles clenched, his buttocks like rocks. Soapy water dripped down his spine to the cleft between. She washed her way down his biceps, his forearm, to his hand. She worked lather into his palm.

"If you wish to wash yourself, Mr. Fox, I will pretend not to notice."

A hoarse laugh escaped him, and was strangled when her hand slipped around, soaping those delicious ridges at his hip.

"Be practical in this matter, Mr. Fox. We will wake up in Vienna, where we might be chased by zombies. You can try to run after staying awake half the night with a stiff cock, or try to hide what you are doing in your bunk—or you can take care of it now."

"Ever so practical." His hand slipped forward. "Sensible."

Not at all—this was madness for her, too. She listened to his harsh breathing, watched the long stroke of his hand. She could not see anything of what he did but the movement of his arm, but she knew what it would be to bed him. He would be slow. She would scream.

But for now, she wrapped her arms around him from behind and used both hands to soap his heaving chest. His free hand clutched at hers.

"Yasmeen." He groaned her name.

She slid her inner thigh up the outside of his. She was wrapped almost completely around him now, his shirt wet between them. He stiffened, shook. His back bowed. He brought her hand to his lips and pressed his open mouth hard against her palm. His tongue tasted her flesh as he came.

His breathing slowed again. Reluctantly, she unwound and found a handkerchief to wipe his palm. "Wash this when you've finished," she said. "I recommend doing it last."

He nodded, gaze roaming all over her face. She rinsed his body with handfuls of clean water, wiped him with the towel. After taking off his shirt, she hung it on the hook to dry and climbed into her bunk.

A few moments later, wearing only his drawers again, Archimedes crouched next to her with a cigarillo between his lips. He lit the end and passed it to her. His emerald eyes regarded her, and for the first time, she could not discern his thoughts from his expression.

Between them, they'd smoked almost to the end of the cigarillo before he said, "Was it all practical?"

Yasmeen smiled. "No."

"You also don't like to owe."

"No, I don't."

"It wouldn't have been a debt. I enjoyed touching you, too."

"As much as touching yourself?"

"No, touching you was . . . different. More pleasurable than orgasm. And even stroking myself, I felt more than I usually . . ." He trailed off, his gaze caressing her face. "How goes your heart? Still of steel?"

Like a strongbox, battered on all sides. She took a final drag, passed the stub back to him. "I have not kissed you yet, Mr. Fox. Is your longing strong enough to initiate it, instead?"

His serious gaze never left hers. "I think my longing will be much, much greater than I thought."

"You *mean* to break your heart against mine," she realized, and understanding slid through her. He'd been terrified of the Horde tower's dampening effect on his emotions. "You want to feel as much as you can, even if it hurts. You never want to feel anything so shallowly again."

"Yes."

So he planned to have her break his heart. "And what will you do if I fall in love with you, instead?"

He grinned. "Then God help us both."

Chapter 9

The forest had reclaimed most of Vienna. The old walls marked out a rough perimeter of the city, and ruins were marked by sparser growth, long grasses upon heaps of stone. To the east, the twisting branches of the Danube flowed in a meandering path. When the initial wave of zombies had spread west from the Hapsburg Wall, that river had helped slow the zombies' progress and saved many of Vienna's residents . . . for a time.

Vienna had been one of the first cities affected, and the number of zombies had still been relatively few. The river, city wall, and a garrison of soldiers had served as adequate defense, giving the Hapsburgs and their generals opportunity to study the creatures—and, when it became clear that the zombies' numbers were growing and that the infection spread so easily that one loose zombie could destroy a city, to plan an evacuation. It had been similar to a story repeated across Europe: At the first sign of the zombie mobs, the populations of many great cities had used the rivers to protect them, rushing in a panic to the opposite bank. Once there, they destroyed the bridges and executed or confined anyone discovered with a bite. The water only held the zombies off for a while, however—if only one bite was overlooked, or concealed by someone still hoping to find a cure, the infection spread.

The stories had taught Archimedes well, though. From the airship, he scouted the locations of the nearest water—even if it was nothing more than a big puddle. Aside from the river, however, he wouldn't find much water in the snow-covered landscape, so he took other precautions.

He'd traded the bright waistcoat and breeches for heavier, darker clothing that wouldn't shout his presence to the zombies. Leather guards buckled over his neck, his arms and legs—if he went down under a zombie, the guards might save him from a bite long enough to get back up. His shoulder harness carried his grapnel and pneumatic launcher, rope, a handwinch, a miners' drip lamp for underground and darkened chambers, extra ammunition, a prybar, and machetes. Though revolvers were holstered at his hips, he preferred blades when fighting zombies: they were quiet and never needed to be reloaded. He kept several strapped to his thighs and sheathed in his boots, and two foot-long blades in the spring-loaded mechanisms embedded in his leather forearm guards.

Guillouet cut *Ceres'* engines as they passed over the city, allowing them to sail in silence toward the foothills. Archimedes saw Ollivier's confusion when he came up to the deck and looked out, and remembered his own disorientation upon his first visit. Almost every painting of Vienna showed the hills close in the background, but in truth, they were still some distance away.

The quietness of the engines was welcome after a full day and night of huffing and vibrations, and the look on Yasmeen's features even more so. Her expression was pure pleasure as she lifted her face to the wind, her heavy lashes lowered against the morning sun as if she were soaking up the warmth through her skin.

Had she looked half so satisfied last night? Unable to see her face as he'd dried her body, he didn't know—and he hadn't seen her expression when she'd wrapped herself around him, either.

She'd been so hot against him, so sleek. He still reeled from the memory of how she'd purred against him, then so easily offered the means of his release without touching him.

He had few inhibitions, but he'd never pictured stroking himself off while a woman washed him like . . . a wife? He didn't know; he'd never imagined having a wife at all. She'd washed him as if she were completely content to do only that, though he knew she wanted him in the bed. More like a mistress, or a concubine, though Yasmeen fit neither. He didn't keep her.

Perhaps it was the opposite. Perhaps *he* was to be the concubine, serving her every need.

A tempting thought.

Almost an hour later, a signal from one of the marines at

the bow pushed him out of those imaginings. Amid the first rise, within a stand of tall trees, stood a stone tower—round and solid, and more like the cylindrical Rouen keep than the arches and peaks of the contemporary Viennese buildings. Snow topped a conical roof—parts of it had collapsed, though not badly, as if the roof structure was well-supported beneath. A pass overhead didn't reveal any gaping holes that would allow Archimedes to rappel directly into the keep. Only narrow arrow slits opened the stone walls.

Archimedes circled the deck as the airship began to turn for another pass, taking a layout of the surrounding area. Trees made the zombies more difficult to spot, but if he and Yasmeen were quiet, it meant any zombie would have more difficulty spotting them, too. Still, in a forest it often seemed as if the creatures sprang from nowhere—many lay motionless and mindless until something caught their attention. Archimedes had been surprised more than once, saved only by his reflexes, leather guards, and luck.

He glanced at Yasmeen and his heart constricted.

God. The mere thought of her hurt down there destroyed him—a fear that stabbed at his chest, just as painful as he could have hoped. This was part of love, to suffer. He'd planned to do it in silence, to experience the beautiful agony of the great romantics.

Faced with it, however, beautiful agony was shit. He'd crow if it meant she was never in pain. Quickly, he made his way back to her side.

"I ought to go alone," he said.

She narrowed her eyes at him.

"One person makes less noise. And—"

"I'm coming," she said.

He reached for the buckles on his arm. "Take my guards, then."

"They'll only slow me down."

Panic caught in his chest. He stepped close, spoke so only she could hear. "Watching *Lady Corsair* burn was hell. But I think now, it would kill me. And if you were bit by the zombies . . ."

No, he could not even *think* it. His breathing stopped when she pushed her face close to his, looked into his eyes with an expression that was almost gentle.

"Stop letting yourself fall for me, Archimedes. Anything that makes you worry for someone else's ass over your own does you no favors, and I like you too well to see you die."

He couldn't have stopped now if he tried. "I'd die to protect you."

"Idiot."

Why, when he *knew* she'd have done the same? "Don't tell me that you wouldn't have risked your life for your crew."

"That is duty, loyalty. Not a foolish reaction based on unsupported fears." She studied him. "Did I tell you of Constantinople? I was raised within walls, and only allowed out into the city on rare occasions."

"A crèche."

Many cities within the empire had them. Not to the extent that the outlying territories did, where almost all of the children were raised in them until they were sent into labor. Within the empire, the crèches functioned more like orphanages, the children educated and given assistance in finding a suitable position afterward.

"No, not a crèche. More like a palace, where I was given the best food and education—and trained to fight. I fought every day of my life until I was fifteen, beginning in the morning and then again at night. When Temür destroyed the city and I escaped, I could count on my fingers the number of full days I'd been outside those walls. Yet I journeyed on foot alone across Greece, armed only with two knives and my wits. I am not like a crèche baby, born, fed, and then changed into a laborer. I was *bred* to be fast and strong. I was bred to be quiet. And I was bred to kill. You want to protect me, but in truth, I'll protect you. It was what I was made for. So let me do it."

That was incredible. *She* was incredible. And yet . . . His jaw clenched, despair tugging at his heart.

How was he to do anything for her?

"Ah," she said, watching his face. Her sneer mocked him. "It is easy to fall in love with a woman who is always making you feel more of a big, powerful man. You ought not have picked me, after all."

"That isn't it." He didn't question his abilities. "It is simply difficult to know that I offer nothing at all to the woman I'm falling in love with."

Her expression lightened. "You offer me nothing? Stupid man. You already give me what few men could. It is rare the man who has the confidence to let me be what I am, whether it is captaining an airship, climbing atop you in a steamcoach, or brawling in a tavern."

She thought she wouldn't make him feel a bigger man? Hearing this from her, it was all he could do not to swagger around with a puffed chest.

But it was a chest that deserved deflating. "I haven't always let you be," he reminded her. "I tried to take your ship in Venice."

"With a gun that didn't work." She surprised him by knowing. "It was the stupidest thing I've ever seen. Still, I admired your balls."

"You knew the gunpowder was wet?"

"I didn't know if it was wet or if you were out of bullets. But we found you on a raft in the middle of the canal, safe from zombies, and yet you were shouting across a pile of ruins to our ship in the middle of the night. If you could have, you'd have signaled with a gun—either then or earlier."

He would have. For a week, he'd been praying for the airship to notice him, but by that time, dirty and starving, he'd resembled the zombies more than a man. He'd have given anything simply for a bright waistcoat to wave on a stick.

"Would you have still forgiven me if it was properly loaded?"

"No, Mr. Fox. If you'd aimed a properly loaded gun at me, I'd have shot you dead. I threw you over the side for being an idiot, pulling it on me in front of my crew and then ordering me about."

Had there ever been such a woman? "The idiots are all of the men who want you to be something else."

"Ah, well. Quite a few of them are dead now." She grinned at him. "I'll help you not to join their number."

Until Bigor and his marines met them at the rope ladder, Archimedes hadn't known that Guillouet had told the men to accompany them on the ground—but as long as they could be quiet, Archimedes didn't care. He shook his head when the man drew a gun, as if in preparation to go down.

"Try to be silent. If one or two come at us, kill them with your machetes or crossbows. One shot will bring the others, and they'll be a little slower in the cold and snow—but against a mob, that won't matter."

The man gave a short nod. While the other marines holstered their guns and readied their weapons, Bigor pointed to each. "Dubois, Durand, and Laurent—representing a combined forty years serving our king, and one year in Europe. Your assistance yesterday was appreciated."

"My pleasure. The worst way to begin an expedition is by dying in an exploding tree harvester."

"I believe you are correct, Mr. Fox." Bigor's flat gaze moved to Yasmeen, then back to Archimedes. "Shall we precede you?"

"No."

Archimedes stepped to the side, and though she didn't need the support, took Yasmeen's hand in his, helping her over the gunwale and onto the ladder. Her eyes met his briefly. He let go.

She slid down. Quiet, so quiet. On the ground, she remained crouched and listening, looking into the trees as they followed her down. Archimedes led them across the snow to the keep. Behind him, three of the marines spread out, keeping watch in all directions. Yasmeen at his side, Archimedes moved around the tower. Halfway around, they located the arched doorway—the entrance sealed up with stone blocks.

Moving almost as quietly as Yasmeen had, Bigor joined them. His voice was low. "Protecting something inside?"

Probably. He'd seen the same in other cities, other villages. Many strongholds became depositories for treasures that the fleeing citizens couldn't carry with them—and everyone assumed they would eventually return. Archimedes' first find had been something similar, a journey begun after months of sifting through fragments of letters and cryptic references.

He retrieved his iron prybar, fitted the end between the blocks. The stones didn't shift. Christ.

"Anything we use will make noise," Yasmeen whispered.

Archimedes nodded, studying her face. She already had a solution, he knew, but she wouldn't like depending on Guillouet to carry it out. "A distraction?"

Her teeth clenched. She tilted her head back and looked up

the side of the tower, then at the surrounding terrain. Weighing her options, he thought. Finally, she nodded and turned to Bigor.

"We need Guillouet to fly *Ceres* to that stand of trees, so he has a clear shot at this door. His boilers need to be at full steam before he starts her engines up, and run half power into the electrical generator. He'll use the rail cannon to take out these blocks." She took a deep breath. "The zombies *will* come. So as soon as he fires on the keep, he needs to kick in the propellers and take *Ceres* at least two or three hundred yards off. Once there, that crew needs to shoot their rifles, drawing the zombies to that location while we head inside the tower—and once we're in, even two of your men guarding the entrance can handle any strays. When we signal, *Ceres* can pick us up."

Bigor nodded. "All right. What signal?"

She glanced up. "We'll be on the roof. Even if the zombies follow *Ceres* back, we're out of reach."

"They won't climb up?"

"They don't climb," Archimedes said. "They'll go up an incline or stairs, so they might follow you up onto a pile of ruins, but they don't have the brains for vertical."

"All right." With another sharp nod, Bigor ran for the rope ladder.

Archimedes followed Yasmeen away from the keep. The rail gun's accuracy meant they didn't have to go far, and they waited, back to back, watching the trees. A soft moan came from the west; Durand took the zombie down with a crossbow bolt shot through its eye.

Bigor returned to the ground. Above, steam boiled from *Ceres*' tail as she sailed into position in line with the tower's entrance. So far, Guillouet was following Yasmeen's instructions.

She turned her head to whisper, "Shall we make a wager? What do you think might be inside? Gold, jewels? If I'm very lucky, cigarillos?"

He grinned but shook his head. It was impossible to know, and depended upon the manner the zombie infection spread, and whether the population had time to gather more than a few items before they fled. Some cities had time to contain the infection and to prepare—and until the very end, Vienna had been one of them. Blocking the entrance to this tower could have been to protect something inside, or simply to keep the zombies out until they returned.

"Don't bet on the last. There was no tobacco in Europe," he said.

"No tobacco, no opium; no wonder the Horde thought they were barbarians."

A high-pitched whine suddenly ripped through the air as the engines started, firing the electrical generator. Yasmeen tensed, watching the woods. The rail cannon fired, silent until the ball rammed into the blocks, blowing through the entrance in a shower of shattered stone. The marines moved toward the entrance to search out any zombies inside—just in case.

The whine faded. *Ceres'* propellers began to spin, the engines huffing. The airship retreated west, the crew already shouting, shooting, making noise. Yasmeen ripped off her hat, angling her head as if trying to listen for moans over the ruckus.

She suddenly stilled. "I hear them. A *lot* of them."

Archimedes took her hand, started toward the keep. "Let's get inside."

"No." She set her feet, eyes wide. "Oh, by the lady. Run, Archimedes! Bigor!" she shouted. "Come away from the keep! Run! To the ship!"

The marines were already backing away from the keep— and now Archimedes could hear them, too: moans and growls, all coming from inside, nearing the shattered entrance.

When the zombies burst through, he was already turning to run.

Yasmeen kept pace with him, suddenly sprinting ahead to meet a zombie that darted from between the trees in front of them. Her machete chopped through the zombie's neck, its head flying. The moans behind them became louder, more, closer. He heard the marines shout, the cracks of their guns. Ahead, Yasmeen whirled, revolver in hand, aimed at Archimedes. Her weapon sounded, again and again, each bullet whizzing past him, striking flesh.

He didn't want to know how close the zombies had been. His boots crunched through the snow, and he couldn't think about slipping—only about running and making sure they both made it back to the airship. When he caught up, Yasmeen traded her gun for her machetes and ran with him.

"She's coming back around!" Yasmeen shouted.

Someone on the airship must have seen the mob and alerted the captain. Above the bare trees, *Ceres* was making a slow turn, the crew's rifles picking off zombies below. Oh, Jesus. Their distraction had worked too well. Even if they outran the mob behind them, the noise of the airship drew more from all directions, too many for the crew to shoot. The rope ladder dropped, and Yasmeen's scream of *"No!"* was lost in the moans and the huff of the engines. Zombies attacked the swinging ladder, emaciated hands gripping the ropes, pulling—cutting off their easiest escape.

Movement from the corner of his eye warned him. Archimedes pulled his gun, fired. The zombie dropped. They were almost to the airship but more were racing toward them, some abandoning the ladder, others coming in from the forest.

Machetes flashing, Yasmeen sped ahead and killed three with astonishing efficiency. She whipped around, shot another. "Tree?"

Not good enough. Archimedes reached back, gripped his pneumatic launcher. He aimed for the airship, fired. The grapnel arced upward over the side, the long rope trailing behind. Steel hooks caught the gunwale, held fast.

He heard Yasmeen's wild laugh. She leapt for the rope, began climbing. Archimedes waited for her to climb high enough, three zombies falling to his bullets before he followed her up. Clawing hands grasped his boot, almost yanked him down. A crack sounded from above; the zombie's head exploded. He looked up. Holding herself steady with the rope between her thighs, Yasmeen hung upside down, the barrel of her gun smoking. She grinned before rocking back up, hauling herself upward with astonishing speed.

The rattle of the cargo lift joined the moans and gunshots. The crew dragged the rope ladder up halfway, shooting a path clear for the marines. They dropped it again as Bigor reached the airship. The four marines began climbing all at once, as if this weren't the first time they'd had to share a single ladder in a rush.

Yasmeen reached the deck. She leaned over the side,

hauled Archimedes over. Chest heaving, laughing, Archimedes turned to look below. Jesus. The zombies were *still* coming out of the keep.

"Well—" He had to stop, catch his breath. "Now we know where they confined the infected."

Yasmeen laughed. Her bright eyes met his, her smile brilliant. He watched it die as her gaze lit on something beyond him.

"Oh, fuck," she said softly.

He looked around. Near the rope ladder, the marines were huddled over one of their men. Bigor had torn away Durand's sleeve. The bloody marks couldn't be anything but a bite.

The crew hushed.

Without turning his head, Bigor asked, "Mr. Fox, how long?"

A ball of lead settled in Archimedes' gut. "If he has nano-agents, a few days. If he doesn't, a few hours."

Durand closed his eyes. Bigor bent his head toward the other man's, said something too low to hear. A moment later, he stood and faced Captain Guillouet. "Will you please clear the deck, sir? We would like to say our farewells."

Though his expression looked suddenly weary, Guillouet's shoulders straightened. "I have to stand witness."

"He's our brother, sir."

"That's why I have to stand, marine."

Bigor's face tightened, but he nodded.

Yasmeen tugged on Archimedes' hand. "Come."

He followed her to the hatchway, where the deck crew was gathering, waiting their turns on the ladder. Softly, he said, "Should we say something to him before we go?"

"What can we say?" She slid down the ladder and waited for him below before starting along the passageway to their cabin. "He asked to have the deck cleared. That was his request. So we honor it."

"And the captain?"

"Too many people try to hide their loved ones after a bite." The weariness on her face matched the captain's. "Guillouet standing witness isn't personal, it isn't an insult. It simply says: The crew comes first."

And her crew had also always come first, Archimedes knew. "You've done the same?"

"Too many times. And too many times, I've been the one pulling the trigger." She stopped as a gunshot sounded above. Her eyes closed. After a long moment, she looked up at him. "If I'm ever bit, please do the same for me. Don't make me do it myself."

"I will." It was the most difficult promise he'd ever made. "I'd ask the same, but there's no question that you'll shoot me—even if I wasn't infected."

A smile touched her mouth, but her eyes remained serious. "It might take more for me to shoot you than you think. I suppose that means I'm not as dangerous to you. Is that disappointing?"

Was it? He recalled the pounding of his heart as he'd shot her with the opium dart, the delicious fear that had accompanied him back to *Lady Corsair*, certain she'd try to kill him at any moment. That fear *had* gone, but it wasn't a loss: every moment with her was more thrilling, more fulfilling, even if she wasn't trying to shoot him.

And he had more fears now to replace it: fear for her life, fear that when this expedition was over and her vengeance satisfied, he'd never see her again. And though he knew her heart was steel, though he looked forward to the longing of an unrequited love, he also knew the fear that she'd never feel the same in return.

She might not kill him, but he was still on a path that didn't lack for danger. It lurked behind her every touch, her every smile, her every word. With each one, he fell a little more—but instead of hope, his shattered heart waited below.

"I'm not disappointed," he said.

He was terrified.

Unsurprisingly, the airship's galley provided Hassan's table with marginally better food and the luxury of wine—which, Yasmeen noted, Hassan didn't touch. Conversation was subdued. She and Archimedes barely mentioned the morning's adventure, though she knew if there'd been any other outcome with Durand, neither one of them could have resisted upstaging the other.

Instead, she refilled her wine and listened as Archimedes told Hassan of an island in Venice that had been used in the

same way as the keep, then of another island on the Seine. He
mentioned dates and names with no effort, no pausing to
recall details—as if history were as familiar as his own
family.

In the serial adventures, Archimedes Fox never studied. He
never sought mysteries; they simply fell into his lap. But in
truth, Archimedes Fox was a scholar with a gun, a grapnel,
and a need to fling himself into danger.

That made the real man infinitely more fascinating.

Not to Hassan, however—or because he'd known the real
man for longer. And though he was subtle, steering the discus-
sion to Venice and Archimedes' recent journey aboard *Lady
Corsair*, she could see that his route would take him to her.
Archimedes must have seen it as well, and—perhaps protecting her from questions she might not want to answer—
not-so-subtly turned the conversation back around. Amused,
Yasmeen watched their back-and-forth until she sensed a hint
of frustration in Archimedes' reply. Their maneuverings had
been entertaining, but not worth hard feelings.

At a pause in their exchange, Yasmeen met Hassan's eyes
and said, "I won't think it rude if you ask."

The man colored slightly. Archimedes lifted his wine
to her.

"Then tell us all, my wife."

She narrowed her eyes at him, but Hassan didn't waste any
time. Shaking his head, he said, "Not all, please. I merely
wondered if you were from the same house as Nasrin."

Nasrin, the wild rose. "Temür Agha's guard?" she guessed.

Hassan nodded. Archimedes had gone utterly still, his gaze
fixed on her face as if not to miss a word. Because she'd mentioned the guard, or because he was learning more about her,
information that didn't come from stories or rumors?

The idiot. If he wanted to know, he only had to say so. She
would tell him.

Not here, however. No, there was another story that she
wanted to hear, and it wasn't her own. She needed a full picture of the man who might be responsible for the death of her
crew, not rumors and stories. She wanted to hear it from a man
who knew him.

"I knew of several *gan tsetseg* by that name," she said, "but there are also many I don't know. I was raised in Constantinople."

"It is unlikely you know her, then. Nasrin was from the Punjaab, but was raised by the house in Daidu." Then, in a careful tone, "Constantinople?"

"Yes." She held his gaze. "I escaped while Temür Agha razed the city."

He gave a deep, resonating sigh. "You must have been young. That is why you were not altered."

"Yes." The mechanical flesh and weapons weren't grafted on until after they were fully grown. It had been near that time for Yasmeen—but this was also not what she wanted to hear, and she didn't care to be subtle when she steered. "Archimedes told me that I was wrong about Temür—that he hadn't been the one to burn the city."

"No," Archimedes jumped in immediately. "He did burn it. I only said he was a Horde rebel."

"He was *destroying* the rebellion."

"You are both correct," Hassan said. His hand shook slightly as he reached for the teapot, but Yasmeen couldn't determine whether it was with emotion or age. He paused before refilling his cup, as if noticing that she'd finished her glass of wine. "Shall I pour some for you?"

"Is it from the New World?"

Humor brightened his face. "Yes."

"No, thank you. Drinking nothing is better than that."

"I must disagree; even this tea is better than nothing." He grimaced slightly as he took a sip. "Though I wish I had thought to stock my own supply. Captain Guillouet does not trust any foods or drink that do not come from the Americas. He fears infection."

So that was why nothing was fresh. Centuries before, the Horde had concealed the nanoagents in the tea and sugar they'd traded in Europe and northern Africa. By the time they activated their controlling signals, much of the population was infected and helpless to fight back, making their invasions as painless as slipping a greased finger into the barrel of a gun that didn't hold any bullets.

Setting his cup down, Hassan continued. "There are those in the empire who would not blame him for his fear. When

word of the occupations in England and Africa reached Xanadu, it made many uneasy—as uneasy as news of the zombies
had a century before. What if the creatures crossed the
empire's walls and great rivers? What if the Great Khan set up
towers to control his people instead of the barbarians? Few
would speak out against Argon Khan, however, under whose
rule the occupations were ordered—but it was then that the
rebellion began to form."

Yasmeen hadn't known that. She'd been taught that Argon
Khan had been as wise as Manduhai Khatun, as generous
as Toqta Khan. To learn differently didn't surprise her,
however—every Khan was powerful enough to write his own
history.

But it also meant there was only one way that Hassan had
heard differently. "Temür Agha told you this?"

"Yes. Perhaps it is true; perhaps it is not. Perhaps it is only
what he was told by others in the rebellion. But it is important
to know that there was also *another* rebellion, though the roots
of that go deeper, and was one that challenged the seat of the
Great Khan."

Yasmeen knew of this one—the heirs of Ögedei, the youn-
gest son of Genghis Khan, could not have been more reviled
in the histories. When the great general Batu, son of Genghis
Khan's eldest son, had been named his grandfather's succes-
sor, Ögedei's supporters had called Batu's legitimacy into
question, reminding all that Genghis Khan's wife had been
raped in captivity before the birth of Batu's father. Though
Batu had crushed the opposition, he allowed his uncle Ögedei
to live, sending him to secure the peninsula ruled by the
Goryeo emperors.

Ögedei's descendants did not forget the question of legitimacy, however—and the blame for many assassinations
within the royal line were laid at their feet. Yasmeen didn't
know if that were true, or if Ögedei's heirs were simply a con-
venient scapegoat.

"Twenty-five years ago," Hassan said, "Kuyuk the Pretender began amassing an army in the White Mountains east
of the Black Sea, claiming to be Ögedei's heir. The Horde's
generals searched for him, but even though a generation had
passed since the great plague, they had too few soldiers to be

thorough, and for a decade Kuyuk remained well hidden—then the Great Khan sent Temür to flush him out. Kuyuk ran northwest, around the sea, then southeast."

"On a route to Constantinople," Yasmeen murmured.

"Even Temür doesn't know whether that was the Pretender's intention, or if it simply lay in his path as he returned east. His army must have been exhausted by the flight, low on supplies and starving—perhaps he only attacked the city to replenish his provisions. But Kuyuk claimed that he would prove to Xanadu his royal blood, a direct line from Genghis Khan, by sacking a city in the same way. Temür was not far behind him."

The man paused, sipped his tea. Though he gave little indication of it, Yasmeen sensed that his thoughts were troubled, his emotions suppressed.

"Temür had long been embroiled in another battle, though it was one that took more care and diplomacy—to convince the Great Khan to strike down the towers in the occupied territories. But the territories are lucrative, so the Khan would not. Temür requested the governorship of the northern African territories, but the Khan wanted to keep him close. But the Pretender's sacking of Constantinople posed a real threat to him—not that he feared Kuyuk would march on Xanadu, but that the people's confidence in him would be further damaged, and support for the rebellion—the *true* rebellion—would grow. So the Khan made the promise that if Temür stopped the Pretender, he would have Morocco."

"But he didn't just stop Kuyuk," Yasmeen said. "Temür *obliterated* him, along with the city. There were still citizens there—citizens of the empire."

"Yes," Hassan said. Though he said it unflinchingly, a deep weariness seemed to settle over him. "He wanted to make certain that the Khan feared him enough never to go back on his promise. Then he sent Nasrin to destroy the Khan's stable."

"What?" Still trying to take in the implications of Temür's actions, trying to decide the sort of man they made, the shock of that statement sent her reeling. "Did she succeed?"

Hassan nodded. "Almost completely."

"The stable?" Archimedes leaned forward, frowning. "For his ponies? I haven't heard this."

"Mongols don't put their ponies in stables. It was a prison, a workhouse for the European mathematicians and philosophers that the Polo brothers and the fool Marco introduced to Toqta Khan." Feeling light-headed, Yasmeen reached for her cigarillo case. *Damn it.* She clenched her fist, took a breath. "But they are all dead, of course, replaced by those from within the empire. They are called the Khan's magicians. But that word is wrong—there is no magic; it is only superstition. They are his inventors. The cleverest children are picked from the crèches and the villages, and brought to Xanadu—and of those, the cleverest are chosen for the stable." A golden cage, much like the houses of the *gan tsetseg,* and those chosen were never allowed to leave. "The stable has been available to the royals, *only* the royals, for centuries. Their technologies are guarded like no other secret, though of course we *see* what they have created every day. But how does it work? So it is magic to many of those in the empire."

"The nanoagents," Archimedes realized.

"Those," Hassan said. "But it began earlier: the war machines that were sent west."

"The kraken, the megalodons, the giant eels," Yasmeen put in. "All created when the European navies began to put steam engines in their ships, the better to take the war to the Horde empire—so the Horde created monsters drawn to the engine vibrations. The *gan tsetseg,* the mechanical flesh, the towers, the boilerworms . . . There is too much to name, and I'm certain that even I have not heard of it all. But all of it was theirs, all of it designed to strengthen the empire and protect the royal family." She turned to Hassan, still disbelieving. "She destroyed the stable? She killed them all?"

"Yes. Perhaps a few were left. It's impossible to be certain."

All of that knowledge, the brilliance, the centuries of work . . . but Yasmeen couldn't be sorry. That was too much power in the hands of one man.

"But of course, the truth is hidden," Hassan said. "Temür has made certain the rebels know, but to most of the empire, the Khan's magicians were only a story to begin with, so the tale of their destruction makes no difference. The truth about the Pretender and the sack of Constantinople has been squashed as well, and instead, Temür Agha crushed a rebellion."

"And now you hope to crush him," Archimedes said.

"I don't hope for that, no." Hassan shook his head. "If God wills it, Temür will understand that it is best for all if he steps down. For as long as he governs, the people of Rabat will not *see* the difference between his rule and the Horde's—and they will always fear. But if one of our own governs in his stead . . . ? They will have hope."

"And if he's killed?" Yasmeen asked.

Hassan closed his eyes. "I cannot think of that. I pray that when the tower comes down, he will see that Rabat cannot be truly free until he has gone."

Until he has gone. If he had the wrong sketch, then Yasmeen would help him along.

The older man sighed again, and Archimedes met Yasmeen's eyes. She nodded. Yes, they had almost stayed too long—and Hassan was likely looking forward to his midday rest. She'd discovered almost everything she wished to know, anyway.

Almost. "Why don't you drink the wine? Do you fear poison?" The corners of Hassan's eyes creased with his smile. "No. It is because the sin is greater than the benefit."

Yasmeen recognized those words. "So you have also taken up the old religion—as Kareem al-Amazigh has."

"As Temür Agha did," he corrected gently. "When trying to restore a city after two hundred years of occupation, one can't simply erase everything the Horde has put into place— there would be chaos. The Horde's support will be gone, and so we searched for new rules of governing, new policies . . . and the economic rules from the Qur'an were very good, very fair. They resonated with us, as they do the people—as does the faith. But I will admit, we are feeling our way. Much of the scholarship was lost, and there is still conflict in our hearts."

"You could appeal to the scholars in the Far Maghreb," Archimedes suggested.

"We have. They will not return from the New World as long as Temür is still governor." He smiled again. "Until then, I will follow my conscience—and drink tea fit for camels rather than wine."

Chapter 10

Archimedes followed Yasmeen out of Hassan's stateroom, before spinning around and entering again. Curious,
she stopped to wait for him, then had to laugh when he came
back out with the bottle of wine in hand.

Yes, they could put it to much better use. His grin wide, his
long stride carried him close, but she didn't back away. She
loved to look at him—his wicked smile, his active expressions, his handsome features. She *wanted* him close.

If only his longing would grow deep enough to kiss her.

She felt his breath instead, the dip of his head as he bent to
her ear. "Did you find out everything you wanted to know
about Temür Agha?"

"Mostly, yes."

"Good."

He didn't move. She was listening for others; so was he.
His gaze roamed her face, fell to her lips. "When I kiss you, I
don't know if I'll stop."

She didn't want him to. Her heart pounded as his mouth
moved across her cheek, hovered over her lips.

"Now, I breathe your breath, and it's sweeter than any kiss
I've ever had." His thumb dragged over her bottom lip. "When
I'm finally inside you . . ."

He trailed off, his eyes glazing as if imagining it. Yasmeen
did, too—the heavy thrust, the slide of sweaty limbs. Opening
her mouth, she bit the tip of his thumb, and with a flick of her
tongue, tasted the salt of his skin. His eyes met hers, and the
world stilled.

A door opened farther down the passageway.

He drew back, pushed his fingers through his hair. His

breathing wasn't steady. "I'll see if Ollivier has those notes ready."

"Don't drink anything."

"I won't."

She looked down the passageway. "If Bigor's in the wardroom, I'll talk to him about tomorrow."

"We'll go in before dawn?"

"Yes." They'd reach the pass by the middle of the night. Using the darkness for cover, they could slip in—or they could wait a day. She didn't want to wait. The more quickly this expedition finished, the more quickly they'd fly to Rabat.

Archimedes stopped at the next cabin, knocked. Yasmeen continued aft. Amidships, she met Deflowered Henri, who paused and fidgeted, mouth flapping like a fish as she passed. She'd seen that look before on young aviators: anxious to speak with her, but lacking the position to address her without being acknowledged first.

Because she could still remember his feet twitching on a tavern table, his stiffened toes spreading wide—and because the memory still amused her to no end—she stopped. "Yes?"

Bright red, he said, "Is it true you only gave your crew fifty percent, ma'am?"

It was true. "Why?"

"Last year, your girl Ginger said she earned three livre. But the engine stoker's boy says he's heard only a fifty percent split between *Lady Corsair*'s crew. Even Guillouet gives us seventy, so I told him that couldn't be true. And as she's dead, I won't stand for him calling her a liar."

The boy was defending Ginger's honor. That was sweet. "Ginger's still alive, Henri. She's with a friend of mine in London. If you like, I can pass on a message for you."

"No." His blush deepened. "Thank you, ma'am. I just wanted to know, so I can tell the stoker what you said."

Was it so important? Interesting. In Yasmeen's experience, if the boys on a ship were discussing earnings and percentages, then the rest of the crew was, too. She might as well set straight whatever rumor was flying around.

"I gave them fifty percent," she said and watched his face

droop. "But she did earn three livre last year. Most of my crew earned five each."

"Truly?" His eyes widened. "And Ginger said that if they lost a hand or an eye, you paid for a replacement, too."

"Yes."

"I *told* him that. He said: But she can't replace their lives."

Yasmeen hoped she didn't run into this stoker's boy anytime soon. "That's also true. Now go on, before the captain finds you talking with me and thinks you're staging a mutiny."

Face suddenly pale, he ran off. Yasmeen grinned. Young boys were so serious. It was only a bit of humor at her own expense, but he must have taken her at her word.

She continued down the passageway. The wardroom lay all the way aft, two decks above the engines. Already huffing along, it wouldn't be long before *Ceres* arrived at Brenner's Pass. She hoped Guillouet had experience with the mountain winds.

Before she had a chance to knock, Laurent opened the door, obviously on the way out. He stopped suddenly, brows lifting.

"Is Mr. Bigor in?"

Stepping back, he gave a little jerk of his chin, inviting her in. A man of few words, apparently. He held the door open for her, then Dubois followed him out.

A designated cabin for officers to dine and take their leisure—or on a private ship, the senior crew, purser, and surgeon—the wardroom was larger and better appointed than the berth deck and mess. A small shelf held a selection of leatherbound books. Several comfortable chairs and a writing desk sat on one side of the room; the dining table filled the other.

All of them had been pushed aside to make space for the marines' equipment. Yasmeen's throat tightened. Eleven, twelve years ago, *Lady Corsair*'s stateroom had often looked the same.

Though they'd been hired for defense on this expedition, *marsouins* had specialized in aerial and water infiltrations during the war. Brass diving suits were mounted along one wall. Collapsible gliders were folded next to them. Crates held other gear, weapons. They'd carried their own arsenal and equipment, not relying on the airship's—apparently, that still held true.

Bigor sat at the table, a small chest open in front of him. He stood as she entered, gestured for her to sit.

A stack of personal effects lay next to the chest, and one by one, Bigor packed them inside. Letters, a rag doll, a ferrotype photograph of a woman and a baby . . . the chest was full of Durand's belongings, she realized. Bigor was preparing to send them off—probably to the woman in the photograph.

"I'm sorry about your man," she said softly.

Jaw hard, he nodded. "It's not often we have a chance to say good-bye."

"I know." And that was better than nothing.

"We might have all been the same if not for your bullets. Thank you."

She nodded her own acknowledgment. There was nothing to say. It hadn't ended up being enough—but he was likely counting his every shot, too. Wondering if he'd just pulled the trigger one more time, maybe he'd have killed the zombie who bit Durand.

"Only one letter left to add now—mine." He closed the chest, but didn't lock it. "He has a wife in the Antilles."

"You'll send her a good story, I hope."

"He has many worth telling. But today, I'll probably put his name on a few of your bullets."

So that his wife could hear that Durand had died after saving his comrades; that they only lived because of him. "That's fine."

He gave another sharp nod, but this time, it seemed rough around the edges. "You don't expect it to be this. The war, yes. You fight for a reason and shoulder a burden of responsibility, duty—and of doing things I'd never want my wife and children to know. In the war, they send a letter home that only tells the family that he fought with honor, he fulfilled his duty— and it's truth. But I'm still doing things I don't want to describe in a letter, and when I go, a good story is all I can hope for. And like Durand's, it will probably be sprinkled with lies."

The lies didn't matter to Yasmeen; she'd built her reputation on bits of truth she'd chosen other people to know, and that would be all anyone knew of her when she died. But responsibility and duty . . .

Only a few months ago, she'd looked at Nasrin and pitied the *gan tsetseg* for the chains that bound her. But Yasmeen had her own; her airship gave her freedom but had bound Yasmeen with duty and loyalty to the men and women who served it. She'd willingly borne those chains—and when the links snapped, it had been a physical pain.

Yet to never feel their burden again was unimaginable. To never feel the wind in her face, *her* wind. To never feel her engines beneath her feet. To never feel pride in her aviators, to know a job well done. She would be willing to bear those chains and risk the pain again—for the right ship, the right crew.

She thought of Archimedes, and an unfamiliar ache bloomed in her chest. Would she be willing to risk the same for the right man? One who knew her now, better than anyone else ever had. But that wouldn't be risking pain; it would be risking her heart, exposing her belly. Yasmeen didn't know if she could do that—even if, like Archimedes, she wanted to.

And she didn't.

Bigor locked the chest. "But you aren't here for Durand."

"No. It's about tomorrow, and the pass. Mr. Fox and I have been discussing strategy—and we agree that our first priority is avoiding notice from the Horde outpost."

He nodded once—his default response for any statement, apparently. "And you need me to put it forth to Guillouet."

"Yes. Hassan has already heard and approved it, but the captain might want another opinion."

Bigor undoubtedly understood the rest: Another opinion, as long as it wasn't hers or Archimedes'. He nodded.

"The Horde outpost is directly across the valley from the old fortress. We plan to come in the early morning, before dawn—sailing straight through, and using the gliders so that *Ceres* doesn't have to stop and hover. But once we're in the fortress, we won't be able to see if the Horde has noticed and if they're coming."

"So you want us to stay on *Ceres* and keep watch."

"Yes." If the Horde came, it wouldn't matter if two were at the fortress, or five. But three skilled men on *Ceres* might make all the difference. "If she sails farther down the valley, she can hide out of the Horde's line of sight, but you'll still be able to see if they begin to cross the valley. If they do, *Ceres* can fire her engines and reach us before the Horde. With the three of you on watch, Mr. Fox and I won't have to keep looking out the windows—and we'll go through the fortress more quickly. We'll be picked up after nightfall on the second day. The new moon will help conceal the balloon—and if we need the cargo lift, it'll be there."

He nodded. "And so will we."

She went above decks, where the wind cleared her head, allowed her to think of absolutely nothing but the mountains passing beneath her feet, the route they were taking south. *Ceres* was a good ship, bucking the wind with barely a sway. Nothing like her lady had been, but solid. When Guillouet was finished flying or dead, she would serve another captain, and perhaps another. Hopefully, she'd be treated well, loved, and serve many more.

Near the end of the afternoon watch, she reluctantly started for the ladder. She couldn't remain up on deck all day. She passed one of the Vashons—with his black eye hidden under his goggles, she couldn't tell if it was Peter or Paul—and acknowledged him with a nod.

"How goes the sky, Captain?"

Yasmeen almost missed a step, so great was her shock. Even on a mercenary ship, his familiar address was a severe break of protocol. But she'd sensed no enmity from either twin the evening before; he might have simply been pushing to see her reaction. She wouldn't give him one—and he wasn't hers to discipline. Smoothly, she turned her stumble into a pause, and responded as if he'd addressed her formally. "Very well, Mr. Vashon."

She continued on and had to stifle her groan when Guillouet abandoned the quarterdeck and intercepted her near the ladder.

Quietly, he said, "You will not speak with my crew, Mrs. Fox."

Her brows lifted. Ordering her about was the surest way to make her do the opposite.

His jaw was tight. "I'd heard rumor that you've been stirring up my men with talk of low wages."

Was that what this was about? Fuck. Though it rasped against her pride to do it, she said, "If there is any talk, Captain, it was in your favor. In conversation, they asked what percentage I gave. I told them fifty percent. Less than you."

Satisfaction briefly loosened the tension in his features. He had his own pride, and discovering that he paid a higher percentage than *Lady Corsair*'s captain obviously soothed it. "This was conversation in the mess?"

"Yes." No need to point a finger at Henri. "I haven't spoken with your crew outside of it."

Some of the tension returned, but this time, Yasmeen sensed that it wasn't directed toward her. Holding her gaze, he said, "Beginning this evening, I would like for you to take your meals in your cabin, and to remain there as much as possible."

This was also an order, but Yasmeen's instincts didn't immediately rise against it. Though he didn't explain it, Captain Guillouet's concern was clear—and a mutiny could be dangerous for anyone who wasn't a mutineer. "And my husband?"

"Can eat where he chooses."

She nodded. Whatever rumors had reached his ears, Guillouet obviously believed they'd been sparked by her presence, even if she hadn't sparked them herself. "We will be away from the ship for two days, Captain, beginning tomorrow."

"Yes," he said, and she saw relief lighten some of his tension. And it might be true: The talk might settle without her presence to prompt it. Crews often grumbled, and rarely did it escalate into something more—but whether it did would depend on Captain Guillouet.

And in this instance, at least, he'd done exactly what Yasmeen would have. So she returned below, prepared to keep her mouth shut, her eyes open . . . and her gun within reach.

In the cabin, Archimedes was in his bunk, lying on his side with elbow propped as he paged through Ollivier's notes. Ah, but he truly was a fine specimen of a man. He looked up, met her eyes. His smile faded. "What is it?"

Yasmeen held up a finger. She didn't want to talk with him from across the cabin, even as small as it was. With the pipes running through the ship, sometimes voices carried over the engines, and she wasn't familiar enough with *Ceres* to know where the dangerous spots were.

After shedding her coat and hat, she went to the side of the bunk, crossing her forearms on his mattress. He leaned forward, and she said softly, "Captain Guillouet fears a mutiny."

His brows shot up. He drew back to study her face, as if to determine whether she was serious. "We are but two days out."

"*We* are," she said. "They left the New World many weeks ago. If there was already dissatisfaction, then seeing Guillouet's reaction to my coming aboard and the insult of him sending me down might have sparked more."

"But they didn't seem insulted by you. Well, not all of them."

"That doesn't matter so much, does it? The grumblings would not truly be about me. But, regardless—I am confined to our cabin until we leave tomorrow morning."

He stared at her. "And you agreed to that?"

"Mutiny is never to be taken lightly. Even if this is not a navy ship, the crew would fear anyone witnessing what happened. Perhaps we'd be safe simply by staying out of the way, but it's impossible to know. So we ought to ready our packs and gliders for tomorrow, but *keep* them ready, even after we return."

She'd rather take her chances in the wilds of Europe than stay aboard a mutinous ship.

Archimedes seemed to agree. He nodded. "All right."

"When you go to dinner, bring back my plate first so I can taste it." It all came from the same pots; he should be all right to eat his afterward. "When you eat with them, listen—especially to what isn't being said. Last night, I didn't sense anything of this sort, but most mutinies are whispers in the dark, not out in the open."

"I'll do that," he said.

She sighed. "And then I will be glad we are not on this ship the next two days."

"And Hassan?"

"If it does happen, tell him to stay in his room, to be quiet, and if they come for him, to offer money—and to give them all the wine."

"And remind them he is a friend to Temür Agha."

His gaze was flat and hard, reminding her that a dangerous, clever mind lay behind those emerald eyes. Archimedes wasn't thinking of what Temür might do; he was thinking of what *he* would do if Hassan were harmed.

"Yes," she said.

"And the marines?"

"If the crew is riled to the point of mutiny, the marines' presence alone might be enough to suppress it. But I will add that they rarely are riled to that point, no matter their complaints. Your father was *much* worse than Guillouet, and though we hated him, we'd never have attempted mutiny. Even the man your father tried to roast had only been overheard complaining—he could have been set down instead with strong discipline. If the example needed to be made, maybe a whipping." And though Yasmeen didn't hesitate to kill when necessary, the entire situation had been horrifying. First the roasted mutineer, and then the number of men she'd shot just to stay alive . . . She couldn't regret it, but there was nothing good in it, either. "Even if he'd ordered a whipping for *me* after I'd shot the roasting man, I wouldn't have mutinied. If *Ceres'* crew rises up because of wormy bread and a lack of women, they are not much of a crew at all."

Mouth firmly set, Archimedes shook his head. "And hearing all that only makes me more glad that you killed him."

"Then why didn't you? And how is it that an educated son of a fanatical mercenary became a weapons smuggler with the Horde rebellion?"

"Why not kill him? I thought I'd eventually prove him wrong. And as the war heated up, he was home less often, and left us there. I don't doubt that if he'd gone back for good while Geraldine—Zenobia—was still living there, I would have." He swung his legs over the side of the bunk, dropped to the floor. "As to the rest, I was just trying to get away from my father as much as possible. That meant supporting whoever he didn't."

"The Liberé?"

"Yes."

Going down on his heels, he dragged their trunk from under the bed—intending to start on their packs as they talked, she realized. Not yet. When he stood and reached into his watch pocket for the key, she hooked her foot behind his knee and pushed against his chest. Unbalanced, he sat down hard on the trunk's lid and almost tipped over backward, stopping when he braced his hands against the bunk behind him. She straddled his hips, smiling, looking down at his face as his expression moved from surprised to amused . . . and then, with a subtle shift, gained a wicked edge.

"I think you like this position, Mrs. Fox."

She rasped her claw across the rough stubble beneath his jaw, marveling at how easily he lifted his chin, exposing his throat. He wasn't stupid, so that had to be trust.

"With you between my legs, at my mercy?" She squeezed him with her thighs. "Yes, I like this position very much. So do you, I think."

His cock was already rigid beneath her. She rocked forward, loving the way his eyes closed, his teeth clenched. He shifted his feet, widened his legs. Yasmeen's breath caught as she settled more firmly against him.

"I like it," he said. "Very much. Now hold still."

"I don't take orders well."

"For this, you will." He sat up. At her back, his hands slipped beneath her shirt. His strong fingers began slow circles up the length of her spine.

"Oh, yes." Yasmeen's eyelids seemed suddenly heavy, weighed down by the pleasure sliding across her skin with each circular stroke. She all but melted against his chest, slipping her arms around his back to hold herself against him, and let him do as he willed. "But tell me about the smuggling."

"There's little to tell. Bilson was a friend from university. We both supported the Liberé, and he knew someone who needed men to bring weapons in from Horde territory. So we did."

But that wasn't all, Yasmeen wagered. "And it was dangerous."

"You have me down, don't you?" His mouth curved into a wry smile. "Yes. Almost all of the meet-ups with suppliers were at the Hapsburg Wall, or at the edges of the empire. The first was on the southern coast of the Baltic Sea. I saw my first megalodon, my first zombies, spent the whole journey with my heart pounding, certain I would die. And the moment we were done, I couldn't wait to return."

She laid her cheek onto his shoulder. "According to the stories, you were good at it."

"I was."

"Until you lost your cargo." The smooth motion of his hands faltered slightly, and made her wonder—"*Did* you lose it? Did you sell it to someone else? What did you do with the money?"

"I didn't sell it. I sank the barge." His voice was low. "This was not long after I was shot, after I was infected by nanoagents, was affected by the tower. My emotions were a wreck—and Temür was shipping war machines to the Liberé."

She opened her eyes, stared blindly past his neck to the porthole. That sort of power would have ended the conflict quickly. But, no—he'd changed his name six months after Bart had stabbed her, she remembered. "But the war was over by then—the Liberé had already won."

"Aside from a few skirmishes, yes. The Liberé said they wanted to have the machines, just to make certain the French weren't a threat again. But I was convinced they'd use them, and war machines on any side tipped the scales too far. So I sank them."

While his emotions had been in turmoil. "And now what do you feel?"

His hands lazily stroked up to her shoulders. "I don't regret it."

"Despite all of this trouble now with your debt, the search for the sketch."

"Yes."

"My crew is dead, my ship gone."

His hands froze. Obviously, he'd never put it together like that. "God, Yasmeen. I can't . . ."

Lifting her cheek from his shoulder, she shook her head. "I don't blame anyone but the person responsible—and the person who gave the order."

Fingers gliding down her sides, he asked softly, "And if it's Nasrin, how will we kill her?"

We. She liked the sound of that too well. "We don't have to kill her. If we kill Temür, she'll die. Of course, getting past her to Temür is another problem entirely." She smiled when his brow furrowed in confusion. "You cannot release a weapon like Nasrin without some tether. When she was altered and the royal she served was chosen, her nanoagents were aligned to his. Even if duty failed, she would save his life simply because hers is also at stake."

"So if he dies, she dies."

"Yes."

"That's . . . barbaric."

Perhaps. "But to her, it's beautiful."

"And to you?"

"It's both." To the *gan tsetseg*, whose very existence was created to honor an act of love and protection, those bonds of loyalty and duty *were* life—and there was nothing else. Yasmeen couldn't believe the same, not anymore, but she couldn't shed everything from her upbringing, and there were memories and stories that she held close. So, too, would the other women. "I'd never wish it for myself. I'd have hated it. But I've also recently thought that there are some bonds that I do welcome, because I receive something that makes the burden worth bearing in return. So I understand her a little better."

"Perhaps you do. But even if you loved me, I wouldn't want you to do that. I would rather you never loved me at all than to know my death killed you."

Such a romantic. Sitting up, she cupped his strong jaw. His gaze locked with hers. She lowered her head, breathing his breath. *Yes.* He was right: This was almost better than a kiss. When he whispered her name, she pressed her face into his neck, smelled his incredible scent.

How could she know what this bond between them was? Friendship, yes. A common purpose. Perhaps the rest was only lust. Perhaps it was more.

Right now, lust was enough.

Dropping her right hand between them, she loosened her breeches, slipped her fingers inside. By the lady, he made her so wet.

"Yasmeen."

She loved the sound of his voice, the need in it as he rasped her name. She loved the boldness of his fingers replacing hers. She loved his heavy groan when he found her, slick and hot, loved the tension in his lean body. Purring when his fingers pushed deeper, she rose and fell against him, and he shook with agonized restraint.

"You torture yourself so well." Panting, she licked his throat, felt him shiver. "Come, Archimedes Fox. Torture me, too. Make me scream."

But the only real torture would have been stopping. He explored instead, discovering what gave her the most pleasure, his fingers clever and adventurous. He learned her quickly. Writhing against his hand, Yasmeen hovered over him, lips all but touching his, breathing his breath—until she did finally scream, muffling her cries against his neck.

Chapter 11

Archimedes forced himself out of bed when the soft knock came at the door, hoping it didn't wake Yasmeen. He loved how irritable she was when her knees hurt, but couldn't love the reason for it—and at least he could support her through it. In just a few days, their mornings had become ritual: a quick wash, followed by pacing. Today, that ritual had to begin earlier, but they'd start with a meal.

As Archimedes had requested the night before, a galley assistant brought their breakfast to them—two bowls of oat porridge and black coffee. Yasmeen hated the coffee, but Archimedes would drink hers, too. She lifted her head from her pillow when he pulled the trunk from beneath her bunk— God, what she'd done to him on it yesterday—and used it as their table. Eyes still heavy, she began pacing right after eating, hobbling along. She didn't seem to have slept any better than he had—wondering half the night if they would be under a mutiny, perhaps.

Finally, she dressed in extra layers, strapped on her weapons, and gathered their packs: food in both, a bedroll to share in his, a change of clothes for each of them in hers, in case those they were wearing became wet. Not much, but the packs had to be light, especially with the excuses for gliders that were aboard *Ceres*. All airships carried them for emergencies, but hers must have been purchased at the start of the war twenty years prior.

Yasmeen would take the lead when they jumped from the airship. With no light from the moon and the deck lanterns extinguished, Archimedes could only make out the shadows of the peaks rising around them, the faint lights from the Horde outpost—he wouldn't have been able to spot the fortress against the opposite mountainside. The ship sailed silently, the wind biting his cheeks. Bigor met them on the main deck, looking as straight and fresh as if he never needed sleep. He held up two folded batwing gliders, and Archimedes saw Yasmeen's relief.

"Thank you, Mr. Bigor."

He nodded. "You'll probably hit crosswinds. Not strong, but enough to toss those older ones over. These were made to maneuver in inclement weather, and the wing size can be adjusted. You're both familiar with them?"

"Yes," Archimedes said. Uneasily familiar with them. These gliders maneuvered so well, even acrobats used them— and the *marsouins* were trained for aerial infiltration.

Yasmeen joined him at the side of the ship. Her eyes narrowed when she saw his face. "What is it?"

He shook his head and slipped on his goggles. Now wasn't the time to tell her of his sudden suspicions, but they nagged at him, dimming his usual thrill when they jumped from the airship, caught the wind.

Though he couldn't see the fortress, Ollivier's notes had included drawings and floor plans. Designed with the simplicity of a monastery and the strength of a citadel, high stone walls formed three sides of a rectangle, with the mountainside serving as the fourth. At the corners and at the main gate, crenellated towers overlooked the valley. Instead of a keep, a two-level stone barracks supported the interior base of the curtain wall, strengthening the defenses and providing chambers for storage, quarters for the soldiers, engineers, and laborers, a foundry to produce the steel needed for da Vinci's machines, and a smithy to shape the parts. The walls and barracks surrounded the enormous courtyard, where the machines were constructed before they rolled out of the main gate.

Yasmeen banked as she approached the southwest tower, aligning herself over the curtain wall and extending the glider's wings, allowing the greater surface area to catch the air and slow her down. Skimming over the crenels, she landed atop the wall and ran along its wide surface, folding the wings back as she came to a stop. Archimedes came in right after her, snow hardened by wind and sun crunching beneath his boots. Yasmeen was a dark silhouette against all the white; over the side of the wall, the courtyard lay in dense shadow.

"There are footprints," she said quietly.

Zombies, then, somewhere. The fortress wouldn't have been constructed with defense against them in mind; it had been built before the zombie infection. He followed her to the southwest tower, where an arched doorway led to a spiral stair, the wooden door long rotted away. All was darkness inside, but Archimedes didn't dare light the drip lamp until they were behind the curtain walls.

"I can see," Yasmeen said. Drawing her machetes, she entered the twisting stairwell. Snow covered the first steps, but the stone was bare past the turn. His palm against the rough block wall, Archimedes felt his way in the dark, and almost bumped into Yasmeen when she stopped.

Her whisper was irritated. "It's too dark for me now, too."

With a silent laugh, he opened the valve to start the gas and lit the lamp. The reflector bowl cast a wide, bright light, revealing granite blocks and steps. A few more turns, and the stair opened to the barracks' second level.

Yasmeen hesitated briefly. "This one first?"

He nodded. Better not to have a zombie at their backs.

They stepped out into the corner chamber. The barracks ran north into the side of the mountain and east along the face of the wall toward the main gate, a long series of chambers connected by doors. To the north, the chambers were all but empty. Either the departing soldiers had taken everything with them, or the Horde outpost had done some scavenging of its own. A few tables remained—perhaps too big to take down the stairs. Arched openings in the stone walls served as windows overlooking the dark courtyard, and small mounds of snow piled on the sills and the stone floor.

No zombies.

They returned to the tower and started east. Debris on the floor gave Archimedes some hope of a find, but he'd sift through it after they secured the fortress. They reached the gate, where the fortifications were twice as thick and separated the barracks that ran along the curtain wall. Another twisting stairwell led below, and with the top level cleared, they didn't have to fear zombies coming at them from above.

"Shall we make a stand here?" Yasmeen murmured. "We can escape through the stairs if we're overwhelmed."

By all appearances, they wouldn't be. There were fewer zombies in this region to begin with, and only one set of footprints above. Though they might simply be lying quiet, as they had been in the Vienna keep, it was more likely that only a few were here.

He nodded. "Yes."

They dropped their packs, readied their weapons. After a glance confirming that she was ready, he gave a whoop that echoed through the chambers. Removing her hat, she exposed her softly pointed, tufted ears. She turned her head, listening.

"Anything?" He didn't need to whisper now.

"Not yet." She drummed her machetes against the stone wall, making racket enough to wake the dead. "Hiyoooooo, *zombieeees!*"

When the echoes and his laughter faded, she shook her head. "I don't hear anything."

"All right. Let's move on."

They cleared more chambers, arriving at the southwest tower again, then heading north toward the mountainside. The snow outside had piled higher than the window openings, drifts spilling into the chambers in large mounds. In the courtyard, dark machinery jutted up through the white, huge and indistinct—war machines abandoned in the middle of construction, or simply the scrap heap from what was left. Yasmeen stopped at one of the windows, peering out, her head tilting back as her gaze continued upward.

Her lips parted. "There's snow all over so I can't see what it is . . . but it's huge. Not like one of da Vinci's. More like one of the Horde's early war machines, the domed clambering ones that looked like turtles."

Unease rippled through him. That didn't make sense. How could something that big get into the fortress—or out? It would have to crash through the walls, and they were intact.

A rumble sounded from the courtyard. Yasmeen froze, eyes wide. Archimedes doused the light, heart pounding. That hadn't been zombies.

That had been a steam engine.

The clank of metal against stone echoed through the chambers, followed by a huffing snort. Then more clanks, in a recognizable rhythm: walking on four feet. A wolf, a horse, a cat. God knew. Maybe something like the ratcatchers in London, cats changed by the Horde into large, vicious hunters with steel armor, razored teeth and claws . . . only by the sound of it, much bigger.

Archimedes stared through the dark, listening to the clanging echo. He couldn't get a fix, though it had to be in one of the barracks. The snow in the courtyard would have muffled those steps. "Which direction is it coming from?"

"South." The way they'd come. Her hand grasped his as an orange glow appeared in the farthest chamber, near the tower. "Let's go. We can cut through the courtyard to the barracks on the opposite side."

She led him to the window. They scrambled up the mound of snow, slipped down the drift pile into the courtyard. They went quickly, knee-deep in the snow, Archimedes praying that zombies weren't under it. The mountainside lay to their left. Machinery rose through the snow on their right, dark amid all the white. Good. Lots of places to hide.

The huffing of the engine quickened, the clank coming faster—galloping. Then suddenly, not clanking. Archimedes' heart raced. It was in the courtyard. Yasmeen suddenly darted to the side, pulled him down next to a piece of machinery. Another snort sounded. Closer. Crouching, they felt their way along the machine, searching for the end, a corner to go around, something to hide behind. The orange glow suddenly offered more light, and Archimedes saw: There was no end to the machine until it reached the other side of the courtyard.

That meant as soon as the thing following them entered the corridor created between the mountain and the machine, it would have them in a direct line of sight.

"Fuck." On a desperate breath, Yasmeen pulled him down again. She sheathed her machetes, drew her guns. "Whatever it is, I'll distract it. You run to the barracks, to the southeast tower. I'll meet you there."

No goddamn chance in hell. He'd run out there naked before he let Yasmeen use herself as bait. But as a sensible man, even when stalked by a giant huffing animal, he put it to her in the least likely way to piss her off.

"No," he said simply.

"Archimedes—"

"Let's see what it is first. If it's faster than you, running out there would be suicide."

She nodded and stood. Archimedes rose with her, his hands searching the side of the machine. He found pipes, riveted panels. Plenty to grab on to. They could climb, and—

Oh, good God.

A giant mechanical horse galloped toward them, but it was a horse made in hell. Eyes glowed with orange. Steel spikes jutted from its chest and neck. Two rapid-fire guns were bolted to its sides, both aimed forward. Fifteen yards away, it came to a sudden stop on legs made from thick pistons. Iron plates formed the skin. At least ten feet tall at the withers, its barrel-shaped body was big enough to hold the devoured remains of twenty men.

Or just a few men, if they were driving it. But how would they see? In the orange glow and changing shadows, Archimedes spotted the narrow vertical slots on its chest.

"Eye slits," he said. "Between the spikes."

Someone was in that thing and looking back at them.

The rapid-fire barrels spun.

"Oh, you fucking bastard." Yasmeen swore at the machine and grabbed his hand. They raced, and it came after them, pounding and snorting. Yasmeen whirled, whipping a knife through the air. The blade slammed into the center eye slit, stopped only by the hilt.

Then she was simply gone.

Archimedes stopped, turned. She was running straight at the giant machine, her long silk kerchief in hand.

He sprinted after her. "Yasmeen!"

She impaled the scarf over the chest spikes, covering the eye slits. With a leap, she was up on its neck, scrambling across the back. Looking for an entrance, he realized. The horse reared, huffing steam from its nose—and from its ass.

Suddenly laughing wildly, Archimedes raced toward it, straight on as she had, out of the firing line of the two guns. The barrels spun. No ammunition. Faintly, he heard shouting from inside, muffled by steel and drowned out by the engine. The horse came down from its rear in a hard stomp. The ground shuddered. Rattled by the impact, Yasmeen fell over its head, thumping to the snow at its front feet. Archimedes dove for her, rolled away as the steel hooves stamped again.

A long piece of wire stabbed through the eye slits, dislodging the scarf. Yasmeen crouched beside him, both motionless, waiting to see the direction the horse moved before they sprang.

The machine quieted, instead. A panel opened in its belly. Guns aimed, they waited.

A young man tumbled out and fell to his knees beneath the mechanical beast, hands outspread as if to show he had no weapons. His face downturned, he was almost crying, Archimedes realized—and his mouth was moving. Over the rumble of the engine, he heard the apology in the Horde language: "I didn't know it was you, *gan tsetseg*, but thought one of the soulless had come. Forgive me, lady."

Gan tsetseg. A flower of steel—the same thing Yasmeen had called herself and Nasrin.

Yasmeen stood stiffly, gun still pointed. Archimedes holstered his.

"He says he's sorry, steel flower," he told her in French. "He thought we were zombies."

Yasmeen blinked. "I couldn't make it all out. His accent is strong." She lowered her gun and spoke in Mongolian. "Stand up now."

Her accent was strong, more like Temür's than the common Horde rebels that Archimedes had met, but the young man immediately complied. About eighteen or twenty, with rounded face and teary brown eyes, he stood in a long quilted tunic split up the middle and belted with a sash. Boots of leather and fur protected his feet.

Yasmeen holstered her weapon. "How many are in the fortress?"

"Only me and no one."

"Where is no one, then?"

A name, Archimedes realized. Nergüi.

"In our chamber. She sleeps heavy with opium."

"She?"

"My grandmother."

Yasmeen nodded. "And you are?"

"Terbish." *That one.*

She smiled faintly. "Your family had bad luck come calling for you before, yes?"

Though his mouth didn't curve, Terbish's eyes crinkled at the corners. Both tears and fear vanished from his face. "Yes."

She gestured to the horse, quietly rumbling behind him. "Did you build this?"

"Yes."

"It's incredible. Will you let us look inside?"

His eyes widened, and he stepped back, arm extended. "Please, lady."

Terbish and Nergüi had taken one of the chambers near the foundry. To keep the heat from escaping, they'd covered the windows with thick wooden planks from the tables and the entrances with heavily woven curtains. Two pallets lay close to a hearth built from stone and steel, making an efficient oven. A gray-haired woman snored lightly on one.

Terbish bent to wake her. "It will be a few minutes before she rouses. Please, sit."

Yasmeen glanced at the woven mats beside the pallets and sank down, crossing her legs. Archimedes crouched, and she had to smile. He wouldn't relax yet. She could move quickly enough it didn't worry her.

The older woman stirred. Not blissed on opium, Yasmeen saw, but probably drinking a medicine before she slept. The stiffness of her movements suggested arthritis. Nergüi's eyes widened, then she stilled when she saw Yasmeen's ears. Quick fear appeared, and then she was up, pushing Terbish off to collect food from their stores. She stoked the fire, and poured fermented milk from a horsehide bag hanging nearby.

Yasmeen accepted the small bowl. After the snow outside, the thick drink was pleasantly warm, slightly sweet and pungent. She passed the bowl to Archimedes.

"I didn't hear ponies," she said. Aside from the terrifyingly huge mechanical one. "Do you keep them here?"

"Across the valley." Nergüi settled onto her mat, crossing

her legs as Yasmeen had. "We return to the outpost each week to replenish our supplies."

"You don't live there?"

"We do. But what is there to do in the winter? There is nothing to harvest, everyone only sits and waits for something to happen. The soldiers are gone, so all of us that are left have only our own families to feed."

And so it was with all of the outposts: the workers allowed outside the walls, but locked in by zombies and their duties. "The soldiers are gone? Where?"

"To Xanadu, to defend against the rebellion, though the news we receive from outside says there is no rebellion to crush." Nergüi grinned and clicked her tongue, obviously not fooled by the official statements. "Perhaps they have flung the rebels all away."

To the Horde outposts. Just as governing an outlying territory was a punishment, so too was this. With many soldiers about, the outposts effectively became a work prison for entire families. "And what will you do with no soldiers about?"

"Me? I only cook. The boy only builds."

Ah. She was being careful with Yasmeen about—not a soldier, but uncertain why a *gan tsetseg* and Archimedes were here. Yasmeen gave the old woman a quick explanation, saying that they'd only come to collect some of the barbarians' equipment, before suspicion led her to ask:

"Did Terbish build his machine from the parts that were left here?"

"Yes."

So they might not find much at all. But why the horse? If they were rebels, did they plan to use it? It did seem the sort of fanciful machine a young man would make. "And one day, will he ride his pony across the empire?"

"No, no." Nergüi's smile bunched cheeks as round as Terbish's. "That is just to cross the valley."

When the sun rose, Terbish showed them the courtyard. Five airships could have been tethered comfortably within its walls, and it was taken up with a dark machine. Yasmeen stared up at it. Roughly shaped as if someone had chopped off the top of a mountain and placed it in the courtyard—but it was a mountain made of propellers and pistons, valves and pipes—too large to be anything but awe-inspiring. She couldn't make sense of its purpose. Propellers might have been for direction, but couldn't provide propulsion—not for something this massive.

"What is it?" Archimedes said, and Yasmeen was thankful she was not the only one who hadn't yet figured it out.

"A flying machine. Of course it is not finished. But in another five years, it will rise."

Oh. How to say this without offending? Yasmeen settled for, "It's very heavy."

Terbish stared at her. Then a bright smile widened his mouth. "No. This is only the shape. Come."

He raced around the machine.

Archimedes grinned and walked with her—neither one in such a hurry.

"This is a surprising find," he said, and she knew he was not speaking of the machine, but Nergüi and Terbish.

"That is the very best kind."

"Yes. We won't find much here. Nergüi says the fortress is almost picked clean."

"Then we'll enjoy two days of food that doesn't crawl with worms."

"Will they have enough?"

"Will you offend them by asking?" She lifted her brows. "Me neither. It sounds as if they replenish often, but we'll give them what we have in our packs, too."

And try not to be embarrassed by the offering. The mare's milk alone had been richer in flavor and more satisfying than anything she'd had aboard *Ceres*. Still, Nergüi and Terbish might enjoy the novelty of barbarian food at its worst.

The young man waited for them near a small ledge jutting out from the machine, and hauled himself up. "Come inside!"

He led them to an opening of a large pipe. More tubes lined the interior. Bent over at the waist, she followed Terbish inside. The pipe narrowed until they were crawling across the metal. Feeling squeezed from the outside in, Yasmeen forced herself to keep following the young man, and when there was no more light, following the sound of him.

"I think God is angry with me," Archimedes grumbled in French. "My face is all but buried in your delectable ass, and I can't see to enjoy a moment of it."

Yasmeen laughed, then her palm encountered more metal—smooth, slightly warm. Unsettled by the unexpected texture, she yanked her hand back. Ahead, Terbish lit a lamp, and she found herself at the entrance to a small, spherical chamber, without enough room to stand. The walls were gray and looked softer than they felt.

Mechanical flesh.

Terbish ran his hand along the curving wall. "It has to grow, and it will cover all of the iron and steel like a skin, using what it needs from them and discarding the rest. It will be light"—he tilted his head, as if considering—"Light*er*. Much lighter. And it will be able to lift itself."

Yasmeen had no idea if that were true. But how could he have this? The Khan's stable had been destroyed. She looked to Archimedes, who was also taking in the chamber with an astonished expression.

"Where did you find the mechanical flesh?"

"It was given to me." He stroked the wall again, and Yasmeen thought that it responded—a slight flexing, like a muscle tensing beneath skin. "One summer when I was still a boy, a man came through the pass. He met with my mother, who was alive, and grandmother while they worked in the valley. He spent the night in the fortress, and my mother, grandmother, and I avoided the soldiers that evening and brought food to him, and we ate with him. They knew he was a magician, and asked him to take me on his journey, so that I could leave this place. They brought a toy that I had built, to prove that I was clever enough to join him—but the magician said he did not know where the road would take him, and to wait, and to build a machine made of my changing dreams, and he would return and help me leave."

Obviously not recognizing this for a well-told story, and a family favorite at that, Archimedes interrupted the young man's telling of it. "How did they know he was a magician?"

"Because he was made from this. Very big, all gray, no hair."

Yasmeen laughed in surprise, and looked to Archimedes. He wore an expression of disbelief. "The Blacksmith?"

She couldn't be certain, but the magician's description resembled his. The Blacksmith of London was the only man she'd ever known made almost entirely out of mechanical flesh.

Terbish shook his head. "I don't know that name. He said he was also Nergüi. He left, and I began to make the biggest, grandest machine that I could think of. My first was the pony, as strong as any that Genghis Khan used to ride across the steppes. Then my grandmother pointed to the mountain peaks, so near to the Eternal Sky, and I began to build that, instead. A year ago, the magician returned. He gave to me a piece of mechanical flesh no bigger than this"—he held his hands cupped together—"and told me to put it in the heart of my machine, and she would grow. And she has."

Astonishing. Yasmeen could not stop grinning, imagining it. "And what will you do with your flying machine?"

"I will take my grandmother, and we will either travel everywhere in the world or return and lead the rebellion. Perhaps both."

"The Blacksmith didn't tell you what to do with it?"

"He said it was mine. He said it was for kindness." Terbish stroked the metal again. "And that I only have to keep my heart big enough to match it."

Chapter 12

After crawling out into the sunlight and dropping into the courtyard's deep snow, Archimedes turned to her. "Are you as certain as I am that this thing will eventually fly?"

"I don't know." But he could see that she did. She was certain it would.

"I feel like I should be terrified. Can you imagine this in the sky?" He shook his head. "But I'm . . ."

"Overwhelmed."

"Yes."

"It's a good story. Let's hope Terbish doesn't grow up to be a dictator."

He looked to her. "And when will you tell me your story, steel flower?"

"Tonight. It isn't something to tell by sunlight, but with firelight and food and wine . . . or mare's milk." She smiled. "Should we begin our search? Perhaps we will find something."

They didn't, but it was still incredible to walk through the fortress, to feel the size and strength of it. With the soldiers gone from the outpost, the worry of discovery was all but gone. That afternoon, he and Yasmeen added their supplies to the food stores, and though Nergüi looked doubtful as she sniffed the dried meats, she cooked a thick stew from it, made hearty with roots and onions and seasoned with herbs. With more fermented mare's milk, he finished the day pleasantly full and warm. Terbish brought out an opium pipe, and for long, quiet moments, Yasmeen shared it with Archimedes. When she returned the pipe, she looked as fully relaxed as he felt, sitting cross-legged on the bedroll with Archimedes stretched out behind her, up on his elbow and his knee cocked, giving light support to her back. Terbish lay similarly stretched out on his pallet, and the older woman sat on her mat, taking her draught.

Archimedes wondered, "Do you have nanoagents, Nergüi?"

She gave an amused cackle. "So that the Great Khan might control us, too?"

"Rebels have much in common with the New World," Yasmeen said in French. "But I would never tell either of them that."

Archimedes laughed, and watched as she seemed to settle in without moving much at all—just a sigh, and a slight pressure against his leg as she rested more fully against him. "So what sort of story are you telling us?"

"A tragic one," she said. "It began with love, as tragedies always do."

"If that is your opinion, no wonder your heart is of steel."

A sharp *shht!* from Nergüi. Archimedes stifled his laugh. It had been some time since he'd been hushed, but he settled in, too, watching Yasmeen's face as she began.

"There was a warrior queen, clever and strong, who held together the empire through turbulent times. Manduhai the Wise, wife to the Khan and Khatun herself after he died of long sickness, she ruled and all of the empire loved her, but for the heirs of Ögedei, who wanted to tear her throne away."

This was not her story, he realized. At least, not as Terbish's had been, but something she must have heard again and again. Blissed, her voice had taken on the cadence of a poem in the Horde language that her heavy accent seemed to emphasize, lift.

"She bore many sons and daughters, and taught them all in the ways of the Eternal Sky and the Earth Mother, and taught them to love the mountains that brought men close to the sky, and the rivers that were the mother's blood. All her children were favored, but none more than her son Barsu Bolod, the Steel Tiger, who everyone agreed would be Khan when her eyes had closed. She told him that he must find a wife, but only to marry one who was as strong and as fierce, as noble and as wise as she. Barsu Bolod searched the empire, looking for such a woman, when he was beset upon by bandits trying to take his gold. He fought, but there were too many. But his warrior's cries were heard in a nearby village, where there lived a maiden of beauty and boldness. Taking up her spear, Khojen slew the bandits, and their blood spewed into the earth like a thunderstorm. Barsu Bolod saw her, and loved her, and knew that she would stand beside him when he was Khan, and if ever he fell too early, she would defend their people with the ferocity of a tiger. He brought her back to Xanadu, and presented her to the wise queen, who saw that Khojen's soul was a mirror to her own. They were married, and in their happiness, they agreed to the queen's wise advice to travel around the empire, so that the people would know them both."

She paused. Not to wet her lips, Archimedes saw with astonishment, but because she was overcome with feeling. Her eyes glistened and her throat worked. Perhaps it was only the opium—but whatever she claimed of her heart of steel, she burned with deep emotion.

What would it be to be loved by her? God, he would give anything to know.

"They traveled to the lands of Goryeo and read the carved blocks. They walked through the flowered temples of Khmer. They bathed in the sacred river, and floated lamps filled with oil across her waters. They reached for the Eternal Sky upon the highest mountains. They crossed the deserts and walked three times around the house of God.

"Everywhere, they were welcomed and showered with gifts. But although Lady Khojen was given gems and gold, treasures uncounted, she would not be parted from the gift of the Persian lynx, the caracal with the tufted ears and golden fur. It sat upon her lap, always, purring as she stroked its soft side, and would not allow anyone but Lady Khojen and Barsu Bolod to caress it. Like Lady Khojen, it hunted with ferocity and defended its mistress from those who might come near. But as they traveled, the wise queen grew old. Her heart and her eyes began to fail. When the happy pair heard news of the wise queen's illness, they returned across the empire, full of all they had seen and heard, their own hearts wise and good. But the heirs of Ögedei had news of their route, and while they rested at a trusted house, they were set upon by the traitorous dogs."

Tears gathered in her eyes, began to slip down her cheeks. Her voice never faltered, her breath never sobbed. Nergüi sat across from her, weeping softly. She knew this story, too, Archimedes realized. Perhaps all of the Horde knew it.

"Warriors in full, they fought, but Barsu Bolod fell. Lady Khojen, the mirror of his mother's soul, threw herself upon him and took a blade meant for his heart, but it could not save them. Impaled together, they breathed their last, and the heirs of Ögedei raised their knives to desecrate the bodies. But the caracal, who knew by the scent of blood that her mistress had fallen, would not let them touch the once-happy couple. With teeth and claws, it defended them. When friends of the wise queen came to the house, they found the caracal had slain all that attacked her beloved son and his fierce wife. When Manduhai the Wise heard this, she knew the animal would always be friend to the Khan and to the empire, and ordered her magicians to create a woman who would never falter in her guard, a woman of teeth and claws, a woman as beautiful as a flower and as strong as steel, with the loyal heart of the caracal. And so it was done—and the *gan tsetseg* have served the true house of royal blood from that day."

Silence fell. The fire crackled. Yasmeen stared into it, pupils dilated, cheeks wet. After what seemed an endless time, Nergüi gave a snore. Terbish lay with his back to them—sleeping or quiet.

Yasmeen looked to him and said softly in French, "Except for me. I don't serve anyone but myself."

"And Lady Lynx was more accurate than Zenobia knew."

Smiling, she lay down beside him. "Yes."

He thought of the rumors that the Horde bred animals with people. He'd never believed it, discarding the talk as the vicious sort that people spoke of their enemies. But there was some truth in it, bits and pieces. Not that women had lain with apes, but they *had* been mixed, in some way. "Is it through the nanoagents?"

"Yes. The inventors at the stable combined the essence of the caracal with that of our mothers. I don't know how. And I don't know who she is," Yasmeen added. "The mothers are chosen through the crèches, and we never see them."

"And when the *gan tsetseg* have children? Are they still like you?"

"I don't know. I never will have my own—after Bart stabbed me, it was too much for my nanoagents to heal, though they worked so hard they began killing me with the fever.

Eben also tried to repair my womb in surgery, but . . . he could not, though he fixed what he could. I would kill Bart again, just for that loss. And the others cannot—they are metal all below. But there must be some in the houses that can't be altered now that the Khan's stable is gone, and they will bear children. Perhaps then we will see."

All metal below. "Can the others . . . ?"

She grinned. "Your brain works exactly as every other man's. Of course they can."

"But they don't have to serve that way, too?"

"No. If she's treated like a whore, she can crush them. Quite literally, in every way." She turned her head, looked into the fire again. "Doesn't it bother you to know?"

"What?"

To his surprise, she flicked her ear. But they were not even so very different: the same shell as any person's, though slightly tapered at the tip and topped by that short tuft.

"No." He reached out to trace the curved edge, and she drew away, smiling.

"Not here, Mr. Fox."

"Why?" He knew she loved it when he stroked her—and he had scratched a cat's ears before, had seen the reaction. He lowered his voice. "Are they sensitive? If I stroke them, will you embarrass yourself in front of our hosts?"

"No, Mr. Fox." She rolled to face him and came up on her elbow, her mouth almost to his. "It's just that they're very, very . . . ticklish."

He squeezed his eyes shut, stifling his laugh.

Her fingers stroked the side of his jaw. "Do you stay awake first, or do I?"

"I will." Though they didn't have to worry about the soldiers, it was still best to keep watch. "Five hours?"

"Yes." Softly, she pressed her lips to his neck. He heard her deep inhalation, as if drawing in his scent. "Do you know that I have read all of your stories?"

He didn't. But now his mind sifted frantically through them, trying to remember what Zenobia had included, what was fact—and what he might hate to have Yasmeen know. Carefully, he asked, "What did you think?"

"Archimedes Fox did some very stupid things."

Ah, yes. Some of those were fact, too. God. Gritting his teeth, he said, "You think so?"

"Yes." She sighed against his throat. "And yet, I could never get enough of him."

And while he was still trying to find the words to reply, she climbed into the bedroll and closed her eyes.

Yasmeen would be sorry to leave. The freezing cold, empty fortress, and the two days spent walking through it with Archimedes Fox had been perfect in every way. Yet as they climbed to the southeast tower after saying their farewells to Nergüi and Terbish, his expression was thoughtful, maybe troubled.

He doused the light at the top of the tower, and they waited atop the wall. Fresh snow covered the flying machine in the courtyard, making it difficult to see even with her eyes. Terbish and Nergüi had agreed to their request to meet the airship alone; knowing that she and Archimedes had been friendly with two members of the Horde might raise suspicions against them, and she didn't want to add to the crew's tension.

Farther up the valley, *Ceres* approached under full sail, her deck lanterns dark. Apparently they hadn't mutinied yet.

And Archimedes had nothing to show for this expedition thus far.

"Are you worried because there was nothing to find?" she wondered.

He shook his head. She couldn't read him—only that something was wrong.

"Have I already broken your heart?" She hoped not. She hoped she never did. She hoped that if he loved her, that he would go on, content to love her.

"Not yet." His gaze softened. He stroked his hand down her cheek, then suddenly cupped her jaw in both hands and his head fell, hovering, hovering just above her mouth. His ragged breath across her lips seemed to echo the shaking of her body.

Her heart pounded. "Kiss me."

"Kiss *me*," he said.

Damn him. Why did he never follow orders? "I can't. But I want to finish this, and I *need* you in my bed. How can your longing *not* be great enough, when I want you so much without love? When will you love me, long for me enough to kiss me?"

"When will *you*?"

Her chest ached suddenly, painful, deep. "That was not part of this. You know I cannot."

"I don't know that anymore. Ah, God. And that makes the pain worse. If you *can* love me but *won't* . . ."

Torment filled his eyes, his voice. He clutched her against his lean body, face buried in her hair. She kissed his neck, jaw, wrapped her arms around his shoulders, holding him tight.

And he said softly against her ear, "I saw gliders that night."

"What?" She drew back, looked up into his face. "What night?"

"Just after I left you on *Lady Corsair*, while I was hiding from Nasrin behind the crates. I thought they were acrobats, practicing—as they sometimes do late."

"So?" They did practice late.

He looked to the batwing gliders that Bigor had lent. "There were four of them."

Her stomach suddenly seemed filled with hot coals. He thought Bigor and his men had boarded her lady? But that was exactly the type of work they did in the war. Quiet, quick, and then erase the evidence.

She remembered Bigor's voice. *Doing things I'd never want my wife and children to know.* Had that been an apology? An explanation? An excuse?

Just something said from one person who'd lost their brother to someone who'd lost their crew?

"How can we know?" she whispered. "What happens if we ask them?"

"I think they could very easily kill us."

"Not *easily*."

"No—the decision would be easy for them."

And so it would be. They didn't leave evidence. "Who hired them before al-Amazigh did? Does Hassan know who recommended them, what contact they used? You can't find a team like that in a tavern."

He nodded. "We'll ask him."

"Yes." By the lady, she could not imagine . . . And now she was sorry she'd saved any of them from the zombies.

No. She was still glad she'd saved three of them. Not just because they might be innocent.

But she'd rather kill them with full knowledge if they weren't.

Suspicion was like a toothed saw through her heart, rasping away. *Ceres* came in over the wall, dropped the rope ladder. Yasmeen reached for it, then glanced back, over the dark courtyard.

"I think I will come back in five years, just to see whether it flies."

"And I will come with you."

Together? She held his gaze long enough to say it, but didn't say it aloud. Turning away, she started up the ladder.

No sign of Bigor and his marines on deck—just Captain Guillouet. Definitely no mutiny, then, but it had been a rough few days for some. Hassan stood next to the captain, face slightly pale, weary. "Did you find anything? Do we need to lower the cargo lift?"

Archimedes came up behind her. "Those at the Horde outpost must have taken everything. There's nothing left."

The old man gave a resounding sigh and nodded. "We will go south, then. It will be warmer, if nothing else." He looked to Captain Guillouet. "We go to Italy."

The captain moved off to give the necessary orders, and Yasmeen was left, feeling more stupid than she'd ever felt. It was warmer on the boot of the Italian peninsula, though not significantly at this time of year and on an airship. Hassan might feel better.

But he shouldn't have been feeling poorly at all. Older men and women felt their age, just as Nergüi did . . . unless they were infected with nanoagents. Except for a fever now and again as the nanoagents fought off severe sickness or attempted to heal a badly injured body, the infected were almost always healthy. Thousands of people in England had lived their lives without so much as a sniffle, and Yasmeen would have wagered anything that the same was true in Morocco.

Yet if it was poison, no one else was suffering from it. The other men who'd been eating at the captain's table showed no sign of sickness . . . and they would have exhibited symptoms faster, because they weren't infected. But Hassan consumed one thing that no one else did.

"Hassan," she said quietly. "No more tea. Drinking nothing is better than that."

He frowned, and then understanding came over his features. "Who?"

"We will speak in your—"

Near the rail behind her, one of the crew called out, "Zombie on the tower wall, Captain! May I fire?"

Her breath caught. There were no zombies in the fortress. *Oh, no.*

"No!" Yasmeen said sharply. "Hold your fire."

Quiet fell over the ship. Guillouet stared at her, face darkening in fury.

Oh, by the lady. She had not even thought—hadn't checked herself. Opening her mouth was the hardest damn thing she'd ever done. "My apologies, Captain, but—"

"You're giving orders on my ship? Fire, Mr. Simon."

Yasmeen turned, but Archimedes had already whipped around. His foot struck the back of Simon's knee as he pulled the trigger. The gun bucked upward, bullet whizzing past the envelope.

Yasmeen faced Guillouet again, hands outspread to placate. "Please understand, Captain. It's not a zombie. It's a boy."

Shock registered on his features. "A *boy*?"

"From the outpost."

"From the Horde?" Shock became distaste. "And yet you stopped my man from shooting it."

It? Rage swept through her. Archimedes tackled her from behind, wrapped his arms around her stomach, pinning her hands to her sides. Quickly, he said, "Apologies, Captain. I'm sure this is only a misunderstanding."

"Captain," Hassan said easily. "The shot might have alerted the outpost."

A shout came from the starboard side. "They're lighting up across the valley, Captain!"

"Fire the engines!" Guillouet called out, and stepped forward. "Mr. Fox. You will keep your wife in her place and her mouth closed or I will do it for you."

Yasmeen felt Archimedes' nod.

"She's to be confined to your cabin. She is not to speak to any man aboard this ship. When her meals are brought to her, she will face away from the door so that my men do not even *look* upon her."

"I'll beat her, too," Archimedes said.

Guillouet was not amused. "Frankly, Mr. Fox, it would not be amiss."

"A war machine, Captain!" The shout sent a hail of responding cries through the crew, panic as sails were drawn in, orders yelled down brass tubes. "They've lit it up! One of the tentacle machines that rip airships from the sky!"

The captain gave a final look to Yasmeen. "Get her below."

Then he was off, and over the starboard side Yasmeen caught a glimpse of the gigantic machine, body rising like a cone as high as the citadel, illuminated by the tall acetylene lamps that lit the outpost walls.

"Should we tell them that there aren't any soldiers to man it?" Archimedes said against her ear, and without waiting for her to answer, "No, I don't think so, either."

Still holding in her fury, Yasmeen shook her head—and walked quietly to the ladder while the crew panicked around them.

Keep your wife in her place.

It echoed in Yasmeen's head until she couldn't shake the rage. Not at Archimedes—she knew it wasn't at him. But as soon as they entered their cabin, she couldn't keep herself from rounding on him with a snarl. "You stopped me!"

His eyes were suddenly bright, hard emerald. "And you let me! I couldn't have held you back if you hadn't allowed it—and that couldn't have ended until one of you was dead."

"It would have been him!"

"I know."

Her teeth clenched. That wasn't enough. She screamed, whipped toward the bunk. The upper mattress shredded to pieces under her claws. It still wasn't enough. She whirled back to Archimedes, who watched her with lifted brows.

"Now we both have to sleep on yours."

Yes. That would be enough.

"Come on," she said, chest heaving. "Now. No more nonsense about kissing. I want to be fucked."

His gaze flattened at *nonsense*. "Not like this, Yasmeen."

"This is how I want it. Angry, hard, rough. If you can't do it, I'll find someone else. On a ship full of men, it'll be no problem."

His jaw hardened. "You will *not*."

"Why? Will it hurt you? Oh, tenderhearted Archimedes Fox." Mouth curling into a sneer, she put her face to his. "You say you want to feel everything. Do you want to feel what it's like to watch me fuck someone else?"

"Do it, then," he said through clenched teeth. "Do it."

Idiot. Did he think he was calling her bluff? She didn't want anyone else, but she'd fucked without caring about the man she was with before. Did he truly think she couldn't do it again? Just bodies fucking, it didn't matter.

And she could end all of this now, she realized. This nonsense about falling in love with her, about longing and waiting to break his heart. She could do it now, and no matter what else Archimedes was, no matter what foolish ideas he had about feeling everything, she knew he *wouldn't* keep on this path after she went to someone else. Hell, she wouldn't even have to fuck anyone to do it. She could leave, wait, make him think she had. She'd break his heart, and that would be the end of it. He wouldn't try to win her love or even a kiss after that.

Two steps carried her to the cabin door. She opened it.

And like a fool, looked back.

Archimedes wasn't angry anymore. His face had whitened, skin taut with shock and hurt, eyes bleak as if he were already watching her with another man. Pain slashed across her chest. She'd done that. She'd *deliberately* done that to him, hacking away at the bond that had formed between them. And if she stepped out of the cabin, she'd break it. Maybe she already had.

That wasn't what she wanted. That was not what she *needed*. Bodies fucking didn't matter . . . and Archimedes Fox did.

Yasmeen closed the door. "I can't," she said. "I'm confined."

She smiled, and his laugh sounded, short with disbelief and relief. She went to him, slipped her arms around his waist. His hands were shaking as he pushed them into her hair, but so was she. She recalled his face as she'd opened the door. His pain. Tears started to her eyes, the ache growing inside her chest, as if it were about to rip apart.

Closing her eyes, she pressed her face into his neck. "Lady Lynx also does some *very* stupid things."

"I won't tell Zenobia," he said, his voice rough. "And I can't seem to get enough, either."

"Then take more," she said. "Please."

Still holding her against him, he backed to the bunk. Her fingers found the buckles of his shoulder harness. He shrugged it off, then reached for her heavy coat. Her hat. She unfastened the leather guard around his neck. The knives at her thighs. His holsters. The guns at her belt. She began to laugh when she started on the guards at his forearms at the same time he dropped to his knee, fingers searching out the fastenings to her boots.

He looked up at her, pressed a kiss to her inner thigh. The warmth of his lips penetrated through to her skin, and she shuddered, her laugh dying.

"You can take the top, Yasmeen," he said. "I'll take the bottom."

By the lady. She ripped her shirt over her head, stood bare before he'd unbuckled her right boot down to her knee. Biting her bottom lip, she watched him, the cold frame of the upper bunk pressing into her back. Her dark nipples hardened to small bullets, and to make him hurry, she cupped her breasts, fingers playing with their stiffened tips, craving his fingers, his mouth.

Oh, but it only slowed him. He watched her hands instead of his own, and when she slipped her hand into her breeches, his fingers fumbled on the buckle at her ankle. He groaned.

Yasmeen slid her hand deeper, lightly pinched her clitoris and imagined his lips, his teeth. Her knees almost folded. She gripped the bunk for support. "Hurry, Mr. Fox. I'd hate to do the job myself."

With a sound almost like a growl, he gripped her hips,

tipped her back onto the lower bunk, ass barely supported by the edge of the mattress.

"Now, *wait*." He finally pulled off her right boot, pressed a hot kiss to her ankle. His jaw rasped up the length of her calf. His fingers tugged the waist of her breeches.

She laughed. "My boot—"

"I don't care." He stripped her breeches fully down her right leg, lifting her knee to maneuver them off. The left leg, he simply pulled down as far as he could. "My God, I forgot there's more."

Just the small, loose pants that fell to mid-thigh—and then she'd be open to him. Yasmeen lifted her hips, pushing them down, the same way he had her breeches: off her right leg, just as far as she could on her left. "Hurry."

"Oh, no. None of that here." Still fully clothed, he pushed her legs apart, strong fingers pressing into her thighs. "You like to be tortured, Mrs. Fox. You like to be stroked, to go slow."

She loved all of that. Anticipation wound through her, tightening her muscles, building the hollow ache at her core into agony. He wasn't going to fill that completely, she realized. Not tonight.

"This isn't the kiss I expected," she panted. Though she wasn't about to complain.

His handsome features stark with need, Archimedes bent his head. "I've wanted this almost as long."

And he definitely wasn't in a hurry now. He began with a slow, broad lick up her center. Yasmeen gasped, her back arching. Another slow lick, his tongue spreading her slick folds, the tip flicking against her clit. She cried out, and barely had time to catch her breath before he was there again, his tongue pushing into her with a leisurely thrust and then sliding up, slow, thorough. He didn't stop, didn't stop, thrusting and licking so slowly, her clit aching for release but he kept that slow, even pace, lapping at her until she was so wet that even with his continual licking she could feel the slickness on her inner thighs, sliding along the curve of her ass. Her body writhed, as she tried to find another angle, another pressure, but his tongue swept through again, that devastating flick at the end that brought her so close, so close. She screamed his name, begged. His tongue came up and swirled, and she bucked against his mouth, sobbing. His long fingers pressed into her, and she couldn't take any more. His lips closed over her clit and his tongue ran over her like a succulent kiss and she was over, broken. Her body clenched, again, again.

She finally fell back, sweating, her body still shuddering. Then Archimedes climbed into the bunk, and she was wrecked.

Lying on his back, he hauled her over his chest, her limp legs straddling his thighs. His hand swept her body, soothing, pleasing. He kissed the wet from her eyes, but he didn't kiss her mouth, didn't fuck her, he simply stroked her skin until sweet lethargy weighed her down like opium.

"You're an idiot to love me," she whispered.

"Am I?" He didn't sound convinced.

"Yes." She drew in his scent, so strong and warm. "But, still—it is a fine thing, to be loved."

And tucking her face against his shoulder, she slept.

Yes. It would be a fine thing, to be loved.

When they'd made their agreement in the Charging Bull, Archimedes hadn't lied when he'd told Yasmeen that falling in love with her wasn't a game. But until now, he didn't know how wrong he'd been.

He *had* been playing a game. A game of luck, a game of chance, with his heart as the stakes, deep emotion and heartbreak the prize—and he hadn't known what any of that meant. But he'd had the smallest taste of it when she'd opened that door, and he never, *ever* wanted to feel like that again. So he could continue on, trying to feel every single emotion, and finish the game broken and poor.

But now that he was in love with her, Archimedes simply wasn't playing anymore.

Chapter 13

Yasmeen stirred when Archimedes slipped out of bed, but she didn't lift her head. He didn't bother with his boots or a jacket, and picked up his dagger from the cabin floor. Silently, he made his way to Ollivier's door and inside.

With a single bunk and room for a small desk, Ollivier's cabin was more spacious than theirs. The man slept on his side, facing away from the door. Archimedes slid his dagger against the man's neck, nudged him awake. Ollivier opened his eyes, his hand moving beneath his pillow. Archimedes let him feel the blade. He froze.

"Put your hands on your head, Mr. Ollivier. Very good. Now, stand up—Nuh-uh! Hands still on your head. There you go. Let's take a walk, have a little drink together."

In a nightdress that came to his knees, Ollivier was silent until they reached the door. Then he tried for outrage. "This is an affront to my dignity, Mr. Fox. If you don't want to share the credit of the find—"

"There's no find yet, Mr. Ollivier. Now close your mouth until we reach the stateroom, or I'll cut out your tongue."

Archimedes wouldn't, actually; the whole point of this was for the man to talk. A toe would do just as well. A finger. The head of his prick—which, apparently, had begun dribbling piss during the short walk to Hassan's stateroom.

On second thought, the tongue would be fine. Ollivier could write his answers.

He wasn't surprised to find Yasmeen already in Hassan's cabin, heating a pot of tea over the small gas burner. How had she fastened her boots so damn quickly? Obviously Archimedes would have to practice.

"Sit here, Mr. Ollivier," Hassan said, gesturing to the chair opposite his. "I thought we might have some tea."

Shaking, Ollivier sat.

Hassan poured his cup. "You'll forgive me if I only watch. My French is poor."

"A scream for mercy sounds the same in any language," Yasmeen said, sliding the teacup across the table. "Did you make it strong, Mr. Ollivier? His nanoagents fought off the poisons, but what about you? What would a sip of this do?"

"I don't know what you're speaking of."

Yasmeen smiled.

"Very well." Ollivier wiped his sleeve across his forehead. "What is it you want to know?"

Archimedes took the chair next to him. "We want to know why."

"Because I was hired to."

"By *whom*, Mr. Ollivier?"

The man was breathing hard, sweating. "I was given orders by the *marsouins*. But al-Amazigh is paying me."

Hassan's expression didn't change. "Kareem al-Amazigh?"

"Yes."

"Why?" Yasmeen asked.

"He doesn't trust Mr. Hassan. Your association to Temür Agha is too close." He spoke directly to Hassan. "He believes you will eventually betray him."

God. Then al-Amazigh didn't know Hassan at all. Archimedes shook his head. "Then why this expedition? Why not a more direct assassination?"

"Temür Agha is a powerful man, Mr. Fox. Al-Amazigh wanted the death to appear natural, the result of sickness, so that there would be no retaliation."

"But he also needs the money," Hassan said. "Is that right?"

"Yes. So he hired me to look for the treasures."

Archimedes leaned forward. "Al-Amazigh didn't want me included on the expedition, initially, because of my association with Temür. Are you supposed to kill me, too?"

"No." He shook his head. "That is not mine to do."

Yasmeen hissed. "Whose is it?"

"The *marsouins*'. After the expedition is over."

Archimedes looked to Hassan. The man showed little, but he'd had years of practice concealing his emotions.

"Al-Amazigh must desperately want that money," Yasmeen said.

"I do not know," Ollivier said. "I was not told more."

A feral expression slipped over her face, lips drawing back over sharp teeth. "And what of *Lady Corsair*?"

"I don't . . . What of her?"

"Two months ago, she was boarded in Port Fallow and my crew slaughtered. Do you know anything of that, Mr. Ollivier?"

"No." He shook his head emphatically. "No. Two months past, I was in Martinique. I did not even speak to Bigor until six weeks ago."

"Why you?" Archimedes said. "You have no name for yourself in this field. You sympathized with the Liberé. How did they know to choose you for the expedition?"

"Bigor discovered me dosing the coffee in a noble's house. He was there for another reason, and couldn't risk the questions raised by my disappearance if he had killed me. But he has known of me since then. He remembered." His hands clenched on the table, tears filling his eyes. "I was done with this! For ten years, I have only studied, taught. I wanted my name to be spoken in the same breath as da Vinci—but not like this!"

"Come now," Archimedes said. "You wouldn't have minded that so much."

Ollivier wiped his eyes. "No. In truth, no. It would be worth it. Or even to have it spoken in the same breath as Archimedes Fox."

Yasmeen grinned, leaned across the table, raised the teacup to his lips. "How about, 'Vincent Ollivier, slain by Archimedes Fox's wife'?"

"Oh, God, please no—"

"Stop." She pulled back, her eyes hard, no humor left. "Understand this, Mr. Ollivier: You are leaving this cabin alive tonight. You are to give no indication that we've spoken of this. If you must, poison yourself to give the appearance of sickness, and remain in your bunk for the remainder of the expedition. Can you do that?"

"Yes. Yes, yes."

"Wonderful." She stood, gestured to the door. "Go now. And sleep well, Mr. Ollivier."

After the smile she gave him, Archimedes would be surprised if the man ever slept again. He waited at the door, watched Ollivier enter his cabin before turning back to the others.

"So, al-Amazigh has arranged to kill us all," he said, and looked to Hassan. "Why? Do you think Ollivier knew the truth of it?"

Tiredly, the old man shook his head. "I could not say. It is true that he worried about your association to Temür, but of mine? He must know I would not compromise the freedom of our people. Perhaps it was to keep some other truth from me."

"And what of the *marsouins*?" Yasmeen asked. "Do you know how or when he became acquainted with them?"

"Yes. There is a man—a weapons smuggler, the one who will provide the explosives for the tower. He told Kareem of the *marsouins*, and said that if ever he needed to complete a job, they were the men to contact. This was several months ago. Kareem has contacted them several times, I believe."

"What is the smuggler's name? Do you recall?"

"Of course. He is called Mattson."

Miracle Mattson, who Yasmeen had shot in his sister's home. He watched her eyes close as the full realization swept over her. Mattson had known of the da Vinci sketch, and must have told Bigor and his men—or perhaps he'd told al-Amazigh, and the rebel had sent in the marines to collect the sketch. They must have reached her strongbox before the timer closed, then attempted to erase the evidence by blowing her ship.

A short expedition, and much more lucrative than the current one. Though the sketch was a fake, Yasmeen's gold had not been.

Had al-Amazigh discovered that he possessed a forgery? Had he heard of the sketch that Temür Agha had now . . . or, even if he had heard, did he think Archimedes had found two?

"Hassan," she said, and he heard the roughness in her

voice, the pain that must be lodged deep within. "How did al-Amazigh pay for this expedition? How did he pay for the *marsouins*?"

"He went to Port Fallow three months ago to sell the jewelry that I gave to him. Temür has been generous to me these many years. I had a small collection."

A small collection wouldn't amount to much—and probably not enough to fund an expedition. But the final connection slid into place. "Did he sell the jewelry through Franz Kessler?"

"That I do not know."

"How long was he in Port Fallow?"

"A month or so." Clearly troubled, he glanced from Archimedes to Yasmeen. "There is something here you have not said. Is this what you asked of Ollivier—about *Lady Corsair*?"

Her mouth tight, Yasmeen nodded.

"You believe al-Amazigh ordered it? That Bigor's men carried it out?"

"Yes," she said. "It begins to seem that way."

He tapped the ends of his broad fingers together, his face thoughtful. "Will you kill them tonight?"

"I haven't decided." She banged her fist on the table. "*Goddammit.* If we were not aboard this ship, I wouldn't hesitate."

Because of the precarious tension within the crew, Archimedes realized—surprised, he had to admit—that it was even a consideration for her.

"I understand that this is not my place," Hassan said carefully. "But I would ask that you wait. If they have no plans to kill you and your husband until after some treasure is secured, then you are safe until then. Perhaps, in the meantime, I can discover more about why Kareem has chosen this route."

Archimedes wasn't so certain. He cared much less about al-Amazigh's plans than he did Yasmeen's life. "And what if Ollivier gives us away?"

"Then I suspect Bigor will be surprised by your wife's capabilities. You probably ought not to be with them by yourselves, however. Tomorrow morning, we will be over Brindisi."

The site of their next search. "We'll go down alone," Archimedes said.

* * *

In their cabin, Yasmeen lit one of their few remaining cigarillos and paced while Archimedes settled onto the bottom bunk. Sleeping together now. That was all right. That was good. *That was the only damn thing that was good—*

Pain struck at her chest. She paced faster, but couldn't outrun it. She dug her fingers into her hair, tried to stop it, but the agony only settled in her throat, welled tears in her eyes. Instead of standing there, shaking, she crushed out the cigarillo and slid in next to Archimedes, and he wrapped her in his arms as she cried silently against his throat.

He kissed the top of her head, simply held her until she stopped. "You wanted to kill them tonight."

She wanted her *crew* back tonight. But she'd have settled for ripping out throats, tasting their blood and pain.

"Yes," she said, and rolled onto her back, relit the cigarillo. She passed it to him when he came up on his elbow. "But I can be patient."

Though he didn't make a sound, she felt his laugh against her side. She narrowed her eyes at him.

"You doubt me?"

"Yes."

"You're wrong." She plucked the cigarillo from his lips. "And you also take a very long time to pass this back."

He grinned.

"I said that to make you laugh," she told him. "You didn't get the better of me."

His smile became tender, and he brushed a stray hair from her forehead. "No. You have definitely gotten the better of me. This might be the wrong time to tell you, I don't know."

"Tell me what?"

He took a deep breath. "I love you."

Oh. Her lips parted. He slipped the cigarillo from between her teeth, bent his head. His mouth brushed hers, so sweet. When she lifted to deepen the kiss, he drew back.

That was it? Yet, in its perfect way, enough.

Smiling, she lay her head on the pillow again. Despite everything, she felt almost settled now. She *would* be patient. She *would* avenge her crew.

And she would hold the heart of Archimedes Fox very, very close.

"Not the wrong time at all," she said.

Why had he never been to Brindisi before? Aside from the zombies, it was a near-perfect city, full of churches and forts and castles whose thick walls stood for hundreds of years without crumbling to ruins. Clear turquoise waters filled the harbor, and on one of the islands—free of zombies—sat an enormous red structure that had been called only "Sea Fort" in Ollivier's notes.

It was far more than that—it was a hoard of relics worth salvaging. Archimedes only picked a few to take back to *Ceres*; finding nothing at all would raise suspicions, and too many would be a treasure and a signal for Bigor to kill him. So he found small painted icons in the chapel, and would return later for the altarpiece. He found a faded tapestry, and left a sundial in the shape of a lute.

But although Hassan might have been satisfied by the few things he'd brought back to the ship, Archimedes knew not to stop there. They had discussed Brindisi with Bigor before they'd learned of his connection to Mattson, so the marine was aware that several locations in the port city were to be explored. He and Yasmeen dutifully crept through a church, and he found a diptych of an archangel and the Virgin, and a lead bowl plated with gold.

If it had been solid gold, he'd have left it.

He could have easily spent weeks here, but he settled on two days. They remained out until after midnight the first day, and almost immediately dropped into sleep on return to *Ceres*. He woke to the cracking of Yasmeen's knees. As soon as she loosened up, they scouted a new building from the airship and went down again, lowering the rope ladder to the roof. After a cursory search, they climbed back up, scouted another building, then a castle overlooking the harbor. A number of zombies milled around in the courtyard, so many that it took Archimedes a few moments to recognize what they were milling *around*. His heart thumped against his chest, and his head swam.

Yasmeen caught his arm. "Archimedes?"

He forced the excitement from his expression, though he wanted to shout and laugh. In a low voice, he said, "It is his *crane*."

"What?"

"The pile of rotted wood below. Do you see the shape of the iron that used to bind it, the giant wheel, the long arm? It's a machine for lifting. I saw a replica of da Vinci's sketch once. This is his crane, almost exactly."

"Ah." She studied the shattered remains. "So what was he lifting?"

Archimedes almost didn't care. He wanted to slide down into the courtyard, simply *touch* the iron. But the number of zombies made that impossible, at least until he returned. He judged the length of the crane arm, followed the arc of it in his mind.

"There." He pointed to the curtain wall nearest to the harbor. "Something could be lifted to the top of the wall and taken into that tower."

"All right." She met his eyes. "There's a lot of stairs."

She was right. The castle didn't possess a regular, symmetrical structure, but sprawled across different levels of walls, towers, halls, and courtyards. Stairs running up the side of the curtain walls gave zombies easy access to the tower—there were already several stumbling along the stone walkway atop the wall.

"We kill those, then we make certain we're quiet," he said.

They did, and even better, the tower had a door—partially rotted, but intact, so that if any more zombies climbed up to the wall, they wouldn't see Archimedes and Yasmeen moving around inside. So long as they were quiet, they shouldn't capture the zombies' attention.

They waved the airship away and went inside. The tower had been designed for defense. The chamber was round, with only a few small openings set at an angle high in the thick stone walls—shafts for ventilation, perhaps, or to let the light in. Dust and stone debris covered a slate floor. Feathers were scattered about, the remains of nests visible in the ventilation shafts and the rafters. Heaps of old cloth had molded in piles and gave home to mice that scattered when he lifted one dark, stiff edge. A bed had collapsed on itself—and on the far side of it, lying on the floor, he found the clockwork man.

"Yasmeen," he whispered, and slipped to his knees.

He felt her fingers against his shoulder, heard her sharp breath.

Shoulders of iron and the gear guts had rusted. A copper pendulum at the heart had tarnished and warped. The fingers were nothing but steel tubes, the arms a system of pulleys whose ropes had long disintegrated. It had no legs and no head. Just a torso with arms, partially finished and abandoned—it was the most wonderful thing he'd ever seen.

And they had to leave it here.

"Ah, God," he said. "Ah, God."

She crouched beside him, her arms wrapping around his shoulders. "We'll come back for it."

He slipped out of her arms and lay on the floor. "I'll stay and guard it."

Yasmeen snorted softly, her half laugh quickly muffled. "You don't even—"

The crack of a gunshot sounded outside. Archimedes sat up, pulse racing. He stared into Yasmeen's eyes, saw the same shock and surprise.

"Was that from the airship?" she whispered.

The airship that was hovering over the harbor, not far from the tower—and the curtain wall lay in a direct line between *Ceres* and the zombies that would be rushing to investigate the sound.

Over the pounding of his heart came the pounding of feet, the moans and growls. Jesus. He raced for the door. *Thank God, thank God*, it opened inward—though chunks were missing in the rotted wood, big enough to shove hands through. With enough pressure, those holes would likely become bigger.

It couldn't be helped. He braced the door with his weight, set his feet. "Is there another way out?"

But Yasmeen was already racing through the room, feeling along the walls, looking for one. She turned back to him, eyes wide. "No."

"Take my grap—"

The first zombie hit. The thud reverberated through his back, but he held fast. Yasmeen shoved her palms against the door beside his shoulders, adding her weight.

"My grapnel," he said, and two more rammed into the door. Or the same one, with a friend. His boots skidded, just a tiny bit—and he could hear more coming over the ravenous growls. "The ventilation shafts. We'll climb out."

Maybe. The openings weren't big.

"All right. Go," she said. "Shoot it."

No, no. She hadn't—

"Archimedes." She met his eyes. "You've practiced shooting that launcher; I haven't. I'll hold the door. You'll need to go up first, anyway, because the second person is going to have to sprint and climb—and I'm faster."

"I'm stronger." And the zombies weren't hitting the door now, but piling against it—pushing, pushing.

"Yes. So you'll need to be fast," she said.

Goddammit. But he nodded. "On three, we switch."

At her nod, he counted. She slipped smoothly into his place, feet braced, jaw clenched with effort. An emaciated arm snaked through a hole, grasping hand waving near her leg.

"Hurry," she said.

He raced to the nearest ventilation shaft, took a second to breathe, to steady his arm. The grapnel launched, hitting the ceiling of the shaft but bouncing through. Behind him, Yasmeen laughed with relief.

"Go up!"

He dropped his shoulder harness—no chance he'd make it through with it. He climbed, digging his toes into the wall to go more quickly. He pushed his head into the shaft, felt the sun, the breeze.

His shoulders didn't fit.

He tried again, another angle this time, diagonally in the square shaft. His hands were sweating on the rope, his arms aching. Every second was another that Yasmeen was holding the door. No matter how he squeezed, his shoulders didn't fit through.

Chest heavy, he dropped back to the floor.

"No," she said. "Don't you—*No!*"

"Yes." He braced his hands against the door beside her—
Thank God—slimmer shoulders, and smashed the heel of his
boot onto a hand groping along the floor. "It has to be this way.
My manly physique is simply too powerful."

Her eyes filled. "No."

"Yes. Now, on three—we switch."

He began to count, and *God*, he wished he'd kissed her
properly first. He wished he'd made love to her as she'd
wanted. Hard, fast, angry, slow . . . it didn't matter now.

"Three," he said and took her place, feeling the hammering
against the wood, the reverberating growls. "Now shoot me
and go."

Her gaze lifted to his. The tears were gone, he saw. Her
eyes were clear, and hard, and cold. Her killing look, he
knew—that heart of steel wrapping completely around her.

And then she kissed him.

Warm, firm, his mouth was everything she wanted,
needed. But the zombies were growling behind him, and she
couldn't linger. She didn't have much time, not if she wanted
to save him.

She *had* to save him.

Yasmeen drew away, and saw his astonishment, his agony,
his hope. It changed to flat denial as she said, "I'm coming
back for you."

"No—"

"Don't you *dare* die," she said. "I'm coming. And if you're
not here, you're going to break my heart, Archimedes Fox. So
hold that door."

She sprinted for the rope. Seconds later, she stuck her head
out of the shaft, looked up. *Ceres* hovered above—coming to
rescue them, after some fucking idiot had nearly killed them.

Her shout was met with several from the decks. The rope
ladder spilled over—out of reach, but she leapt for it, swinging
above the harbor cliff.

On the deck, she ignored everything but the man she
wanted.

"Bigor! I need your diving suit. Now, now, *now!*"

With a sharp nod, the marine ran for the ladder. Yasmeen

stripped off her jacket, her boots. "Captain! Bring that rope ladder right to the tower door!"

He stiffened like she'd shoved a burning rod up his ass. "Mrs. Fox, you don't—"

"Some bastard on your ship fired a gun and *he's going to die down there*! Give me the fucking ladder!"

Though Guillouet shook with rage, he nodded to the mate. Good. If he hadn't, Yasmeen would have killed him.

Bigor returned, carrying half the suit. The two other marines carried the rest. With amazing speed, they helped her into the thick canvas, fastened and buckled the brass over her limbs. The zombies might get a bite in between the brass plates, but wouldn't break through the canvas. The brass helmet reduced her sight to nothing, but it didn't matter: If it moved, she was going to kill it.

The canvas gloves were too heavy for a gun, but machetes were just fine. She gripped the handles. The suit felt like moving with chains tied to her ankles, her elbows. Bigor yanked the hose out of the top of the helmet, and fresh air came in.

She clanked over to the rope ladder, grabbed on, and dove in. *So heavy*. She fell to one knee on the stone wall as she landed, and they were on her, but Archimedes was waiting. Her blades hacked and chopped. The zombies growled and moaned, and there were so many but she would not stop, *she'd never stop—*

A crack sounded, the snap of wood. The tower door. Oh, by the lady—the door. She whipped around, and through the tiny, blood-streaked window of her helmet, she saw the zombies pushing against it, she saw the door shatter.

Her heart shattered with it.

I'm coming back for you.

Archimedes held on to that. He held and held—the door didn't. Wood shattered. Hands grabbed at him. He raced across the chamber, heading for the grapnel rope. His shoulders were too wide, but *by God*, he could hold on until she arrived.

Boots digging into the wall, he hauled himself out of reach.

He heard a sound like a muffled scream of rage and pain. *Yasmeen.* She'd seen the door go down.

So he'd let her know he was still inside. His revolvers were in his holsters. Gripping the rope with one hand, Archimedes aimed, fired. God, how many were in here? Thirty or forty? He'd take a good number down, but prayed for a reload to drop out of the sky.

Or for a woman with a brass suit and machetes. He laughed as she came through the door, mobbed by zombies but slashing them down with brutal efficiency. There was nothing elegant about her movements now, just vicious hacks of her blades that sent heads and arms thudding to the floor. The brass plates were covered in gore.

"I love you!" he called out, then shot a zombie coming at Yasmeen from behind, and another trampling the clockwork man. He heard more shots now, too—and there were fewer new zombies racing in. The crew on the airship must have been clearing off the wall leading to the tower. He fired until he was out. Only a few zombies left in the chamber. He dropped, triggered the springs at his forearms, and hacked the blade through the zombie that came running at him. Yasmeen finished off the last.

He heard her laugh, muffled by the helmet. The chamber floor was an inch deep in blood, deeper in twitching body parts. He wiped off the blades usually hidden in his forearm guards and pushed them back in. His shoulder harness dripped; he didn't think about it, just slung it over his arm.

The cargo lift waited outside. They stepped aboard, and Archimedes unbolted her helmet, lifted it off, tossed it aside. Her face was streaked with sweat—and tears? Her chest hit his with a clank, and she was laughing again when he kissed her, so deep, unable to stop until they were almost at the deck. He unbuckled the blood-streaked plates, the soaked canvas. Her breeches and shirt were clean, her calves and feet bare.

When the lift clanked into place, they faced Captain Guillouet's loaded gun.

Yasmeen stilled, her hand tightening on his. Archimedes waited, then realized—she didn't have a gun, and his revolvers were empty.

"Mr. Bigor, please escort Mr. Fox to the wardroom, and guard him while I speak with his wife. Keep a gun on him at all times, so that she knows not to step out of place."

Bigor hesitated for only the briefest moment. Then he drew his weapon, aimed it at Archimedes. "Mr. Fox."

"If you hear any kind of commotion from Mrs. Fox, shoot him."

"Yes, sir."

"Take him below."

With her gaze locked on Guillouet's gun, Yasmeen let go of his hand. As Archimedes stepped from the cargo lift to the deck, he said softly, "I'll be coming for you."

Then he saw her eyes, and *now* he knew cold. Now he knew hard.

"You'd better hurry," she said.

No commotion. Yasmeen could have disarmed Guillouet and taken him down with barely a sound, but she couldn't halt a commotion if everyone saw her do it. So she would be patient.

Obviously feeling bold with his pistol aimed at her face, Guillouet stepped close. "Come to my cabin, Mrs. Fox."

Wrapping his fist in the hair at her nape, he shoved her in front of him, tucked the gun barrel behind her ear. She walked obediently, noting the expressions of the crew around them. Vashon with jaw set and a disapproving glower, and the twin with an angrier match. Some shock. Some who wouldn't look her way. Guilt? Uncomfortable?

As they should be. When a man forced a woman into his cabin, it usually only meant one thing.

"Who shot the gun?" she wondered aloud. Their quick glances and the pain lancing through her scalp told her without a word. "*You*, Captain?"

"Twenty years on a ship and I have *never* had to shout over my own men," he said. "And I will not talk over you. Do not speak again until I tell you to, Mrs. Fox."

So he'd had to shoot his gun to get the attention of his crew. What had they been arguing over? Wages? Women? Did it even matter?

Not really. Captain Guillouet wouldn't be a captain much longer.

He held the gun on her as they went down the ladder. He pushed her past a staring, wide-eyed Henri.

"Even the boy paid for his," Yasmeen said.

Pain exploded in the back of her head. She stumbled, and black spots danced in her vision. Her claws dug into her palms. He'd whipped her with the gun butt.

Now, she might not even make it quick.

He shoved her through the cabin door, locked it behind him. "Stand next to the table, Mrs. Fox, and turn around."

With her back to him, her hands flat on the surface. She complied, then watched him over her shoulder. "Will raping me truly make your crew behave, Captain?"

"I don't want to do this. I don't want to touch you." His hand tugged at his breeches. "But they will see you put in your proper place."

"My proper place?" She laughed. "And so this is why you won't have women on the crew. You can't stop yourself from raping them after they dared to climb out of bed."

"You've brought this on yourself."

"Oh, yes? Well I must say, for someone who doesn't want to touch me, your prick seems eager."

"Eyes forward!" He moved in behind her, pressed the gun to her shoulder. "You're fortunate I did not do this in front of my crew and then toss you to them!"

She was fortunate? No. That might have saved *him*.

His hand curved up her ass. Yasmeen whipped around, dropping her shoulder. His pistol fired, the bullet digging into the table, wood chips striking her cheek. Her elbow smashed into his ear.

He staggered back. Her foot struck his hand. The gun went flying. He turned to run, and she caught him before he made another step, bringing him to his knees with her forearm locked against his throat and her hand in his hair.

"Alive," he wheezed. "You need me alive. Or they'll kill him."

"Maybe. But I think I'll get them first."

She twisted past the crack. He dropped to the floor.

A sudden commotion of running feet sounded down the

passageway. The door crashed open. Archimedes burst through, the long blades at his forearms dripping with blood, eyes wildly searching the cabin. They stopped on her.

She arched her brows.

His gaze dropped to Guillouet. "Goddammit. Can't I save you just *once*?"

"You've already saved me twice, just using your grapnel." She lifted her gaze to the bruise forming on his cheekbone. "Who was that?"

"Bigor." His fingers gently traced her jaw. "He's still alive, but tied."

"Good." She'd deal with him in a bit.

He held up his hands, showed her the bloody blades extending from his wrist guards. "And I'm sorry, I surprised and killed the other two marines while getting away. Are you all right?"

"Just a headache. Why are you sorry?"

"They murdered your crew."

Oh. She shook her head. "I don't *like* killing. But I'll do it if it needs to be done. I'm just glad it's done."

He glanced down at Guillouet and sheathed his blades. "So am I. Now what?"

"Do you want her?"

His brows drew together. "Do I want who?"

"The ship. *Ceres*. Do you want control of her?"

"No."

"Then she's mine."

For now. *Ceres* was a lady, but would never be *her* lady.

Archimedes followed her as she started for the door. "All right. And then?"

"And then . . . I'm ready to head to Rabat."

Chapter 14

By the lady, she hated leaving Archimedes this quickly. There was much to say—but there was also now a ship to manage.

His voice caught her in the passageway. "Yasmeen."

She turned, caught sight of Guillouet's body in the cabin before the door closed. That would need to be removed, the wardroom cleaned. "Yes, Mr. Fox?"

"I kissed you on the cargo lift. Do you need to hang me over the side of the ship?"

Her gaze snapped to his. His emerald eyes were steady on hers, his features set with determination.

He would let her, she realized. If it meant making certain her position was secure, he would let her strip him naked and humiliate him.

Such a man, to let her be, to give her so much. Why had it taken her so long to see?

She shook her head. "No. That kiss was personal, and nothing to do with rank or our relative positions. All who saw would know that."

"All right." His grin held more than a hint of relief. "I'm glad to hear it."

But because he also needed to know, she said, "But now, there is a line, and it will end at that cabin door. When I tread her decks, I am captain. When we're alone, we can do whatever we like."

"Or when we've just been saved from zombies."

"Yes." She approached him, took his hand in hers. "And even in that cabin, I will not kiss you while we stand over a dead body. I will not kiss you when there is work that *must* be done. I want nothing more than to kiss you now, as I desperately need to."

"But you won't."

"I can't." She sighed. "And I can't order you to do the same, because you are not part of my crew—but I ask the same of you."

"You will have it." His fingers squeezed hers. His gaze didn't waver. "And I am not crew, but I would like to stand behind you. Not above, not below. To back you up, should ever you need it."

Her heart filled, and she nodded. "Thank you, Mr. Fox."

"Always, Captain—" He paused. "Are we still married?"

She laughed. There was no need to be; they no longer relied on al-Amazigh for their passage to Rabat. But, in truth, Yasmeen had come to enjoy it. What did it matter that these bonds were not official? She liked to bear them.

"I think we must be," she said. "I don't know an institution in the world that would grant a divorce to us."

"True." With a grin, he bowed over her hand, pressed a kiss to her palm before letting her go. "Then we are well and truly stuck, Captain Fox."

Unsurprisingly, she encountered a mix of emotions and shouted questions when she went above and called for all hands on deck. Though some were dismayed when Yasmeen succinctly laid out that she'd killed Guillouet while he attempted to rape her, she didn't see blame. That, more than anything, gave her hope for this crew.

For almost an hour, she fielded questions about wages. *I will split between you whatever the captain held in his strongbox, minus* Ceres' *costs. The purser will verify my numbers.* About their destination: *We will continue our expedition to Rabat, and deliver Mr. Hassan home.* About taking women into the crew: *I will be here, but I do not intend to stay aboard long enough to hire new crew.* How long would she stay? *We will return to Port Fallow, where Mr. Fox and I will depart and leave the airship in your hands.*

The last surprised them. The speculation about who would become captain then overtook the decks. Yasmeen held up her hand. When they quieted, she gave them the only advice she could: "Choose a captain who knows that he serves the ship and the crew, first. You will be taking orders from this person; choose someone that you trust will have your interests at heart, as well as his own, every time he makes a decision— even if those decisions are not what you want to hear."

She looked to the Vashons. Her gut told her that one of them—or both—would be *Ceres'* captain. That could be either a brilliant arrangement, or a disaster. "And if it is between the two of you, do not treat her like a whore, fighting over who will have a first go."

They both grinned.

Probably a disaster. "Now, there are bodies on this ship that will be cared for and given proper send-offs, and a wardroom to clean. Aviators on watch duty, attend to your posts; all others report to the first mate for your details. In an hour, I want to see all mates and masters in the wardroom with their ledgers. Heave around, then."

They broke up and headed to their posts, a few muttering . . . but fewer than she expected. Not a bad crew at all.

She didn't know what the hell Guillouet had gotten so wrong with them.

She was incredible. Archimedes watched Yasmeen take over the ship, and by mid-afternoon, all was running smoothly. Even Engels the bitter navigator deferred to her command as they plotted the course to Rabat. She hadn't yet fired the engines, however. They still hovered over the Brindisi harbor as most of the crew went to the mess, and Yasmeen asked the Vashons to bring Bigor up on deck.

Hands bound behind his back, his nose broken from Archimedes' fist, clothes askew, the marine no longer appeared buttoned up and straightened out, but still held his shoulders back, head high.

The Vashons pushed him to his knees near the cargo lift, and he kneeled, his expression flat—not resisting, not trying to escape, which made Archimedes wonder whether his sanity had broken or his pride was indestructible.

"Clear the decks, please," Yasmeen said.

The crew still on watch didn't hesitate. Archimedes wasn't crew—and he wouldn't leave her alone with the marine, anyway. He stood behind her, ready to back her up if needed.

When the last aviator had descended the ladder, she said, "Mr. Bigor. You understand that this has nothing to do with your following Captain Guillouet's orders today."

He gave a sharp nod.

"If you did *not* board *Lady Corsair* two months ago, slaughter my crew, and steal my gold, please say so now."

She wanted him to, Archimedes realized. Even though this meant she could avenge her crew, she didn't want it to be Bigor. Respect for him, perhaps—it was easy to respect such quiet strength.

"I did," he said.

If Yasmeen was disappointed, she didn't show it. Instead, she hardened. "Ordered by al-Amazigh?"

"Hired."

"Is that different than ordered?"

A nod. "Only my superiors give me orders. A man who simply possesses money is not my superior."

"And there's no loyalty to him, which is why you're telling me this now."

Another nod.

Yasmeen advanced on him, crouched a few feet away. "I'll trade you a story, Mr. Bigor. You tell me why al-Amazigh wants Hassan dead, and I'll write a letter to your wife and children that doesn't mention the slaughter of an entire ship, murders that *weren't* in service to your king."

"But they *were*, Captain Fox." The big marine stood.

Archimedes drew his gun. Yasmeen might not use hers as a warning, but by God, he would. "One step toward her and I pull the trigger."

The man didn't move, his eyes locked on Yasmeen's face. "They will receive a letter, Captain, but not from you. One that tells them how I was instrumental in assisting the French take their first step back into the Old World. That is an honor that needs no lie—and it is with that honor, I die."

Without warning, Bigor threw himself backward. *What the hell?* Archimedes rushed forward as the marine flipped over the rail. He didn't make a sound as he dropped into the harbor below. A splash swallowed him up.

Archimedes looked back in disbelief. Yasmeen hadn't moved, her face thoughtful as she looked out over the side of the ship. Her fingers reached for her sash—for her cigarillo case, he knew—and only when they encountered nothing did she shake her head, focus on him.

"It always seems a shame not to let a proud man go his own way," she said.

"You knew he'd do that?"

"I thought he might. And I am so tired of shooting people."

"Perhaps you should have." Archimedes looked over again. "You know what will happen now? He'll return when we least expect it and take his revenge."

She snorted. "That only happens in Archimedes Fox serials. His hands are tied."

"I returned from Venice," he said.

"So you did." Yasmeen pursed her lips, approached the side, and looked over. "If he bobs up again, feel free to fire. But don't wait too long for him to appear—you'll miss dinner."

Yasmeen would have been happy to miss the meal itself, but she'd always enjoyed sharing dinner with her passengers—and eating with Hassan and Archimedes for company was just as pleasurable. If she'd planned to stay on as *Ceres'* captain, she'd have eventually traded the stiff chairs for pillows around a low table, but this would do for the two or three weeks she intended to remain aboard.

The low thrum of the engines could be heard and felt from all the way aft, the conversation was entertaining, and for a short time, it was almost as if Yasmeen was exactly where she belonged again. In an odd way, Guillouet *had* put her back in her place.

But this lady wasn't hers, and so it wasn't quite where she belonged—and the only perfect thing was that Archimedes was sharing the table with her.

Tonight, they'd share the bed.

She could not stop imagining it. Not when he sat so close, so quick with a grin or a clever reply. Not when he swallowed his wine, and she couldn't take her eyes from the strong column of his throat, remembering how he smelled, how he tasted. The way he held his fork, the thickness of his hair, his rough jaw—every detail recalling what it was to touch him, to be touched, to be *loved*.

"You've grown quiet, Captain," Hassan said.

Lusting after my husband. Something that Yasmeen had never imagined herself doing, and yet she enjoyed every delicious second of it.

But of course she lied, and mentioned another matter that wouldn't have made for pleasant conversation during dinner but was acceptable over wine. "I am thinking of what Bigor said just before he jumped over. Did al-Amazigh have other French contacts aside from the *marsouins*?"

"Yes." Hassan sipped his—unpoisoned—tea. "For some time, he considered bringing in allies to help overthrow Temür, and to ease the transition from a Horde territory to an independent state. But I argued against it. I could too easily see that we might simply trade one occupying force for another, especially as the French had asked for portions of the city to be given over, so that their citizens could also settle here."

"One foot back in the Old World," Archimedes said. "After losing so much territory in the Liberé war, they've been feeling the pinch."

"Yes. Eventually, Kareem abandoned the idea, agreeing that the change needs to come from our own people."

"What of the two French officers I saw him with in Port Fallow?" Archimedes asked.

"We still must find friends in the New World," Hassan said. "To make certain that our trade routes are secure, that tariffs are reasonable, that our people will be able to travel without incident. We have met with a great number of men wearing many different uniforms."

"But al-Amazigh wanted to kill you," Yasmeen said. "Perhaps he had returned to his original intention, and didn't want your opposition."

Hassan nodded thoughtfully. "Perhaps. But if he brings the

French to Rabat's doorstep believing that it will accomplish anything, he has sorely underestimated Temür Agha."

"They could begin a siege, cut off trade to the city." If Yasmeen were to attack it, she would begin that way. Rabat was isolated; an ocean on one side, a desert and zombies on the other. They depended on goods brought in by the Horde and other sources. "They could try to starve Temür out—or wait until the starving people ousted him themselves."

"A siege with what? Sailing ships on the water, dreadnoughts in the air?" Hassan looked amused. "Wolfram did not destroy *all* of Temür's war machines. He has hidden them in the desert so they will not loom over the city, but they are accessed easily enough."

"Oh." She glanced at Archimedes—who was staring at her mouth. "I suppose Rabat has nothing to worry about, then. Right, Wolfram?"

It took him a moment. His gaze lifted from her lips to her eyes, then like a man dying of thirst, he threw back the rest of his wine.

"I suppose not," he said.

Guillouet had kept his papers in good order, so that her evening's entries into the records were not the chore she'd been expecting. On the opposite side of the desk, Archimedes was making his own records: a rudimentary map of Brindisi, an inventory of the items they'd gathered, the locations of the items they'd left behind. It had killed him to leave the clockwork man, she knew—but he'd agreed it was best not to bring something of that value aboard a ship with a new captain, on an expedition where mutiny had threatened and blood had been shed.

Even if they had been the ones to shed it.

"You are the perfect match for me," she said.

He stilled, then slowly lifted his head. His gaze caressed her face, emerald eyes dark and intense.

She leaned back in her chair. "But I think, for you, that simply being a match for me is probably not enough."

"It is." His voice was rough.

"No. Not for Archimedes Fox, who throws himself into

every danger, every excitement. 'A good match' would not be enough for me, either. It would be like drinking saltwater after wine. It is like lining up two people in bed like figures in a ledger. It adds up, but gold in hand is so much better."

He tossed down his pen. "What are you saying?"

"I'm wondering what you thought when I kissed you today. About to be killed by zombies, perhaps you thought it for pity—or to give you reason to hold on."

Wood shrieked as he came up out of his chair, braced his hands on the desk. His gaze bored into hers. "No."

"I could not blame you. Because what followed then? Crew and dinner and ledgers. Hardly the passionate responses of a woman who declared the softening of her heart with a kiss just that morning."

His jaw clenched. "Why are you saying this?"

"Because I am about to kiss you as I want to. As I would have, if zombies had not been at your back, and a new responsibility laid on mine the moment we stepped aboard." She rose slowly. Lifting her knee to the desk, she stalked him across its surface, put her lips almost to his. "Because I cannot believe I almost lost you today, because it still hurts, and I only have to close my eyes to see that door shattering again."

"Then don't close your eyes," he said softly.

"How can I not? Without that pain, how could I have ever known?" She breathed in his breath, loved the taste, the warmth, *him*. "So I tell you all of this because you are a man of deep emotion, Archimedes Fox, and I want you to know: *We are a perfect match.*"

For a long moment, his breath stilled. "So you are warning me."

Her lips curled. "Yes."

"And God help us both."

"There's no help for this," she said.

Rising up, she threaded her fingers through his hair. Silky and thick, unlike the rough scrape of his jaw beneath her lips. She tasted his skin, drank in his intoxicating scent, filled just by that, still empty and needing more.

And as her mouth opened over his, this was more than wanting, needing. It was *longing*, the slow, perfect pain of being so close but not yet having.

She had not had many things, had not wanted others, but here was both, having and wanting, built into a man who simply let her be who she was. Even Yasmeen had never allowed herself that, not completely. She'd never let herself be a woman who poured her heart into a kiss. She'd never let herself fall into the sensation of a man's mouth against hers, the stroke of his tongue, the tease of his lips, until she was hardly aware of anything else. She'd never let herself trust a man so much that when he lifted her with incredible ease, she did not even break from his kiss long enough to see where he was taking her.

Archimedes let her be, and she loved him for it—and she told him with her kiss.

He replied with his own need, his groans that said he loved her mouth on his jaw, her tongue tracing the straining tendons of his throat, the trail of openmouthed kisses down his chest. His stillness, his rigid abdomen betrayed his anticipation. Then his hands in her hair, his hoarse chanting of her name as his body shuddered beneath her tongue told her that she could do this forever, and never tire of his heady taste, his complete abandon to her mouth.

And he was magnificent as he rose over her, eyes so brilliantly green, his fingers strong, his body lean. Her thighs opened at a touch, her longing deep, having him, but not all of him yet, until he came into her slowly, so slowly. Her body arched as she fought to take him all, her nails digging into his shoulders, lips parting on a soundless scream.

His muscles bunched beneath her hands. He drove deep, and she'd never been this before, either, a woman crying out her lover's name, desperate to have him inside her again and again. She'd never brought his head down to hers, their kiss a frantic echo of each thrust, with everything wet—mouth and sweat and the slick push and pull.

She couldn't let him go. Her fingers and her body gripped him tight as she felt the end approach. Then she was gasping, shaking, trying to get away from each overwhelming thrust, opening wider to take more. He gave it, as hard as she wanted, needed, longed for.

Never this much before. Never this much.

She shattered beneath him, and he broke with her, shaking,

shuddering. Through ragged breaths, she kissed him again, deep and slow, and let everything slip away.

No zombies. No airship. No treasure or ledgers.

But still her perfect match.

She'd warned him. Archimedes stared up at the ceiling, faintly visible in the predawn light through the porthole, and tried to think of anything, *anything*, that had been more exciting, more dangerous, more incredible than Yasmeen unleashing herself upon him. There was nothing. She'd probably ruined him for treasure hunts. Zombies wouldn't even raise his pulse. Hell, meeting Leonardo da Vinci in Heaven surrounded by nude singing virgins and endless hits of opium couldn't compare to the bliss of one kiss.

He was never going to leave the bed again.

Others on the airship had already left theirs. He heard the footsteps of the deck crew on watch above, the clatter of pots in the galley below. The engines rumbled, carrying him toward Rabat, the tower, and . . . nothing.

At his side, Yasmeen stirred. Eyes still heavy with sleep, her sleek body arched in a long stretch. Her knees cracked. She tensed, drew a sharp breath.

There. His reason to leave the bed. Archimedes could support her even when he felt almost nothing. He stroked his hand down her spine, smiled at her purr. She flipped her hair back, sat up, and stiffly straddled him, her knees popping again as they folded beneath her.

"Yasmeen—"

He broke off as she reached down, took his cock in a firm grip. Already roused by the morning and the memories of the night, he stiffened quickly against her stroking palm. She leaned over and kissed his lips, his jaw. Against his ear, she said, "I'm tired of pacing a cabin again and again. If you don't mind, I'd like to loosen my knees up another way."

Mind? He was already so hard he ached. "Use me," he said. "For as long as you like."

He felt her smile against his skin. "It takes me about half an hour."

Oh, God. His fingers gripped her thighs, and heaven surrounded him as she sank onto his shaft, softly biting her bottom lip, eyelids half closed as she worked herself down his length. He slipped his hand between her legs, thumb stroking through her dark curls.

"Oh." Her head fell back, the ends of her hair brushing his thighs. "By the lady . . . I can't even feel my knees anymore. Just . . . you."

And then she rocked, and before the half hour had passed, she'd ruined him for pacing a cabin again, too.

It was for the best that she'd drawn the line at the cabin door, but she still missed Archimedes' touch, his wicked replies, all the things that couldn't be said or done in front of a crew. At least she could read his smile and his eyes—and that morning, both were telling her that he was troubled.

He stood beside her on the quarterdeck, flying over the sparkling Mediterranean. A perfect sky lay before them, brilliantly blue, yet he looked inward, his eyes unfocused.

Perhaps he felt her gaze. He glanced at her, the corners of his lips tilting in the same smile that Yasmeen found herself giving when she met his gaze after a long time apart—not amusement, but simply the pleasure of seeing him, having his attention again.

"You looked very serious," she said.

His brows rose, and he nodded. "I suppose I am. I was attempting to judge our speed, and the distance to Rabat. We will arrive tomorrow, I think?"

Why guess when he could ask her? "Twelve hundred miles from Brindisi," she said. "A full forty hours, with this wind against us. We'll reach the city the morning after tomorrow."

"And how long until we are within range of the tower?"

Oh, lady. She had completely forgotten that he was susceptible to that signal. It was just . . . *impossible* to imagine him subdued in that way, with every strong emotion turned mild. Shallow happiness, shallow anger, no desire. She didn't know whether he could bed her, but he wouldn't *want* to bed her.

How could that ever be Archimedes?

"Rabat's tower has about a 250-mile radius," she said. "It will be late tomorrow night."

He nodded, watching the sky ahead. Terrified, yet not showing a bit of it. Such a man—and her line at the cabin door said nothing of hands. Silently, she laced her fingers through his, faced the oncoming wind. His throat worked.

"I will still love you," he said.

She squeezed his hand. "Yes. And it is only temporary. A few days, at most."

Not much time at all.

But the day felt as if it flew by, and though Yasmeen reminded herself that they would only be in Rabat a short time, she could hardly bear the thought of watching everything lively in him fading. Where was her heart of steel now? She skipped her recordkeeping and pulled him to the bed early, as if somehow she could sink deep inside him, put herself between his nanoagents and a radio signal. In the morning, she loosened up over him and then paced the day away on her quarterdeck, watching the height of the sun. When it began to slide west, she couldn't stay past the cabin line any longer.

With a clipped, "Mr. Vashon, the helm is yours," she asked Archimedes to accompany her to the cabin, and had barely closed the door when she was on him, tearing off his clothes, desperate to kiss him *enough* so that the next few days wouldn't matter, wouldn't hurt so much, wouldn't look so bleak. She leapt up around his waist, loved his hunger and ferocity as he pounded her back against the wall.

"Hard," she told him. "So hard we feel it until next week."

Pain, if nothing else. And that would have to be enough.

That would have to be enough.

Hassan appeared in a cheerful mood at dinner. Perhaps he enjoyed having his emotions castrated. Archimedes hated his own glower, his dim mood—but that would be cured soon, ha!

The older man's gaze rested on his face for a moment, then moved to Yasmeen's. She gingerly ate her beans one at a time, but she was moving everything gingerly. Archimedes hadn't been getting around so easily himself. He'd never have imagined it, but it was possible that they'd actually fucked *too* hard.

God, what a woman she was.

He glanced at the clock. A few more hours. They'd move into range just before midnight. Christ, he felt so maudlin, as if he were waiting to die. He should be sensible, instead.

"When the tower comes down," he said, "don't you worry that the people will have the same reaction they did in England?—the panic, the chaos?"

Hassan shook his head. "No, it is only the symbol."

"But when the signal suddenly stops, and they are flooded with emotion . . ." He trailed off as Hassan's brow furrowed. "What?"

"The signal is gone. It has been these past five years."

Next to him, Yasmeen dropped her fork. She put her elbows on the table, her face in her hands. Her shoulders shook.

Was this a joke? Archimedes stared at him. "Five years?"

"Yes. Temür reduced the signal gradually so that we wouldn't have the same panic. A period of several years at reduced strength, then gone altogether for the past five." Hassan gave him a strange look, as if suddenly wondering if he was talking to an idiot. Archimedes began to wonder, too. "Those towers are part of the reason the rebellion gathered such support. Why would Temür keep it on after he secured the governorship?"

"Why is the tower still *up*?"

"It is built on part of an old minaret, a site that many consider a tie to their past and the old religion—something from before the Horde. He did not want to antagonize the recent converts."

"But you will?"

"It needs to fall," Hassan said. "It is an old and valuable minaret, but Rabat would be stronger if we built something new in its place, together."

Not a joke, then. Yasmeen lifted her face from her hands, wiping her eyes. "Oh, damn. I can barely even *sit*," she cried, and then burst into laughter again, not bothering to quiet it, this time.

The older man's eyes were bright with laughter, darting from Yasmeen to Archimedes as if he was enjoying the hilarity without fully comprehending what had happened. Then his head tilted back, as if lifted by realization. "Ah, I see. He thought the tower would affect him."

Christ. "You talked of blowing it up, just like the Iron Duke had in England."

"And I see that you ran full bore with the assumptions you made from that, as per usual," Hassan said, and his laugh echoed in his air tank, reverberating through the cabin. "You fear more, you dare more—and now you love more. It will not be taken away from you in Rabat. Do you know, it was seeing what happened to you that prompted Temür to turn off the signal earlier than he intended?"

Yasmeen's brows rose. "Truly?"

"Yes. He'd always intended to power it down, but very gradually—over a generation, perhaps. We had heard of England and did not want a repeat of that. But when Wolfram was shot, when we saw the change in him after the infection . . ." He shook his head. "We have seen many who have lived beneath the tower, and then were released from it. The reaction of most warned us to go slowly. There was too much fear, too much wildness. But Wolfram was one of the first we knew who had been free, and then yoked by the tower. It was devastating. Even I felt the horror of it, and I was still under the tower's suppression. When Temür saw that bravery itself was squashed, he could not bear the thought that there was a city of brave souls, all squashed in the same manner."

"Temür Agha," Yasmeen repeated. "The same man who literally squashed a city of brave souls?"

Hassan frowned at her. "You break a man's neck with no regret before he carried out his intended rape, and yet you let the man who slaughtered your crew choose his own method of death. I love a man like a brother, yet I also know that the best thing for the city I love is to remove that man from power. We are none of us so easy to peg."

"I am," Archimedes said.

"You are the worst of us," Yasmeen said. "Everything you seek, every fear, every thrill, is something that is also gone like"—she lifted her fingers, *snap!snap!snap!*—"Done so quickly, and you run off to find the next. But you seek love, intend to run to heartbreak, and then you stick with love. You do not regret losing war machines that would lead to too many deaths, and then kill two marines following orders on their ship with barely a blink."

Mortally wounded, he flattened his hand over his chest. "I had to rescue my beautiful wife."

"So you did." She gave him a laughing look from beneath her lashes. "Perhaps next time I'll wait and let you break a neck."

He looked to Hassan. "Do you see? She makes offers like that. It would be impossible to fall out of love."

Chapter 15

Two Horde outposts guarded each side of the mouth of the Mediterranean, overlooking the narrow entrance to the sea. Unlike a sailing ship, Yasmeen could detour around the outposts, taking a southern route directly overland to Rabat. A jewel of a city with a river running through its heart and nestled between the wall and the ocean, there was only one port that all airships and sailing vessels used—and it was under siege.

A fleet of French ships patrolled the waters, supported by two airships overhead. No airships were tethered at the port. They must have let all of the merchants leave, but no one through the blockade.

But unlike most of the airships, Yasmeen wasn't coming in from the west. She could approach the city from the eastern walled side before they could intercept her . . . though that offered its own dangers, and not only from the French fleet.

At the port, four of Temür's war machines stood at the edge of the sea, great hulking colossusi guarding the city. Two vaguely resembled elephants, with enormous bodies supported by sturdy legs, and at the front, a bank of long cannons that could be manipulated, elongated to defend at a distance or contracted to fire a barrage up close. The other two were equally bulky and enormous, like an octopus brought out of the water—each tentacle working like a giant grapnel, pulling down airships within range. All four machines had firebomb launching stations, a battery of self-reloading cannons, rapid-fire guns that could be manned from inside or from one of the stations connected by ladders and lifts surrounding the outside. Though at rest, with steam drifting lazily from the vents, they would be ready to stoke at a moment's notice, pushing them into lumbering mobility and engaging the electrical rail guns—and even with boilers cold, could still use all of its weapons.

Manned by a crew of thirty men, protected by the thick steel hide, a single one of the machines could devastate a city—or a fleet of ships that came into range of its firebombs.

But Temür had not posted them only on the seaside. Two more machines stood at the wall, overlooking the desert. Slightly shorter than the machines at the port, but no less dangerous, they were shaped almost like a Buddha sitting atop a giant mobile chamber that rolled on plated tracks. A body squat and wide housed the bulk of the weaponry, and it was so large that if it had hands instead of two grapnel arms that could easily pull them down into the zombie-infested desert, *Ceres* would have settled comfortably into its palm.

On the quarterdeck, Yasmeen lowered her spyglass and told the aviator at the helm, "Take her in directly between those machines, at the height of its shoulder. Follow the path of the river into the city."

"Ma'am? Between the machines?"

"Yes."

Archimedes said, too softly for anyone to hear, "Are we out of the tentacles' range?"

"No." She glanced at him. "No one has begun shooting yet. They likely won't start for a sugar sloop."

"Even one with a Huguenot cross emblazoned on her balloon?"

A French symbol. That was unfortunate. "Do you think your luck is still holding up?"

"Well enough."

Hassan came onto the quarterdeck, peering across the city to the water in the distance. "So they have begun a siege."

"Yes."

He sighed. "Let me go to the bow so that they will see that I am aboard."

After sharing a glance with Yasmeen, Archimedes went with him. Yasmeen ordered the engines cut, and slowly, they sailed toward the city.

The great machines rose on each side. Though far enough

away that Yasmeen couldn't have hit them with a thrown rock, their sheer size made it seem they passed at an arm's length.

And it was, she supposed. The machine's arm's length.

A shout rose from the starboard bow. And there she was. On a path from the city wall to the machine, zombies began to fall in the wake of a small figure robed in black. Moving with astonishing speed, Nasrin cleared the half mile between the wall and the machine's squat base in the space of ten breaths. Leaping up, she caught the edge of a ladder with gray fingers, flipped up onto the rolling tracks. She climbed to the torso, the shoulders, simply pushing with a foot, a hand, and launching herself higher with each push, so swiftly that she all but flew to the machine's shoulder.

The crew looked to Yasmeen, wild-eyed, as if waiting for her order. A few had started toward the gun stations.

"Attention!" she shouted. "A lady boards us. You will treat her as such. If you cannot stand as gentlemen, leave this deck."

Or die.

On the machine's shoulder, Nasrin flicked her wrist. Several of the men cried out as her hand detached and streaked toward them, trailing thin chains of mechanical flesh. Disembodied gray fingers gripped the gunwale. Nasrin leapt, the chain winding swiftly back into her arm. Within moments, the seam of her wrist sealed, and she climbed over the side of the ship with infinite grace. Her gaze touched Yasmeen, held for a long second, before moving to the men at the bow.

"Hassan, my friend," she said in Arabic, her voice like honey in spiced tea. "Have you been treated well? You appear sickly, as I have never seen you before."

Yasmeen curled her fingers to hide the trembling of her hands. The fate of this entire crew likely rested on his answers.

"Very well, Nasrin. The food and cold climes have not agreed with me."

"And are these friends?"

"Yes. Very good friends to me."

"And are you still friend to us?"

"Always. To Temür and to Rabat."

"I am pleased to hear that, Hassan." Her gaze moved to Archimedes. "Mr. Gunther-Baptiste. It is also good to see you in full, rather than peering at me through a peephole in a crate."

"You must forgive me," he said, grinning. "In the New World, men are taught that peepholes are the only proper way to catch a glimpse of a beautiful woman."

"Then you must have spent every moment aboard looking through a peephole." She looked to Yasmeen. "Is he yours, sister?"

"Every man aboard is, Lady Nasrin."

"Then I will call every man aboard a friend. You may enter our city without fear." On silent feet, she came up to the quarterdeck. "I will show you where to tether your ship. Will you tolerate the company of an old woman while we fly?"

Yasmeen would, gladly—but even if she wouldn't, it wasn't as if she had a choice.

Rabat was unlike any city she'd seen before. Though many things were the same—the smoke pouring from the factories along the walls and beside the sea, streets crowded with steam-powered vehicles and pedal-carts, people walking between them, it was also lusher than she expected, even with the presence of the river. As they flew over, there was hardly a building that did not have a garden on its flat roof. Goats and chickens were plentiful.

"If they plan to starve you out," Yasmeen said, "it will take awhile."

"Yes," Nasrin said. "Supplies from the east are not as plentiful, and Temür did not know if we could make friends with the west. So we prepared to have no friends at all. We have transformed two of the salt factories into water factories to ease the burden on the river, and have spent years laying the pipes that bring fresh water to every part of the city."

"It is incredible."

"It has been much work, but well worth it."

But Nasrin did not smile in full, and her eyes softened as her gaze swept over the city—almost with longing, Yasmeen thought. A city that wasn't fully hers.

She pointed to a sandstone fortress near the sea. Walls surrounded a palace and the great tower, made of red stone and rising tall over the city, impossible to miss. One only had to glance that way, and their vision would be filled with that tower. It looked indestructible, immovable, imposing.

Perhaps Hassan was right. Perhaps such a thing would serve as a constant reminder . . . and even powered down, the fear that it might be turned back on.

"Come in over there," Nasrin said. "Near the *kasbah* wall, you may tether your ship."

Near a large section of the city under tents and stalls. "Is that a marketplace?" Yasmeen asked.

"Yes. But please understand—I know that some of the ports to the north are rough, Captain, especially as regards to the treatment of women. I see that there are no women on your crew, and so your men cannot have much practice with them. I ask that, unless necessary, they remain aboard the ship."

Yasmeen flushed. Because there were no women aboard, Nasrin thought that Yasmeen could not control her crew or depend on them to behave. But she had never been one to offer excuses. "Our supplies have spoiled along the way. If I may send my steward and one other man to restock them, it would be greatly appreciated. I will remind them to be gentlemen."

"That would be allowed. If they do not speak the language, I will be happy to send a guide to them, so that they might find everything more easily."

And keep an eye on them. Though Yasmeen bristled, in truth, she knew little of the crew's behavior at port except for what she'd seen in the Charging Bull.

To avoid any trouble at all, an escort might be a very fine idea. "Thank you, Lady Nasrin."

"Very good. Perhaps you would like to speak with your steward now, while I go and properly greet Hassan. As soon as you have tethered, perhaps you and Mr. Gunther-Baptiste would accompany me to the *kasbah*."

Such polite orders from a woman who had decided that Yasmeen was a complete barbarian. "We will."

The heat was welcome after so much cold. Though not sweltering, as he'd experienced it before in Rabat, warm enough to soak into skin and bones. He expected Yasmeen to lift her face to the sun after they came down the cargo lift and climbed up into the crawler's box, but the expression that he had seen aboard *Ceres* as she'd spoken to Nasrin—a tight combination of embarrassment, frustration—had given way to the cool amusement that tried to express everything was going her way.

On the padded seat bench behind Hassan and Nasrin, he gave her a searching glance. She met his eyes, gave a tiny shake of her head.

Well, they were not on her decks. He slid his hand into hers, offered the little support he could, and her amusement softened and warmed.

The crawler rumbled lightly and lifted its body from the ground on segmented legs. On its back, their small box of cushioned benches rose too, high enough that the steamcarts and wagons they passed would not belch into their faces. The rounded back allowed them to see over the driver, seated at the crawler's head, offering a perfect view of the green of the city, the blue of the sea—with the war machines and dreadnoughts the only marring.

Temür had rebuilt this into an amazing city. When last he'd been here, all had been yellow from the desert, a city baked and a people who simply lived and worked. But now, almost all of the buildings had been painted in whites and blues, and trees sheltered the streets from the sun. The people no longer looked so downtrodden. Several called up to Hassan with warmth. But on every face, there was still the wary glance, the tight pinch of a mouth—only the children playing seemed to lack it.

The gates in the *kasbah* walls were open, and Archimedes saw no guards. The enormous tower filled up the corner of the courtyard on Archimedes' right. A fountain spilled water on their left. Farther inside, only two guards stood at the palace entrance, and those not heavily armed—and not a single man wore the Horde's walking suit, that machine of steam and steel that could crush a body beneath its massive feet. A masjid had been built at the end of the courtyard, a simple dome and four minarets. He caught Yasmeen's eye. Her small nod said that she thought the same thing: Temür had been working very hard to bring the people to him. Judging by the small number who milled about, they hadn't been coming.

Nasrin turned in her seat. "I have forgotten to tell you, Mr. Gunther-Baptiste—I have greatly enjoyed your stories."

He was surprised. "You've read them?"

"Of course. We have many of the publications from the New World sent to us, and Temür and I have long followed the adventures of Archimedes Fox. We have missed a few chapters, however."

Yasmeen frowned. "You knew he was also Archimedes?"

"Yes. We were not certain at first, but in every story, a new brightly colored waistcoat for Mr. Fox was faithfully described as if dictated." Her laugh was delicate, the ringing of a silver bell. "We knew he could not be anyone else."

"I thought he didn't know," Archimedes said. "That the assassins only found me by luck—there were so few."

"Oh, no. Those are men who Temür deemed incompetent, but for one reason or another, it would have been . . . delicate, to dispose of them. So he sent them to find you, knowing they would not be returning."

Taken aback, Archimedes shook his head. "That's oddly flattering."

Yasmeen said, "So it wasn't regarding Archimedes' debt?"

Nasrin's brows lifted. "Archimedes? You use that name at all times now?"

"Yes," he confirmed.

Her gaze slipped to Yasmeen. "And you are Captain Fox. I thought you were untethered."

Untethered? After a second, Archimedes understood. Nasrin's life was dependent upon Temür's continuing; she wondered if Yasmeen's life was tethered to his in the same way.

"She's not," he said, but Yasmeen added, "I might as well be," and he couldn't speak again immediately, so great was the emotion crushing his chest. She had not even said that she loved him yet, not in as many words. But now she declared, so very simply, that his death would be like her own.

It wouldn't be—and thank God for it, because that meant if he was ever killed, she would likely go on a tear of vengeance unlike the world had ever seen.

Nasrin's gaze held Yasmeen's. "Hassan has also been telling me of your journey, and how you came to captain the airship. I offer apologies for my insult."

"Thank you, Lady Nasrin, but there was no insult taken."

"You are very kind, and a liar."

"And you are fully altered."

The women smiled at each other for a long moment. Nasrin looked to Archimedes again, whose bemusement must have been clear. She said, "It is true. When you are fully altered, you have not much need to use lies as protection—though they are still useful when protecting others. Your name is a lie like that, I suppose, though you hardly needed protection from us."

"No?"

"Temür was angry after you destroyed the barge, it was true—but we also recognized that sending you out so quickly after you fell under the tower had been *our* mistake."

"He didn't care about the money?" Yasmeen said doubtfully.

"Of course that would have been of great use to us, but he did not *lose* money. He lost war machines—and as you must see, he already has more than most men could ever use. What are two or three more?"

Like Yasmeen's puddings. Like an extra five thousand livre. Archimedes couldn't ever recall falling into hysterical laughter, but he was afraid it might be coming. His brain felt as if it would soon explode. "So there was no debt?"

"Oh, there was a debt. But it was of obligation, an explanation." She gave him a disapproving glance. "You ought to have come to us. Every assassin we sent had the same message: come to us."

Now he did laugh, on a memory of slashing knives, quickly drawn guns. "I never let them get round to it. And I have spent ten years trying to find something of value enough to replace the money."

"If there was no debt, why did you steal the sketch?" Yasmeen asked. "It wasn't necessary."

"It was necessary to save his life," Nasrin countered. "One of those assassins would have eventually killed him. His luck cannot last forever . . . though I suppose with you at his side now, he does not need luck to protect him. And I knew that he would come for the sketch, so Temür and I let others know that we had it."

"Why didn't you just send him a letter, requesting him to come?"

Nasrin smiled faintly. "A request from Temür Agha is an order—and an obligation fulfilled under order is not one truly fulfilled. So my seeing him in Port Fallow was a happy accident, an opportunity opened to give him reason to come. I took it."

"Then you weren't there to kill him."

"Not at all." She looked to Hassan, and her smile was sharp. "I was only there to see why our friend Hassan was selling his jewelry."

That announcement killed any further conversation. Though Yasmeen could clearly read the resignation on the older man's face, there was not much to be done. Nasrin told them they would meet with Temür Agha after he'd spoken with Hassan, and she left with him for his audience with Temür. Yasmeen and Archimedes were escorted through the open, airy palace to a chamber that looked much like her cabin aboard *Lady Corsair*—though with many more pillows, a breeze that blew the silk curtains over the bed, and live birds singing in a small private garden.

"Are they going to kill us?" Archimedes wondered.

"I don't know," Yasmeen said. "It will all depend on Hassan, you realize."

"Yes."

"Do you think he was a true friend to Temür?"

"From everything I've witnessed between them, yes."

Yasmeen smiled faintly. "Then that might make Temür more lenient, or make the betrayal seem that much worse. It is impossible to know."

A serving girl bustled in, pulled a chain over a large marble tub. A clanking echoed through the floor, and a tile opened, spilling steaming water.

Yasmeen began unbuckling her jacket. "And it appears that if we are going to our executions, we are to be clean."

"Anything else would be rude. I hope we are also fed," he said and joined her.

* * *

Though she kissed him in the privacy of their bath, she dared not lose all awareness and make love. They were fed flaky pastries filled with beef and spices, a peppery stew over couscous, breads stuffed with honey and almonds. Yasmeen tasted each for poison, then for flavor, then his mouth after they drank the mint tea with rosewater.

She dared not do more, so she lay against him on the pillows, thinking of how she might possibly kill Temür if the man *did* intend to execute them. She would have to be quicker than Nasrin, to take the woman by surprise. After Temür was dead, she didn't know how quickly Nasrin would also fall. Hopefully it would be immediate. Hopefully, if the woman had time to strike at all, she would only have time to strike at Yasmeen—and Archimedes would live.

"I ought not have come here with you," she told him.

He frowned. "What?"

She sat up. "We could have left Hassan somewhere safe. We didn't have to bring him back to the city. You know why we did: Kareem al-Amazigh might be here, and I need to kill him."

"I know," he said, and her chest squeezed almost to nothing.

Of course, he understood. Like her, he did not live in civilization, not truly. He did not live under the safety of rules and laws. No, the only rules and laws they lived by were their own.

But that also meant that when the seas ate up someone she loved, whether it was in lawless Port Fallow or the Ivory Market, whether it was aboard a ship on the ocean, that there was no one to seek justice. Murder was not illegal in a land without law, and so the only possible recourse for Yasmeen, the only loyalty she could show to her crew was to seek her own justice, to apply her own laws.

That didn't mean they had to be *his*.

"I could have come later," she said. "I didn't have to risk you. I should have been patient. I understand the *gan tsetseg* now, Archimedes. If the man I need to protect is hurt, a part of me will also die. I don't know if it is beautiful or barbaric, but I *know* it now."

"Yasmeen." Roughly, he took her face between his hands and kissed her—and kissed her again. "I will stand behind you. I will *always* stand behind you."

But he wouldn't, she knew. If anything ever threatened her, he would jump in front and take the first blow. Just as she would for him.

Hours passed. By the afternoon, they heard a growing commotion, of many voices shouting together. They had no view from their chamber, and so Yasmeen climbed quietly to the roof to look over, and saw the courtyard filled with men and women. Together, like this, the effects of the Horde occupation were still shouting as they did: almost every man and woman had been modified by the tools of the occupation. Legs had been altered into lifts or rollers, arms augmented with steel and iron or replaced altogether. But although they shouted, they did not seem angry. Determined, rather—and all of them seemed to be waiting, expectant.

Nasrin was waiting in their chambers when Yasmeen climbed back down, her amusement plain. "We are sorry to have kept you here, but the talks were long, and the councilors have only just left."

The talks with the French? But Nasrin didn't say. She led them to a great columned hall that might have once held a throne, but now was only laid with a thick rug. Temür sat at the head, his legs folded beneath him. Hassan sat at his right side.

Temür gestured for them to sit on his left. Smaller than she'd always imagined, with shrewd eyes and iron-gray hair gathered at the top of his head in a narrow tail, he was quiet, and still—much like Nasrin now, standing slightly behind him. He did not appear the clenched-teethed madman she had always pictured, ordering a city razed to the ground; nor did he appear the generous, impassioned man that had built another city up. He simply looked like a man, seated in front of a game of strategy—and she could not determine whether he was winning or losing.

"Our friend Hassan has told us of your journey, and all that you suspect of Kareem al-Amazigh."

Archimedes nodded, obviously relieved by the "our friend." "Yes."

"He is aboard one of the French ships laying siege to us now. They demand entry for their soldiers, and to allow al-Amazigh to destroy the tower."

He ought to have listened to Hassan, Yasmeen thought. Such an action might make him a hero, but he would lose the city to a foreign power.

Either way, he would not be a hero for long. Yasmeen pictured the line of ships. She would have to discover which he was on, and then fly *Ceres* close enough that she could infiltrate . . .

No. That wouldn't do, not unless she flew her alone. She could not risk the crew with this. She would not risk Archimedes—though she didn't know how she would stop him from risking himself.

"She is already determining how she will kill Kareem al-Amazigh," Nasrin said. "You had best talk more quickly, my love."

Yasmeen's eyes locked on the man's face. "You don't want me to?"

"An assassination aboard the French ships would be akin to shooting a first bullet. My war machines *will* destroy the fleet, but that would also destroy many of the trade agreements we have set in place with their allies in the New World. I do not wish to embroil my city in a war."

And a request from Temür Agha was an order. Yasmeen was not foolish enough to defy it. "And after he is not aboard the ship?"

The corners of his eyes lifted slightly. "Do as you like."

"How long will the siege last, do you think?"

"Not long. They will have no reason to stay, and their demands will shortly mean nothing. I am bringing down the tower tonight. Or rather—" He glanced to Hassan. "My friend will, after he steps into my place."

Shock silenced them both. Tears glistened in Hassan's eyes, sadness—the weight of responsibility.

He was a good man to bear it, Yasmeen thought.

Archimedes shook his head. "Truly?"

"Yes," Hassan said. "We are going out into the courtyard shortly, where we will make the announcement. I wanted to extend an invitation for you to see."

Yasmeen nodded, then glanced to Nasrin. "And you? What will you do afterward?"

"We will go somewhere. We have not decided yet."

"But for safety, and because it would not be expected, we would like to be aboard your ship," Temür said.

Yasmeen laughed. A rich, powerful man, planning to relocate using only *Ceres*? "She's a small ship. She can't carry much. She could probably not even fit your collection of robes."

"We will not take anything but what we wear."

"And perhaps we will read the wooden blocks in Goryeo," Nasrin said. "We will walk the flowered temples of Khmer, and bathe in the sacred river."

Yasmeen's throat tightened. Her eyes filled. She could not hear a word of Lady Khojen's tale without being overwhelmed—and it was more than a request. The iron in Temür's hair said that he would have more years, but they could not number many.

"All right." She nodded, then realized, "And your man is already putting the provisions aboard the ship. The one you sent as a guide for my steward."

"Yes. Your steward was very glad not to pay for anything."

So was Yasmeen. But that didn't mean she would take this job for free. "The price of passage—to wherever you like—will be Archimedes' sketch."

"Of course."

She glanced at him, saw his grin, and whispered, *"Fifty percent."*

"You will have it," he promised.

As the sun set, Yasmeen sat with Archimedes at her side, watching from the palace roof as the tower fell—not with an explosion, but pushed over by a squat war machine, under Hassan's first order.

Inside the courtyard, outside—the cheers rose over the rumble of the war machine and the crash of stone, just as Hassan had hoped. Then the people themselves rose up, sparked by the tower's fall—which Hassan had predicted, too.

But perhaps he hadn't anticipated the speed with which they would come for Temür Agha.

Yasmeen and Archimedes had cheered with the rest, but as the tenor of the cheers and the chants began to change, she rose uneasily to her feet. A crowd had started toward the palace, where the former governor stood at the entrance with Hassan's council.

She turned to Archimedes. "We need to get to *Ceres*. Quickly. Nasrin and Temür will have to catch up."

They returned to their chamber, where the sketch still lay in Archimedes' converted glider. He scooped it up and strapped it onto his back, and by the lady, Yasmeen was glad that he was a fast man, a strong man. He did not need to stop and rest as they raced through the palace. Behind them came shouts, the sound of stone shattering. They reached the palace wall, and he did not hesitate—not climbing the laurel tree as quickly as she, but just as surefooted.

The gardens behind the palace were quiet. They were on the eastern side of the *kasbah*, and the mob at the west courtyard. Still, it would not be long before they would spill all through this area, searching for Temür.

A crash made her look around. The war machine loomed over the palace, giant arms swinging, breaking it open for looters. Also under Hassan's order? Probably not. But perhaps it would fulfill the same need as destroying Temür Agha. Cannons fired, crushing sandstone walls. People shouted over the rumbling, huffing machine. Steam spewed into the air as it squatted, lifted, and came down to crush the palace roof like a child stomping a grape.

"Good God," Archimedes breathed, looking back.

Yasmeen didn't dare look back again. *Ceres* hovered just outside the *kasbah*. Her eyes searched the dark for a gate, a tree, anything that would allow them over. The *kasbah* wall was too high, too smooth. Without a rope, Archimedes wouldn't make it to the top. Yasmeen wasn't certain *she* would make it.

"Can we signal them?" he asked.

She did not know with what. She and the crew of her lady had many signals, but she'd never established them with this crew.

"We might have to run through the crowd," she whispered. "We need to find robes."

Anything, anything to hide, anything to be safe—to make certain he made it to the airship.

"Find robes in there?" He looked to the palace again, eyes widening as the ground suddenly shook under an enormous impact. "Not in there. We'll knock someone out, take their clothes."

A dark figure in a robe swept past them, easily carrying a hooded man. "Come," Nasrin said. "We knew that they might storm the palace, but now they have taken over the war machine. So come quickly."

Hope lifted through Yasmeen again as they raced after her, until a shout from behind them gave away their presence. Nasrin reached the wall and leapt, flying halfway up. Her foot struck the smooth side and propelled her the remaining way to the top.

If anyone had doubts about who had been fleeing, they would not now.

"Nasrin!" Yasmeen shouted.

She turned, flicked her hand down to them. Yasmeen grasped the smooth mechanical flesh, held on to Archimedes. Nasrin wound them up with dizzying speed, and Yasmeen might have laughed if the mob were not closing in.

Atop the wall, they looked to *Ceres*. "She is too far away for me," Nasrin said.

People were in the streets below, but not rioting. Still cheering, many of them, others confused by the commotion inside the *kasbah*. She and Archimedes would be safe, for now, if they escaped here.

A rock whizzed past Yasmeen's head—thrown by a mechanical arm, altered and strengthened by the Horde.

Nasrin jumped from the wall, landed easily, then looked up at them.

"Jesus," Archimedes said. "I think she intends to catch—"

A rock slammed into the wall just below their feet, breaking apart in a shower of shards.

"You go first," he said.

Yasmeen laughed, turned to jump. The whizzing sound

warned her, and she ducked. Pain shot through her brain, and everything went dark as she fell, instead.

"Yasmeen!"

Archimedes leapt for her, missed. Overbalanced, he toppled over, barely gripped the edge of the wall. He hung over the side, desperately watching as Nasrin caught her.

But, God—how badly had she been struck?

He flung himself away from the wall the moment Nasrin put her down. He crashed into her, and he felt her mechanical body warp beneath her robe, cushioning the impact. Still, it slammed the breath from him, and his chest was a molten hole as he scrambled for Yasmeen. Blood flowed heavily from her scalp, over her ear.

"She's alive," Nasrin said. "Pick her up. Let us go, go!"

He gathered her up, trying to let her breath and her heartbeat ease his fear. Behind them came shouts, the crash and huffing of the war machine. He ran, carrying his life, as he'd never run before.

They reached *Ceres*. Nasrin's hand shot upward, her arm wrapped around his waist. They were carried up, onto the deck, where the crew waited, eyes wide as they looked over the *kasbah*. The war machine had begun rolling toward them.

The crew looked to Yasmeen, then to him. And holding her, *God please let her forgive him*, Archimedes took command of her ship.

Chapter 16

When Yasmeen awoke, the morning sun was shining through the portholes. Bandages wrapped her head—so that was why it pounded so badly. She couldn't remember drinking *that* much.

Archimedes sat in a chair next to the bed, eyes closed, jaw rough, head in his hands. He looked exhausted.

"Idiot," she said. Her mouth felt parched, her tongue huge. She hadn't drunk too much; she *needed* a drink that much. "You should have slept."

He looked up. His eyes suddenly glistened—oh, beautiful man. She felt the smile curve her mouth, the one she could not help every time she saw him.

"Yasmeen," he said, and his voice was as rough as hers felt. He started for her, as if to pull her into his arms, before stopping himself. "How do you feel?"

She pushed up to sitting. Her knees cracked. She froze, then let the tension out on a sigh. "I feel like I need to loosen up—and I have to piss."

"Not at the same time, I hope." Gently, his arms slid under her. "A whipping, I can take. But I am not quite adventurous enough for that."

She laughed, then had to stop at the ache in her head. He lifted her against him to carry her to the privy, but halted halfway across the cabin, suddenly shaking, holding her tight.

"I love you," he said. "Please remember that when I tell you—I have taken over your ship."

Yasmeen stared at him. Eyes bright, jaw tense, he appeared as if he were waiting for her machete at the back of his neck. "You ordered the crew to take her out of Rabat, I hope?"

"Yes."

"Which way have we gone?"

"North."

"Are we completely lost? Is the navigator dead?"

His tension began to ease. "No."

"All right, then. You have said you would back me up if needed, and you have done a perfectly fine job of it." She pointed to the privy. "Please."

He had her morning water heated when she was finished, the soap ready. And being injured was not so terrible at all when it was followed by Archimedes carefully washing her from head to toe, then drying her with slow strokes of a soft cloth.

Retrieving one of his shirts, he slipped it over her head, and put his arm about her waist so that they could begin to pace.

Outside the porthole lay a rolling plain covered in snow. They must have gone farther north than she'd realized. "How long has it been?" she wondered.

"Three days."

"And Rabat?"

"The mob stopped their looting after the palace. All is quiet again, and the French fleet is leaving."

She began to nod, then realized—"If you fled, how do you know this?"

"Ah, well. I ordered the ship south first, and then west, and then back north over the sea. And when we approached the French fleet . . ." He paused as Yasmeen choked. "We are obviously still alive."

Alive, and Archimedes would never be so stupid to approach them without a purpose. "Why did you do it?"

"We had a French academic aboard who had been part of a recent expedition that ended in Rabat, and he was seeking safe passage back to the islands. They recognized my name, of course—"

She snorted. "Of course."

"And when they saw the items we gathered in Brindisi, were happy to take them aboard—especially as Ollivier also knew the location of da Vinci's clockwork man."

Her breath left her. "You told him?"

"Well, yes. Because in a few days, he will be eager to meet another man he has heard is in their fleet, one who has possession of a da Vinci sketch . . . that Ollivier will recognize as a fake. And then that man is going to die a very natural-looking death. I made certain he knew that 'natural-looking' was most critical."

Al-Amazigh. Archimedes had arranged for Ollivier to kill the man who'd ordered the slaughter of her crew, yet do it in a way that wouldn't begin a war. And this man was hers?

Her eyes filled. "Thank you."

"I am sorry you couldn't do it yourself."

"It only matters that it is done." Finally done. It would not ease the pain of losing her crew, her lady, but the debt of their deaths had not gone unpaid. "And the French let you fly away?"

"I had a Vashon for a first mate, and this is an airship *very* loyal to their king. We even sport a Huguenot cross on our balloon."

That ugly, horrible thing. "And to think I said that Guillouet was treating her like a whore for it."

"She is definitely a lady," he said. "Are you sure you will not keep her?"

"She is not *my* lady."

"All right. We will buy another one." He stroked her back. "Temür Agha and Nasrin are waiting for you to awake before they go."

So soon? But it was probably for the best. "Then let us go see them off."

Ceres hovered over the edge of Paris, the sunlight glaring on her white balloon. A gorgeous day. The air above decks was crisp, zombies moaned below, and she had Archimedes by her side.

Temür Agha stood on the cargo lift, waiting for Nasrin. The *gan tsetseg* glanced at him before turning back to Yasmeen. "If the lady allows it, I will see you again, sister."

Perhaps. After learning that the Horde soldiers had been abandoning the outposts, Temür Agha had decided that, rather than wandering the empire on Lady Khojen's path, he would start at the outpost near Paris and begin gathering up rebels, slowly marching east. They would be in Europe for some time . . . and so, yes, it was possible that Yasmeen would meet them again.

"I look forward to it," she said.

Nasrin leaned forward, kissed her cheeks, then kissed Archimedes'. With a smile, she turned toward the cargo lift—but of course she did not go down that way. She leapt, and by the time the lift rattled its way to the ground and Temür stepped off, a mob of dead zombies littered the snow.

Yasmeen smiled, watching them begin their long walk before looking to Archimedes. "I would have chosen Lady Khojen's path."

"So would I. But for now, our path goes to Port Fallow." Archimedes took her hand. "Where does it go from there? I am an adventurer, you are a mercenary, but with the sketch, we will both have money enough to do whatever we like. Will you still be with me?"

"Idiot. I just said, I'd have chosen Lady Khojen's path." She lifted onto her toes, kissed him. Why not? This would not be her crew for much longer. "That path is to go traveling the world with her man—except I will not die at the hands of bandits. And I will still take passengers, and make more money."

"I'll make it with you. And I will still throw myself into crypts filled with zombies."

"Then I will throw myself with you," she said. "But first we need a lady to throw ourselves from."

The Vashon shipyards seemed to be the perfect place to find her. Three weeks after selling their sketch for five thousand more than they'd anticipated, and four days after receiving a letter from Ollivier confirming al-Amazigh's death, Yasmeen and Archimedes traveled to the New World to search for her new lady. They took out a two-seater balloon, weaving around the airships tethered above Port-au-Prince's turquoise water.

"That would match my waistcoat," Archimedes said, pointing to a bright orange balloon, then laughed when Yasmeen gave him a look to kill. "You're right. The zombies would probably be leaping into the sky trying to catch us."

"And I would die of embarrassment before I ever stepped aboard."

He had never dreamed that choosing an airship would be like taking his sister to buy a hat for her birthday. He only cared that they had a cabin big enough for a small library and their bed made of pillows, and that it wouldn't fall out of the sky on the first run. "You have said that of most these ships."

"It is true of most." She pushed the steering lever and pedaled, circling around the orange envelope. A skyrunner appeared in front of them.

Archimedes had hope. "She looks like your lady."

"Too much," Yasmeen said, and her eyes softened as her gaze ran over its lines. "She is the same model, but I hate her for not being the same. And—*Oh*. There."

Had she ever looked at another person with such longing, Archimedes' heart would have broken. But he understood too well that the sleek airship was something else to her—a life with no walls. She felt the wind on her face; he ran from zombies. They could not choose what they loved, but he thanked God for his luck in finding a woman to share it.

They rode the two-seater to her decks, and he heard Yasmeen's sigh as her feet touched the boards. Her fingers trailed over the wooden rail as she walked along the side, and he saw the shaking of her hands as she stepped onto the quarterdeck and looked out over the bow.

A Vashon came up the rope ladder. Having seen several members of the family now, Archimedes wasn't convinced that Peter and Paul had been twins. They all looked alike: tall, dark, and trouble in their grins.

This one looked surprised, however. "This one, Captain Corsair? She is a sound ship, but she has been used before. You were supposed to be told of the markings on the tails that would indicate which ships were new."

"We were, and I don't care. Used only means that she has been tested—and she still flies, so she must have passed all her trials. How much?"

"Don't you want to see—"

"No. She'll need alterations. Rail cannons at bow and stern. More shelves installed in the captain's cabin. A different cargo lift, capable of raising . . ." She looked to Archimedes.

"What is the biggest thing you have ever found, and wanted badly, but were not able to take with you?"

God, he loved her. "The bronze horses at the basilica in Venice."

Her brows rose. "Back to Venice?"

"Yes."

She turned to the Vashon. "Capable of raising four bronze horses, and to store them in her hold. You'll probably need to enlarge the exterior hold doors, as well."

"I would have to speak with the carpenters and recalculate the figures. The price will be—"

"Do it. I'll pay it."

"Yes, ma'am." He ran for the rope ladder.

Archimedes moved about the deck, looking down the hatchway, making his way to the quarterdeck, where Yasmeen stood with her eyes shining. Not tears now. Already feeling the wind.

"What shall you name her? She will be a lady, I think."

"Yes. Always a lady."

"Lady Luck? Lady Love?"

Her sneer was ruined by her laugh. "Those are horrible. You don't name your own adventures, do you?"

"No. Zenobia never allows me."

"I see why."

"She has named Lady Lynx's skyrunner *Steel Flower*."

Yasmeen smiled. "This one has the same feel about her: fierce, loyal. She will fly *so* well."

He grinned. "Lady Caracal? Lady Tiger?"

"Stop," she said, laughing. "Those are awful. Perhaps she will be Lady Nergüi—and she will be no one but my lady." She slid her hand through his. "You'll treat her well?"

His lady. "Always, my captain."

"Then we will see what adventures await us, Mr. Fox," she said, and met his lips for a kiss.

Turn the page for a special bonus—
a new, never-before-published
tale of the Iron Seas featuring
the further adventures of Archimedes Fox
and Captain Corsair, in "Tethered,"
exclusively with this edition only.

The Further Adventures of Archimedes Fox
and Captain Corsair

Fladstrand, Upper Peninsula, Denmark
August 23

Dearest Archimedes,

One day philosophers will weep as they ponder the following questions: How is it that a brother often managed to write his sister even when he was hiding from assassins hired by one of the most dangerous men in the world, yet cannot put pen to page now that the threat is annulled? How is it, after securing a fortune and a permanent residence aboard Lady Nergüi, *he allows five months to pass without a single word sent?*

I do not weep over these imponderables, however. Those philosophers do not know your character as I do; I know you would never have been so remiss if any possible opportunity to send a note had arisen. Quite obviously, your hands have been devoured by zombies, preventing your fingers from lifting a pencil, and your tongue must be roasting on some barbarian's fire. Otherwise, surely, you'd have asked someone to post a message when Lady Nergüi *flew into a port for provisions—as airships frequently do.*

So I can only conclude that you are crippled, starved for lack of supplies, and your skyrunner is lost among the clouds, thousands of miles from any friendly port. I also assume that, in addition to all of these terrible calamities, you have been inconsolable knowing that had you been near any city with a postal drop, you could have read the recent editions of The Lamplighter, *which contain my first Lady Lynx adventure. But do not despair, dearest brother! When you return to Port Fallow and collect the mountains of letters that have accumulated during your absence, you will find that I have enclosed the full manuscript of* Lady Lynx and the Cutthroat of Constantinople.

My generosity overwhelms you; I know it must. No doubt you are sobbing with gratitude even as you read this letter. Stay your tears for a few more paragraphs, however, for I must also relay news that you—or Captain Corsair—might find troubling.

You need not worry that it pertains to the story itself; it is quite the ripping adventure. My concern is thus: When I broached the idea of a new serial with Captain Corsair and solicited her help in the creation of Lady Lynx, she made only two requests—that Lady Lynx would not easily soften, and that I would not reveal who provided the foundation for Lady Lynx's character. I believe she will not be disappointed by the first; Lady Lynx is appropriately ruthless in the story. The second, however, is now completely beyond my control.

I did try, Archimedes. I took my usual liberties with your version of events, changing names, altering descriptions, and creating a fictional plot to carry the action along. At my request, The Lamplighter *broadly hinted that Lady Lynx was, in fact, based on the Wentworth woman in London.*

After the newssheets reported that you accompanied Captain Corsair to the Vashon shipyards, however, and that you now resided aboard her new skyrunner—and what could be more shocking and worthy of gossip than the famous Archimedes Fox taking up with a notorious mercenary?—the speculation about Lady Lynx's true identity gained a life of its own. Perhaps it is unsurprising. Everyone has long believed that you are the author of the Archimedes Fox adventures; of course the readers assume that the Lady Lynx adventures are thinly veiled stories about the woman most closely connected to you now.

I debated for some time whether to write Captain Corsair directly, and to inform her that the dangerous reputation she so carefully cultivated is now jeopardized by Lady Lynx's heroics. You know her better than I do, however, and can better judge her moods; so I have put this intelligence in your hands to impart as you see fit, and in the hope that I have not jeopardized something far more important to me: your happiness, which you have miraculously found with this woman.

Also, she is less likely to kill me if you deliver the message.

With no small measure of love or cowardice,
Zenobia

P.S. I will begin writing the next Lady Lynx tale soon. If you have any new adventures to report, your contribution will be, as always, greatly appreciated—and perhaps I will not title it Lady Lynx and the Horribly Neglectful Sibling.

Nova Lagos, Lusitania, the Americas
September 4

O! loveliest Zenobia!

I imagine you receiving this letter with a great cry of relief— and an equally great cry of guilt for all of the abuse that you have undoubtedly heaped onto my handsome head these past few months. Neglectful! Idiotic! Ridiculous! *Oh, how you must have wailed these sweet words during my absence.*

You may now cease your seething, dear sister, for Yasmeen and I have finally flown into a port where the express post can be depended upon to deliver my letter within a month, rather than sometime within the next five years. I have also included a packet that contains all of the unsent letters describing the particulars of our journey; I believe you will find the contents useful.

We will remain at least a few more days in the New World. Some of the aviators in Lady Nergüi's *new crew have not worked out to Yasmeen's satisfaction, and she must find their replacements. If all goes according to plan, we shall return to Port Fallow not long after you have received this letter. Do not worry, however, if you don't hear from me directly after that. Very little has gone "according to plan" in the few months we've been aboard* Lady Nergüi, *beginning when a band of idiotic pirates tried to board our lady without knowing who her captain was (if ever you write about it, let free your pen; their expressions of horror upon recognizing Yasmeen could not be overstated—or more comical) and ending but two days ago, when we scouted the Castilian border to assist a group of rebelling laborers.*

Going off course is exhilarating—but although the events narrated within that packet have thrilled me, they might cause some concern to you.

I'm sorry to tell you that the secret of Lady Lynx is out. I know you spoke with Yasmeen about how you intended to conceal the truth, but I suppose that became impossible after I married her. You may heap invectives upon my head for that, dear sister, without fear of injuring me. I can never regret it.

In any case, it seems that little harm has been done. Though there have been some who assumed that our marriage meant Yasmeen had gone soft and attempted to take advantage of her, they quickly discovered how mistaken that assumption was.

Ah, and here is my love now, stalking into our cabin with her incomparable scowl riding her divine lips. As you close this letter, pray for our quartermaster. I believe he will need it.

—Archimedes

P.S. Please forgive my hasty adieu; every moment spent writing is a moment I cannot worship Yasmeen. In my rush, however, I forgot to mention that I have also included the preliminary research for a salvaging run in Cordoba. I found a reference to a statue of Marcus Aurelius that had been carried from Rome to that city ahead of the zombie menace, then abandoned as the population fled to the New World. If all goes according to plan, we will fly to Cordoba shortly after reaching Port Fallow. I have already thought of a title for that adventure—or any other: Lady Lynx and the Absolutely Besotted Husband.

Fladstrand, Upper Peninsula, Denmark
September 29

My absolutely besotted brother,

You are as ridiculous in love as I always knew you would be; thankfully, however, you are not as foolish in love as I feared. I cannot express the depth of my relief upon receiving your letters yesterday, and knowing that Captain Corsair weathered this first patch of rough air with you. No doubt, you will say that I am too cynical, but not without reason. Remember, I have seen a man who claimed to be your friend abandon you at the first sign of trouble. A man who ran even as you thrashed in your bed, delirious and still vulnerable from an assassin's poison.

That man is also the reason I am sending this letter now, rather than waiting until I have had an opportunity to read through your packet. Only this morning, I received a visit from Miles Bilson. He claimed he'd heard that Temür Agha's assassins had been called off, and wanted to know whether the rumors were accurate. I assured him that indeed, it was true, and that he was free to roam about the world again. He then asked me how to contact you, for he would like to hear the details of Temür Agha's change of heart in person.

I am certain Mr. Bilson's sudden desire to speak with you has nothing *to do with the enormous fortune you received after auctioning off da Vinci's sketch—an amount which was reported in every newssheet on either side of the Atlantic.*

Do not *laugh at my cynicism, Archimedes. His timing is rather suspect, don't you agree?*

At any rate, I could not think of a good reason to conceal that you collect your post in Port Fallow; he would simply discover the boardinghouse directions from another of your acquaintances. And knowing Mr. Bilson, you will not find a letter waiting for you, but the man himself. You will easily recognize him; he is as handsome and as charming as ever, and likely just as inconstant.

Forgive me. I know he was your friend. Perhaps my bitterness is disproportionate to his sin—but I once held him in such *high regard, and cannot forget my disappointment upon learning how quickly he abandoned you. But do not fret, brother. If there is but one aspect of his sudden reappearance for which I am grateful, it is learning that he no longer poses a danger to my emotions.*

Perhaps this means my heart has grown as steely as Captain Corsair's—not that it did her much good.

With all the love that my icy, hardened heart can manage,
Zenobia

P.S. I have had opportunity to read through a few of the letters in your packet, and I beg you, Archimedes, and I beg Captain Corsair, too—please take a little more time before killing the people who threaten you. Aside from descriptions of their clothing and their death throes, you leave me with absolutely no impression of their characters. Can you not chat with them a bit before shooting? If not, soon I shall be forced to title every adventure *Lady Lynx and the Hair-Triggered Buffoon.*

Chapter 1

Chat with them a bit? Grinning, Archimedes folded Zenobia's note. Of course his sister knew that taking time for a chat also gave someone the opportunity to carry out their threat—just as she knew that making Archimedes laugh was the easiest way to reassure him that the disappointed feelings she'd revealed weren't a source of any suffering now.

He didn't doubt her resilience. Still, a visit wouldn't be amiss. Fladstrand was only half a day's flight from Port Fallow aboard most airships—and faster aboard a skyrunner.

Automatically, his gaze went to the opposite side of the boardinghouse's tiny attic room, where the afternoon sun streamed into the garret through a small window. Beyond the cracked pane lay a view of Port Fallow's docks. Boats crowded the harbor, their tall masts and branching spars resembling a bare, wintry forest rolling gently over the water. Two dozen airships floated in the brilliant blue sky above them, their wooden cruisers suspended beneath white balloons, as if dangling from dense clouds.

Lovely ladies, all of them. Archimedes only had eyes for one.

Sleek and swift, *Lady Nergüi* had been tethered along the south dock—directly over the spot where her predecessor had fallen earlier that year. That skyrunner's charred bones lay at the bottom of the harbor now, and though it was impossible to see them, he knew that Yasmeen felt their presence as keenly as she would a harpoon through her gut. He couldn't imagine what it had cost her to tether *Lady Nergüi* in the same location, where the newly rebuilt dock's clean boards served as a constant reminder of her airship's demise. But he also understood that Yasmeen would never allow her lady to be tethered anywhere else, not while the loss of that airship and crew was still so sharp.

Archimedes had hated leaving her there alone, even for a short run to the boardinghouse. After they'd docked that morning, he'd delayed his departure as long as possible. He couldn't prevent her from feeling any pain, but he could stand beside her through it.

Of course, as soon as Yasmeen had realized why he was waiting to disembark, she'd laughed and told him to go. And he'd gone, because although their fights were always entertaining and would serve as a distraction for her, an argument wasn't the sort of support that he wanted to provide now. He'd use this jaunt into Port Fallow as an opportunity to find something to help her ease the ache. Zenobia's manuscript was the perfect start. A visit to the silversmith's would hopefully offer more.

He added his sister's note to the pile of envelopes on the desk, then grabbed up the whole lot and began stuffing them into his shoulder pack. Zenobia had marked the most recent letter as an express, and so he had immediately read it, but he would have to spend the better part of a week to make his way through the rest of the correspondence.

"Oh, it is you!" The exclamation came from behind him. "Is everything as it should be, Mr. Fox?"

He looked toward the open door. The house matron stood on the landing, her stern face softened by the two brown curls that framed her broad forehead. Pink tinged her cheeks and chin—not a blush, but the kiss of the brisk autumn air. She hadn't even taken the time to remove her sturdy walking jacket, but had come directly up the three flights of stairs with a folded parasol clutched in her hand, as if sensing that danger had entered her home.

Archimedes adored her for coming to confront that danger herself. But then, he'd always had a soft spot for bold and self-reliant women. "It's all in order, Mrs. Kohen. You have my gratitude."

The matron harrumphed lightly, her keen gaze settling on his canvas pack. "You won't be staying in the room?"

"I'll be aboard *Lady Nergüi*," he said. "But I'd like to continue our arrangement, if possible. I'll pay the full year's rate now if you hold the room for me and receive my correspondence."

No fool, Mrs. Kohen immediately nodded. "That's acceptable."

Of course it was. An absent boarder who paid in advance had to be the best sort. "More acceptable than watching me stumble up the stairs every night, reeking of liquor—and not wearing a stitch?"

"Go on, you scoundrel." Lips pursed, she pointed down the stairs with the tip of her parasol. "I'll be happy to see the back side of you again."

Archimedes laughed. A hint of a smile lifted her mouth. Then her brows shot up, and she patted the side of her skirts, clearly searching for something.

"I nearly forgot." She produced a pale card from beneath her jacket. "This gentleman called on you as I was going out."

Miles Bilson. Archimedes wasn't surprised when he read the name. "Thank you."

Nodding, Mrs. Kohen started down the stairs. "If you leave any valuable sketches in your room, Mr. Fox, please remember to lock up this time."

He would, even though the lock wouldn't stop anyone determined to get in. Thoughtfully, he glanced down at Bilson's card. A direction had been scrawled on the back. Archimedes recognized the hotel in Port Fallow's second ring of residences—Bilson and he had stayed there several times in their smuggling days, more than a decade before.

Unlike his sister, Archimedes felt no ill will toward the man. Given his tendency to mine every emotion to its furthermost depths, if he *had* felt the least bit betrayed by Bilson's abandonment, Archimedes would have hunted down his friend and taken his revenge.

There was no need for vengeance, however. He'd often thought that if anyone had been betrayed, it was Bilson. Archimedes had been the one to destroy a shipment of war machines. Archimedes had been the reason Temür Agha sent assassins after them. Bilson's life had been threatened and a fortune lost, and it was all due to Archimedes' impulsive action.

But Archimedes didn't suffer any guilt for that, either—and that was another emotion he'd have wallowed in, given half a chance. Instead, he only felt a faint curiosity, wondering why the man sought him now.

Strange, that. Archimedes rarely felt anything "faintly." Yet even with Bilson's card in his hand, he had no real desire to visit his old friend. As far as he was concerned, his accounts with Bilson had been settled long ago. It was possible that Bilson didn't feel the same, and Zenobia had reason to be worried—but if that was the case, there was no reason to go looking for the man.

Shaking his head, Archimedes tucked the card into his sack and locked the door behind him. If trouble was coming, it would find him soon enough. It always did.

And he always enjoyed the hell out of it.

His visit to the silversmith's shop had been even more fruitful than Archimedes had hoped. He returned to the south dock with a light step—no, a light step wasn't enough. This sort of success called for dancing.

Fortunately, the crowded walk was filled with partners. As he passed a tinker's cart, Archimedes caught the eye of the attending blacksmith—difficult to do, as she was staring at his lime green breeches. Then her gaze rose to his face and he saw recognition fill her eyes when the pieces fell into place: his loud clothing, his astonishingly handsome features, his dashing grin. Yes, she knew who he was.

Archimedes Fox, Fearless Adventurer.

With great formality, he bowed—and caught the blacksmith around her aproned waist, swinging her about. Her shriek of surprise became a laugh. Her strong hands tightened on his shoulders, her feet quickly finding the step. Heads turned.

He dropped a kiss to her flushed cheek and spun away. Nearby, a stout washerwoman with red hands and sleeves rolled to her elbows was watching, smiling. Archimedes started for her. She winked and met him with a saucy toss of her hips. God love bold women. Laughing, he promenaded with her past a group of hooting sailors. He left the washerwoman with a flourish, then picked a little girl in threadbare skirts, her eyes wide and fingers sticky, dancing a wide circle before returning her to a beaming mother. A burly stevedore was next, gamely allowing Archimedes to twirl him around a huffing steamcoach, though with his steel prosthetic arms and hydraulic shoulders, he could have tossed Archimedes over it. As it was, when the stevedore saw a pretty partner more to his liking, Archimedes found himself spun directly into the path of a matriarch wearing velvet gloves and a fashionable lace ruff, and whose protest only lasted until the shouts of encouragement around them spurred her into Archimedes' arms. Light and quick, her first step was a challenge that he almost failed to meet. The haughty lift of her brow delighted him, and he attempted to lead her on a merry chase, only to find she outstepped him on every turn. His deep bow conceded defeat; she nodded, her mouth disapproving, her eyes sparkling. He winked and turned, spotting a gray-haired woman in traveling clothes sitting atop a trunk, her face lined and weary. With only a bit of encouragement, he pulled her up on top of the trunk and into a jig. She hiked her skirts, exposing a brilliant pair of red stockings. The laughter and the clapping began in earnest then, boots pounding a rhythm on the boards. A jaunty accordion started up somewhere—a street musician would likely be earning a few more coins that day. Exhilarated, Archimedes led them into faster clapping, louder stomping. The docks were always noisy, but this sort of commotion wouldn't go unnoticed above.

Nor did it. Archimedes looked up toward *Lady Nergüi* as he leapt off the trunk, and caught a glimpse of Yasmeen's blue kerchief, her dark braids, her grin.

Perfect.

Dizzy and out of breath, he reached *Lady Nergüi*'s docking station. An Amazon in a sharply tailored jacket and trousers waited beside the cargo lift, her black hair cut short and exposing a neck like an Egyptian queen's. His final partner, then— but as he spun toward her, her look of absolute horror made him pause. When her gaze flicked upward, he understood.

He stopped and held out his hand in invitation, his grin wide. "So you are not a mythical Amazon, but Adèle Vashon, our new quartermaster?"

She looked to him, to the crowd behind him—which had been shouting encouragement all the while—then up to the airship again. A hint of panic had widened her brown eyes. "Yes."

"Your new captain watches," he said, his hand still extended. "Do you dance like a fool, or snub her husband?"

The Amazon closed her eyes. "I snub you."

"Good choice. My life would be nothing if she caught me with my arms around another woman." He heard the rasp of a rope overhead, and his racing heart skipped in anticipation. The laughter and clapping around them quieted. "And here she comes now."

And what a woman. Lithe, strong, Yasmeen slid down the rope as easily as a dancing man took a step. Like the quarter-master, she wore a short aviator's jacket, but had brightened the dour blue wool with a crimson sash that cinched her waist. Cold steel glinted at her thighs, where her daggers were tucked into the tops of her tall leather boots. With barely a flex of her hand, she stopped ten feet above the boards.

She looked down at the quartermaster. "You are welcome aboard, Mademoiselle Vashon. Strike the chains when you're ready, and they'll start the lift. I'll meet with you in my cabin as soon as I've gone back up."

"Yes, Captain Corsair."

"Captain Fox," she corrected. Her gaze fixed on Archimedes, and he saw no limit to the warmth there. Slowly, with her thighs clenched on the rope, she turned upside down—her cat-green eyes even with his, her hair hanging in a thick curtain. Her voice softened. "And after creating such a spectacle, what do you have to say for yourself, Mr. Fox?"

He placed his hand over his heart and sank to one knee. "I've come to ask you to marry me, my gentle captain."

Laughter lit her expression, and was matched by the sound in the crowd. "My current husband might object."

"Do you care what he thinks?"

"Perhaps not. But I ought to warn you—he's a jealous man. And quite dangerous."

That description pleased Archimedes to no end. "I will fight him for your hand."

"Only my hand?"

"All of you. But if your hand is all that I can have, it would be far more satisfying than what I have without it: my dreams of you . . . and my own hand."

"I won't cry for you, Mr. Fox. I know how satisfying your hand can be." Her wicked grin took his breath. Her gaze held his for a long moment, then flicked up . . . *down* his length. "I like your daggers."

"I found them at the silversmith's." His hands went to the new weapons sheathed at his hips, and he stroked the scrolled guards with his fingertips, watching her face. "As soon as I saw the crimson grips, I was lost."

So was Yasmeen, as he knew she'd be. "Are they for me?"

"I chose something else for you. But I'll sweeten my offer of marriage by allowing you to touch them now and again."

"With an incentive such as that, I *must* accept." Her full lips curved, and her eyes met his again. "Shall I be called Captain Fox-Fox now?"

"You shall be called nothing but my wife." He looked to the crowd and called out, "She agreed!" Over her laughter and the cheers, he turned back to her and asked, "Now, will you dance with me as they did?"

He knew it wasn't a simple question, and he anticipated her refusal. Yasmeen lived by her reputation, and although they'd found that they could express their affection onboard, in front of the aviators, even that was almost always in a playful manner, never in a way that undermined her authority. They'd also had serious moments, quiet and intense amidst a working airship crew, but there was always a line they didn't cross until they were alone in their cabin. That line was typically any form of embracing, or any display of passion—any act that might make the crew wonder whether her captain's responsibilities held Yasmeen's full attention.

All of which was perfectly fine, in Archimedes' mind. It made no more sense to kiss Yasmeen while she was performing her duties than it would to stop for a cuddle while they were searching through ruins and trying to avoid zombies. At any rate, their self-imposed restrictions possessed a wonderful benefit: The hours on deck became a delicious tease, building anticipation for the moments they were alone—when he could hold her in his arms, and do anything they wished.

"I would dance with you on this dock," she said.

Taken aback, Archimedes was speechless for a moment. Her smile widened. She'd meant to shock him, he realized. But still, what he'd intended to say *had* to be said, even if it meant refusing her acceptance.

"I would not," he said. "I could never dance with you as I did with them."

"Why?" Her brows lifted, her eyes bright with amusement. "Do you think I don't know a step or two?"

"I'm sure you do. But dancing with them was only for fun. A dance could never be only for fun when you are in my arms—not after wishing you were there for so long, and not when I love you so ardently now."

She stared at him, all humor bleeding from her expression. Tension quieted the crowd, and they gasped as she let go of the rope, flipping around and landing lightly on her feet. Archimedes rose from kneeling, and though he was taller than she, his shoulders broader, no one could have doubted who was the more dangerous, the more deadly.

And she gave him no warning. Her fingers suddenly fisted in his hair, hauling his mouth down to hers. He heard the relieved laughter and the applause, then there was only the heat of her kiss, the pounding of his heart. Christ, but he loved a fierce woman. She was an answer to his every prayer. His hands circled her waist and her body pressed against his, telling everyone who could see what he wanted everyone to know: By God, he was hers.

But they wouldn't know the rest, the part he'd asked them to play that afternoon. Because now, when Yasmeen looked down from her airship at these docks, when she walked their length, she wouldn't just see their fresh boards; the sight wouldn't just serve as a reminder of how they'd burned when her lady had exploded, a reminder of why the dock had to be rebuilt. Now, she'd remember the man who loved her dancing his way down the length of the dock in his lime green breeches and orange jacket; she'd remember the laughter and the music, and a kiss beneath the shadow of her airship.

All of it for her—and never *just* for fun.

She drew back, her gaze lingering on his, the grip of her

fingers softening in his hair. "You're an incredible man, Archimedes Fox."

He often thought so, too.

As if reading that from his expression, she suddenly laughed and stepped back, catching hold of the rope again. "I'll see you on deck, my husband."

And he would wait a few seconds, enjoying the view as she climbed. No matter how many cities he searched, Archimedes doubted he'd ever find a statue as perfectly sculpted as Yasmeen's backside. Her black breeches hugged each curve and the length of her thighs . . . where the crimson handles of his new daggers currently protruded from the tops of her boots. She must have lifted them in the second between releasing his hair and taking hold of the rope, and he hadn't felt a thing.

With a grin, he started up after her. Some things were *mostly* for fun—and now he needed to steal his daggers back.

It would undoubtedly be much easier than stealing her heart had been.

Chapter 2

Some days, Yasmeen didn't know what to do with him. Archimedes truly was the most incredible man—and, she suspected, a far better husband than she was a wife. He displayed affection so easily, so unexpectedly; Yasmeen had no idea how to do the same. She wasn't even certain how *he* managed it. How could a man so openly state his possession of a woman without also claiming ownership? Yet he did. How could he create a singing, dancing spectacle of himself, and still quietly soothe her heart? Yet he did.

She knew exactly what he'd done on that dock. He would never reveal his reasons or take credit for it—just as he never said a word when she woke from nightmares of shattering doors and ravenous zombies, and simply held her quietly, without questions, without asking her to acknowledge her terror by speaking of it. This had been the same. He'd *known* how she'd felt when they'd tethered *Lady Nergüi* on this spot, but he would never ask her to admit to her grief. He simply tried to make it better.

Yasmeen wished she could do the same for him. Of course, that would mean finding something that grieved her husband—not so easy when he was so determinedly good-humored, and he confronted every obstacle with an exuberant whoop.

By the lady, how she loved that about him. And she had no wish to pain him, simply so that she could soothe it. Better to leave such emotional manipulations to those who'd enjoy expending their efforts on them.

She would expend her efforts on enjoying her husband and commanding her lady. Aware that he was climbing the rope after her, however, and with her lips still warm from their kiss,

Yasmeen was sorry that command had to take precedence at that moment.

On deck, she spotted the new quartermaster waiting by the gangway. Adèle Vashon was observing the crew, her gaze moving from aviator to aviator, as if judging their performance—as if judging whether it was a crew worthy of the time she'd be putting into it. The woman didn't have to straighten when the second mate announced the captain on deck; her shoulders were already back, her spine ramrod straight—and when Vashon faced her, Yasmeen saw that same considering look directed her way, as if deciding whether she would be a worthy captain.

Yasmeen's throat tightened as grief suddenly slipped up, took hold. *Goddammit.* She could never prepare for this. She only had to hear a laugh, to catch a movement at the corner of her eye, and for an instant she would see her old crew, before losing them all over again—and Adèle Vashon's assessing, critical gaze reminded her so much of Rousseau, the Frenchman who'd been her right hand for a decade. Hell, but she missed him. And if Vashon was even half the quartermaster that Rousseau had been, Yasmeen would be satisfied with her.

With a scrape of his boots against the hull, Archimedes came up over the gunwale. She caught his eyes, lifted her brows, and stroked the handles of her new daggers.

His grin promised retribution. Yasmeen looked forward to it. Later.

"Mademoiselle Vashon—with me, please."

The quartermaster joined her at the ladder leading to the second deck. The woman was taller than Yasmeen; not many women were, and it would be to Vashon's advantage with the crew, helping to command their respect—at least initially. The first quartermaster Yasmeen hired for *Lady Nergüi* had been tall, too. No matter how much he'd demanded respect, however, he'd never been able to command it.

Yasmeen was glad to be rid of him. Despite impeccable references, he hadn't known how to handle a crew; she hoped that a woman whose family name was synonymous with excellent aviation would. Having met two of Vashon's mutinous cousins, however, Yasmeen wouldn't count on the name alone.

At least this Vashon had the good sense not to comment on the unusual décor in Yasmeen's cabin. In *their* cabin. Archimedes loved the low dining table and lounging pillows as much as Yasmeen did, and so they'd kept that part of their living quarters the same as Yasmeen's previous cabin. The shelves of books were new, however, and all his—as were the two additional crates of books waiting to be unpacked, and the oversized wardrobe. The desk allowed them to work facing each other, and had been clearly set up as a shared space, with two inkwells and chairs for them both.

Now Yasmeen slid his chair out and gestured for Vashon to sit. As she took the opposite side, with her back to the shelves, Archimedes entered the cabin.

Yasmeen wasn't surprised. He'd taken an interest in every aspect of her—*their*—airship, and though he'd pretend to be occupied by another task, she knew he'd be listening to every word, coming to his own conclusions about their new quartermaster.

If any other man had done the same, Yasmeen would have been irritated by how far he'd overstepped. Not with Archimedes, however. He had no desire to run her ship, only to know everything about it—just as she often read the research that preceded his salvaging runs. She wanted to better know what he loved, to understand it. Luckily, his work was just as fascinating as the man, and she enjoyed it almost as much as he did. He'd become equally invested in her ship.

He tossed his bulging canvas pack onto the low table. "If you don't mind, Captain, I'll lounge here and sort my correspondence."

"Very well, Mr. Fox."

In truth, Yasmeen was happy to have him there. He sank onto the pillows centered in the pool of afternoon light that spilled in through the two large portholes, directly in her line of sight—and an appealing sight it was. Summer had streaked his brown hair with gold, and as the months passed without a cut, he'd tamed the ragged length with a leather tie at his nape. After a lazy morning, he'd skipped a shave, leaving his jaw roughly shadowed. Now, making himself comfortable, he loosened the linen around his neck. What an incredibly appealing combination that was—the orange silk of his waistcoat, the white shirt, the tanned skin at his throat. She loved to bury her face in that spot, to feel the lean muscles underneath that outrageous clothing.

It was strange how many people underestimated him, who only saw the color he wore and not the strength beneath it. That had been another failing of the last quartermaster, who'd acted as if Archimedes didn't exist—who'd treated him like a pretty boy with an empty head.

Her husband was anything but.

She met Vashon's eyes again, aware that the other woman hadn't looked away from her face during the exchange with Archimedes. Had she noted that Archimedes hadn't actually asked for Yasmeen's permission to remain? No, he was simply making certain that the new quartermaster saw his respect for Yasmeen's position.

Judging by the hint of uncertainty in the woman's expression, however, Yasmeen would soon have to clarify Archimedes' position aboard this ship. But first, she needed to clarify exactly what Vashon's would be.

She leaned back in her chair and pinned Vashon with a sharp stare. "Before I make your appointment official, mademoiselle, I have questions regarding your record and recommendations."

"Of course, Captain."

"Your references from your family are quite favorable, as are those from your former commanders. Normally, that alone would recommend you to any captain."

Yasmeen paused, creating a silence that seemed significant—but Vashon didn't rush to fill it. She didn't try to second-guess Yasmeen, but waited to discover what the problem was before addressing it.

Good.

"With your qualifications, you ought to be seeking command of a Vashon ship. Why aren't you?"

"In my family, Captain, there are two options: to serve the king in the navy or to serve aboard the Vashon fleet. I'm loyal to my king and I'm loyal to my family, but I wanted a broader experience than that."

"All well and good," Yasmeen said. "Except that you've already gained plenty of experience aboard different merchant carriers—and all without lowering yourself to a quartermaster's position aboard my airship."

Vashon's gaze held steady. "I was given to understand, Captain, that unlike a merchant or navy vessel, the quartermaster's position aboard a mercenary airship is to act as second in command, and that I'd be your first in the deck department. That isn't lower than any position I've held previously."

"It's true you'll be my first, but the rest is utter shit. Whether captain or cabin boy, the only thing lower than a mercenary is a pirate—and you won't be expecting any invitations to your family gatherings while you're aboard my lady." Yasmeen rocked forward, eyes narrowed. "Don't feed me a cock's tale, mademoiselle. What the hell is someone of your background doing aboard *my* ship?"

Vashon's fingers tightened on the arms of her chair. Rattled, but only a little. "Two months ago, I took passage aboard *Ceres*. My cousins Peter and Paul are still co-captaining her."

The twins hadn't destroyed each other? Incredible. Yasmeen had doubted that they'd ever stop squabbling over possession of *Ceres* long enough to properly command her. She'd liked them well enough—who couldn't appreciate such good-natured mischievousness and charm?—but that didn't mean they were fit for a captain's position.

"I've known them all my life, Captain—and for as long as I've known them, they've been a disappointment to the family. Undisciplined, careless, impulsive. But although they were still utter rapscallions, I couldn't mistake the change in them—a change for the better. They told me it was because, in the weeks they served under you, they'd finally seen what a good captain should be." She paused, her mouth twisting briefly. "I'll confess that I was angry, at first. It was an insult to our family, to each Vashon who'd ever borne a captain's responsibility. I soon realized, however, that every Vashon was expected to bear that. But even though we also expected it of Peter and Paul, they wouldn't live up to those expectations—they didn't, they couldn't. Yet you *inspired* it in them. I want to know what did it. You are a mercenary, but there's obviously more to you than your reputation—and obviously some truth to the Lady Lynx story."

By the lady. Yasmeen hadn't expected any of *that*. She glanced at Archimedes, saw his grin. No doubt he was enjoying her discomfort.

And she needed to read that damn story. What sort of captain did it suggest she was? "Why would you assume any of that ridiculousness is true?"

"Even though the twins' names and descriptions were changed, and though they told me that none of the events were quite the same, the two brothers in the story were unmistakably Peter and Paul. Their characters were captured perfectly."

Even though Zenobia had never met the twins, and had to rely on Yasmeen's and Archimedes' descriptions of them. How much of that was luck?

And how much of *Yasmeen* had Zenobia captured? Whatever the level of accuracy, hopefully Lady Lynx's personality had been determined before Yasmeen's heart had softened. There was no need to have that sort of reputation spread around.

Yasmeen shook her head, suddenly realizing that the very existence of Lady Lynx forced her to consider something she never had before. "Do you hope that this position will secure a bit of fame for you, as well?"

It was almost unthinkable. Work aboard a mercenary ship was often dangerous and always difficult—there had to be easier ways to earn a mention in a newssheet or an adventure story. But it was impossible to guess what drove someone seeking such things.

"No, ma'am. In fact, it was the one thing that threatened to put me off. I'm rather terrified of discovering what Archimedes Fox sees when he describes a dull arrow like me."

Yasmeen had to admire her balls. She'd confessed to terror without revealing a bit of it in her demeanor, yet Yasmeen didn't doubt its truth. She suspected that Vashon admitted to the fear only to prove—to her new captain or to herself—that she could overcome it. "You're quite safe. My husband doesn't write those stories."

And he only faintly resembled the Archimedes Fox that Vashon probably thought she knew. Even Yasmeen had long been fascinated by the fictional version of her husband—yet that adventurer was nothing compared to the reality of the man.

"I thought he did, ma'am. But if you say otherwise, then I'm obviously mistaken."

Despite Vashon's words, she clearly didn't believe it. Behind her, Archimedes heaved a dramatic sigh and shook his head.

Amused, Yasmeen leaned back again. She still had a few more questions—though she already knew the answer to this one. "Your last assignment aboard a merchant vessel ended six months ago. What have you done since then?"

"I spent time aboard my mother's airship."

That was the truth, but not all of it. "Smuggling rebels into Castile, as I've heard it. Do you make a habit of bucking authority?"

"Not my captain's authority, ma'am."

She hadn't even hesitated. Perhaps she ought to. Yasmeen pressed, "Even if that captain once took jobs that helped the Liberé during their war with your king? You've already stated your loyalty to him."

"As I recall, you also took jobs that helped the French. I understand that a mercenary ship is loyal to no one, Captain, except for when it serves your interests."

"And what if my interests conflict with yours? If I ordered you to board a Vashon ship, would you comply?"

Yasmeen was pleased to see the quartermaster take more time considering that. After a moment, Vashon replied, "In all honesty, ma'am, I don't know. If I can't fulfill my duty, however, I won't take a coward's way out of it and work against you behind your back. I'll tell you if I've turned."

"Good. I'd kill you for going against me, but only toss you off my ship for refusing an order." When the other woman nodded, acknowledging those consequences, Yasmeen continued. "Is there any order you categorically refuse to carry out? If so, you'd best tell me now."

"I won't kill a child, ma'am, or murder an innocent. But I wouldn't be here if I thought you'd ask me to do either."

Fair enough. Yasmeen would have thrown Vashon off *Lady Nergüi* immediately if the quartermaster had been willing to do either. "Are you infected?"

For the first time, Vashon seemed taken aback. She hesitated. Deciding whether to lie?

Yasmeen couldn't blame her. In the New World, most people feared the Horde's nanoagents. Though the tiny machines strengthened anyone infected by them, the Horde had also used radio signals broadcast from enormous towers to control occupied populations. The signals dampened emotions such as fear, love, and hate—anything that might provide a motivation to rebel—while increasing obedience, pliancy. The nanoagents and radio towers created the perfect workforce.

The perfect hell, for many. Now so many New Worlders feared the nanoagents that no infected person was allowed past their port gates, and they were convinced that the infected became zombies after their deaths. The infected themselves were often treated like lepers, as if the nanoagents spread with a touch rather than a transfusion of blood.

If the woman was infected, that might serve as another reason for her joining Yasmeen's crew. Though the Vashon family likely had enough money and pull to bribe port officials and let her enter the New World countries, Yasmeen doubted that the quartermaster wanted to rely on that.

"If you are infected," Yasmeen said, "you will be in good company. I am. My husband is. Many of the crew are—several have been augmented with mechanical prosthetics and tools."

"Yes. I saw that as I came aboard."

"Then perhaps you fear being infected by one of us?"

"No. It is simply a more intimate question than I was prepared to answer, Captain."

Ah. Of course a New Worlder would think so. "There's nothing personal in my interest," Yasmeen said dryly. "I simply want to be prepared. *Lady Nergüi* flies routes that other airships do not—including routes that will take us over Horde-occupied territories. If my quartermaster suddenly begins responding like an automaton, I'll have a better idea of why it might have happened."

"Well, then." She nodded. "Yes, I am."

"What strain?"

"Ma'am?"

"English, Moroccan, Egyptian? Some other tower? Obviously, if you have a Moroccan or English strain, you are in the clear, because those towers are gone. But others are still active, so if you are infected by bugs from Egypt or the territories in southern Africa, I will know to fly clear of their towers."

"English, I believe." She blinked. "I didn't realize they were different, ma'am."

Unsurprising. Of the New Worlders who had infected themselves, most could trace the nanoagents back to the Horde occupation in England—and most didn't know that the towers operated at different frequencies.

"Just be glad that the zombie strain is different," Yasmeen said, and leaned forward to brace her elbows on the desk, satisfied with the interview. The woman hadn't squirmed much, which pleased her. Yasmeen needed someone who could stand up to fierce scrutiny without flinching—and in the air, Yasmeen would be much harder on the woman than this.

"All right," she said. "After you sign your contract and stow your trunk, you'll find the first mate, Mr. Longcock, on the deck."

Vashon grew very still. "Mr. Longcock?"

Yasmeen smiled. "Many people on this ship have chosen their own names, and for their own reasons. I don't question that—or whether it's an accurate name."

"Yes, ma'am." It emerged on a choked laugh.

"Accurate or not, however, you won't be required to identify him by that description. He's the big one."

"The big one?" The quartermaster's mouth rounded as she realized who Yasmeen meant. Of course she'd seen him on deck. George Longcock was impossible to overlook. "The one with . . ."

"Guns grafted to his arms and chest, yes."

"A *lot* of guns, ma'am, if I can be so bold."

"There are more that you can't see." Yasmeen held in her laugh when the other woman's face registered disbelief. She had to admit, her first sight of the man had struck her speechless, as well—though a part of her understood exactly what he'd done, *why* he'd done it. A factory builder in Horde-occupied England, he'd already been modified with steel arms. After the revolution, he'd added weapons to protect himself. Then, after leaving England for the high seas, he'd added more . . . and hadn't stopped.

After the occupations, some people turned to the opium dens. Longcock had grafted weapons to his body. Yasmeen thought both reactions were exactly the same, in their own way.

"I've asked him to walk with you through my lady," Yasmeen continued. "In the weeks since we've left Lusitania, Longcock has acted as *Lady Nergüi*'s quartermaster—and he was quartermaster aboard *The Flying Spear* until a month ago. You'd do well to listen to him. He has rough edges, but he knows what he's about."

Vashon nodded, then asked, "*The Flying Spear*? A pirate ship, ma'am?"

"Quite a few pirate ships have come upon us lately, and many of them have experienced crews. I offer better pay, however, so some of those pirates now serve aboard my lady."

"If he was a quartermaster aboard *The Flying Spear*, why isn't he yours?"

She was already trying to figure out whether Longcock's demotion would pose a problem, Yasmeen realized. He wouldn't—Longcock preferred the first mate's position—but Yasmeen would let Vashon determine that for herself. "He can't read and write. I need you to do both at times. You are my right hand with the aviators."

"Yes, ma'am." She took a deep breath. "And which hand is Mr. Fox?"

Archimedes looked up from a letter, brows arched in surprise. Yasmeen smiled. Though the question was impertinent, she was pleased Vashon had asked. It was best to lay out the rules now.

"As far as you are concerned, he is me," Yasmeen said. "If he ever makes a request, you will consider it an order."

"Yes, ma'am." After a brief hesitation, she asked, "And if his order conflicts with yours?"

"Tell him so. If he still insists that you carry out his order, then do as he says."

Both stared at her—Vashon in some confusion, Archimedes in absolute shock.

Yasmeen pretended that neither of them was gaping at her like a fish that had been coshed over the head. Though she had never imagined making such a decision, the past few months had made it a simple one. She knew Archimedes would *never* undermine or question her authority on this ship unless absolutely necessary—and to him, that necessity would be saving her life. If Archimedes Fox, Fearless Adventurer thought any situation was that dire, it was worth pausing and reconsidering.

And she didn't want to lose him, either.

Yasmeen continued, "Then come and let me know that he's countermanded my orders, of course—if he does not beat you to it. But if he feels it necessary to overturn my orders without first consulting me, I know he'd have a damned compelling reason. That's worth listening to."

Slowly, Archimedes sat up, holding her gaze. By the sweet heavens, he was a beautiful man. The shock had fled, leaving an expression of incredible intensity that all but shouted the depth of his love. Yasmeen's throat constricted. Why had she never said this so clearly before? She thought he'd known. Perhaps he had—but had just never thought she'd say it.

Beautiful, incredible man.

And if he kept staring at her like that, she would soon throw herself into his arms. Shaken by the strength of her reaction, Yasmeen forced herself to look away from him. Vashon had managed to close her mouth, but clearly had no idea how to respond.

Yasmeen cleared her throat and helped her out. "It probably won't happen, you realize. He won't even make any requests. In the unlikely event that he does, however, these are my instructions."

The quartermaster released a long breath. "Yes, ma'am."

"All right." Yasmeen slid a sheaf of papers across the desk. "This is your contract. Your duties are listed; if you have any questions, I suggest that you ask the steward for clarification before you sign it. After you have signed it, he'll add you to the payroll. Your wages and share are noted on the second page."

Vashon's eyes rounded. "That's incredibly generous, ma'am."

Only if she lasted long enough to collect it. "Don't be

fooled by the number, mademoiselle. My last quartermaster thought that amount of money made him a man of leisure— but I will work every single denier out of you."

"Yes, ma'am."

"Then welcome aboard *Lady Nergüi*, mademoiselle. You're dismissed."

The moment Vashon made her exit, Yasmeen's gaze returned to Archimedes. He rose from the pillows, so lean and strong.

The roughness of his voice was a caress up her spine. "Why?"

"Why do I state what has become obvious to all of the crew? I am still captain, but this ship is your lady, too. I trust you to care for her, for *us*, if the need arises. I trust that you will do it, even if by undermining me you risk my anger—I trust that you will do it, even if it's at the expense of your own heart." Yasmeen stood and came around the desk, her pulse racing. She wasn't adept at these sorts of declarations, not like he was. Still, she was glad to make it. "But I would never ask you to risk your heart. I want you to know that if you ever do need to override me, you can without fear that I'll resent you for it. Because *I* have no fear that you would ever do it without great reason."

He crossed the cabin, caught her face between his hands. His emerald gaze searched her features, as if seeking any doubts. "You don't fear at all?"

"No." Not that he would take her ship. She only feared losing him.

His focus dropped to her lips. "Kiss me, then," he said.

Gladly. He met her halfway—and oh, his mouth. So sweet. His arms slid around her waist. She clung to his shoulders, sought a deeper taste, and with the parting of his lips she began shaking from the intensity of the emotions tearing through her. How could he do this to her so easily? Often, their kisses were playful, fun. Not this one. It brought her heart up out of her chest, filled the space between them.

Yasmeen never knew what to do when he left her so vulnerable, so open. She kissed him—by the lady, how could she not when it felt as if she would die without it?—and she loved him. God, how she loved him. But she knew the only thing that saved her when she exposed her heart was Archimedes himself, and that she trusted him never to crush it.

He knew, too. When he lifted his head—not far, just enough to look into her eyes—his breathing was as rough as hers, and already he was helping her find a more comfortable tack. "You made me lose my head, Mrs. Fox. I meant to steal my daggers back."

Smiling, she pressed another kiss to his mouth and dropped her hands to her thighs. "Look again, Mr. Fox. I didn't take them."

He was quick, but she was quicker. By the time his hands fell to his hips, she'd already slipped the blades into his sheaths and returned her arms around his neck. His grin matched hers.

"You gave them back?"

"I saved you the humiliation of fumbling when you attempted to steal them."

"Truly?" His eyes narrowed. "No. You've revealed yourself, Captain. Now I know you love me."

"It must be love," she agreed. "You humiliate yourself so regularly, yet I try to spare you whenever I can."

Laughing, he caught her waist again, dragged her against him. "And this time, I'm grateful for it. Because God knows, I would only have to touch your thighs and completely forget why I was attempting to grab a pair of knives, instead."

He only had to touch her, too—though right now, they couldn't follow through. With a sigh, Yasmeen laid her head against his shoulder.

Archimedes groaned. "Our daily visit with Mrs. Fortescue?"

"Yes." Though rather than simply adjusting and verifying their direction, they would be meeting with the navigator to establish their new course when they left Port Fallow. Such consultations always took more time. "A longer visit."

"I prefer this," Archimedes said.

She preferred this, too. His taut muscles, his warmth, the slide of his fingers up her back . . . Yasmeen couldn't stifle her soft sound of pleasure.

"You should stop," she said.

He didn't, and there wasn't just simple pleasure now, but heat. His hands cupped her bottom, lifted her against him. His mouth sought the curve of her jaw, the sensitive skin at her neck.

With a moan, she let her head fall back, giving him better access. "I'll kill you for this."

A shudder ripped through him. "Good God, that was cruel. You know how that arouses me."

She did. Lowering her face to his, she scraped the sharp tip of her forefinger beneath his jaw, watched the ecstasy tightening his features. Archimedes Fox relished a bit of danger—in any form.

He closed his eyes. "Don't sneer at me," he said. "If you do, I'll probably come."

The laugh burst from her, soothing the burn between them. Yasmeen kissed him, hard, and his reluctance echoed hers when he slowly let her down. She looked away from his flushed features, searching for a distraction. A few minutes remained before Fortescue arrived, but if Yasmeen didn't find something to occupy herself, their navigator would find them writhing naked on the desk, instead.

Probably best not to look at the desk now, either.

Her gaze lit on the pile of correspondence on the table. Not just letters—packages, too. Some that might have been stacks of pages bound together. "Is the Lady Lynx story in there?"

"It is." His long stride carried him to the table, but he picked up a small envelope rather than a manuscript. "I plan to read it to you tonight."

She would love that. "And is there any other news?"

"Zenobia wants us to know that the origin of Lady Lynx has been found out."

A bit late. Yasmeen automatically took the letter he held out, then read the direction in surprise. She rarely received correspondence, and none of it came to Port Fallow—she collected it from her solicitor. "This was addressed to me?"

"From Scarsdale."

A good friend, but not usually the writing sort. She broke the seal, and her belly seemed to drop. Not a letter. An invitation.

Watching her face, Archimedes frowned. "What is it?"

"His wedding."

"To a woman?"

Unfortunately, it was the only sort of marriage Scarsdale could have. "It's his duty to produce an heir," she said. "Goddammit. As long as his prick still works, he can do his duty. Why couldn't he go on as he was and marry when he was an old man? And why the hell invite *me*? Perhaps he hopes that my presence will horrify the wedding party so much, the bride will flee."

But, no. Though she wished it, Yasmeen knew that wouldn't be why. Scarsdale had many friendly acquaintances, but few friends. She was one—and he wanted her there for that reason alone. Still, as his friend, she'd make damn certain he absolutely wanted this.

Casually, Archimedes said, "Since the navigator is coming soon, perhaps we ought to decide where we're heading next."

Yasmeen glanced up at him. "Not Cordoba?"

"Eventually. But I thought we might visit Zenobia first, to make certain she's all right. Afterward, why not detour to England and visit Scarsdale?"

"Oh, you are a brilliant man. Unless I'm convinced that he truly wants this marriage, we'll abduct him and tell his bride that I had my way with him. No gentle-bred miss would want him after that." She narrowed her eyes at him when he laughed. "Why do you think Zenobia might not be all right?"

"She received a visit from my old partner. It upset her."

His old partner . . ."Bilson?" She headed back to the desk after all, and found a note she'd tossed there earlier. "This arrived shortly after you left this afternoon. Then you distracted me with your dancing, and I forgot. It's from Miles Bilson."

Archimedes' dark brows drew together as he read the note. "He's requested a meeting. He thinks I can help him."

No doubt Archimedes *could*. But Bilson had probably asked because Archimedes was the sort of man who *would*. "What kind of help?"

"It doesn't say."

And he wasn't expressing much interest in finding out. "You don't seem that eager to meet your friend."

He glanced up. "I enjoy his company quite a bit. But I know him well; he always has some sort of game in play. Perhaps not this time, but I'd be a fool not to wonder if I'm part of a greater plot."

And he wasn't a fool. "Why was Zenobia upset by him?"

"She had tender feelings for him—I hadn't even realized. But she's also certain that he's here for money, and that he felt cheated when I sank those war machines."

Yasmeen's protective instincts sharpened. "Do *you* think he felt cheated?"

He shook his head, studying the note again as if to discern Bilson's intentions from the slant of the letters, the darkness of the ink. "I can't say. I don't think so. But it's been years."

A seed of resentment could have grown enormous in that time. "And you're famously rich now."

"Yes."

"Do you feel you owe him for the botched job with the war machines?"

"No." He glanced up from the note with a wry grin. "But if he asked, I'd probably give the money to him."

That was the lovely thing about possessing a ridiculous fortune—they could give away small fortunes, and hardly notice the difference. "And if it's not money that he's after?"

Yasmeen would deal with Bilson herself, if Archimedes asked her to. She knew he wouldn't, however, and left the decision open to him.

"I'll go out and meet with him tonight," he said. "Then at least I'll know what he wants."

"Invite him aboard for dinner, instead," Yasmeen suggested. "And introduce your old friend to your new wife."

She met Archimedes' sharp look with a smile that had terrified other men. He only chuckled, shaking his head—not refusing, but considering. She watched him struggle against his hope that Bilson's request would be nothing, and his worry that if it wasn't, Yasmeen might be caught in between.

Just as protective of her as she was of him. Yasmeen softened her smile, stepped close. When he met her eyes, she said quietly, "Why did you dance on those docks today? *Lady Corsair* wasn't yours, her crew wasn't yours—you didn't love them as I did. Yet you helped me today, when everything else I saw reminded me of how much it hurt to lose them. And your dealings with Bilson aren't my business, I know—but if he's here to take some sort of revenge on you, to hurt you . . . then let me stand behind you and help you in return."

His throat worked. He lowered his head, dipping his mouth close to hers. His voice was rough as he said, "You have my heart, Mrs. Fox."

"Good. After you stole mine, I'm in need of one."

He smiled against her lips. "Bilson's request will likely be nothing."

"Does he have a brain in his head?"

"Yes."

"Then it will be nothing," she said, and reassured him with a kiss.

Only an idiot would believe he stood a chance in hell against this.

Chapter 3

Thankfully, Miles Bilson didn't seem like an idiot, though it was difficult to be certain after only a few hours' acquaintance. He proved to be an affable, charming bastard, and—as Archimedes had said—good company, but Yasmeen might have enjoyed his company more if she hadn't read Zenobia's letters before he'd arrived to dinner. Though she'd known that Archimedes and Bilson had parted ways to better avoid Temür Agha's assassins, she hadn't realized that Bilson had abandoned Archimedes while he still suffered from a poisoning.

No matter how amiable Bilson was, the knowledge guaranteed that Yasmeen would never trust him.

Despite her reservations, however, Bilson's jovial greeting to Archimedes seemed genuine, and his interest keen as Archimedes introduced Yasmeen. She welcomed him aboard and saw that Archimedes' friend was made to feel at ease in her cabin, which he did quite readily, sinking into the cushions surrounding the low table. As the cabin girls brought in the first course, Bilson launched into conversation with Archimedes, filling in the years that had separated them, and allowing Yasmeen time to sip her wine and observe him.

On the surface, he was much like Archimedes—or perhaps like a brother to Archimedes—sharing many of the same interests, but not so similar that they bored each other. Physically, he held himself in the relaxed manner that Archimedes did. His features were undeniably handsome, though more roughly hewn, and he was barrel-chested where Archimedes was lean. He wore the full beard that the Europeans on the northern American continent favored, and his brown hair was neatly trimmed, his jacket and trousers smartly tailored.

That neatness wasn't what Yasmeen had expected of a man who'd leased a farm from the natives in the American interior, though she knew her expectations might have been wrong. The interior was one of the few places Yasmeen hadn't been. Only chartered airships could fly over the native territories, and only along established routes that were strictly enforced by the trade confederacies—which deployed too many mechanical air-walkers to make the attempt to fly off-route worth the risk. She'd never seen an airship consumed by a clockwork swarm, only heard secondhand rumors and tales, but she didn't intend to test the truth of them with her lady.

Bilson shared tales from the interior, too—and Yasmeen couldn't decide whether they were true, or whether he might have heard them from someone else—but there was no doubt that he possessed an engaging way of telling them, and a robust laugh that was infectious.

She could see why Zenobia had feelings for him. Under other circumstances, Yasmeen would have quickly warmed to him, too. Perhaps it was because of his familiarity and long history with Archimedes, but he fit quite naturally into the spot across the table, seemed completely at ease. Some men never looked comfortable lounging on rugs and cushions during a meal, as if a simple pillow was a shocking decadence—and perhaps it was. The cushions seemed to invite intimacy, and Yasmeen could not count the number of times she and Archimedes had eaten together, all but entwined, progressing from dessert to lovemaking with barely a change in position. They maintained a small distance when they dined with passengers—or old friends—but that space between them was for their guest's comfort rather than their own. Yasmeen suspected, however, that Bilson would have appeared just as relaxed if she and Archimedes had been stroking each other in front of him.

And she saw why Zenobia worried now: despite the surface similarities, Bilson wasn't like Archimedes at all.

That sort of immediate ease simply wasn't natural. Even Archimedes watched new acquaintances for cues, soliciting their opinions and weighing their responses; he only truly relaxed after taking their measure. For a man of Bilson's experience, it would be the height of stupidity not to do the same, particularly in the company of a mercenary with Yasmeen's reputation. Yet he didn't. As a result, his easy manner seemed to be something that he deliberately put on.

But why? Perhaps only to heighten that sense of friendly intimacy, to remind Archimedes of their long familiarity before asking for his help. Perhaps to avoid any awkwardness, given the way he abandoned his friend. Perhaps he was the sort of man whose pride wouldn't allow him to show that he was the least bit concerned about Yasmeen's reactions, no matter how dangerous offending her might be.

Whatever the reason, his manner confirmed Archimedes' earlier claim: his friend always had a game in play—even if that game was nothing more than maintaining a certain attitude.

Yasmeen hoped that was the only one he intended to play tonight. If it was, she'd be willing to forgive him much, because his presence offered her a glimpse of Archimedes she'd never seen before. Except for Zenobia, she'd never met anyone who'd known him so well—and she was far less interested in the native interior than she was in her husband.

As the cabin girls removed the lamb course and set out the plates of cheese and fruit, Yasmeen took advantage of the pause in conversation. She refilled Bilson's wine, subtly forcing his attention toward her with his thank-you.

"My pleasure, Mr. Bilson. It isn't often that we have an opportunity to entertain friends—we are usually en route to some abandoned city or other."

Her smile must have been as engaging as she'd hoped. With a laughing glance at Archimedes, Bilson said, "I recall months where we never saw the inside of an alehouse, let alone entertainment of any sort."

"So you often lamented." Wineglass in hand, Archimedes sank deeper into the pillows, resting his thigh lightly against hers. "I always had a smashing time."

Relishing every hardship, no doubt. What had driven Bilson to go along with him? "With such adventures in the New World, Mr. Bilson, I imagine that you haven't missed salvaging?"

"And the zombies?" He laughed. "Not at all."

Archimedes would have missed them—or rather, the danger and the excitement they offered him. Apparently, Bilson hadn't experienced the same thrill.

"I do wish I'd seen that da Vinci sketch he'd found, though." Bilson exhaled on a low whistle, as if in astonishment that Archimedes had ever come across such an artifact. "I'm not sure what's more impressive—what that sketch is or what it was worth."

"What it is," Archimedes answered.

His response drew a chuckle from Bilson, and he looked to Yasmeen again. "That's why I don't miss it much. Salvaging was always a puzzle to him: finding a clue in some old letter, searching through journals, trying to figure out where everyone left their valuables. Not that I didn't feel that same thrill when we found something—and not that I didn't appreciate the money. But I'd have been just as happy getting in and out, and calling the job done."

"That's also why he's never been popular with the ladies," Archimedes said.

Yasmeen grinned. Bilson laughed and turned to her, as if looking for an ally now that Archimedes had begun firing. She would be glad to act as one, as long as his return fire told her more about Archimedes.

To her pleasure, Bilson's first volley did. "Ladies? Let me tell you this. The first year at university, there wasn't a man less likely to speak to a woman than him. Always dressed in black and buckled up to his chin, and he never took a step out of line. You couldn't get more than a word or two out of him— and that only if he ever glanced up from a book long enough to look at you."

Though Yasmeen hadn't expected that, she also wasn't surprised. Archimedes had been known as Wolfram Gunther-Baptiste then—and Yasmeen had known another Gunther-Baptiste, once.

She held Archimedes' gaze. There wasn't as much amusement there now, but an emotion flat and hard. "That's how your father expected you to behave?"

When he nodded, Bilson grimaced. "I forgot you know about that bastard well enough, Captain."

Yasmeen did; she'd killed Emmerich Gunther-Baptiste

after he'd tried to roast her alive. Years later, Archimedes and his sister had thanked her for it.

"We assumed he was one of those Separatist revivalists that were cropping up in the northern principalities," Bilson said. "And though all of the first-year students were quartered together in the same hall, we paid him no mind. A handful of us would often gather in the great room and confer upon ways of getting into trouble—but not him. He was always in the corner, studying the lives of dead men."

"The dead were more interesting than anything you were up to." Archimedes turned to Yasmeen. "It was all bluster. They'd formed a brotherhood—"

"*La Confrérie de la Vérité,*" Bilson supplied, saluting Yasmeen with his wineglass and a wink.

"And it was even more ridiculous than it sounds. They hoped to impress everyone in Johannesland with their anonymous ramblings printed on handbills, but they only impressed themselves."

"We were quite the radicals."

"You were all balloons filled with hot air, with no course in mind and no rudder. You weren't even half the radical that Yasmeen is, and she doesn't put any effort into it." At her narrowed look, he lifted her hand, kissed her fingers. "You're a complete anarchist, my captain. Admit it."

"I won't, because it's not true."

"Ah, yes—that one exception." He widened his eyes a bit, laughing at her. "Anarchy has no place aboard your lady."

"Or any airship," she agreed. "On the ground, however, it seems a better option than the governments and corruption that most people suffer under now."

"So you are not a *complete* anarchist."

She gave him the sharp edge of her smile. The answering curve of his mouth kindled an immediate need to move closer, to slip into his arms and taste the heat of his lips. God, but she couldn't think properly when he looked at her like that.

Sipping wine to soothe that familiar burn, she turned to Bilson. Perhaps he hadn't been radical, but why had Archimedes dismissed those ramblings so quickly? "Now I'm curious as to what you wrote in those handbills."

"Only the truth," he replied solemnly, before the humor returned to his voice. "No, Archimedes had it pegged. We didn't lack for topics, not with the Liberé war and the native disputes in full force, but we only said what everyone else was thinking—though written in a manner that we thought profound and rebellious."

Archimedes looked heavenward. "Show me a boy in first-year university who *doesn't* think he's both profound and rebellious."

Bilson ignored him, rocking forward slightly, gaze fixed on Yasmeen. "But one was different. The high magistrate had been exposed for keeping a mistress—which was nothing, except that she was bound to him under an indentured contract. There had been a general outcry, but nothing came of it. The magistrate made apologetic speeches and yet managed to justify his behavior, and soon enough, no one was speaking of it . . . except some of those justifications began to spread, repeated by other officials, all but overturning the protections in the Laws of Indenture."

"And somehow, it was all for the indentured's moral good," Archimedes said dryly.

Bilson shook his head. "It was an insult to our people. The principalities of Johannesland had been built on the backs of the indentured, and then united under the laws protecting them. So we—*La Confrérie de la Vérité*—met in the great room, wondering how to expose the hypocrisy, to strip it so bare that no justifications could cling to it. We debated for hours, but had nothing.'"

"God, the noise." Archimedes closed his eyes, as if remembering. "I couldn't have borne another hour of the brotherhood's bellowing that night."

Bilson snorted. "So we discovered. This one pulls his head up out of his book and says, 'Good God, you imbeciles! Two hundred years ago in Lusitania, Father Jacobus excoriated the Archbishop of Alagoas for the same hypocrisies. Read his journals, and you'll find that he's done all of the thinking for you.' So we did—and our handbill spurred the reforms later that year. And *I* discovered that Wolfram Gunther-Baptiste wasn't just some dull inknose, so I brought him into our brotherhood."

Ah, of course he had. "And you led that brotherhood, I imagine?"

"We didn't have a leader, but—"

"You were," Archimedes said.

Bilson conceded with a nod. "If leadership was determining a direction, I suppose I was."

So he was. Yasmeen thought she was beginning to see Bilson better now. Archimedes said he always had a game in play, but she'd assumed that his schemes led to some other end: money, excitement, power. Now she suspected that the game itself was his reason. Smuggling would have put him in the thick of power struggles and negotiations . . . until Archimedes had destroyed Temür Agha's war machines.

Perhaps that was why Bilson hadn't enjoyed salvaging itself, despite the money and excitement—while partnered with Archimedes, he hadn't been the one making all of the decisions and determining a direction. Archimedes wasn't the sort to take orders; he did as he damn well pleased, and the salvaging runs they'd made had depended upon his research.

Yet Bilson had remained in the salvaging business for years—and Yasmeen would have wagered that Bilson stayed because there was one part of salvaging that he did enjoy: the negotiations with dealers afterward.

And it had all begun with a pamphlet. Knowing Archimedes, however, Yasmeen thought that Bilson hadn't perfectly understood what had happened. He might have invited Archimedes into their group, but Archimedes had likely joined for reasons of his own—probably because they'd finally begun talking about something that mattered to him.

Hell, he and Bilson had probably been partnered for so long simply because Bilson had been engaged in something that Archimedes also wanted to do.

Bilson sipped his wine, gaze unfocused as if lost to memory. "The brotherhood was stronger for having him. We never had quite the same success at home again—perhaps because the Liberé war was such a distraction."

"But you were all quite the rebels," Yasmeen said, sending a teasing look to Archimedes. He answered it with a flutter of his lashes.

"No. Not truly. We wrote the handbills anonymously, and

we all walked the straight and narrow in public." Bilson's gaze sharpened on Archimedes. "Except *he* didn't. Not after our second year."

Oh, she truly did enjoy having this man here. Yasmeen leaned forward. "What happened?"

"He came back to university after the summer recess wearing a god-awful green waistcoat."

"It was *emerald*." Archimedes smoothed his hand down the green silk of his current waistcoat, as if protecting it from similar abuse. "It matched my eyes."

"And it got him tossed out of the first lecture."

"The bright color was disruptive to learning," Archimedes said when Yasmeen looked to him for an explanation. "But I wasn't tossed out until I asked whether I should remove my eyes for being disruptive, too."

"And he became worse after that," Bilson said. "The waistcoats, the trousers—the *flirting*. God."

Worse? To Yasmeen, that sounded like he got better. "How long before you were expelled?"

"Three weeks," Archimedes said. "But I stayed on. There was still studying to be done."

"He'd won favor with some of the lecturers, in truth. They kept him on to perform their research."

"And because they thought my eyes were distracting, too."

Bilson shook his head. "That's what many of the other lads thought—that all the dandy clothing meant he was visiting the market around the corner."

"With other men?" Yasmeen hadn't heard it phrased that way before, but it wasn't difficult to guess the meaning. Frowning, she looked to Archimedes. "How did you survive that?"

She only realized how much anger and worry had sharpened her voice when his fingers covered hers in a reassuring touch. "By learning to fight," he said. "I took a few beatings, but eventually made certain they didn't bother me anymore."

That probably wouldn't have stopped them—perhaps something else had. "And there were women?"

"A few."

"A few more than that," Bilson countered. "All of the sudden he's this charming bastard, always laughing and singing like a fool—nothing like the buckled-up inknose I'd known. At first I thought it was an act, some ruse to ease his way into their beds. But it wasn't. The laughing fool had been under those buckles all that time, I think, and he'd finally let it out."

"That's a bit what it felt like," Archimedes said.

Bilson nodded, his gaze speculative. "I always wondered what happened to you that summer. Was it a girl?"

"No." His smile held little humor. "A man."

And probably not in the way he suggested, though Yasmeen would have preferred that to the likely truth. Archimedes had reasons for wanting to kill his father. No doubt one of those reasons had been created that summer.

Bilson accepted that without further question. As Yasmeen refilled his wine, he continued, "At any rate, not long after that I heard about a smuggling job through one of my political acquaintances. I asked the others in the brotherhood if they wanted to join me—though Archimedes was the last one I expected to go. He took to smuggling, though."

He'd taken to the danger of it, Yasmeen knew. "Did you?"

Bilson shrugged. "It was a job."

"A job we did well," Archimedes said. "Until I was infected in Morocco."

"We did well even after that, when we began salvaging. It wasn't exactly the same, but we muddled through together."

"Barely." Archimedes looked to Yasmeen. "He accused me of running after death."

"Deliberately running up against zombies is the same thing," Bilson said.

No, it wasn't. Not to Archimedes.

After being shot during a smuggling run, one of Temür Agha's men had saved Archimedes' life by infecting him with nanoagents—and the influence of the Moroccan tower had all but stifled his emotions. Archimedes had always loved danger and excitement, but after the tower, he'd *needed* it.

For Archimedes, running from zombies wasn't seeking death at all; it was just a way of making certain that he was alive.

"I understood why you did it, after a fashion," Bilson said. "Seeing you affected by that signal . . . it was like someone blew out a lamp. I hope never to see it again."

"Me, too," Archimedes said softly.

Yasmeen slipped her hand into his. It wouldn't happen again; the tower was gone. Unfortunately, that didn't erase the memory for him.

Bilson's gaze flicked to their linked hands. With a deep breath, he abruptly set his wineglass on the table. "You must be wondering about the help I mentioned in my earlier note."

"I assumed you'd come to it in your own time."

"Time I shouldn't be wasting." He sighed. "Do you remember my brother?"

"Joseph? Or the younger one?"

"Joseph." Bilson added to Yasmeen, "He was part of our brotherhood, too."

Archimedes said, "And only there because we always had liquor."

"True enough." Bilson's smile was short-lived. "He began trading weapons not long after we left the business. I gave him some of my contacts, and now he makes regular runs round the bottom."

To the smuggling dens in southern Australia. Yasmeen nodded. It was a well-sailed route for both legitimate traders and those carrying illegal Horde technologies, though not one that she often made herself. If Bilson planned to ask for their help smuggling an item, however, she wouldn't mind flying that course again.

"He'd been doing well enough until a few months ago," Bilson said. "I didn't hear from him for a bit. Then I got word that his airship had been taken by New Eden."

Oh, damn. She met Archimedes' eyes and saw the dismay that matched hers.

Led by the idealist William Bushke, New Eden was a floating garden city made of airships tethered together—and almost all of them had been taken by force. After capture, no one was allowed to leave the city. Yasmeen had heard rumors of a few escapes, but only knew for certain of one made by her friend, Scarsdale, and the pirate captain Rhys Trahaearn.

And now she saw where Bilson was headed. Archimedes apparently did, too, though he tried to stop his friend before getting there.

"So he'll be given hard work and religion," Archimedes said. "Both are likely doing him some good."

"Maybe." Bilson's gaze held steady on Archimedes' face. "I want to hire you and this crew; I want you to help me get him back."

Yasmeen's mouth tightened. So he hadn't come asking for Archimedes' help, not truly. He wanted hers, and had just used Archimedes as a connection—all the while reminding Archimedes of their old friendship in order to deepen the obligation her husband might feel.

"No," Archimedes said. "Not this ship, not this crew."

Bilson didn't react, except to look at Yasmeen.

Was he waiting for her to contradict Archimedes? Amusement mixed with sharp anger. Did he think that just because Archimedes had made a decision on her lady, she'd counter it to assert her authority? She didn't need to prove anything to him.

He apparently tired of waiting for her response. "You let him give the orders on this ship, Captain?"

Humor lightened his voice, as if he were making a joke, but Yasmeen assumed that she was supposed to feel its bite.

She merely lifted her brows. "If he doesn't think your brother is worth the risk to my crew, why would I?"

And it *would* be a risk. Aside from the enormous, rigid dreadnoughts that accompanied naval fleets, airships weren't built for battle; it was too easy to incinerate the balloon. The etiquette of the seas demanded that enemies didn't target an airship's envelope, though the wooden cruiser beneath was a fair target. Only the dirtiest pirates and mercenaries fired on a balloon.

William Bushke was dirtier than any of them. As soon as he spotted an airship in the distance, he sent out steam-powered flyers to pursue it. Every captain prayed for cloudy skies if they were unlucky enough to come close to the floating city—and once those flyers came, prayer was all they had left. Bushke gave them a choice: surrender or die. There were no further negotiations, and the flyers *would* fire on the balloon.

It would have been a terrible risk . . . yet if Archimedes had wanted to go, she'd have gone with him. She'd have helped him if her husband felt he owed his friend that much.

Thank the blue heavens, he didn't seem to feel that obligation.

Still, that didn't mean her husband wasn't willing to help. He offered, "If you need money to buy mercenaries and an airship willing to go, I'll give it to you."

"I have money. And I've found someone who would go— but they wouldn't be good enough to get away. No, I need someone who can get in and out, and get the job done. Someone with expertise." He looked to Yasmeen. "You. After you killed his father, Archimedes followed your career, sought every mention of you. I heard all about how you scouted for the Liberé and French, how you brought in infiltration soldiers to garrisons fortified with more weapons and men than Bushke has. I know what you can do."

"And most of it over jungle canopy," Yasmeen said. Infiltration was far more difficult over the wide-open sea. "I know people who can do it for you, and they might be persuaded by money more readily than we are."

Bilson's jaw clenched, and his frustrated gaze shot to Archimedes. "Do the years we spent as partners mean nothing to you? Every time I saved your reckless ass, every time I stood behind you. You won't even consider honoring that debt of friendship?"

Archimedes met that accusing stare without flinching. "They mean quite a bit, and are the only reason I did consider it. But I won't risk Yasmeen and this ship."

Bilson closed his eyes. A long silence followed. Finally, with a tired smile, he shook his head. "You understand I had to try."

By questioning Archimedes' honor? If not for that, Yasmeen could have felt sympathy for his dilemma. She left it to her husband to express any, instead.

She was surprised when he remained quiet, watching his friend. He held his wine lightly, but she could see the tension in his forearms, felt it in the tautness of his thigh against hers. Archimedes was on his guard, though his expression gave away none of his wariness. He regarded Bilson with solemn regret—not regretting his refusal, Yasmeen thought, but sorry that his refusal had pushed his friend to insult. Her husband forgave personal transgressions quite readily, but after such words had been said, Yasmeen couldn't see how they could be completely easy with each other again.

Already, awkwardness had set in. Bilson cleared his throat and attempted to rescue the conversation. "Well. Where are you off to next?"

"England, to kidnap an earl," Archimedes said, his manner affable. "Then on to Cordoba to look for a statue."

He didn't mention their planned visit to Zenobia. Of course, Bilson hadn't mentioned his visit to Fladstrand the week before, either, which had prompted Zenobia's express. That hadn't struck Yasmeen as strange until this moment, but Archimedes must have noticed and wondered why Bilson hadn't spoken about the meeting with his sister.

Now Yasmeen wondered, too.

"An earl? I hope you receive a hearty ransom for him." Bilson chuckled, all ease and comfort again when he settled against the cushions. "If you are flying to England, may I ask a different favor? I have a contact in London who might be able to assist me. I would have arranged for passage tomorrow, but if you are—"

"We'll take you," Archimedes said, then glanced at Yasmeen. "Captain?"

"Of course," she confirmed. Archimedes apparently wanted to see his friend off in the direction opposite from his sister's—and though she didn't quite understand the source of his worry, she'd do anything to help him. "It's the least we can do."

In no time, they'd hired a porter to retrieve Bilson's belongings from his lodgings and bring them to *Lady Nergüi*. While Archimedes showed Bilson to the stateroom on the third deck, Yasmeen informed the steward of their new passenger and returned to their cabin.

She removed her jacket, boots, and weapons, then settled into the cushions around the table and helped herself to the wine. Archimedes' expression was still pensive when he let himself in.

Yasmeen waited until he closed the door. "We're no longer visiting Zenobia?"

He eased down beside her, and Yasmeen automatically curled against his side, her head on his shoulder. His hand rested on her hip. His thumb stroked circles just above the edge of her sash, where only thin cotton separated him from her skin. A purr rumbled through her chest. God, but she couldn't help it. That absent little touch was pure pleasure to her.

And the touch wasn't so absent now. Archimedes smiled, pulled her closer. "Bilson usually has a standby plan, in the event that his first doesn't pull through."

Was that to warn her or to reassure her? "So he'll ask another mercenary to help him?"

"No, he'll try to convince us again. He'll have some reason for us to help him held in reserve."

And he would need time to deploy it. "Was that why he asked for passage, then?"

"Probably."

"Will he try to lay more guilt on you?" Or, if he was clever, attempt to convince Archimedes that infiltrating New Eden would be the height of excitement, more dangerous than zombies. "Or will he try to entice you into it?"

He slanted her an amused look. "Do you think I would be enticed so easily?"

If *Lady Nergüi* wasn't at risk? "Yes."

"Yes, perhaps I would be." His sudden laugh shook through her. "You know me well."

So did Bilson. Perhaps he hadn't anticipated that Archimedes' love for Yasmeen would override his need to pursue a thrill—but surely he must have realized how protective Archimedes was of the people he cared for. After all, Bilson had known Zenobia.

"Would he use your sister in some way?" She hoped Bilson wouldn't be that stupid, but it would be an effective play. For Archimedes, there could be no more powerful incentive than protecting Zenobia—except, perhaps, protecting Yasmeen . . . but threatening her never seemed to work out well for anyone. "Is that why we're making certain he travels to England?"

"I don't know if he would use her," Archimedes said. He tilted his head back and stared up at the ceiling, clearly troubled. "I didn't think so . . . until he called my honor into question. He's already gone further than I'd have expected."

"Would he *hurt* her?"

"No. Not physically. But he might try to manipulate her, use her to persuade me—especially if he has guessed her feelings toward him."

His sister was too practical and too clever for that. "She wouldn't let him."

"True. Still, it's better to take him to England, then let Zenobia know what he wanted so that she's prepared if he attempts to work on her. He'll be at least two days traveling back to Fladstrand; we'll have alerted her before then."

"Shall we send the express now?"

He nuzzled beneath her ear, sending a shiver racing over her skin. "I'd rather do this."

So would she. But they'd both make Zenobia a priority.

"I won't kiss you until it's done," she said.

Eyes narrowed, he lifted his head. "You're sending me away so that you can begin reading her manuscript."

Yasmeen laughed. She'd forgotten about the story, in truth. Lady Lynx would never come before Archimedes Fox, not for her. "Perhaps," she said. "But I'll give you reason to hurry back."

She slipped her hand into the warmth between her thighs. Archimedes caught his breath and scrambled to his feet, dumping her face-first into the cushions.

"Christ." He raced across the cabin, followed by her laughter. At the desk, he stabbed a pen into ink, and spoke aloud as he scrawled:

Zenobia—

Bilson is aboard. His brother has been taken to New Eden. He wants us to mount a rescue. We refused. He might come to you, hoping that you'll help him to persuade us. Remain steadfast, O! brilliant Zenobia. Neither my darling captain nor I wish to become praying gardeners.

Yours,
Archimedes

He suddenly paused, frowning.

"Lady Lynx and the Smuggler's Secret Scheme?" Yasmeen suggested.

"By God, that's awful," he said, even as he added it to the postscript. He tossed down the pen and lifted the paper, pursing his lips and blowing to dry the ink.

Oh, his mouth was beautiful. Watching him, Yasmeen slid her hands beneath her shirt, and gave her imagination full sail—his hot tongue on her skin, the gentle suction of his lips. Her nipples hardened between her fingers.

Her back arched. "Hurry, Archimedes."

With a tortured groan, he shoved the letter into an envelope and ran for the door. He stopped before opening it, abruptly faced her.

"Don't move," he commanded, and turned to lift the latch—then spun around again. "Unless it's to take off your clothes. And prepare a cigarillo for afterward."

Yasmeen grinned. "Is that an order, sir?"

"Yes."

He rushed into the corridor, slammed the door. With her muscles warmed by anticipation and desire, Yasmeen stretched luxuriously, then dipped her fingers beneath her red sash.

She paused. The shape and feel of her cigarillo case had changed . . . but both were still *so* familiar.

A heavy lump formed in her throat even before she saw the silver case, its decorative engraving almost rubbed away from years of constant use. *Oh, Archimedes.* He'd said that he'd chosen a gift for her at the silversmiths, but she'd never dreamed he would know to buy this—one of the few items to survive the explosion that had destroyed *Lady Corsair.* Yasmeen had lost everything else, and she'd been forced to sell the case just to have money enough to pursue her revenge.

She'd never said anything about it, but Archimedes must have known what she'd done—and he must have known that she would never return to the silversmith's, afraid that her case would already be gone. It was easier to tell herself she didn't want it than to know she'd lost it forever.

So he'd gone for it. She'd never said anything, but he'd gone for it, and slipped the case into her sash without her noticing.

She looked up when Archimedes came into the cabin. His warm gaze lifted from the case in her hands to search her features. She blinked away the burning in her eyes, swallowing hard.

"*You*," she said. It was all that she could manage. *Incredible man*.

"And you're still dressed," he said softly.

She rose from the cushions and met him halfway. His lips parted against hers, yet a kiss wasn't enough. Through the swelling in her chest, the ache in her throat, she said, "I love you."

"Of course you do." Despite the teasing reply, his voice was rough with emotion. "I'm far too manly to resist."

So he was. And he was the only man she'd ever allow to sweep her up into his arms. She brought his mouth to hers as he crossed the cabin, loving his easy strength. He shouldered through the heavy curtains surrounding their bed, laying her in the center and following her down.

He pulled her shirt from her breeches, found bare skin beneath. His touch sent fire racing across her nerves, searing her senses, taking her breath. Panting, Yasmeen rolled him over, straddling his lean hips.

"Let me, Mr. Fox," she said against his lips.

He smiled. "I'm all yours, Captain."

He was, thank the lady. Her fingers made quick work of his waistcoat buckles, but as she spread the emerald silk to reveal the white linen beneath, memory of their conversation with Bilson intruded. She met his eyes. "What happened that summer?"

"I picked a flower, brought it home to my mother, and put it in her hair." He untied the silk tails of Yasmeen's kerchief, and coiled one of her narrow braids around his hand. "She blushed and smiled—her smiles came rarely then. When we were children, they came more frequently. But this was the first I'd seen in some time."

"Your father ruined it?" Yasmeen guessed.

"Adornments are for sodomites and whores. And when he was done with me, he started in on her. Not with his fists," he added. "He didn't usually need them."

With words, then. "But you finally had enough?" When he

nodded, Yasmeen stroked her fingers down the green silk. "So you told him with this."

"Well, it matched my eyes—and I'd always been fond of adornments, anyway."

His grin wrecked her. She buried her face against his neck, breathed in his warm scent. "I'd kill him again for you."

"I hope you'd let me have a turn," he said, running his palms along her spine.

"If you ask nicely."

"I would."

"Then let me be nice to you, first," she said, sliding down.

His groan was the perfect answer. She bared his stomach to her mouth, tracing the ridges of muscle with her tongue. Anticipation pounded through her, was echoed in the thud of his heart. Oh, beautiful man—every morning, an hour spent sparring with a pugilist's automaton in the cargo hold kept him strong, always ready to run, ready to fight. The life-sized windup machine had cost them a hefty amount, but was worth every denier. His body was a wiry sculpted marvel, taut and aroused beneath her hands, her lips.

A gentle nip low on his abdomen made him shake, hands fisting against the sheets. He shuddered when her mouth closed around him—rigid and thick, hot against her tongue. His moan seemed torn from his chest . . . then he quieted, as if the sensation overwhelmed even that response.

His erection softened in her mouth.

After a moment of shock, Yasmeen choked on her laugh. Had she finally scared the arousal out of him? She glanced up, ready to tease.

Archimedes wasn't laughing. A slightly puzzled expression settled over his features as he looked at her.

That was all she saw. No love in his eyes—not even lust.

Pain stabbed her heart. She fought against the instinctive need to curl away from him, to protect herself from that empty gaze. By the lady, what had she done? What had happened?

Had she lost him already?

An uncontrollable ache bloomed through her chest. With effort, she battled the panic threatening to overwhelm her sense. He'd never *not* been responsive. He'd never *not* wanted her. Something had to be wrong.

"Archimedes," she said softly. "Are you all right?"

"Yes." Realization slipped over his expression . . . but not in the way that she was accustomed to seeing it. Rather than lively and mobile, his features seemed wooden, his attitude disinterested. "I'm not feeling much."

His flaccid cock attested to that. She attempted a smile. "Do you need me to do something else?"

"No. I don't want you now."

So blandly stated, his words hurt more than a vehement rejection might have. The ache became teeth that ripped at her throat. She stared at him, trying to see beyond the pain, beyond the terrible feeling of helplessness. What was happening?

"Archimedes?"

His gaze locked with hers—and she finally saw an emotion, faint though it was. *Fear.* "It's the tower, Yasmeen."

The tower? She sat up, heart pounding. Bilson had compared the effect of its signal to a lamp burning out . . . but Yasmeen had never been this afraid of the dark.

"I don't want this," he said, and there was no color in his voice, no life . . . nothing that was Archimedes. Nothing of the man he was.

And he knew. *He knew.* Even with his emotions muffled, she could see his faint horror bleeding through.

God. How could she help him? Closing her eyes, she forced away the terror, forced herself to think.

"Not the tower," she said. It had been destroyed in Morocco—but something was broadcasting a signal that affected his nanoagents, stripping away his emotions. Yasmeen had seen a small device like that before: a twelve-inch obelisk atop a heavy base. "I know of something similar to it, though—and I'll find it. By the lady, I swear I'll find it."

She kissed him, and his lack of response tore her heart out all over again. Feet bare and throat aching, she paused only long enough to tuck a pistol into her sash. She wouldn't have to go far; the device didn't have a wide range. She would search every person between her airship and the end of the south docks—and search twice, if they appeared wealthy. The device was difficult to obtain, and had to be smuggled in from Horde territories. It wouldn't have come cheaply.

She glanced back at Archimedes, now sitting at the edge of their bed. He regarded her without a hint of fire, without a hint of laughter. *Who the hell had taken that from him?* Anger swelled, replacing the pain and fear.

Perhaps the person who'd activated the device hadn't meant to affect him. Yasmeen would tear them apart anyway.

She hauled the door open, stepped into the corridor—where Bilson waited, sorrow etching deep lines beside his mouth.

Bilson, who'd once smuggled Horde weapons, who would know how to procure such a device . . . and who would know exactly which signal would affect Archimedes.

Goddamned *Bilson*, who always had a plan on standby.

He only had enough time to open his mouth. Then her fingers were around his throat, slamming him back against the wooden bulkhead. His hands clamped on her wrist, desperately tried to force her to release him. He froze when her claws dug into tender flesh, drawing blood.

"Three seconds," she hissed. "Tell me where the device is."

"I'm not alone." It emerged on a wheeze. "Kill me and he'll die—and you won't ever know who did it."

He'll die? Yasmeen snarled. It wouldn't be Archimedes who died here. She'd rip through Bilson's neck . . . except he didn't have the device with him. A quick look confirmed it. And he wouldn't have been stupid enough to just leave it in the stateroom. Someone else had to have it.

She drew more blood. "Who is it?"

Bilson looked to the side. Yasmeen followed his gaze. Archimedes stood at the entrance to the cabin, watching them without expression.

Beneath her hand, Bilson's throat worked. "I'm so sorry, my friend. But my brother needs your help."

Archimedes gave no response. Not concealing his reaction—not even *having* one.

A scream ripped through Yasmeen's chest. She refused to voice it. Archimedes had made his way into her heart, but it was still made of steel. Maybe she couldn't kill Bilson right now. She could give him a reason to tell her where the device was.

Bilson's body tensed when she pulled her pistol from her

sash. Ah, yes. He'd probably read that Lady Lynx never drew her gun unless she intended to use it.

That was one thing Zenobia had gotten perfectly right.

Yasmeen placed the muzzle against his left shoulder and fired. Bilson howled, then clamped his mouth shut. His feet stomped the boards as he attempted to manage the pain.

Gunpowder smoke stung her eyes, her nose. Over the ringing in her ears, she heard the shouts of her crew. Ginger popped her head out of the cabin-girls' berth, saw Yasmeen, and waved the other girls away from the door. Longcock's heavy step sounded on the deck, with Vashon's quick behind him.

Yasmeen glanced at the quartermaster. "See that the aviators on watch hold their positions, mademoiselle. Tell the others to stand down."

"Yes, ma'am."

Vashon disappeared up the companionway. The first mate didn't move, his augmented bulk filling up the corridor.

"Mr. Longcock?"

His pale gaze moved from Archimedes to Bilson, pinned against the bulkhead and breathing shallowly through clenched teeth. "I'm not on watch, ma'am."

All right, then. He wasn't needed on deck, and was also Archimedes' friend. Obviously, a much better one than Archimedes' stinking rat partner. She focused on Bilson again. "Is the device on my ship?"

Bilson didn't answer—but he didn't need to. It would have to be aboard *Lady Nergüi* to pose any real threat. The device had such a short range that they could fly out of danger within minutes.

But that also meant his associate was a member of her crew. They hadn't taken on any other passengers in Port Fallow . . . only Vashon, the new quartermaster.

No. That was a dangerous route for a captain to take; an airship couldn't function if she couldn't rely on her aviators. So she would trust each member of her crew, until one of them proved untrustworthy.

Or until Bilson gave up a name. She pressed the muzzle harder against his shoulder. "Who has it?"

Bilson's face whitened, but he shook his head.

In a flat voice, Archimedes said, "That won't work, Yasmeen. He won't break."

Perhaps not, but as the minutes passed and Archimedes remained smothered by that device, Yasmeen thought that she would enjoy trying.

"Go on," Bilson rasped. "Torture me, and my associate will realize that you won't help me—and use the device to kill him for that, too. You have no choice, Captain. Help us, or Archimedes will pay for your refusal."

Idiot. If the device was on her ship, it was only a matter of time before she found it.

She smiled, and Bilson tensed again. Good enough. She released him, stepping back. "If your associate stops the signal, I'll see that a surgeon is brought to you. If it remains on, you'd best pray that wound doesn't turn gangrenous before we rescue your brother."

Bilson hunched over, holding his shoulder. "If you take us to New Eden, we won't activate it again—and won't kill him. Do we have an agreement, Captain?"

"We do, Mr. Bilson."

The lie came easily. Yasmeen only intended to discover who held the device—and then destroy them both.

He nodded and turned toward the third deck companionway. Would he be foolish enough to lead them straight to his associate?

Farther down the passageway, Longcock met Yasmeen's gaze, his blond brows lifted in query. She nodded. The first mate would keep an eye on Bilson, then, and let her know who the man spoke with. She would stay with Archimedes until this horror had passed. While under the device's influence, perhaps he didn't care enough to need her with him—but by the lady, *she* needed to be with *him*.

The glint of steel in Bilson's hand stopped her from returning to the cabin. Wary, Yasmeen watched him. Surely he wouldn't be foolish enough to attack Longcock? But, no. Injured arm held awkwardly to his side, he swept the dagger over his head. The blade clanged against an exposed copper pipe running the length of the deckhead.

The slick bastard, Yasmeen realized. He was using the pipes to signal someone on the ship.

A terrible, haunted moan came from behind her. *Archimedes?* The hairs on the back of her neck prickled.

He charged out of the cabin, unleashing a primal scream of rage and hate, unlike anything she'd ever heard from a man . . . and had *never* imagined coming from Archimedes. Stunned, Yasmeen barely had a moment to step out of the way. He tore down the passageway, face contorted with fury. Bilson's eyes widened and his grip on the dagger firmed.

He wasn't as fast as her husband. Archimedes dodged the slashing blade. His fist smashed into Bilson's jaw. Yasmeen watched in fierce satisfaction as the man staggered. Archimedes' knee rammed into his stomach, crumpled him to the boards. Pinning Bilson's dagger to the deck with his foot, Archimedes yanked the man up by his bloodied shirt, then pounded another blow to his face.

Was Archimedes going to kill him? Yasmeen's relief at seeing her husband released from the device transformed into mounting worry. She rushed forward, caught his wrist as he brought his fist back for another strike.

Yasmeen held on as he attempted to swing, and was almost hauled over his shoulder. God, he was strong. She braced her feet.

"Stop! Archimedes, you have to stop! If you go too far, they'll use the device to kill you!"

"Good." Roughly, he shoved her back. His voice was hoarse, his eyes tormented. His knuckles bled. "I'd rather be dead than feel nothing again."

Gutted, she stared at him. *He'd rather be dead?*

No. She was *never* going to lose him.

He picked up Bilson again, drew back his fist. Yasmeen leapt, grabbing Archimedes' hair, yanking him away.

"Enough!" she shouted into Archimedes' ear, whipped him against the bulkhead. The wood shuddered against the impact. Blindly, he fought her, trying to rip out of her grip—a man driven mad by what his friend had just done. His pain overwhelmed her, became her own. By the blue heavens, how could she help him? How could she ease this? She didn't know, and her fear and horror reached up to choke her. "Please, Archimedes. *Please.*"

His eyes seemed to clear . . . not completely, but just

enough. His devastated gaze locked on hers. He stopped struggling and began to shake, uncontrollable tremors that rattled
his frame.

"You're all right. I'm here." Yasmeen released her grip on
his hair and gently cupped his face between her hands. His
beloved features blurred in front of her. "You're all right."

With a ragged, sobbing breath, he clutched her to his chest.
His face buried in her hair. His shaking intensified when,
behind them, Bilson's gave a pained groan.

Archimedes lifted his head, the sheen over his eyes making them appear brilliantly green. His hair had come free of
the leather tie, an unruly tangle that looked as wild as he had
moments before—and still was, she saw. He was just barely
containing the emotional eruption.

"God, Yasmeen. I have to go. I need to run."

Her throat aching, she nodded. Archimedes wasn't like her.
The airship wasn't big enough for him—he needed more, and
especially now. "I'll come with you."

"No." A violent shake of his head followed the response.
"No."

God. How could she agree to that? She couldn't let him go
alone when he was like this.

But she also couldn't imagine what was going through his
head. Whatever it was, he obviously couldn't bear for her to
see it.

"Not to the city wall," she said. Zombies crowded Port Fallow's wall—and even though he needed to bring himself back,
to seek danger . . . out there, he wouldn't be reaffirming life.
He'd only find death. "Promise me, Archimedes. There's too
many. Promise me."

Nodding, he pressed an unsteady kiss to her lips. "I love
you." His voice was broken. "More than I can . . . *God.*"

He abruptly pulled out of her arms. Yasmeen watched him
disappear up the companionway, trying to breathe past the
pain in her chest. She looked to the first mate. He glanced at
Bilson, who was struggling to his feet—the bastard obviously
wasn't going anywhere, and he'd already communicated with
his associate on board.

With a short salute, Longcock headed off after Archimedes. Whatever her husband got into, the first mate could help him if he needed it.

And Bilson . . . She wasn't done with him yet.

Archimedes' old friend spit blood from his mouth as she approached, regarding her with disgust. "You let him go alone? You ice cold bit—"

She whipped around. Her bare heel cracked against his jaw. Bone snapped. Bilson's eyes rolled back, and he dropped to the boards.

Yasmeen looked up at the sound of steps. Vashon stood at the head of the companionway, staring at the unconscious man, her expression impassive except for the barest widening of her eyes.

"Would you like us to move him, ma'am?"

"In a moment." They couldn't kill him yet, but they could make certain the device wouldn't only affect Archimedes. She glanced toward her cabin, where Ginger still waited by the girls' berth. The girl hadn't flinched—but then, she'd seen much worse. "Run for Tom Blacksmith and Anisa Stoker, and bring them both to Mr. Bilson's stateroom."

As the girl started off, Yasmeen reached for Bilson's uninjured arm and sent a significant glance to his boots. Vashon caught on, lifted his feet, and they began sliding him toward the companionway.

Walking crab-like to avoid the trail of blood they were leaving, the quartermaster asked, "Do we need to call for a surgeon, Captain?"

"No." And normally, Yasmeen wouldn't cross this line and infect a man without his consent—but Bilson's goddamn game had pushed her over. *He'd hurt Archimedes.* The man was lucky she wasn't flaying him alive. "He only needs the blacksmith."

The nanoagents would heal him more quickly than any surgeon's tricks could. And if he was smart, he'd be damn grateful that Yasmeen hadn't ordered the ship's blacksmith to bolt his mouth shut while he was at it.

Chapter 4

A system of copper and brass pipes ran all through the ship—some for heating, others for communication. The pipe that Bilson had clanged ran through the aviators' mess. Several crew members were seated at the long table that dominated the midsection of the berth deck, engrossed in a game of Five Click Mérelles. Others came and went without notice—particularly tonight, while *Lady Nergüi* was still docked and lightly manned.

Yasmeen firmed her mouth against a sigh of frustration. Following the pipes hadn't helped. Anyone on the ship could have listened for Bilson's signal and deactivated the device without drawing undue attention.

Anyone but Yasmeen.

Despite having just swigged a mouthful of grog, the second mate abruptly stood when she saw Yasmeen. The table jolted, scattering the marbles across the rotating game board. A shout of dismay went up, a jeer at her clumsiness—then they were suddenly on their feet, too.

The second mate swallowed and announced, "Captain on deck!"

"Thank you, Mrs. Markel. Please, return to your activities."

They immediately sat again, though all were clearly uncomfortable—and would have been with any captain. This was one of the few places on her lady that Yasmeen rarely visited, because a simple statement inviting them to return to their game became an order to sit. A crew shouldn't always have to be mindful of a captain's presence. Even Archimedes—whose relationship with the crew was both less formal and far more complicated than Yasmeen's—rarely intruded here, accepting only spontaneous invitations during celebratory occasions.

She wished he was here now. Not knowing how he fared was killing her. She had to trust that he'd be all right . . . he was Archimedes Fox, after all. But he'd been so enraged, so devastated—nothing at all like the Archimedes Fox she knew, the man who rarely even worked himself up to a temper. How could she guess what he would do, what he was thinking? Never before had she seen him in such a state.

And she'd never let it happen again. Only a thin thread of self-control had kept her from tearing through her lady, searching for the device. Quietly, she walked the length of the aviator's mess, and even though she rarely visited, Yasmeen knew her lady and the look of her decks well enough to know that nothing appeared out of place, as if recently moved or used to conceal another object. Of course, she hadn't expected to find anything. There was little hope of locating the device before Archimedes' return. Eventually, Yasmeen would find it, but not in any obvious spot. Bilson had prepared too well.

She could destroy all of those preparations now by leaving Archimedes in Port Fallow and flying out of the harbor. Her husband would be safely out of range, and she could search every inch of the airship.

Except . . . she couldn't. That was Archimedes' decision to make. Perhaps later, when he was thinking clearly again, he would choose to leave the airship until she found the device. And even though distance would be safer for him, she wouldn't abandon her husband while he was still reeling from Bilson's attack.

Bilson. The fucking bilgewater trout.

Unfortunately, whatever happened to the man was also up to her husband. Though Yasmeen would have liked to toss him straight into a kraken's clutches, and though Bilson deserved much worse than what she'd already done, his fate was Archimedes' to determine.

If he gave the bastard over to Yasmeen, though . . .

"Captain?"

The query came from the table, where the aviators were watching her. When she turned, the second mate's eyes widened. The others paled and hastily looked back to their game. Apparently, the fierce and bloody vengeance she'd been imagining had found its way to her expression.

Still, Mrs. Markel had balls enough to ask, "Are you searching for something, ma'am? May we help you?"

Could they? Yasmeen stopped, her heart stuttering with the sudden realization: she could lose her crew over this.

She hadn't thought of it until now—how could she, while Archimedes was out in Port Fallow somewhere, trying to jettison the effects of the device?—but the simple truth was that Bilson had come aboard her airship and taken command. Until they found the device, that bastard would determine where they flew.

She'd killed several people who'd tried to take control of her airship before. She'd even tossed *Archimedes* off her lady and into a zombie-infested swamp for attempting the same. Each time, there'd been some risk to her life, a weapon aimed her way, yet she'd never submitted to the demands—and she'd stopped every single bastard who had ever tried to steal her ship.

Yet now, it wasn't her life that had been threatened, but Archimedes'. . . and she'd backed down. Even if only to give herself time to find the device, she'd backed down, and allowed Bilson to live in order to save her husband.

Yasmeen couldn't regret it, not even for a moment. All the same, a sick uncertainty began roiling in her gut. How could she prevent Bilson's blackmail from destroying the crew's confidence in her? Someone had seen her weakness and exploited it. Why would they follow someone who couldn't maintain command of her own airship?

Thank the lady, the danger wasn't immediate. For now, the aviators knew that she'd shot Bilson, but not *why*—and Bilson's associate probably wouldn't reveal himself by talking about it. George Longcock and Ginger knew of the device and its effect on Archimedes, but Yasmeen didn't doubt their ability to keep their mouths shut. She'd already asked Ginger not to mention the device, in case the associate *did* inadvertently expose himself, but also to avoid a panic; many of the crew were infected by nanoagents, and few cared that none of them shared the same strain as Archimedes—except for Anisa

Stoker, who'd been in her bunk and sleeping while the device had been activated.

Ginger wouldn't talk; the girl's loyalty had survived the explosion that had destroyed *Lady Corsair*, and nothing Bilson could do would shake it. Though an excellent first mate, Longcock's loyalty to Yasmeen ended at the bottom of her purse—but not his loyalty to Archimedes, whose quick thinking and pneumatic grapnel launcher had once saved the first mate from a megalodon's jaws, even though Archimedes had risked his own life to do it. Already an admirer of the adventurer Archimedes Fox, George Longcock had become a devoted friend of the man himself after that brush with death.

An impossible friendship, Yasmeen would have thought, but somehow, Archimedes easily navigated through the lines of position and ranking aboard *Lady Nergüi*.

Though not as close to him as George Longcock, many other members of the crew felt similarly toward Archimedes—either because they'd read his serial adventures, because of some kindness, or simply because he was always good company. Her husband wasn't part of her crew, yet beloved by them. None of the aviators would have wondered why their captain had a soft spot for him, too.

They wouldn't have wondered why . . . but they might have wondered whether that soft spot made her too vulnerable to properly command them.

She wasn't. Yasmeen had no doubt of that. Still, she was shaken by the realization of how much damage Bilson's scheme could do to her position. Perhaps she would have reason to kill him herself, after all.

But not yet. She wouldn't risk Archimedes.

The second mate was waiting for her reply. Yasmeen came to a decision, shook her head.

"No, Mrs. Markel. Thank you." She wouldn't send her crew scuttling about in search of the device, driven by fear. Better to determine a course, to prepare. Both would be easier to do after Archimedes returned and her every thought wasn't consumed by her worry for him. "As you were."

She started aft, toward the galley kitchen. The aviators' sighs of relief as she left the mess would have been inaudible to most people; Yasmeen heard them, smiled slightly—then wondered if she *was* too soft on them.

The galley was empty, except for the scullery woman. Of course it was. This late, Cook was already abed. She'd have to speak with him about securing enough provisions for a months' long flight tomorrow.

The scullery woman glanced up, her hands red from the scalding wash water and the fringe of her brown hair curled by the steam. Yasmeen immediately saw the same discomfort that the aviators had shown, but held out her hand to stop the woman's attempt to stand. "As you were, senhora. I'm only passing through."

Though clearly uncertain, the woman eased back down on her cushioned stool. "Yes, Captain."

The galley was spotless and in perfect order. Though there were likely more places to conceal the device here than anywhere else aboard her lady, Yasmeen suspected that Cook would have ferreted out any foreign object in *his* domain and made everyone aware of his displeasure long before Bilson's associate had managed to use it.

Indeed, the only thing out of place in Cook's firmly regimented kitchen was Maria Barriga de Lata—the scullery woman. It was a bit late for scrubbing pots, yet Yasmeen wasn't surprised to see her. She'd heard that Cook had been allowing the woman to rest during the last dog watch. Typically, all cleaning duties would be completed before the eighth bell had been struck, but Barriga de Lata had difficulty sitting for long stretches of time, thanks to the blacksmith butchers in the Lusitanian mines. Yasmeen didn't know what they'd been hoping to do to the woman—aside from making their own strong laborers who came cheaper than those abducted from Horde-occupied territories—but all they'd managed to do was replace most of her abdomen with a tin can filled with guts and useless clockworks. Only her nanoagents kept her alive.

By the time Yasmeen reached the end of the galley, Barriga de Lata was diligently scrubbing again. Out of pity or some other reason, Cook had relaxed the strict order of his kitchen for this woman—and Yasmeen didn't care whether she worked the usual schedule, either, as long as her duties were completed every day.

But was Yasmeen being too soft on her, too?

Sense told her that she wasn't. Still, the question of her softness nagged at her—and in turn, *that* nagged at her. She'd never been uncertain like this.

Perhaps it was impossible to be certain of anything when her life and emotions had suddenly been turned on their heads by one goddamn device, when the man she loved had been so devastated by it . . . and hadn't yet returned.

Though she wouldn't find the device before he came back, she could help him by making certain that Bilson's associate had no reason to activate it again. Letters needed to be sent to Scarsdale, and to the Blacksmith in London—she didn't want to see even a glimpse of New Eden, but by the lady, she would be prepared for it. Instructions had to be written for her steward, lead engineer, and quartermaster, ordering them to secure enough provisions for a long trip. She could help Archimedes best by returning to her cabin, by being the captain her lady needed.

And by being here when he came home.

Archimedes ran.

He ran the length of the dock that he'd danced down that afternoon, each step just as quick, quicker—but no partners now, except for those that veered out of his path or jumped out of his way, and no music, only cries of surprise or anger as he rushed past. Past the bridge choked with steamcoaches, the light from their hissing gas lanterns flickering over the surface of the canal, gilding the floating refuse and gleaming in the eyes of swimming rats. Though contained by water and walls, Port Fallow was endless, the curving streets and twisting alleys forever leading to others. Everything that could be felt was here to see and hear, the despair of digging through rotting scraps, the joy of laughter between friends, the sorrow of the lost-and-couldn't-be-led, the passion of lovers coupling in the dark, the terror of cold nights and rough hands. Like a boilerworm leeching minerals from dirt, he wound his way through the city, drawing out as many emotions as he could. His lungs became a fiery bellows and his thighs screaming pistons, and the pain and exhaustion helped more than all of the rest because it was *his*.

But it wasn't enough.

He could still picture the stabbing hurt in Yasmeen's gaze when she'd looked up at him, could still feel the *nothing* inside as he'd looked back. He hadn't cared. God, *that wasn't him*— but the memory of her expression was his, the vision of her pain that he hadn't even *tried* to protect her from, and it ripped him open now, filled him with shame.

Even that wasn't enough.

Every time he turned toward the harbor, the sight of *Lady Nergüi* was a razor to his gut. He couldn't go back, not yet. Not until he was himself again. But he couldn't go to the wall, where armed men fired into the night, where the ravenous moans and growls never ceased. There were other places, though—zombies couldn't be found in Port Fallow's worst rum dives, but when the patrons had enough to drink, they were almost the same. Stinking, vacant-eyed, and willing to tear a man apart at the slightest provocation.

Archimedes couldn't see much difference—and shortly after provoking the right one, he couldn't see anything past the blood and the sweat dripping into his eyes.

This, too, wasn't enough. But it was something.

Something absurd. Laughing wildly, he swung at a drunken giant and was pummeled in return. Ah, God, yes. *This* was pain, rupturing through his chest and gut, eating away the edges of his memory until the agony of remembering her face and his nothing in response began to blur. Until the goddamn mechanical bugs in his blood were forced to begin healing him, until they had a use other than smothering him into oblivion.

A fist sent him into that void, instead. Archimedes reeled back, hit a wall. His knees folded. The world spun and darkened.

That wasn't enough.

Killing Bilson might be. That duplicitous bastard had used him to get to Yasmeen. She'd found a new ship and new crew and Bilson had ripped it from her . . . using her love for him. God. Would she resent him for that? Hate him for it?

That pain of that thought was too much, shredding everything, leaving only despair. It had to be Bilson, instead, the utter betrayal of using that device. Embracing his horror and anger, Archimedes pushed the darkness away and lifted his head.

Longcock squatted in front of him, a foaming pint in hand, and more foam dissolving in his blond mustache. His rough blue tunic bulged over his arms and chest, covering the guns beneath without concealing them. Behind him, the drunken giant was on the floor, rubbing his jaw.

"And he's awake," the first mate said. "Are you done?"

Hurting everywhere, but not enough. "Not yet."

Longcock nodded, as if unsurprised. "Did you mean to pick out the biggest one?"

"Yes." And would have gone another round, except the drunken giant was hauling himself up and sidling toward the door, keeping one eye on Longcock. "Not that it does me any good now that you've chased him away."

"I thought the device had addled your brains. But any man who salvages rubbish from a continent full of zombies can't have many brains to begin with."

Even smiling pained him, so Archimedes laughed and relished the full-bodied, agonizing effect.

Longcock shook his head. "I can't figure New Worlders. Buggers like me lived all our lives under the tower in London, and when that tower went down we went mad with feeling. I did things during the revolution I can't bear to think of now, that even as a pirate, it couldn't compare. Before that, I thought I knew who I was—and after, I'd have done anything to just stop feeling again, to stop hurting, to know myself again. That's what every bugger did. But you go and do the opposite."

For the same reasons, though. Even as the buttoned-up ink-nose, he'd felt deeply. That signal took it all away—and didn't let him care that it was gone. Longcock hadn't known who he was when the tower went down; Archimedes didn't know who he was when it was up.

He knew who he wanted to be, who he should be—and it wasn't *this*. None of this was enough.

Doing the opposite wasn't enough, either, though that was part of him, too. "If I did what was expected of me, I'd bore everyone."

"True enough. Though that puts another light on Archimedes Fox, Adventurer," Longcock mused. "You're a madman with an airship, searching for danger."

Almost all correct. "It's *her* airship."

"No doubt of that." The first mate nodded, his gaze shrewd. "And you running away from it is the opposite of sense, too. If I was searching for danger, the last thing I'd do would be leaving that ship."

Leaving *her*. Yasmeen. Archimedes' gut clenched. He'd left her. Terrified, he'd left her. Terrified of what he might do, what he might say. His emotions often got the best of his sense—and the last time he'd surfaced out of a tower-induced fugue, he'd sunk Temür Agha's barge and destroyed his war machines. Christ knew what he might have done to her ship or in front of her crew.

But Bilson had jeopardized her ship and her crew, anyway. She might resent Archimedes for making her vulnerable. But, *by God*, he would convince her to let him stay.

He'd seduce her. She admired his clever tongue. He'd use it in every way a man could to win her over again.

Longcock rocked back a bit. "If you're looking at me like that, friend, then I know your brain's addled."

"Not at you." With effort, Archimedes stood. "If I was, you'd already be in my arms."

"And here I thought you were coming to your senses."

He wasn't. His emotions weren't balancing any better than his feet were. But he was finally getting there, heading in the right direction. This felt more like him.

"I'd charm you," he told the first mate. "You'd fall desperately in love with me."

"No man could be more mistaken—"

"I won *her* heart. Yours would be no challenge in comparison."

The other man paused. "You have a point."

So he did, but Archimedes was already losing it. The oily, smoking funk of the harbor led him to the docks, and revulsion disturbed his brief humor. Pain shot through his knuckles when he gripped the rope ladder. With each step, he reminded himself—he wouldn't kill Bilson. Dead was better than nothing, but he couldn't bear seeing her reaction to that statement again.

He wouldn't kill Bilson for that, either.

The crew must have thought he was there to kill *someone*. Wary, they watched him cross the deck. Blood spotted his shirt. His waistcoat was gone. Yasmeen had taken it off of him before she'd taken him in her mouth, before Bilson's device had taken the rest. He shouldn't go to her like this.

But he did, because she was the right direction to take— and because Longcock had been right, too. He'd been an idiot to leave.

She sat at their desk, and looked up as he entered the cabin. Raw emotions raced across her face—fear, pain, uncertainty— and all of them chased by relief.

God. How was it that poets hadn't dedicated thousands of verses to the expressive tilt of her eyes? Where were the songs to her lips, her sharp teeth? He would write them, and sing them, and lay at her feet.

"You're all right." Her gaze lingered on his battered face, the blood on his shirt, but it wasn't quite a question. She knew he was more resilient than that.

But not resilient enough.

"Not yet." He closed the door. "But I realized that there was no need to keep running, to keep fighting. The most dangerous person in Port Fallow is on this airship."

She watched him for a long moment. Then her eyes cooled, and her smile held a knife's edge. A shiver worked up his spine, delicious and terrifying.

"Yes." Slowly, she lay down her pen. "I am."

His heart pounded. Christ, the thrill she gave him with that simple movement outstripped the onslaught of a dozen zombies. Wary, he stalked closer. "Do I interrupt your writing, Captain?"

"No." She watched him come, elbows on the desk and her fingers steepled, clicking her claws together. Her casual posture was deceptive, he knew. She could spring at any moment. "It is only a reply to Lord Scarsdale."

Scarsdale. Though never Yasmeen's lover, the man had touched her, kissed her when Archimedes couldn't . . . when he hadn't wanted anything more than the woman Scarsdale had beneath his hands and lips.

Old jealousy sparked; over the course of a step, Archimedes blew that spark into a conflagration. "I don't want you to write him again. Or see him."

Her brow arched. "No?"

"I'll kill him if you do." And by God, he meant it.

A cruel little smile curved her mouth. "After your performance tonight, maybe I'll go back to him. He doesn't even desire women and managed to get hard with me."

Go back to him? Rage flared, burning hot. Blind with it, fists shaking, he barely stopped himself from charging, rooted his feet to the deck.

Her body smashed into his without warning and sent him staggering. He caught his balance; she caught his hair, yanked his head back. Her strong legs wrapped his hips. Sharp teeth snapped near his ear, then closed over his exposed throat, her tongue hot against his skin. Archimedes froze as she bit, exquisite needles of pain.

She could kill him like this, so easily.

The heat of rage consumed itself, smoldered into lust. His blood raced, the tension in his muscles subtly shifting from wariness to anticipation. His cock stiffened, ached. He held her against him, her taut bottom filling his palms.

Yasmeen.

He breathed her name. She released his throat, dragged her tongue beneath his jaw. Shuddering, he lifted her against his erection, grinding between her thighs, and a groan ripped from his chest. God, this feeling. So rough, so sweet. No other woman had ever excited him as she did. No other woman ever would.

Her breath rasped in his ear, each inhalation ragged, as if her control was as tattered as his, the need to touch overwhelming.

With her legs anchored around him, she loosened her grip in his hair. He caught her hands, drew them down. No need to hold him, to bite him. He was all right now, exactly where he wanted to be, and this was *him*, hungry for her. Her claws thrilled him, but he didn't need them. He didn't need her to threaten him. He just needed her. He just needed to show her that the disinterest had been a lie, that he could never *not* want her, and to soothe the hurt he'd caused. It wasn't the danger that excited him; it was her. Only her.

Her pulse thrummed beneath his thumbs as he captured her hands behind her back, gently shackling her wrists with his fingers. He'd use only his tongue now, and show her—

Yasmeen's body exploded into motion against his. She ripped out of his arms, her foot shoving into his chest—not hard, just enough to get away. Still, shock sent him tripping backward.

The same shock was reflected on her face. Crouching on the deck boards, Yasmeen stared at him, openmouthed. "I didn't . . ." She swallowed hard. "Don't restrain my hands."

Oh, now *that* was pain. Anger came with it. "You don't trust me?"

Her jaw tightened. "That's not what I said."

"I know. You said today, 'I know you'd never hurt me,'" he mocked her accent. "I see how well you mean it."

"You don't see anything." Her eyes narrowed, and she shifted her weight, as if preparing to pounce. Christ, his cock had never been this hard before. "You're a goddamn fool right now."

"*Your* fool." He spat the words, and she laughed. *Laughed.*

"And God help us," she said—but didn't pounce. Her attack was far more liquid than that, a sublime dance of muscle and stealth. He had but a moment to watch, her deadly beauty striking him speechless, motionless.

Then she was behind him, around him, dragging him down to the boards. Her knees pinned his arms; her weight across his stomach stole his breath. She leaned down, her incredible face directly over his.

"Archimedes." She whispered his name and pressed her lips to his jaw. "Archimedes."

He opened his mouth to answer, but she took it from him with a soft, searching kiss. His eyes burned. The ache that filled his chest was unbearable, but he wanted more of it, more of this. A kiss meant she loved him.

Loved him.

God, and this was what he'd come back for. What he'd feared might have been destroyed. And he *had* been a fool— not to run, but to think that he would find what he needed anywhere but here.

He trembled, and she released his arms. He held her to him,

returning the kiss, deepening it. Her breath seemed to catch in her throat, her chest hitched, and then he was lost to the heat of her mouth, the taste of her skin, her shuddering cry as she took him in. Here was rage and sorrow, joy and fear. Despair . . . and love. She gave him everything.

And he would never get enough.

Chapter 5

She couldn't breathe.

She should have been able to. The hole at the top of her brass helmet let in air. But air wasn't the problem—it was her chest. Her heart was giving out.

Ravenous growls filled her head. She chopped away at the zombies. The door was only a few feet away. Archimedes was trapped behind that rotten wood, bracing the entrance against the zombies' attack. He just had to hold on. Only a few more were left, but she had to hack and hack and endlessly hack, and more were coming, and the wood . . . was cracking.

The sound splintered through her chest. The door shattered inward.

Her scream ripped like a knife from her gut to her throat. Staggering, she was hit from behind and then carried along as the zombies crowded, rushed through the door. She swung the machete, hacking, killing—but it didn't matter, because she was dead now, too.

But . . . no. When she made it through the door, all would be right. She would look up and see Archimedes clinging to the rope, above the zombies' reach—holding on, just as she'd told him to. Then sharp relief would wake her.

Except he wasn't on the rope. And there was her heart, gone, gone, as the zombies surrounded him, tore at him, and he looked at her. There was nothing in his eyes. No love, no pain, nothing.

Her screams tore at her throat again, and she hacked, hacked. She couldn't lose him. She couldn't bear it even in a dream, she had to wake up, had to wake—

Yasmeen opened her eyes, her heart racing. With shaking

hands, she reached for Archimedes, as she always did on waking from this nightmare.

He was gone.

She jolted up. Pain shot though her knees, still healing from the explosion that had destroyed her lady. Her relief at seeing Archimedes at the end of the bed only lasted a moment; sympathy took its place. Nude, he sat with his shoulders hunched and elbows braced on his thighs, his head in his hands. Despair and rejection traced every line of his body.

Ignoring the ache in her knees, Yasmeen slid toward him. His head came up, fingers wiping at his eyes. Throat suddenly raw, she slid her arms around his waist, lay her cheek against the back of his shoulder.

"Are you all right?"

"Not completely. But I will be," he said, and she heard his smile in his voice, felt his determination in the long, shuddering breath that he drew. His palm cupped her left knee, fingers softly massaging the stiffness away. "And I'm sorry."

"Why?"

"A few times last night . . . I was rough with you."

That was all? It was true, the instability of his emotions meant that they'd gone a few rounds before exhaustion had finally worn them down, but nothing had been said or done that needed an apology now. Yasmeen gently nipped his shoulder. "And we've never been rough before?"

"Never with anger. Not out of jealousy."

"And I deliberately pushed you to both, knowing that you would squeeze every bit of emotion out of them. Wasn't that what you wanted after the device stole that from you?"

His answer was a kiss pressed to her fingers, and a grin. "I'm squeezing out every bit of shame now."

"So you are." And without needing her to push him to it. Some emotions had been easier to find in him than others. "Are you truly jealous of Scarsdale?"

"No. But I was, once." He moved his attentions to her right knee, fingers gently working. "I *am* envious of how much time he has spent with you, the years he's been your friend—but I don't begrudge him that time."

"You have me now."

"And I often feel like crowing that fact to everyone I see."

So did she. Yasmeen smiled, held him closer. His fingers paused on her knee.

"And your reaction when I restrained your hands? That wasn't deliberate. I scared you. I'm sorry for that, too. I didn't know."

"I didn't know, either," she said. She'd been utterly shocked by her reaction.

Tension stiffened his shoulders. "I wasn't myself."

Oh. He still thought she hadn't trusted him because of the device's effect on his emotions. Even if he were enraged beyond reason, she would put her life in his hands.

She had more difficulty risking *his* life.

"I trust you," she said. "But I don't trust anyone else. When you held my hands, I was terrified by the idea that someone could come into the cabin, and I wouldn't be able to protect you."

Though he was quiet for a long moment, his tension didn't ease. "I would protect us both."

"I know. But it wasn't about *knowing*. It was more . . . instinctive."

Archimedes smiled faintly, reached up to flick her tufted ear—the one ticklish spot she had. Damn him. She squirmed, refusing to voice a single giggle, and retaliated with the scrape of her claws across his chest.

He groaned. "Stop arousing me like that, woman. You've already squeezed me dry."

So she had. She'd enjoyed every second of it.

But she hadn't enjoyed everything that had happened the previous night. Her laugh ended on a sigh, and was echoed by Archimedes'. He was better, but trouble hadn't left their home.

Archimedes hadn't forgotten, either. "Where's Bilson?"

"In the stateroom, recovering. He's still unconscious."

"Unconscious?" His brows rose. "How badly unconscious?"

"I broke his jaw. That put him out. Then I infected him with Anisa Stoker's blood. He's full of opium now. It ought to keep him down for another day."

"And the device?"

Heaviness settled in her gut. "I didn't find it."

"And you can't risk the crew looking for it."

So he'd already realized the threat to her position. She'd planned to keep that knowledge from him, but he understood her ship too well now. "I'll ask Vashon and Longcock to search for it, but to treat the search as an inspection. Anyone whose station or storeroom is out of order will receive scullery duties."

Archimedes nodded, but didn't appear hopeful. "It won't be anywhere obvious."

"No. But there are only so many places to hide it."

"And if we don't find it?"

"Then we fly to New Eden."

"No." He pulled away from her, stood. "You won't risk your freedom and your ship for—"

"Don't think to give me orders, Mr. Fox."

Though softly said, she meant it. He knew it.

His mouth flattened. Frustration glittered in his eyes, a bit of anger—and something more. Fear? "How do you like it, Yasmeen, knowing that I'm your soft spot? That I'm your exposed belly, and that my friend is holding a knife to it?"

"Truthfully? I don't like it at all."

He froze. It was a long moment before he spoke again, his face rigid and voice hoarse. "Do you regret me?"

"Never." It was a vow. Her gaze didn't waver from his. "But I hate that I don't know how to protect you, except by giving in to his demand."

A grim smile tilted the corners of his mouth. "I hate that I don't know how to protect you and your ship, except by giving in . . . or leaving."

"Don't leave. And I'll protect myself and my lady. You don't have to worry about it."

"Only if you don't worry about protecting me."

"I can't."

"Then don't ask me to do the impossible, either." He dragged his hand though his hair. "Christ. As it is, I am behind on the protecting. I have to save your life a few more times just to pull even. I ought to be hiring men to line up and shoot at you so that I can jump in front of the bullet—but God knows, you'd likely get to them first and snap their necks, and I'd end up paying the poor bastards to die."

Despite herself, she had to laugh. He could be so wonderfully absurd.

He flashed a smile, then took a deep breath. "All right. We're *not* giving in—we're delaying while we look for the damned thing. We'll find it, and that will be the end. Yes?"

"Yes," she said, but in spite of his declaration, lines of worry formed on his brow. "Archimedes?"

"He always has a plan on standby." He drew the statement out, as if thinking aloud. "But he didn't try to stop me when I left the ship last night. You could have flown out of range—or I could have walked out of range, nullifying the threat. And he has to know we might find the device en route. No, this was to secure our attention or to serve as a distraction, and perhaps to keep us in line or to protect himself, but—"

By the dawning horror in his eyes, the answer struck him the same moment that Yasmeen realized it, too. They wouldn't risk everything for Bilson's brother. But for Archimedes' sister . . . ?

"Zenobia," he whispered. "Dear God."

His stunned immobility didn't last long. Always ready for action, he started for the door. Yasmeen scrambled across the bed, found his yellow breeches amid the sheets and flung them in his direction.

He snagged them out of the air and stepped into the legs as he went. "I'll wake the navigator."

"The course to Fladstrand is already laid," she reminded him, yanking her shirt over her head. Where were her boots? She needed five minutes to finish her letter to Scarsdale and send the express. "Tell Vashon to pull up our tether and push the engines to full steam. Archimedes?"

He paused at the door, looked back.

"What will it take for Bilson to break?"

"He won't." His gaze was flat. "And if it needs to be done, I'll do it. But I'm not sure it will matter whether we find his breaking point. If he has Zenobia, he's already found mine."

And Yasmeen's. Not just because she was Archimedes' sister—the woman was her friend, too.

"Will he hurt her?"

"He wouldn't have to. He just needs to send her to New Eden."

Sweet heavens. "Who would take her?"

"Someone who'd accept money to go, but who wasn't good enough to get away."

Goddammit. That smug bastard had all but told them how he would do it. She shook her head, saw the same anger on Archimedes' face . . . and the same fear.

"We'll get her back," she told him. "We will."

Grimly, he nodded. "Either that or I'll die trying."

Then they were definitely getting Zenobia back—because Yasmeen would kill everyone in their way before letting *that* happen.

It was late afternoon when *Lady Nergüi* flew into Fladstrand. Yasmeen didn't bother to stop at the harbor, but sailed through the town, stopping directly over Zenobia's home.

Archimedes slid down the rope ladder first, with Yasmeen close behind. Zenobia's orange three-level house stood between two identical buildings, all of them painted in bright colors. Though he didn't visit as often as he'd have liked, Archimedes loved her home, loved watching her put on a display of irritation every time he shoved his loud and ridiculous life into her practical, quiet one.

Now dread weighed heavy in his chest as he let himself in. The house was cold, the air already stale. The express they'd sent the previous night lay unopened, untouched since being shoved beneath the door that morning. He found a note on her writing desk.

Archimedes,

It seems that I am to embark on an unexpected holiday to New Eden. Please do not follow me. I have always wanted an adventure of my own. If anyone threatens you, please kill them as usual. Don't stop to chat.

Your doting sister,
Zenobia

P.S. Lady Lynx and the Damned Deceitful Dolt

Dolt? His sister was far better at ripping a man's character apart than that banal insult suggested.

"They must have been rushing her," he murmured. "Or she was terrified."

Beside him, Yasmeen nodded, her mouth a flat line. "The maids are gone, too."

More people to bring back—but he was glad Zenobia wasn't alone. "We use codes in our letters, sometimes. She didn't in this one, so she must not have known the name of the airship."

"Someone at the harbor will tell us. Fladstrand's too small for a strange airship to go unnoticed."

"Her letter includes today's date." Perhaps early that morning—before Archimedes' express had arrived. Bilson must have sent a message to his mercenaries soon after he'd been invited to dinner aboard *Lady Nergüi*. "Can we catch up to them?"

Her hesitation told him before she did. "Only if we know their exact heading."

That heading would be south, Archimedes knew. But only a degree's difference could mean a separation of hundreds of miles by the time they'd traveled the same distance—and the bastards were already at least twelve hours ahead of them.

They'd soon be farther ahead. *Lady Nergüi* wasn't prepared for a long journey. They didn't yet have the necessary fuel and food, or the equipment needed to infiltrate New Eden. That twelve-hour lead would be thirty-six hours or more before they were ready to follow Zenobia.

Yasmeen touched his arm. "We need to go."

Yes, they did. Zenobia's note in hand, he started for the door. "How long before we're in England?"

"Tomorrow morning."

And the express letters she'd sent from Port Fallow would be arriving in London any moment now. "Will the Blacksmith's people have time to make the autogyros?"

"For as much as we offered to pay his smithy? Yes."

No. Archimedes' jaw tightened. The Blacksmith wouldn't jump at anyone's command, not even for money. She must have been owed a favor, and no one called in the Blacksmith's favors lightly.

For Zenobia's sake, he couldn't ask Yasmeen to reconsider that course . . . not that she would if he did.

Her gaze swept the gray sky when they stepped outside. Steel had hardened her eyes; no man looking at her would have imagined she had any weak points, any softness. Yet here he stood, a vulnerability exposed and used against her.

Truthfully? I don't like it at all.

Archimedes liked it even less. Though strong, he was her soft belly.

Would she resent him for that?

God, the thought gutted him. He knew she wouldn't abandon him for this . . . but perhaps it would be the start of regret. Losing one ship had hurt her so much, more than she probably admitted to herself. What if, in their search for Zenobia, she lost another?

He couldn't let it happen. He'd find his sister.

But he wouldn't risk losing Yasmeen in the process.

Every airship captain who made runs around the bottom knew to avoid Madagascar in the southern spring. New Eden didn't often come within sight of the Horde-occupied island, but the steam-powered flyers traded with the merchants there. Those flyers didn't have a long range. Wherever they roamed, New Eden couldn't be far away.

And as soon as Yasmeen told Mrs. Fortescue their destination, it was obvious that the navigator thought that New Eden could never be far enough away. Her face was pale as she unrolled maps across Yasmeen's desk and began plotting the course. Usually bold and flirtatious, now she was quiet, and within minutes she'd gnawed away the rosy stain on her lips. Beside her, Vashon's tension was less visible, but still apparent in the set of her jaw, and the uncertain glances she cast at Yasmeen's face, as if wondering whether she'd just signed on with a madwoman.

Fuck uncertainty. This ended now.

A crew that didn't trust their captain was as worthless as a crew *she* didn't trust. But goddammit, she'd been tested as they had. She didn't rely on her reputation aboard her own ship—and in five months, she'd led them through dangers that other mercenaries wouldn't have survived. She had no more time for this. They would trust her to do her duty by them, or they could stay behind.

She pinned her new quartermaster with a hard stare. "Would you have signed that contract if you knew we'd be heading straight for New Eden?"

At the table, Archimedes looked up from a journal, where he'd been searching for a colleague's account of William Bushke before the man had built New Eden. His emerald eyes were haunted—guilt and worry were weighing on him. Earlier, they'd eaten a quiet dinner, and for the first time, the silence hadn't been comfortable, or filled with more pleasurable activities. No, it had simply been too difficult to laugh or smile when they'd both been sliced open at the gut by Zenobia's abduction.

Vashon cleared her throat. "Honestly, ma'am?"

"Yes."

"I wouldn't have. But now that I'm aboard your airship, I'll stick with her."

Yasmeen turned her attention to the navigator. "And you, Mrs. Fortescue?"

"I'm still thinking about it, ma'am." Agitation had darkened the woman's plump cheeks, but she held herself calmly. "You're . . . well, you're the notorious Lady Corsair. I know your reputation, and I've seen you wriggle us out of tight spots. And I knew this job meant that I'd be picking up a sword or a gun and using them; I knew I might die on these decks. But I can't say I ever saw myself spending the rest of my life farming in a city in the sky."

A fate worse than death, for some. Yasmeen couldn't blame them for thinking so—she'd have felt the same way.

She couldn't blame them. But she'd be damned before ever abandoning a ship and crew in the wake of such fears. If anyone would rather leave her lady, good riddance to them.

"We'll arrive in Medway tomorrow, Mrs. Fortescue. You have until that time to decide."

"Whether to leave?" She appeared briefly horrified. "It's true I wouldn't like farming, but there's no question. I'll stay, ma'am."

Good. But *all* of them needed to decide by then. Yasmeen

looked to Vashon. "Call all hands on deck. Not just the aviators—everyone. Now."

"Yes, ma'am."

As she turned, Yasmeen said, "I'll see you up top, Mrs. Fortescue."

The navigator nodded and made a hasty exit.

Yasmeen drew a deep breath, then threw back her shoulders. She buckled her jacket, straightened her sash.

"Are you primping?"

Archimedes sounded amused. A glance at his face told her that he wasn't.

"I'm giving them the choice to go," she said.

"Why?"

Because they'd be less likely to change their minds later or to refuse her orders. Because she'd have to kill anyone who did.

"I wouldn't, if this was my old crew." Or even if she'd had more time with this one. "I knew they'd follow me anywhere and without hesitation. Even if they thought I was mad, they'd trust me to pull through. My old crew . . ." Her throat tightened. "My old crew isn't here."

He came to her, caught her face between his hands. "I'm so sorry, Yasmeen."

It wasn't his fault. But she knew that trying to talk him out of that guilt would be useless. She tried to smile—and when she failed, tried to make him smile. "I want Zenobia back, too. Who else would immortalize my adventures? And I still have to convince her to pay me fifty percent in royalties."

The tilt of his lips didn't last long, and the humor never reached his eyes. "What will you tell them about Bilson?"

"Not that he's hiding a device that can kill you and Anisa Stoker," she said. "I'll have to frame his presence in another way."

"One that explains why you shot him."

"Ah, yes. I forgot about that."

Not truly, but she might as well have. Finding the device mattered. Zenobia mattered. When Bilson finally awoke from his opium-induced sleep, Archimedes and she would have to deal with the man . . . but he didn't matter.

She looked up at Archimedes, saw the torment on his face.

Though she knew he wouldn't let go of this guilt easily, she had to try. "Stop blaming yourself for this."

"Oh, I've progressed to blaming him." His smile was short-lived, and that tortured regret appeared again. Softly, he added, "But you shouldn't be forced into this. I'll hire another airship at Medway. I'll go after Zenobia alone."

He wasn't joking. Yasmeen stared at him. She wanted to laugh, but each word resounded in her ears, squeezed painfully at her heart. A sense of unreality descended; she shook her head, trying to clear it. "I'm having difficulty deciding whether I'm moved or offended by that suggestion."

"Moved," he said. "I love you. I can't bear to risk you. And I can't bear being the reason you might lose your crew."

She would hate it, too. But by the lady, she hated this suggestion more, and as the sense of unreality lifted, she wasn't moved or offended. She was *hurt*. He'd wounded her so easily. So carelessly.

"You know everything I am," she said, and hated the strain in her voice, the betraying tremble. "For *me* to let you go alone to New Eden, I would have to be the same person that you are under the influence of that device."

"God, no." He reached for her. "Yasmeen—"

She pulled away. If he touched her now, it would be too much. She had to shut it all away, to steel her heart, or begin weeping, sobbing . . . directly before speaking to her crew. They wouldn't follow her anywhere.

She wouldn't blame them.

His voice raw, Archimedes tried again. "Yasmeen, I just want to protect—"

"Don't. Don't even suggest it." She drew her dagger, held it out to him. "You might as well take this blade and shove it through my heart now."

He didn't take it. Of course he didn't. He hadn't meant to hurt her. She *knew* that . . . but knowing meant nothing compared to the growing ache in her chest, the tightness of her throat. She had to go up top and pretend this pain didn't exist. Had to pretend she wasn't terrified that half her crew would decide she wasn't worth following, and leave.

She paused at the door. Perhaps it was weak, but she needed this from him now. "You'd be risking Zenobia by hiring someone else. Someone not as good. Do you want that, instead?"

He closed his eyes. "No."

Then Yasmeen could hold on to that, at least.

You know everything I am.

God, he did. Bred to guard Horde royalty, she'd grown up expecting to have her very *life* tethered to one person, to guard them or die trying. She'd escaped that life and made her own, but she hadn't discarded everything from her training—she'd said that falling in love had been like tethering to him; her life was bound to his now. She took pride in standing beside him, protecting him . . . just as he did in standing by her.

He'd known all that—and he'd made a mess of it. He'd wanted to see her safe, and slapped at her pride and heart, instead.

But he couldn't repair the damage right away. He could only stand beside her now.

On the main deck, everyone aboard had gathered amidships. The aviators had clustered in front, the engineers and senior crew to starboard, and the others scattered in between. Thirty men and woman—plus five girls and two boys. He knew their names now, most of their stories.

Yasmeen took the quarterdeck. Behind her, steam billowed in great clouds—the boilers at full, but the engines quiet for the next few minutes. The wind wafted thick tendrils of mist around the balloon, as if they were floating backward through a heavy fog. Archimedes stepped onto the quarterdeck, took his place behind her. Perhaps she didn't want him there now; he didn't know. It wouldn't have mattered, anyway. Even if she put a knife to his throat and told him to go, he'd never do anything but stand with her.

It was impossible to judge her reaction. Her expression appeared colder, harder than he'd seen in months—flint and steel, an angry fire waiting to be struck. The aviators quieted. Yasmeen's voice carried over them.

"I am putting to rest the speculation that has run rampant aboard this ship since last evening, when I shot our passenger,

Mr. Bilson—speculation that has increased since our hasty departure for Fladstrand this morning."

She paused, as if in silent reprimand for their gossiping. Archimedes knew that she thought such speculations were to be expected, and mostly harmless. She only ever squashed rumors if they threatened to disrupt the order aboard her ship—and typically, the quartermaster or the mates squashed them, first. But she couldn't mention their speculation without also correcting it, even if that correction lasted only the space of a breath.

A few aviators squirmed. That seemed to satisfy her. "Some of you remember Miss Zenobia Fox, who traveled with us from England to Fladstrand this spring. She is Mr. Fox's sister, and the author of the Archimedes Fox adventures—and now the Lady Lynx adventures, as well. Last night, we discovered that Mr. Bilson had arranged her kidnap."

A murmur passed through the gathered crew, a swelling of outrage and excitement. This demanded action, adventure—and undoubtedly, a fine reward. For many of them, this was probably what they'd hoped to find aboard her airship, and within a few months, she'd served it to them in spades. Escorting pilgrims to Mecca over Horde-occupied lands, encountering airship pirates in Venice and off the shores of the Canary Islands, carrying sharkhunters to the southern tip of the Americas, scouting for rebels in Castile, an unexpected run-in with smugglers at the Hapsburg Wall. Yes, they'd had adventures—enough even for Archimedes.

"Miss Fox has been taken to New Eden," Yasmeen said. "*Lady Nergüi* is going after her."

The excitement turned to disbelief. A discontented muttering began, heads turning as if they were all confirming what they'd heard.

Yasmeen held up her hand. Instant silence fell. "I recognize that to many of you, New Eden is a risk you wouldn't want to take. That any airship wouldn't take. And that you'd think any captain who tried is a fool."

She said what they wouldn't dare to . . . not where she might hear. Clever. On any vessel, whispers in the dark were the most dangerous. She brought it into the open.

And smashed it. "I'm not a fool. I don't plan to fly *Lady Nergüi* near to New Eden, but only close enough to enter the city in another way. There is a risk, however, and you have until tomorrow at noon to decide whether you'll leave this ship. If so, you'll walk away with a full month's wages and a season's share in your purse." Her cold gaze swept over them. "Let me be clear. New Eden poses no more threat than the Coiling Straits, the wall, or anywhere over Horde territory. There will *always* be danger aboard this ship. If you can't face New Eden, then you aren't suited for any other dangers we face—and you aren't suited for my lady's crew."

A brief quiet fell, filled only by the sound of hissing steam and the wind. After a moment, Vashon spoke up. "I don't need to wait until tomorrow, Captain. I'm with you."

Fortescue and a few others nodded their agreement. Archimedes looked to the first mate. The quartermaster's word had some weight, but not as much as she would have if she'd been aboard a longer time. His friend had that weight, but he wasn't throwing it around yet. Longcock regarded the captain in silence as the mutters and declarations of loyalty swelled around them.

Yasmeen held up her hand, quieting them again. "Tomorrow," she repeated. "Make certain this decision is your own."

Longcock cleared his throat. "Captain?"

"Mr. Longcock."

"I'm with you. But as the others make their decision, I'm certain there's one thing in particular they'd like to know: If those flyers come for us, will you let them take us in or blow us up?"

"I'll surrender," she said.

Surprise slapped Archimedes; he stared at her, wishing he could read her expression. Beyond her, the aviators' heads turned again, their faces uncertain. They hadn't expected that from her. *He* hadn't expected that from her.

She continued, "Then I'll kill William Bushke and destroy his flyers, untether my lady from the city, and get us the hell out of there."

Ah. That was more like he'd expected. Thank God she was never boring about it.

Pursing his lips, Longcock nodded. "That sounds all right to me," he said.

She couldn't lose him like this, she couldn't lose him—

Yasmeen woke up, gasping, sweating. Gray, predawn light filtered through the portholes. Through a blur of tears, she searched for Archimedes. He lay beside her—and even in his sleep, he wore a troubled frown.

Not just worried for Zenobia, she knew. Worried for her, too.

She understood that fear, though she hadn't always. She wasn't accustomed to being terrified for the people she loved. Hurting for them. Steeling herself against that pain and fear was the only solution now, the only way to get through this without losing her friend, her crew, her ship . . . and her husband, too. But she couldn't steel herself against him, however much Archimedes might believe she had.

By the lady, she couldn't bear to lose him—and was almost afraid of the lengths she'd go to, making certain she didn't.

The sound of the engines changed, slower, throatier. No longer driving at full bore. She felt the slight shift in their speed, the adjustment in their course. They were coming into Medway, then.

Turning toward Archimedes, she wiped the sweat and tears from her face. When they'd gone to sleep early that morning, there'd been distance between them. No anger, nothing hot— simply exhaustion and weariness. Now she was cold.

She curled against him, her back to his chest. Gingerly, she bent her legs, trying to loosen her knees without disturbing him. He might sleep yet. After discovering that *The Kite*—a mercenary skyrunner captained by Olaf Berge—had flown into Fladstrand early the previous morning, they'd spent most of the night bent over the desk with the senior crew and department heads, confirming inventory and drawing up lists of provisions. All of it would need to be secured and stowed today, stuffing her lady to the deckheads. Most of the expanded cargo hold would be filled with the extra coal they'd need; they'd burn up some on the journey, but it was impossible to

know how long they'd be circling Madagascar or venturing
farther into the Eastern Ocean, looking for the balloon city.

Perhaps luck would be with them, and it wouldn't take
more than a week or two . . . but it might take months. They
could restock their supplies in Australia, but a wide expanse
of ocean and Horde territory lay between here and there. Yasmeen didn't want to run out of fuel and depend on the wind to
bring them in, or risk fishing for sustenance in kraken-infested
waters.

The stiffness in her knees subsided—not enough, but she
couldn't lie abed. Not when there was so much to do. With a
sigh, she sat up.

Archimedes' callused hand slid over her thigh. His head
lifted, his hair a gold-streaked jumble, his eyes still heavy.
"Yasmeen?"

"Sleep. I have to meet with Scarsdale."

"I'll come."

"No." She pressed her palm to his chest, prevented him
from sitting up. Her refusal hurt him, she saw. But she was
afraid of hurting him more if she didn't work through the tangle of emotions that had been tying them up since Bilson had
activated that device.

"Yasmeen." He caught her hand, held it against his heart.
Regret deepened the emerald in his eyes. "What I said about
hiring someone else, that wasn't meant to hurt you."

"I know." And she also knew that he wanted to unravel this
tangle, too. Something wasn't right between them—and somehow, that fucked over everything else. But she couldn't see
what it was yet. She needed to clear her head, to look with new
eyes.

Slowly, she slid from the bed, turning back to collect her
silver cigarillo case from the pillow. His gaze followed her,
and she couldn't bear the torment in his face. Bending, she
kissed him. "I know," she repeated.

He nodded, pulled her down for another sweet kiss. When
he released her, his grin was familiar, perfect. "Remember
that when you're with your fancy earl."

"But he has such fashionable waistcoats."

"Fashionable? How boring."

Yasmeen had to agree—and because she wanted to keep

Archimedes close, she pulled on one of his shirts. Too big, but it carried his wonderful scent. She expected a comment, but when she looked away from the wardrobe, he was watching her with a frown.

"You're all but hobbling, Mrs. Fox. You ought to have loosened up on me."

Oh, but she'd have loved to. Riding him slowly, taking him deep. "Perhaps tomorrow, Mr. Fox."

"Perhaps tonight," he said.

"I won't be stiff then."

"Scowl at me over dinner, and I will be."

She grinned and shook her head, before covering her hair with a red silk kerchief and tying the ends. When she glanced back at him, his gaze had unfocused. Lost in thought.

"What is it?"

He shook his head. "It's all too expected."

"What is?"

"Bilson using Zenobia."

Expected? "It surprised us yesterday."

"Only because the device threw us into a spin. We expected him to go for her—we sent her that express."

"He knows what matters to you. That's not a surprise. It was clever."

"Ah!" he exclaimed, as if whatever idea had been forming in his head seemed to come together. "It *is* clever. But only until we rescue her and Joseph from New Eden. Then . . ."

"We kill him."

"Unless she was never there."

Ah. "*That* would be clever," she agreed. "We fly to New Eden after her, only to find that it was all a ruse. Then he doesn't reveal her true location until we take him and his brother back to civilization."

And the more she considered it, the more sense it made. Bilson and his mercenaries couldn't know where New Eden was with any more accuracy than Yasmeen did. In all possibility, *Lady Nergüi* would find the floating city long before *The Kite* did.

"Yes," Archimedes said. "But it doesn't help us now. We wouldn't know the truth until we were there."

No, they wouldn't. If Bilson claimed that he'd sent Zenobia

to New Eden, and then—under threat of torture—admitted that he'd tried to fool them, they still wouldn't know whether he was telling them what they wanted to hear simply to stop the torment.

And he would still be playing some sort of game. "He can't be holding all of the strings," Yasmeen said.

"He has the strings." With a broad grin, Archimedes leaned back on the pillows, arms folded behind his head. "But I have iron balls and a silver tongue . . . and a fortune."

Oh, but she loved it when he was cocky. It was Archimedes Fox's version of her blades and claws. She narrowed her eyes. "And?"

"We'll play along . . . and call his bluff. If Berge has Zenobia aboard *The Kite*, they're likely waiting for word from Bilson. But if we're supposed to be searching for New Eden, they can't know how long they'll be waiting."

She caught on. "And they would need supplies. They'd need a place to collect messages."

"But we can't wait for an answer—not unless we find that device. So we'll have to fly south, let Bilson think it's all happening just as he planned." He paused. "Would Scarsdale be willing to send the word out, and then send any reply to us?"

"Oh, yes. I'll arrange it with him now." The turnabout might take several weeks to come to fruition, but she was already anticipating Bilson's dismay. Grinning, she buckled her jacket. "In the meantime, the autogyros ought to arrive by midmorning. Will you see that they are properly loaded?"

"You realize I won't be able to resist taking one up?"

Yes. "They'll need to be tested, anyway. Take Longcock, see if they handle the weight. We'll have the maids with us, remember."

"I will."

"And if any of the aviators decide to leave—"

"I'll kill them."

She laughed, shook her head. "No. Send them to the steward for their pay and papers. I should return shortly before noon, so I'll be available if anyone needs to have a word with me before making their decision."

Archimedes frowned. "You'll let them question you?"

"No. If they're still undecided, I'd rather they go. So if they come to me with doubts, I'll push them along."

His eyes narrowed. "Do *you* have doubts?"

In her ability to captain this ship? Not at all. In her ability to rescue Zenobia from New Eden, if necessary? Not many. Yasmeen believed they *would* be successful. But there were always risks. "Realistically, I have to recognize that there's a chance I might fail."

"Well, I don't have any doubts," he said smugly. "Not one."

"That's because you've never approached anything with an attitude that resembled 'realistic.'"

"It's true." He grinned. "That's why you love me."

"Perhaps." Slowly, her gaze slipped over the hard expanse of his chest, the lean muscles of his stomach, the breadth of his shoulders. "But that's not the only reason, Mr. Fox."

His laughter followed her to the door, and Yasmeen couldn't stop smiling. Whatever had been tangled between them had begun to loosen, and already she felt lighter.

Archimedes suddenly stopped laughing. "Are those my daggers in your boots?"

"Mine." Her fingers wrapped around the red handles. "Unless you know a good reason for me to give them back?"

"I'll run after you naked, exposing myself to all of your crew until you return them."

"I asked for a *good* reason."

"They match my favorite waistcoat."

She flicked the tails of her red silk kerchief over her shoulders, then tucked her fingers into the crimson sash at her waist.

He swore. "I *will* have them back, Mrs. Fox."

"I'll enjoy seeing you try, Mr. Fox."

She was still smiling as she came onto the main deck. The sky was dreary, clouded. Drizzle pattered against the metal fabric of the envelope. The deck crew was already busy, readying the airship to take on the extra supplies. With the coal heavy in her lady's belly, she wouldn't fly as quickly, but she was fleet and the engines at her heart were strong. Even weighed down, she'd still make fine time on their journey south.

Her knees had loosened up a bit more, but Yasmeen

descended on the cargo lift rather than risk the rope ladder. The steward had been busy; crates of supplies were already stacking up at her mooring station. The boards were slippery with rain. The naval docks at Medway were never quiet—but never as chaotic as unregulated harbors. Yasmeen hailed a passing cab. The steamcoach driver peered at her through the gray morning light, then blinked hard when recognition set in. She saw his brief moment of panic and indecision before waving her into the rattling carriage. Yasmeen grinned as she climbed in. Her reputation extended far, and still produced the response that she'd wanted.

She had earned that reputation, often lived up to it, and had carefully nurtured the barroom stories of her more ruthless deeds . . . because it was far easier and less time-consuming to let fear deter the majority of the idiots who might attempt to cross her than to actually deal with them.

That reputation would change, she knew. With Archimedes at her side, with Lady Lynx circulating two sides of an ocean, that change was inevitable.

But she didn't yet know what sort of change that would be—or the effect that change would have. Bilson might be one indication of it. Instead of fearing her, idiots might attempt to take advantage of her feelings for Archimedes.

Why didn't that bother her as much as it should have?

She cared that someone might threaten Archimedes; she didn't care whether anyone knew she loved him, even though her reputation could burn on that one detail.

But she didn't care if it did . . . and she couldn't fathom it. For years, she'd labored to prevent vulnerabilities from softening her reputation. Why did it matter so little now? Her reaction was the opposite of what she'd expected of herself— and what Archimedes had expected of her, too.

Perhaps that was the root of the tangle. They'd both expected that her response would be different, and they'd both been reacting as if it had been. Because she *should* have cared.

How odd that she didn't.

The steamcoach rumbled to a stop in front of Medway's finest inn. Yasmeen flipped a coin to the driver and made her way to the door, where an automaton butler welcomed her in. God. These things were all the rage in the New World, but though its hat-taking skills and wax-recorded greeting were impressive, it slowed the normal speed of an entrance down a bit.

Beyond the entryway, the dining room bustled with activity. Well-dressed travelers laughed and chatted, all of them surrounded by an air of expectation. Obviously, none of them were headed to New Eden. A smiling woman in a sensible black dress and widow's cap approached Yasmeen—the hotelier, she assumed.

"Which is Lord Scarsdale's room?"

The woman's gaze flicked up to Yasmeen's kerchief, traveled down to her boots. Her pleasant expression froze in place. "Lady Corsair, how lovely of you to call. I will be happy to notify his lordship that you've arrived."

"Don't notify him." The man was likely too drunk to wake easily; she'd be waiting until afternoon for a reply. "He's expecting me. Just tell me where his room is."

"I'm afraid I can't—"

Yasmeen smiled.

The woman stuttered to a stop. Flustered and wringing her hands, she said, "He's upstairs, ma'am. The third door on the left."

"Thank you."

The stairs made her wish that she'd spent the minutes in the steamcoach massaging her knees. Scarsdale's door wasn't locked—and no surprise there. His quarters smelled like an absinthe factory. She found him facedown on the bed. The poor bastard hadn't even managed to get his boots off before passing out.

An ewer sat on the dressing table. She dipped her fingers inside. The water was cold. Freezing would have been better, but this would do.

At the sound of footsteps, she looked over her shoulder. Wearing a nightgown and a long floppy cap, Scarsdale's valet was attempting to creep up behind her, a chamber pot raised high.

He froze with his arms straight over his head. His nightgown had lifted with the movement, exposing knobby knees. "Captain! It is so very good to see you."

Better than bashing her skull in, at least. "What time did he fall asleep?"

"I'm not certain. He sent me to bed an hour after midnight." The valet tsked, setting down the pot and stepping forward, his gaze fixed on Scarsdale's boots. "The poor dear."

Yasmeen dumped the ewer over the poor dear's head.

Sputtering, Scarsdale reared up, batting wildly at his hair, pushing the sodden brown strands away from his eyes. Bloodshot, they focused on her. "Blast you!"

"Darling," she purred, and tossed him a towel. "You look horrible."

"I look fantastic." He scrubbed at his face, then stopped to weave as if the vigorous moment had unbalanced him. Still, he managed to add, "As always."

"I wake up next to 'fantastic' every day. You're not even within leagues of him right now."

"You've only yourself to blame. You bring me to Medway, Yasmeen? Good God. What is here but sailors and an oddities fair? This atmosphere sucks the life from a man, drains him dry, and the only thing to do is drink. You ought to have had the sense of meeting with me in Brighton."

"Where supplies cost twice as much?"

He laughed suddenly. "Ah, well. That explains the price of my upcoming nuptials. I ought to have insisted on them taking place in Medway instead of Brighton. We could drink together, you and I."

His marriage. Goddammit. So he *was* going through with it.

Maybe. "If you drink enough, it'll be much easier to abduct you."

"Is that your plan—to spirit me away aboard your lady?" He pressed his hand to his stomach, as if queasy. He probably was, and not just because of the drink. Heights terrified him. Even now, the shades over the windows were drawn—not to keep out the light, but so that he wouldn't see the view from the second floor. "I'd rather be married."

No, he wouldn't. "Break it off. The people on your father's estates don't need you. They managed well enough alone for two hundred years."

"They were under the boot of the Horde for two hundred years," he said dryly.

"And the aristocracy is different?"

"It's not tyranny."

Yasmeen thought that everything but willing service was tyranny of some sort. "So you will swoop in and take back what they have earned, and the people on your lands have no choice in the matter."

"Neither do I."

Fair enough—and there was little more to be said. He would no more abandon the responsibilities of his station than she would her crew. But if this marriage would be hell, she would never abandon him to it. "Do you like her, at least?"

"Yes." He sighed. "I like her very well. I will be content, Yasmeen."

That couldn't be enough—but that wasn't her decision to make. "No kidnapping, then? Perhaps it's for the best, since Zenobia Fox has just been abducted and taken to New Eden."

Scarsdale froze. "What do you say? I thought you were after somebody's brother."

"We were at her home only yesterday. She'd been taken by Berge on *The Kite* as an added incentive to the brother's rescue." At the sideboard, Yasmeen poured him another drink. Zenobia and Scarsdale had become good friends the previous winter, inseparable in each other's company. If Zenobia was not secretly as romantic-minded as her brother, it might have been a practical match. "We're off to New Eden as soon as the supplies are aboard my lady. Did you speak with the Blacksmith?"

Slowly coming out of his shock, he took the brandy. "Yes. I saw the autogyros loaded into the locomotive car. So you truly are attempting this madness?"

"Yes."

"I'll come with you."

Despite his terror, he offered. A finer friend was difficult to find. "I need you here. Archimedes and I think her kidnap is nothing but a bluff to ensure Bilson's return."

She didn't have to say more. Even drunk, Scarsdale was always shrewd. He nodded. "What do you want me to do?"

"Lure the mercenaries out. Use the newssheets to advertise our offer. And we'll need to know as quickly as possible if that offer is accepted."

"And if it's not?"

"Then their lives are forfeit. Archimedes and I will hunt them down—and you can add that to the advertisement, as well. Use our names, so that the word spreads. A full-page advert ought to do it."

"If it doesn't, they're complete fools."

"Yes. I also need you to arrange the hire of a fleet to search for them, and give a reward to anyone who locates *The Kite* and relays our offer to Berge." If the advertisement didn't bring them in, the promise of a fortune would. "Fifty livre for finding him and delivering the message, and fifty more if Berge takes the one hundred we're offering to him in the newssheets."

"One hundred? You won't need to hire the fleet. Berge will bring himself in for that."

"He'd cut off his own cock for that. The fleet and the reward are to ensure that he learns about the offer as quickly as possible." Yasmeen poured her own drink. "And you have to promise to come for us if we don't return within six months."

Scarsdale burst into laughter and lifted his glass in a toast. "And so here is the real reason you contacted me. You want me to send in a rescue if it all goes to hell."

Only part of the reason. "Yes."

"Ah, well. I'm glad it's you that's going, then. It means a rescue won't be necessary. Bring that portfolio in the trunk, would you, Hopkins?" He rose from the bed as the valet disappeared into the adjoining room and returned with a leather-bound sketchbook. "On that table, that's fine. I've drawn the layout of the city for you, as requested. But remember, Yasmeen, this was more than a decade ago. He's added more ships since then."

She joined him at the table. "That's all right. The arrangement is probably the same in essentials."

"Probably. Have you seen the city?"

"Only from a distance." It had only been a spot against the horizon, and that had been close enough.

"It's larger than you will expect. Frankly, I was astonished by its breadth, and it can only be bigger now." He opened to the first sketch, a roughly circular overhead view of the city.

His forefinger traced a large ring in the center. "These are the primary gardens. At the aft edge—"

"Aft?" The city was round. "Where's the bow?"

He pointed to the farthest edge of the city, where he'd written "Bushke" in neat letters. "The city can fly in any direction—but typically, it flies with his quarters at its head."

"All right." It made sense. Using his quarters as a reference would be the simplest way to navigate around the city. "At the aft edge of the garden is . . . ?"

"Where new arrivals are taken until they're indoctrinated. Then they're married off and receive their own living section in one of the outlying ships."

So if Bilson wasn't bluffing, that's where Zenobia would be. "Under guard?"

"Two citizen volunteers, very lightly armed."

"Then who has the heavy arms?"

"Bushke's guard. Thirty to thirty-five men, and they're fanatically loyal—they have to be. They're the pilots on the flyers."

And if they weren't loyal, they'd simply use the flyers to escape. "And their watch?"

"Is around the clock."

"The best way in?"

"From underneath." He showed her another page, more roughly sketched and labeled with "hanger shed," "engines," "boiler," and "stoker quarters." Twenty flower-like symbols denoted the propellers. "This is the second level of the city, constructed on the framework that stabilizes the airships. There's the surface and the gardens on the upper decks, the living quarters within the airship cabins and holds—and then this, below the ships. We didn't see much of it from below, so the placement is an estimate, at best."

They'd adjust as needed. "Why is this best?"

"It's all open, for the most part. They've enclosed the quarters, the engines, and the hangar. The rest is just a framework of metal struts with access to the propeller shafts—and access to the surface levels."

Her gaze sharpened on the sketch. He hadn't marked any notable access points. "Where?"

"Everywhere. When they tether the ships together, their bowed sides don't align perfectly. And there's a cushion of space between the hulls to prevent them from smashing into each other during a storm. Most of those gaps are covered over, but there are many left open and used to dispose rubbish or to lower the fishing nets. Some lead down to the lower levels, too, and they have guards. But you won't find a guard on a rubbish hole."

Brilliant. The autogyros were quiet; they could fly up beneath New Eden in the dark, and be inside a few minutes later. She was almost sorry that Bilson was likely bluffing, and that she *wouldn't* be infiltrating the city this way. After she told Archimedes about it, she thought he'd have loved a shot at it, too.

"Thank you, James."

"It's nothing." Scarsdale closed his eyes, rubbed his forehead. "Truly, nothing. It's easy to get into the city—getting away from it is another matter. Do you have a plan for that?"

"No good one yet, but we probably won't build a glider."

His smile was pained. "As long as you don't let Trahaearn build it, you'll likely do better than we did."

He'd survived, so he hadn't done too badly—but it had been exactly the wrong time for Scarsdale to survive. A few years earlier, his lover had been killed by hunters who'd deemed them less than men. Scarsdale had sought his own death after that, aligning himself with Trahaearn, a pirate who seemed bound to die in fiery blaze.

But when they'd been taken aboard New Eden and the glider they'd used to escape had fallen apart while they'd still been in the air, Scarsdale hadn't been as ready for death as he'd thought. He'd been terrified of heights since fleeing New Eden. Though still one of the bravest men she knew, he couldn't even climb aboard her airship without being blissed on opium or unconscious with drink.

She'd always been afraid that love would bring her to her knees, destroy everything she'd earned. She'd never wanted it. But she had love now, and she still stood. Stronger, perhaps, than she'd ever stood before.

But *losing* that love . . . Hell, it had brought a man as strong as Scarsdale to his knees. She wouldn't do any better if she lost Archimedes.

She barely did any better simply *thinking* of losing him.

Belatedly, she realized that silence had fallen between them, with Scarsdale's perceptive gaze monitoring her every expression. When she met his eyes, his smile mocked her. "You don't ask about Bushke?"

"I was waiting for you to tell me."

"He's a kindly looking man with an iron fist."

"Literally?"

"No. But it's easy to believe that he's weak, that he'll have mercy."

"Like General Truss." During the Liberé war, even Yasmeen had been uneasy when she'd accepted a job from him. "Or Saint Marie from *Archimedes Fox and the Pearls of Penitence*."

"Yes."

A benevolent tyrant, then—one who never gave his people any choices at all. "Why didn't you or Trahaearn kill him?"

"We meant to. After the glider was ready, we'd formed a plan to enter his quarters from the lower level—one of those access points is connected to the hangar and comes up right beside his ship . . . probably so that he can escape if New Eden is ever attacked. We were in position, we'd gotten past his guard on that entry, but Bushke was called away from his quarters. We had the glider with us; if we'd waited, if anyone had seen us, we'd have missed our opportunity to go."

And killing Bushke hadn't been a priority. She nodded and glanced down at the sketches. "May I take these?"

"You haven't memorized them?" Laughing at her, he shook his head. "I've seen you plan dozens of missions. You've never been this distracted."

Her smile was slight. It was true. Worry gnawed at her, as it never had before. She thought of Archimedes constantly.

"Is it Fox?" He watched her face, and within a moment, astonishment registered on his. "Unbelievable. I thought you were fond of him, at most."

"At most, that's what I should have been. So I declared anything more to be impossible . . . and it seemed that in the next moment, I was full in. He sneaked up on me."

"He seems that sort." Scarsdale's grin betrayed his genuine delight. "And now that your belly is exposed, whatever will you do?"

Ah, Scarsdale. He always got right to the heart of it. "I don't worry about my belly anymore. I worry about him. I didn't know that would happen."

"I'd have told you, but you wouldn't have believed me."

"Probably not," she admitted. Even when she'd first fallen in love with Archimedes, she'd thought she knew what it meant: that she'd have a friend, lover, someone she'd protect and who'd protect her in return. She'd never guessed how necessary he'd become to *everything*. "It's completely different from what I thought it might be."

Completely different from what Archimedes had thought, too. He'd planned to love her, but only until she inevitably broke his heart. They'd stumbled into forever, instead.

"Love, the great disrupter," Scarsdale declared. "It ruins all of our grand schemes, destroys our reputations."

So it had. She supposed that meant it was time to make a new reputation. But as for schemes . . . love hadn't ruined hers.

Bilson's scheme was another matter.

As soon as the newssheets printed that advertisement, Archimedes' play was going to rip that damn game apart.

Archimedes had never paired his crimson waistcoat with his scarlet breeches before, but he had to admit the effect was oddly dashing. He didn't own a red jacket—an oversight that he'd have to correct upon his next visit to the tailor's—but the sun came out midmorning and shirtsleeves became a viable option. He was waiting on deck in all his monochromatic glory when Yasmeen returned. She burst into laughter upon seeing him, and drew the red-handled daggers from her boots.

"I concede defeat," she said.

"No." Not defeated. "Never that."

"All right." She slipped the left dagger back into its sheath. "You have one. I'll keep the other. Between us, we'll have a matching set."

A perfect match. He accepted the blade, still warm from her thigh—and not half as warm as the emotion that moved through him when she smiled.

She looked round the decks, at the crew engaged in their work. "So how goes the sky, Mr. Fox?"

"Well." He walked with her toward the companionway. "We ought to be finished loading by midafternoon. We're only waiting on the second delivery of coal. And how goes your fashionable earl?"

"He sketched New Eden's layout, and gave us a way in—if we need it. The advertisement will be at the printer's tomorrow, and he'll also be directing a fleet of airships to search for *The Kite* around the North Sea, which is Berge's usual territory. He'll find her."

No doubt. But the hint of trouble in her eyes told him there was more. "And how is *he*?"

"Not well. But he hasn't been for years." She stopped at the head of the ladder, reached up to cup his jaw in her palm. Her gaze captured his, saw through him. "It's . . . difficult, loving someone, and fearing you'll lose them. I say I don't like my belly exposed. You say you don't want me with you when you rescue Zenobia. We don't want someone to be hurt, so we try to protect them, and hurt them while we do it. It's irrational."

Irrational, yes. He smiled against her hand. "That's why I'm so good at loving you."

She laughed. "Probably."

"I want you with me, Yasmeen."

"And I'm not sorry my belly is exposed. Perhaps I'm more vulnerable, but it doesn't make me weak. The opposite is true." She lowered her hand, gripped his, and held him tight. "I lost my crew, my ship. I *know* what it is to lose and how much it hurts, and I'll do anything to keep it from happening again. And so being vulnerable now means that I'm far, far more dangerous than I ever was before."

"My God, that's so arousing." Her grin all but finished him off. "You're a cruel woman, to tell me this while in full view of the crew."

With a wicked tilt of her brows, she stepped closer. "You've been fondling your dagger since I came aboard."

"Only because it was still warm from your sheath, Mrs. Fox."

Her laughter faded; intense heat replaced the humor in her

gaze. She inhaled deeply—drawing in his scent, he knew. All a tease, a delicious and exquisitely frustrating one that aroused her, too. Need quickened her breath, made him ache.

"Tonight," he promised softly. "I'll sheathe myself so deep. I'll make you scream."

"By the lady, you'd better," she breathed, then closed her eyes. "Tonight."

He had to force himself to step away, or tonight would begin within minutes at the head of the companionway. Her skin was flushed when she looked at him again, but she was every inch the captain.

"Has Bilson awoken?"

Archimedes nodded. "An hour ago. Still groggy, but mostly healed. He knows he's infected with my strain of nanoagents."

Her gaze turned speculative. "As soon as we're under way, we'll let him out of the stateroom and move about the airship as any passenger might."

Clever. "And hope he speaks to the person with the device?"

"Yes. Longcock and Vashon know to keep an eye on him." She took a deep breath, met his eyes. "How many of the aviators have decided to leave?"

"One, but not because of New Eden."

"Only one?" Astonishment swept across her expression, and a pained emotion that wasn't relief or gratitude, but somewhere in between. She'd thought it would be much worse, he realized. "Who was it? What was the reason?"

"It was Suskind, the third engineer. A letter caught up to him in Port Fallow yesterday, almost six months out. His wife is due to deliver their first child within a week or two now, and when he saw that we were bringing on three months' worth of supplies, he asked for leave."

"God forbid that it takes three months," Yasmeen said softly. "Suskind? Goddammit. They're already short by a shoveler. Has Farnsburrow said how he'll split the third's duties?"

The head engineer hadn't made that decision yet, because he was waiting for Yasmeen's. "I offered to take them."

Yasmeen frowned at him. "You're not trained as a stoker."

"Not for the engines, but under full steam, the third will spend most of his time shoveling coal. If there's a problem with the engines or pipes on my watch, I'll call on Farnsburrow."

"You *can't* be crew."

Because it would upset the order of authority on the ship—where he already possessed an odd standing outside of the normal rankings, as it was. He knew she worried that his presence in the engine room might put Farnsburrow in the awkward position of giving orders to the captain's husband.

"I know," he said. "I've told Farnsburrow that I wouldn't be signing on, just helping out. Just as I've helped out on the deck before. None of the aviators gave me orders when something needed to be done; they gave me directions about how to do it."

It was a small distinction, but an important one. Her frown smoothed and she nodded. "So they did."

"So I'll just be there to help shovel during the third's watch—and I'll need to do it," he added. "We had to disassemble the pugilist machine to make room for the autogyros and the extra coal in the cargo hold. I won't be off this airship for a while, so I might as well sweat at the heart of her."

Her expression didn't soften, but he saw the sudden understanding in her eyes. Books and journals would keep him occupied on this journey, but not enough. "You'll sweat," she said. "Did Farnsburrow tell you the third's hours?"

Two shifts every day, one in the dead of night. He nodded. "I'll survive."

"He might feel obligated to give you the first's hours. Don't let him."

"I won't."

"All right. Your watch starts in thirty minutes, Mr. Fox." Her lips curved as her gaze moved down his length. "You'll probably want to change your clothing before you begin shoveling coal into a furnace for four hours."

He sighed. "The one drawback."

She laughed and started down the ladder. "I suggest you wear the clothes you use to avoid the zombies. They're already black."

*　　*　　*

It didn't matter which clothes he wore. By the middle
of his second shift, he'd stripped down to his breeches, sweating from the heat of the furnace and the exertion, covered in
coal dust and breathing the engine room's thick air, humid
with steam from the boiler. God, he loved it. Though not exciting in the slightest, the work pushed his body harder than the
automaton had. His muscles would pay for it later, he knew,
with soreness and exhaustion—and it would likely take a few
days to become accustomed to this new schedule. During salvaging runs, he often went weeks on little sleep, but the constant threat of zombies kept him alert, aware of everything
around him, and relishing the thrill of every foreign sound.

This offered a different sort of bliss—not from danger, but
of shutting everything out. He stuffed cotton into his ears to
muffle the deafening roar of the engines, and though his sweat
belonged to the furnace, he had his brain to himself for a
stretch of four hours.

His head was never a dull place to be.

Naturally, on that night Yasmeen occupied most of his
thoughts. She was always a surprise to him. The most incredible surprise. And he'd always known that he'd enjoyed a fair
amount of good luck in his life, but her love for him led to an
inescapable truth:

Archimedes Fox was the single luckiest man to ever walk
the Earth.

So it should be written . . . and as soon as they got Zenobia
back, he'd ask her to.

His entire body was pleasantly aching by the end of his
watch, and the hot water from the evaporators washed away
the worst of the dust and sweat. The sound of the engines
slowly quieted as he made his way to the captain's cabin; after
months on the ship, he rarely noticed the constant vibration
through the decks, aside from the moments when they ceased
or resumed.

Yasmeen wasn't in bed. A lantern burned low on the table.
Before his shift had begun, he'd left her on the cushions there,
naked and glistening, her satisfied smile matching the purr
from her chest. Since then, she'd apparently poured herself a

glass of wine and fallen asleep reading Zenobia's latest tale. Half of the pages were stacked neatly on the table, the others turned facedown beside her. Wearing a blue silk wrap, she slept on her side, curled up on the pillows and with her back to the door.

He hated to disturb her, but he would be glad to hold her. Intending to carry her to the bed, he crouched beside her, then paused. She wasn't sleeping easily. A sheen of perspiration covered her forehead. Her fingers twitched. Each breath was a small, sobbing pant.

Another nightmare. He knew they'd come before, but never this often—and he hadn't asked about them, hadn't needed to. She'd been trapped in her cabin while her crew was slaughtered, and still aboard her lady when it had exploded. That ship had been everything to her.

And this was the third night in a row she'd woken from those nightmares . . . beginning when Bilson had activated that damn device, and all but stolen her ship with his demands.

"Yasmeen." His chest tight, he gently stroked the long muscles of her back. He couldn't erase the devastation that caused these dreams, but his touch soothed her. "Yasmeen."

Her eyes flew open, met his, and the shattering fear he saw there undid him. With a harsh denial, he gathered her into his lap. Clinging to him, she buried her face against his throat. Hot tears burned against his skin.

"You won't lose her," he promised roughly. "I swear to you."

She nodded against his neck—then lifted her head, eyes bright and lashes matted. "Her?"

"Lady Nergüi."

Her lips parted, as if in confusion, before suddenly widening in a laugh. "Oh, Mr. Fox. Is that what you expected? These dreams aren't about my losing my lady."

"Your dreams are about me, of course," he agreed. "The *nightmares* are losing her."

"No. They're about losing *you.*"

He wasn't often lost for words. In the silence, she lowered her cheek to his shoulder, slipped her arms around him.

"You won't," he finally managed.

"I *can't.*" Her breath shuddered against his neck. "It's not what I expected, either. A year ago, losing my ship to New Eden was the most painful thing I could imagine. And if *Lady Corsair* ever fell, I swore I'd go down with her. But when the time came, I didn't. It all changed when I lost my crew, when I saw them bleeding on the decks. They were more important to me than my lady was, and avenging them was more important than dying with her. So I don't dream of losing my ship. That's not the worst I can imagine anymore."

Losing him was. Too overcome to speak, Archimedes' arms tightened around her.

"The irrational part of it is that I *should* be dreaming of the explosion. It truly happened, and *Lady Corsair* was destroyed. The zombies breaking that door really happened, too . . . but you were fine. Not even a scratch. And yet, that's what I see over and over. Just the *threat* of losing you terrifies me. You've become more important than everything else: my crew, my ship. Even my own life."

He stiffened. "No. Don't say that."

"I'm not rushing to jump over the side, Archimedes. Trust me when I say that I'll go to frightening lengths to save both of us . . . and I'm truly not certain whether I'd be saving you or myself. It would destroy me to lose you."

His throat closed. Somehow, he rasped, "I'm supposed to be the romantic one."

"Blame your emerald eyes, if you must. I've apparently looked into them for too long." She was smiling as she lifted her face to his, pressed a soft kiss to his lips. "I love you."

He couldn't answer. He captured her mouth instead, and abandoned everything to this kiss. Every promise, every thought, every feeling, they were all hers. Fierce and sweet, she clung to him, her lips tasting of wine and adventure, her hair smelling of tobacco and coconut, simply the most incredible woman God had ever created. By some miracle, she was his—and she was completely and utterly deluded if she truly thought that *anything* would ever take him from her side.

Her skin was flushed when he lifted his head, her breathing as sharp as his.

"You won't lose me," he vowed. "You could throw me off your ship a thousand times, and even if I landed in the mouth of Hell, I'd always come back to you."

Her arms tightened around his shoulders as he rose to his feet, lifting her against his chest. "You have overtaken me as the romantic again."

"If it pleases you, I will be the realist: after the hundredth time, I might come back as a zombie." Her burst of laughter disarmed him. He couldn't maintain a stoic façade. "But I swear to God in Heaven that even if my brains have rotted and my flesh falls from my bones, my heart will still beat for you."

"Your brains are already rotted. You don't have a bit of sense in you."

"You couldn't be more wrong, my captain. I am everything that is sensible." Though almost to the bed, he turned away from it, and started for the desk. "I will show you the solution to your dilemma."

"Which one?"

"Your fear of losing me." He swept aside a map and set her down, her delectable bottom on the desk and her legs dangling over the edge. "It's very simple."

Her eyes narrowed with amusement. "Is it?"

"It is. Here is one solid, undeniable fact: I will never leave your side. So all you have to do is sit here, forever." He hooked the leg of his chair with his booted foot and pulled it close. "I will be right here. You'll see that I'm perfectly safe, and all of your fears will vanish."

He sat in front of her. With a grin, she rested her toes on his knees and let hers fall open. The shadows in the room became his greatest enemy, preventing him from seeing any of the luscious beauty between her thighs. Ah, well. He'd wage war on those shadows with his hands and tongue, instead.

She nudged him with her foot. He dragged his gaze back to her face. "And when I leave the cabin?"

"I'd still be at your side. But the practical solution is, of course, that you would never leave."

"Oh, so practical."

Leaning forward, he placed his hands on her knees. Her eyelashes fell to half-mast, her lips softening, parting. Anticipation. Already hard, his cock stiffened in response. The need to taste her was almost unendurable.

So he endured it, drew it out further. "I could make it easy to stay, too—there's a simple solution for that."

Her voice was low and throaty. "Tell me."

Her command almost broke his control. He pushed at her knees, widening them, making room for his shoulders. *Tell me.* God. He was a man of endless sense and restraint, yet her words sent him toppling over into mindless need. His brain stopped functioning, and his responses piled up and tumbled out, all of them ridiculous.

"I could lock the door."

She dragged her fingertips up the inside of her thigh, into the shadows. "I have a key."

"I could hire a guard to keep you in."

"I'll tear him apart."

God help him, he had to have her. "I'll tie you to the desk."

Not truly, not after the terrified reaction she'd had when he'd held her wrists together, but by God he could barely think of anything else at this point. There was no other practical course but touching her, nothing would make sense but tasting her. He leaned in—then froze as sudden tension shook her legs.

That wasn't just anticipation.

He looked up. Her jaw had set. She stared at him, her eyes glittering with an unreadable emotion. Because he'd mentioned tying her . . . ?

"I wouldn't restrain you." He ran his hands the length of her legs, soothing. "I wouldn't."

She seemed to struggle with her reply—then finally spoke, and surprised him all over again.

"But I want you to," she said.

He hadn't expected that.

Yasmeen hadn't either. And in truth, despite wanting him to do it, she wasn't certain that *she* would be able to . . . but that only made her more determined to try.

Archimedes must have seen her doubt. "I won't."

"You will."

"You don't have to prove anything, Yasmeen." His hands stilled on her knees, his gaze holding hers. The beautiful flush of arousal still darkened his cheekbones. "If it's instinct, that's all there is to it."

Wonderful man. She had nothing to prove to *him*, because he loved her so well. Proving it to herself was another matter. "I won't be ruled by instinct."

"Or any other tyrant?"

He knew her so well. "Yes," she said, but when he rose and moved to the wardrobe, retrieving two of her long silk kerchiefs, she couldn't stop the shaking that suddenly overcame her. Heart pounding, she imagined them tightening around her wrists, holding her immobile—

He paused, watching her face. "Yasmeen?"

"Just my legs." She could bear that more easily than her hands. Even tied to the desk, she could shoot, she could throw a dagger, she could rip and tear. "This first time."

His jaw tightened. "There won't be another time."

Perhaps not. He'd touched her hundreds of times, thousands—but knowing that he would tie her, it took all of her control not to push him away when he sat again and clasped her right ankle, gently drawing her foot toward the desk's leg. Her ankle touched smooth wood. She trembled.

He closed his eyes, clenched his teeth. *"Yasmeen."*

"Do it."

She had to gasp out the order, then hold herself still when she felt the light tug of silk. He sat back, his expression tormented.

"It's done."

And so loosely tied that if she pulled at the bindings even a bit, the knot would fall apart. Yasmeen stared down at the slack loop around her ankle. It was not restraining her at all; to stay bound, *she* would have to hold her leg immobile. In truth, she was restricted by nothing but her own determination to stay that way.

Perhaps that was for the best, this time. "The other leg now."

He didn't move. With a sigh, she slid her left leg toward the corner of the desk, scooting forward so that her ankle would reach. It wasn't easy. The position spread her wide, stretching the inner muscles of her thighs. She paused at the soft hitch of his breath.

"Christ," he groaned. The remaining kerchief crumpled in his fist. "Christ, Yasmeen. Look at you."

She didn't need to. The roughness of his voice told her, the erection straining at the front of his breeches. Silence fell, and there was only his harsh breathing, the soft vibration of the engines through the desk beneath her, the rapid thrum of her pulse in her ears.

Deliberately, she pressed her ankle to the desk leg. A shiver ran over her skin—not fear this time, though that lurked just beneath the desire.

"Tie me, Archimedes. Please."

With another groan and trembling hands, he did—the same loose knot that forced her to keep her legs open rather than holding them open for her. His callused palm smoothed up the length of her shin, over her knee.

"Stay still, if you can," he said. "And lie back."

Yasmeen didn't ask why. He'd done this difficult thing for her; she would do this easy thing for him.

As her back met the cool surface of the desk, however, she found it wasn't so easy. Holding her legs open wasn't a physical effort, but she'd never been this acutely aware of being exposed. So bare. Was he looking at her? She couldn't see him to know. Lying as she was, with her head resting almost at the opposite edge of the desk, she could only see the rise of her silk-covered breasts, lifting rhythmically with each shallow breath. She fought the urge to pull free, to close her legs, to regain some sort of certainty.

She froze as a soft caress brushed her knee. His fingers? His lips?

His lips. The warmth of his mouth heated that spot as he said, "Untie your wrap."

Leaving her more exposed, though the trepidation that accompanied that realization was being swept away by anticipation, by excitement. There *was* fear here, the need to pull her legs free, that battle against instinct, but it only served to heighten her awareness and every sensation. She yanked her wrap open and pressed her palms flat to the desk beside her hips.

Where was he? A cool whisper of breath against her heated sex told her. A shudder wracked her body and she immediately stiffened, desperately trying to remain still.

"It's like your zombies," she panted. That terrifying, wonderful thrill—and she might become as addicted to this feeling as he was. "Oh, sweet lady, help me."

"*This* is like a zombie? No. Though I will soon devour you." His laughing reply was punctuated by a nip to the sensitive tendon at juncture of her inner thigh.

That gentle bite all but devastated her self-control. She cried out, her back bowing. The flames of need that had been licking beneath her skin erupted into a rolling fire that seared every nerve and coiled with liquid heat through her core. His hands gripped her thighs, to support her or to help her stay still, she didn't know, but as his thumbs slid inward, she needed the assistance.

His deep, hungry groan followed the first slick caress. "*God*, Yasmeen. You're like a furnace."

Burning. "Now. *Now.*"

And he did. Devouring, as he'd promised, lips and tongue and fingers everywhere touching, tasting, thrusting. He feasted, eager and abandoned, his rough jaw scraping delicate flesh, his moans laden with unquenchable need, suckling her clitoris until she screamed her finish, and still licking, licking, as if he could never get enough.

She never would.

Leisurely, his mouth journeyed over her stomach, and now she saw him, his eyes glazed with violent need, his control visible in every straining muscle.

He rose over her, his hands braced beside her shoulders. "Like this, Yasmeen? Or do I untie you first?"

With her thighs still spread and her body still exposed, forced to remain almost motionless as he drove his cock into her again and again . . . The same trepidation reared up again—and the same thrill.

Anticipation wound her tight. "Like this."

His face stark with arousal, he straightened and opened his breeches. He was vulnerable now, too. Exposed. Her legs trembled, instinct pushing at her to rip open the knots. If he was threatened, how quickly would she be able to move? Would it be fast enough?

Gently, he pushed at her entrance. Yasmeen sucked in a sharp breath, and the crowding questions fled. She waited in a silent frenzy of expectation, feeling only his blunt intrusion, the stretch of her thighs, the silk around her ankles. Seeing only his love and need, the ecstasy that rolled through his lean body as he pressed forward, filling her so slowly that she was keening with frustration and agonizing pleasure when he finally sheathed his cock to the hilt.

She would not survive this. Every instinct demanded that she free herself, wrap her thighs around him and set a faster, harder pace, instead of forcing her legs to stay bound. Instead of shaking from the effort of lying still, instead of crying out on sobbing breaths when he completely withdrew his heavy shaft before starting that endless penetration again.

There was nothing else. Only Archimedes, giving everything she'd asked of him and more, his hands fastened on her hips, helping her remain tied to the desk but tethered to him.

So sweetly, so deeply, to him.

"Yasmeen." His emerald gaze burned. Her name was a feral command, everything stripped away but primitive need and demand. "Clamp down on my cock now."

Because he loved that, loved how she squeezed him, teased him. God, she did, too. Panting, she clenched her inner muscles around his thick length, and cried out as everything intensified, became sharper, tighter. So much tighter, her taut legs trembling already, and now inside, where delicious friction became luscious resistance that made him force his way deeper, deeper. His body bowed in response, every muscle standing in stark relief. His groan was harsh, fingers digging into her hips.

"So sweet." His head fell forward, his beautiful mouth drawn in a grimace of acute pleasure. "So unbearably sweet."

But he bore it, though his heaving chest and tortured groans told her that he wanted to let go and pound harder, harder. He held on, instead, his gaze locked on hers and slowly riding with her to the edge.

And then she was done, writhing at the end of an infinite stroke, no control left—only the mindless rocking of her hips, taking in those last thick inches over and over again, her arms around his shoulders and his mouth fused to hers in a kiss that could never last long enough. Sweat slicked his lean body; he suddenly stilled and shuddered against her, inside her. She tasted it, tasted him, whispering words of love against his skin.

He groaned her name and collapsed over her, chest heaving. She held him until he suddenly raised his upper body away from her, bracing his arms and meeting her eyes.

"There's only one practical solution now." His expression was solemn. "We must buy enough desks to fill every inch of this airship."

Her laugh lifted through her. "So very practical," she agreed.

"Alas, I suppose it will have to wait until we return from the Eastern Ocean."

"And hopefully that date will not be too far away," she said, thinking of the weeks that stretched ahead.

To her surprise, she felt little dread. The tangle between Archimedes and her had been unknotted. They had a clear course of action ahead. There were still risks to her ship and crew—but so there would always be when flying over lawless seas, and she would never have it any other way.

"I must be mad, Mr. Fox. My lady has been commandeered by your bastard friend, his damned device is still a threat . . . and yet I think I might enjoy myself on this journey."

He grinned and dropped a kiss to her mouth. "I know I will."

Chapter 6

Bilson was not enjoying himself.

On the quarterdeck, Yasmeen watched the slick bastard nod to Longcock, then stop for a moment to flirt with Miss Cheeksankum. She wasn't at all surprised that in the three weeks since leaving Port Fallow, Bilson had charmed his way into some of the crew's good graces; he was simply that sort. Archimedes and Yasmeen remained brief and polite, as if he weren't different from any other passenger, so the crew had initially followed their lead. And after he'd shared the reason behind Zenobia's kidnap—in confidence, and with only a few of the aviators, though obviously knowing that the story would spread—some of the crew's initial outrage had faded, too.

All well and good. He could play his little games; they didn't stop the frustration that she saw rising every time Yasmeen cut the engines and allowed her aviators—and Archimedes—time to take out the autogyros or practice their weapons drills, and passing the time by planning mock escapes from New Eden. To Bilson, this must seem a holiday for most of her aviators, a slow cruise over beautiful turquoise water in the warmth of the late southern spring.

Her gaze moved to Archimedes, standing at the bow with a spyglass in hand. This *hadn't* been a holiday, of course. Ever vigilant, they all searched the sky for signs of the flyers . . . or any other airship.

Yasmeen hoped to spot other airships, first. But even if one arrived with news of Zenobia, it wouldn't be complete freedom from Bilson's demands.

That had been *her* one frustration—they hadn't yet found the device. Frowning over the mystery now, she retrieved a cigarillo from her case. Every inch of this ship had been quietly searched, including the crews' belongings. Archimedes had even scoured the outside hull whilst flying the autogyro, and Yasmeen had personally crawled through the engines, shimmied along the propeller shafts, delving into every crevice and piece of equipment on her ship.

She didn't know where the hell it could be—and still didn't know who Bilson's ally was.

Her eyes narrowed on him as he approached the quarterdeck. She nodded permission when he called out a request to join her, and when his gaze flicked to her cigarillo case, she offered him one.

He leaned closer to the windbreak to light it, then regarded her quietly as he inhaled. After a moment, he looked starboard, toward the southern horizon, where a green sliver of Madagascar was visible in the distance. "Is that the island again?"

Ah, yes. His greatest frustration, quietly expressed. He wanted to venture farther out into the Eastern Ocean, taking a longer, wider route in search of the floating city. Yasmeen had explained that his suggestion would make finding New Eden all but impossible; there was simply too much ocean, and it would be like trying to find a boilerworm in a desert. It made much more sense to wait by a waterhole, knowing they'd eventually come to replenish their stores. In the same way, it was better to let the city come to them, in a location that the flyers were known to frequent.

Of course, Yasmeen hadn't shared that the flyers almost always approached Madagascar from the south. *Lady Nergüi* had been circling the region to the northeast—though not just to avoid New Eden. This was where she'd told Scarsdale to find them; she didn't want to force his hired airships to search for the equivalent of a boilerworm, either.

Nodding, she blew a stream of smoke into the wind. "It is."

His gaze narrowed on her face again. "You must despise me, Captain."

"No." And it was true. Nothing she felt toward him was that strong. "You amuse me."

Oh, he didn't like that. And what would his reply be? She'd wager a full bag of gold on a statement about his mental or moral superiority. It was the typical response from proud men who'd been mocked by strong women.

He nodded, as if he hadn't anticipated anything else from her. "I know you want to kill me for having the audacity to go to these lengths to save my brother. I don't expect you to understand why I would do that."

As she'd assumed. "You know I understand exactly why, or you wouldn't have used the device against Archimedes. Your *audacious* plan hinges on my caring enough not to throw him off my ship the moment he and his sister became a problem for me."

"You call the man that you supposedly care for a 'problem'?"

He truly did amuse her. She smiled, and had to give him credit—he didn't step back, and he only revealed a bit of wariness in the sudden shift of his gaze, the tensing of his shoulders.

"My husband was a problem for you, not me. That's why you used Zenobia. When you asked for his help, you knew he wouldn't endanger me and my ship—so you already had your standby plan in place. And that plan put us both right where you wanted us, made us slaves to your cause . . . and it only worked because you knew very well that both Archimedes and I understand perfectly the risks that love will drive us to take."

"I know *he* does."

He glanced toward Archimedes, who was watching them from the bow. Bemusement had lifted the corners of his beautiful mouth—probably recognizing that his old friend was attempting to cut her down a bit. She saw Archimedes laugh and shake his head.

Yes, it was absolutely ridiculous.

Bilson said softly, "But I also know you, Captain. I heard all the same stories that he did whilst following your career, but I'm not as besotted or as blinded as he is. Your reputation is at stake, and that's the only reason you're still going along with this—so that no one discovers that *I* forced your hand."

That made no sense at all. It would have been far easier simply to kill him if she wanted to preserve her reputation. But she allowed him this little moment, letting him think he'd gotten the better of her.

"Yes," she agreed. "You have all the pieces lined up perfectly. I wonder what happens when one doesn't fall in the direction you've anticipated? I think you'd have nothing left—just as you won't when we find New Eden."

He didn't respond, but she had never been more certain that his kidnap of Zenobia had indeed been a bluff. There was smugness in the set of his mouth, his self-satisfied posture.

"Ah, that look," she said. "That is why you amuse me, Mr. Bilson. You're so certain that you've played your game perfectly. So certain that you'll always have another trick. It's a pity, actually. With this ability to prepare and plan, your ability to align yourself with and understand the people around you, you could have been a fine leader."

His brows rose. "Are you praising me, Captain?"

"I'm not blind. Only an idiot refuses to recognize the strength of an adversary." She let him puff his chest up before adding, "But you're a different sort of idiot. You see the strengths of the people who aren't adversaries, and who would align themselves with you given the right incentive, but you exploit their vulnerabilities, instead. You simply poke at weak spots—just as you did when you were writing your radical handbills. Just a little boy, poking away, and needing the help of someone like Archimedes in order to actually accomplish anything."

His jaw clenched. "Are you claiming that you'd have aligned yourself with me, that you'd have helped me? You refused, Captain. And I knew you would."

"You took the wrong tack from the very start. You knew our strengths. My abilities, Archimedes' need for excitement—"

"That's a strength?"

Anyone who saw Archimedes' willingness to throw himself into dangerous situations as a weakness truly was an idiot. If Archimedes had been stupid or reckless, that would have been another matter. He wasn't either of those things, and he wouldn't have lived this long if he had been. Her husband ascribed much of his survival to luck, but that was wrong, too. He survived because his mind was as quick as his body, because of his unyielding determination to succeed no matter the odds, and because he studied every situation and prepared for the danger before throwing himself into it.

But his willingness to throw himself into the fray extended far beyond "danger." No matter the undertaking, he approached it with that same eagerness, abandoning himself to the experience—whether he was loving her, learning the workings of an airship, or simply shoveling coal.

It was a marvelous combination of traits, and she'd seen how much his wholehearted engagement with life affected those around him, how often he inspired laughter and joy, and how his involvement in the most commonplace activities seemed to imbue them with a bit of adventure.

No wonder that she loved him so. And she could *never* consider that part of him a weakness.

"It's a strength," she told him. But then, seeing that was one of *her* strengths. Just as she often had to do with her crew: recognizing what was best in them, and then making use of it. "Do you know what mine is? But of course you knew—that's why you came to us. You'd listened to all of those stories about me, and recognized that I could rescue your brother."

"And you refused to help," he said again.

"No, we offered to help—we just refused to go. But if you'd asked how we would have gone about rescuing your brother, we'd have told you everything. We would have given you a plan, money, names. But that wasn't exactly the way you wanted it to happen, so you forced our hand." Smiling, she crushed out her cigarillo in her palm. "And that is where you became the idiot, trying to poke us where we're vulnerable instead of bringing out the best in us. Archimedes, because he's loyal, and because when a job needs to be done he prefers to do it himself—and because after studying that job, the risks to me and my ship don't seem as dire as they first did. And me, because I'm proud, and I'll be damned if I let someone else take a job that I could do better. So we'd have aligned ourselves with you and offered to go. If you'd only been patient, if you'd seen that in us, it would have been a manipulation worth being proud of, a game truly well played. Instead, you made enemies of two people who'd have been far more useful to you as friends."

"You think that matters to me?" Frowning, he shook his head. "It's not important how I did it, as long as it's done. There's nothing to regret here."

Of course he would tell himself that. Expressing any regret would be too akin to admitting that he was mistaken—and justifying the means with the end was a coward's way of taking responsibility, and the last resort of tyrants. In Yasmeen's opinion, it took true courage to admit to being wrong. She doubted he had the ability to admit it even to himself.

And any man who didn't regret the loss of Archimedes Fox's friendship was a fool.

Lighting another cigarillo, she regarded him with cool amusement until he'd had enough of it and walked away. A few minutes later, Archimedes joined her, his spyglass in hand and coiled excitement in his posture. Whatever he'd seen, it must not have been one of New Eden's flyers.

Without a word, she offered her cigarillo in trade for the spyglass. An airship was coming in from the north, flying low to the water. At a far enough distance, it would be almost indistinguishable from a sailing ship—a trick to avoid New Eden and used by many airships in the region, including *Lady Nergüi*.

Yasmeen lowered the spyglass, met his eyes, and saw the same hope that this was the message they'd been waiting for. "It might not be," she warned him.

"Such little faith. I, on the other hand, will be waiting for you in the autogyro."

So that they could easily travel to the other airship when it came close. "That's a bit of a wait. It's still a good distance away."

"I'll spend the time composing odes to your lips. But as I can't kiss you now, I will settle for this." He passed her the cigarillo, and watched her mouth as he exhaled slowly. The same taste, the same smoke. Sharing these with Archimedes was one of her favorite intimacies, a simple act that had become an exquisitely sensual ritual—yet one that could be performed in full view of the crew. "What did Bilson have to say?"

"He was telling me how heartless I am and how clever he is."

"You always have enjoyed a good piece of fiction." He lifted the spyglass again. "It's *The Blue Canary*."

One of the skyrunners in Scarsdale's hired fleet. Fierce satisfaction took her in its grip, and she gave Vashon the order to hail the other airship.

Bilson was about to see his pieces all falling down.

Yasmeen had never particularly liked autogyros. Often wildly unstable, they forced the pilot to ceaselessly pedal at high speeds until the rotor blades overhead spun fast enough to lift the machine into the air. The Blacksmith's were even worse—in order to create a profile low enough for an airship's cargo hold, the pilot's seat had been fashioned so that, instead of sitting up, he had to pedal while reclining. Yasmeen could think few other things more stupid than lying in a metal cage and endlessly pumping her legs.

Archimedes loved it, of course. He laughed with every terrifying tilt of the machine, and whooped as a bit of wind sent them spinning about. Her knuckles were white, but he grinned and pulled levers and easily righted their course. She closed her eyes, pumped her feet, and prayed until they landed safely on *The Blue Canary*'s deck.

But she smiled along with him on their return trip to *Lady Nergüi*. Three days after printing the advertisement, Berge had returned Zenobia to her home. *The Blue Canary*'s captain had passed on a letter from her, which Yasmeen read aloud to Archimedes as soon as they were in the air again. The turbulence from the rotor blades made the paper flap and fold, forcing her to straighten it after almost every line—and the words themselves forcing her to pause, laughing after almost every line. Upon discovering that they'd actually flown to the Eastern Ocean, Zenobia's opinion of their mental capacity had apparently plummeted.

"'Now everyone knows that my only two living relations are also the only two imbeciles in the world who have ever deliberately gone in search of New Eden. I will forever hang my head in shame. Yours, Zenobia,'" Yasmeen read, and looked over at Archimedes, who was grinning as broadly as she.

"She's overwhelmed with gratitude, obviously. And the postscript?"

"'P.S. I'm particularly thankful because now that this farce is over, I won't be forced to write *Lady Lynx and the Floating City*. What a terrible title that would be.'"

"I rather like it," Archimedes said.

So did Yasmeen—and unfortunately, the farce wasn't over yet. It wouldn't be until they found the device. She tucked the letter into her jacket. "When we reach *Lady Nergüi*, our story will be that we only asked whether *The Blue Canary* had gotten word of any sightings."

"All right. And should we start for home? Bilson's not likely to kill me now—not when the signal will kill him, too."

"But we don't know what his ally will do."

Perhaps that person had just as imperative a reason to go to New Eden, and less to lose if they used the device. Until they discovered who it was, however, it was impossible to know how much of a threat that person posed.

Frustration pushed her legs faster. "How the hell did they hide it so well? Where haven't we looked? We've all but crawled up the asses of everyone onboard."

"Perhaps we shouldn't have stopped there," Archimedes said easily, and offered an unrepentant grin when she snorted. "I'm not about to rule it out. The device would have to be easy to get to, wouldn't it, because anyone who had to make an effort to retrieve it and put it away would have been noticed."

That was true. Everyone had their place on the ship, and it didn't go unremarked when someone ventured outside of their place.

"We've searched everywhere," he said. "Except where decency tells us that we can't—such as looking under a woman's dress."

"So I'll order them to hike up their hems and give you a good look."

His chuckle stopped abruptly. His brows drew together. "I can't decide if you're serious. Would you?"

"Yes." But not in front of any male, even Archimedes. "There are only four women who wear skirts. It won't be difficult to check each of them."

And at this point, foolish not to check. The device had to be somewhere, and beneath a skirt was as good a place as any.

Archimedes grimaced, clearly not liking the idea. "We're fortunate that everyone else wears trousers. There aren't many

places to carry a foot-long obelisk around without having it
bulge like Longcock's guns . . ."

Oh, hell. She realized at the same moment he did. His eyes
widened and met hers.

"No," he said, though clearly not believing his own denial.

"Yes," Yasmeen said. "It has to be."

He shook his head. "If we're wrong . . . An apology could
never be enough. God, I can't even *think* it."

She couldn't either. So they had to make certain they
weren't wrong, eliminate every other possibility first, no matter how intrusive and awkward. It couldn't be as horrible as
the final option.

"When we return," she said. "I'll ask the others to lift their
skirts."

When the bell for first watch rang, Yasmeen wasn't
surprised to find Maria Barriga de Lata alone in the galley
kitchen. The scullery woman was surprised to see *her*, and her
dark eyes widened farther when Archimedes and Vashon
came in after. The quartermaster slid closed the door leading
to the crew's mess.

"Don't stand up, senhora," Yasmeen said when the woman
made an awkward effort to rise. "Remain on your stool with
your hands to your sides."

The woman's expression fell. Quietly, she complied, looking past Yasmeen to focus on Archimedes. Her bottom lip
trembled. "I am so sorry, senhor."

Until that moment, Yasmeen hadn't been absolutely certain. She didn't feel any better for being so; instead, her heart
felt heavy and tired as she said, "Will you open your stomach,
please? Do it slowly. Mr. Fox, perhaps you might turn around
while she does."

Yasmeen wanted to turn away, too. She'd thought that discovering the device would be a moment of triumph, not a
painful exposure. The woman lifted her tunic. The tin can that
the Lusitanian butchers had made extended from her pelvis to
beneath her breasts. The graft had been horribly done, among
the worst that Yasmeen had ever seen; instead of the smooth
melding of metal to flesh, the edges were ragged and scarred,

the skin pulled tight over the unevenly sawed ends of her ribs. The smooth tin belly latched at her breastbone and opened like the door of an oven. Yasmeen braced herself, willing away the automatic revulsion, breathing shallowly through her mouth. She knew what to expect: guts and gears.

But, no. There were barely any guts. Perhaps there had been, once, but they'd all been replaced with windups and tubes. She shouldn't have been alive—and wouldn't have been, if not for the nanoagents. Yasmeen didn't know how; only someone like the Blacksmith could explain how the tiny machines performed all of the necessary bodily functions, using only a few pipes, hoses and small clockwork devices with winding levers. The rest was an open cavity, empty except for the Horde device.

Maria reached in.

"No!" Yasmeen stopped her. "Please put your hands to the sides again. Vashon?"

Eyes wide and fixed on that dark cavity, the quartermaster came to her side. "Ma'am?"

"Retrieve the device and hand it over to Mr. Fox, please. Be careful not to twist the base. That will activate it."

"Yes, ma'am." Not hesitating, Vashon knelt in front of the scullery woman. Yasmeen heard her murmured *I'm sorry* as she reached in. And she must have truly gone soft, because instead of reprimanding the quartermaster, she was only sorry that she couldn't say it, too. "Please tell me if I touch anything I shouldn't, senhora."

Maria stared fixedly over Vashon's shoulder, as if determinedly not thinking about having another person's hands in her stomach. "You are fine."

Vashon scooted back and rose to her feet with the device cradled gingerly in her hands. Archimedes sigh of relief lightened Yasmeen's heart for the first time since she'd come into the galley.

"Now how do I destroy it?" he asked.

"The furnace would be best," Yasmeen said, still watching the scullery woman. "Please close up, senhora, and explain your reasons for this. How do you know Mr. Bilson?"

"I had no work. I couldn't stay in my country. After I escaped the mines, I was forced to go to the ports because of the infection. I was supposed to leave Lusitania, but I had nothing. No money for passage." Her hands came up to cover her face. "I met him on the docks. I was trying to . . . No one would have me."

Trying to earn her passage by whoring. It wasn't an unfamiliar story. "And what did he do?"

"He wouldn't, either. But he said *Lady Nergüi* was looking for new crew, including a scullery maid—and that he would pay me to carry this thing for him, and to turn it on when he gave the signal." Tears streaked her face now as she looked to Archimedes. "He said it wouldn't hurt you, and that I would only have to do it once. Then I was to give it back to him after you rescued his brother, and he would pay me the rest."

Yasmeen's pity cooled. "What was the price?"

"He told me that I'd receive enough money to pay for a body that allowed me to be a woman again." Her breath hitched, echoed a sobbing rattle through the can of her stomach. "So that someone *would* have me."

Another weakness exploited, and damn Bilson to hell for it. Vashon looked away from the woman, her eyes stricken. Yasmeen couldn't see Archimedes behind her, but could easily imagine his feelings now: pity for the woman, anger toward the bastard Bilson.

And what solution now? Even as she watched, the woman's sobbing quieted, and a stoic acceptance seemed to come over her. With a tired sigh, Maria squared her shoulders and met Yasmeen's eyes.

Ready for death.

Yasmeen had no intention of dealing it out here. "Did you read your contract when you came aboard, senhora?"

"I cannot read." She gave a weary shrug. "The steward offered to read it to me, but I only cared that there was work."

"And there still is, so we will soon leave you to it." Yasmeen gestured to the pots still waiting to be scrubbed. "After we've gone, you will tell *no one* of this device or your part in this plot. Tomorrow morning you will report to the steward's quarters, and ask him to read the section of the contract which states that *Lady Nergüi*'s captain will pay for any augmentation or changes to existing prosthetics that allow a crew member to better fulfill her duties. Then you'll report to Tom

Blacksmith, so that he can clean up the graft and make it easier for you to sit. When we return to England I'll see that you have an appointment with *the* Blacksmith."

The woman stared at her, eyes filling again. "Captain?"

"Don't mistake me, senhora," Yasmeen said. "I will toss you overboard without a second thought if anything of this sort ever happens again. Do you understand?"

Sobbing again, Maria could only nod.

"Mr. Fox, do you have anything to add?"

"Nothing," he said quietly. "I've got what I came for."

Yasmeen nodded. "We will leave you to it, senhora."

Vashon trailed them out of the galley. Though too well trained to gape, the quartermaster's surprise and confusion were almost palpable. "Captain. A word, please?"

Would it be quick? Yasmeen hoped so. She stopped and glanced at Archimedes, who nodded and continued on toward the boiler room and the furnace.

Frowning, Yasmeen looked to the quartermaster. "You have a concern, mademoiselle?"

"Not a concern. Quite simply, ma'am, I can't help but wonder: Is that all you will do to her?"

"Yes." When the quartermaster seemed to struggle with that simple answer, Yasmeen expanded on it. "What should I do with her? She's already so miserable that a whipping wouldn't even touch her. Should I lock her up? She has nowhere to go anyway, unless she wants to jump off the ship—and then we will be short a scullery maid. Do *you* want to take on her duties? Do you think any of the crew does?"

Vashon sighed. "No."

"But she will be damned grateful to do it now. Have you ever seen any person who was happy to scrub?"

A smile touched Vashon's mouth. "This would be the first one."

"And likely worth her weight in gold. I can't tell you how valuable a woman who can smuggle items in her belly would have been during some of my past jobs." Yasmeen fished out the cigarillo case tucked into her sash. "Now, please go up top and throw the engines to full steam. I want to be back to England within the week."

An eager "Yes, ma'am" followed her order, then Yasmeen

was making her way to the boiler room. Covered in coal dust and stripped down to a thin sleeveless tunic, Anisa Stoker stood casually off to the side, her elbow propped on the handle of a shovel. Archimedes waited for Yasmeen in front of the open furnace, looking down at the device.

She touched his arm, spoke over the noise of the nearby engines. "May I see it?"

At his nod, she lifted it. The solid base was heavy, the obelisk more fragile. The black surface was smooth, like polished stone. She turned it over, then closed her eyes in disbelief when she read the Horde markings on the base.

"Yasmeen?" Archimedes had seen her reaction.

"It only has one setting," she told him, then shook her head with a laugh. "It can't kill you. He bluffed."

"No." He took the device and tossed it into the orange mouth of the furnace, where it landed amid the white-hot coals. "That one setting did exactly what he threatened. Perhaps it was only for a few minutes, but for those few minutes, when I couldn't feel my love for you, he stopped my heart—and I might as well have been dead."

She slid her hand into his, threaded their fingers. "But you came back."

"I always will," he said, then sighed. "And Bilson?"

"I leave him to you."

He gave her a wry look. "I wish you wouldn't."

Ah. So he was torn. Like her, he had no compunction against killing someone when they posed a threat. When that person didn't pose a threat, the decisions were more difficult, and his relationship with the man was already complicated.

"Think on it," she suggested. "When he wakes up tomorrow we'll be three hundred miles north and over dry land. Perhaps his reaction to seeing that his plan has failed will help determine yours."

Archimedes nodded and looked into the furnace, then met her eyes again. He didn't have to say it; she already knew what he was thinking.

With a grin, she said, "And after we are back in England, perhaps we'll see about hiring on more mercenaries and a few more airships, and coming up with a more solid plan to rescue his damn brother—and anyone else who wants to escape New Eden. But don't tell Bilson."

"I wouldn't." He shook his head, laughing. "And that sounds like a fine plan."

"It does, doesn't it?" Lighting a cigarillo, she smiled up at him—then stiffened as an insistent clanging sounded through the pipes.

The alarm from the deck. Now, just as they'd turned for home? It had to be a joke. Had to be.

But Vashon wasn't the sort to joke while on duty.

Yasmeen took off at a run, Archimedes' boots pounding behind her, up the companionways. Everyone on board was in motion, shouting as the ship came to full alert. When she reached the main deck, the lanterns had been doused, but everything was bathed in the silvery light of a full moon. By the lady, what terrible luck. The dark couldn't hide them when *Lady Nergüi*'s white balloon was illuminated by that light. All of the aviators stood quietly, waiting—and all staring in the same direction.

Yasmeen narrowed her eyes. Far north, a spot of orange seemed to burn like the beacon of a lighthouse. Vashon leapt down from the quarterdeck, expression tight, spyglass in hand. Yasmeen brought the lens to her eye.

A ball of fire flickered on the water. *Oh, don't let it be.* Dreading the answer, Yasmeen asked, "Is that *The Blue Canary*?"

"Yes, ma'am."

Her stomach plummeted. By the lady's shining teeth. Forty people had been on that airship.

"Their captain must have tried to run," Vashon added, just as Yasmeen spotted the long trails of smoke across the night sky—not from the fire, but from steam-powered flyers.

"May they all rot into a zombie's gut," she said softly, and looked to Archimedes. "It's New Eden. They shot down the *Canary*."

His mouth grim, Archimedes said, "Have they seen us?"

She studied the trails of smoke, and a leaden weight settled in her chest. "Yes. They're flying in this direction."

So that was it, then. Yasmeen lowered the spyglass and

drew a deep breath, hoping to lighten the sudden heaviness around her heart. They'd intended to return to New Eden, eventually. Not like this . . . but they'd make do with what they had.

"Well," Archimedes said, and she saw the determination set in . . . along with the inevitable excitement and anticipation. With raised brows, he glanced at her, and began to grin. "It's fortunate that we're prepared for this, isn't it?"

Chapter 7

Yasmeen wasn't prepared, though it all happened exactly as she'd expected.

Like a swarm of dragonflies, the flyers came. A dozen surrounded *Lady Nergüi*, the pilots' eyes hidden behind the smoked lenses of aviator goggles. They sat astride the flyers' long bodies, and the buzzing of the three propellers on the forward edge of each wing drowned out the huffing of the engines hanging beneath the seat. Yasmeen ran up a flag of surrender. The lead pilot signaled a direction, and *Lady Nergüi* followed him.

It took everything she had not to swat them out of the sky, or die trying.

She understood exactly why the captain of *The Blue Canary* had tried. Yasmeen had met him, knew his reputation—he hadn't been a fool. He'd simply been a captain, and a good one, trying to protect his people.

That wasn't instinct. Accepting responsibility for all of the lives aboard a ship required a certain amount of arrogance. Yasmeen had that in spades as well; she had to. Life aboard a mercenary ship required her to take risks, and to believe that despite the odds, she'd pull them all through. *The Blue Canary*'s captain had had that, too, but attempting to outrun the flyers wasn't simply an act of arrogance; it was also an act of faith. Faith in his ship, that she would be swift. Faith in his crew, that they would be capable. He would have believed in them all, or he'd never have taken such a chance.

Yasmeen might have taken that chance, too. As they flew, she studied the flyers' patterns, their positions. She had no doubt that her crew could destroy them . . . but that wasn't the plan. *Lady Nergüi* would be tethered to the floating city, they'd destroy the flyers there, and make their escape.

Until she saw New Eden, knowing that plan was enough. But when the moonlight picked out the cluster of balloons in the distance, the dark shape moving across the horizon, she wasn't prepared for her reaction.

She should have been. Oh, she should have known. Simply allowing her leg to be tied to a desk had taken a concentrated battle of will over instinct, even though the knot had been tied by someone she loved and trusted beyond any other, because the bonds might have prevented her from protecting him.

It wasn't just Archimedes now, but also her crew. And she had to allow her lady to be tied, the ship that protected them all.

She could barely conceal the shaking that started then. Even knowing that this was the right course, even knowing that their plan was solid and that her crew was capable, her instincts clamored with a desperate urge to rip free and fight.

And unlike when Archimedes had tied her, there was no thrill here. No excitement. Only terror and rage and dread.

She couldn't reveal them, though they howled within her. Outwardly calm, she stood on the quarterdeck with Archimedes, sharing a cigarillo. Then another. When she lit the third, he studied her face, and she knew by the tensing of his shoulders that he'd realized what was happening to her.

"Let me help," he said softly.

There was nothing to be done that he wasn't already doing, simply by standing at her side. "You're here," she said. Where he'd always promised to be. "That's all I need."

She would be glad when it was done, however. By the time *Lady Nergüi* reached the city, her control wavered on a thin thread. Though she hadn't expended any effort during the flight, her body trembled not just from the need to fight, but the ordeal of holding herself back.

Despite that maelstrom of emotion, both instinct and deadly intent kept her mind sharp. Scouting out strongholds, cataloguing their weaknesses and strengths had served her well during the war and in the years since. This was no different.

They approached New Eden at a slightly lower altitude

than the city. Yasmeen studied the level beneath before passing the spyglass to Archimedes. "Can you make it out?"

He made a sound of frustration. "Too many shadows."

"All right." Her eyes were better in the dark, and the reflected moonlight on the water illuminated the underside enough for her to see. "The framework is just as Scarsdale described. Cables tether the airships to the beams, but much of it is open. The engines look to be made up of eight turbines. They're off center and starboard, with the boilers and furnace to port and the pipes running between. Suspended walkways connect them and the stokers' quarters."

"And the hangar shed?"

"Is farther forward. Another walkway from the stokers' quarters leads to it." This would be key. To escape the city, they'd have to destroy the flyers . . . if any pilots were left to man them. "There's also access from Bushke's quarters, and another suspended walkway. Scarsdale and Trahaearn planned to use it to kill him before they lost the opportunity. He said the hangar is guarded at both points."

Archimedes nodded, lifting the spyglass again. After a long moment he said, "It's bigger than I expected."

Bigger than she had, too, even with Scarsdale's warning. "Almost two hundred airships," Yasmeen estimated.

But not all of the ships still tethered to their balloons—or the balloons had been removed and tethered directly to the framework. Closer now and rising in altitude, she saw that more balloons crowded the outside rings of ships, with fewer in the center—most likely to let in the sunlight over the gardens.

Approaching the city, all but two of the flyers veered off toward the hanger. *Lady Nergüi* flew up over the outside ring of balloons. Yasmeen drew in a sharp breath. Beside her, Archimedes' eyes widened. She heard the surprised murmurs of the crew, many of them leaning to look over the side.

Bathed in moonlight, the city could have been a wonderland depicted in the pages of a children's story book. Terraced gardens grew abundantly over almost every visible surface. Not just food, but flowers and climbing vines, trees with branches spread wide.

Long past midnight, the people slept—below the gardens,

within the airships. All was dark, except for the four lanterns lighting an open platform just aft of the central, open gardens.

Yasmeen's throat tightened, her awe and surprise fading. A tin-plated gun sloop was tethered next to the lighted platform. Its cargo doors were wide, the hold empty. The hull gaped open at the tail; the propellers removed, the engines and boilers stripped.

They'd ripped the heart out of her.

The warm pressure of Archimedes hand against her back helped to soothe the ragged shaking that overtook her again. He met her eyes. "Scarsdale said they take an inventory first, yes?"

Too sickhearted to reply, Yasmeen nodded.

"Then we'll have at least a few days," he said.

"We'll do it tomorrow night." No reason to wait any longer than that.

A shout came from below—a call for *Lady Nergüi*'s tether cable. Yasmeen nodded to Vashon, who gave the order. Once fastened, they dragged her lady down, forcing her belly to the ground. Ten guards waited, each armed with blunderbuss pistol and wearing iron-plated gloves and pneumatic arm braces that could make a punch feel like a hit from a cannonball. There were hardly enough of them to pose a threat to a thirty-man crew, but two more waited in the shadows with rapid-fire guns. Yasmeen pointed them out to Archimedes as more instructions were shouted: no weapons, they were to disembark one at a time.

"All right, then." Everyone on board had assembled on the decks. Yasmeen raised her voice. "We do as they say. I'll be the last off. Drop your weapons to the deck."

A clatter of pistols and daggers followed. Longcock looked over at her.

"Make certain your hands are up," she told him. A new man had joined the guards—Bushke, she guessed. With soft white hair and beard and a homespun tunic over rustic trousers, he *did* have a kindly, unassuming look to him. Unlike the guards, he didn't wear gloves, but she wouldn't forget Scarsdale's warning about his iron fist. At the gangway, she called to him, "My first mate's weapons are grafted to his body. He's not carrying any ammunition."

Bushke's gaze narrowed on her face. "Are you the captain, miss?"

"Yes." She saw no hint of recognition—but then, he'd built New Eden before she'd made a reputation for herself. That could work to her advantage, particularly as few people knew her name . . . or Archimedes' given name. "Yasmeen Gunther-Baptiste."

She saw her husband's quick grin, and knew he would use the same name. If any of the guards had only recently come to New Eden, perhaps they might be recognized . . . but it was unlikely. He wasn't the only handsome man who wore loud clothing. She was most commonly known as Lady Corsair, named after her previous ship; and she was not the only airship captain to wear a kerchief over her hair—though most of the others were pirates. Perhaps that was what Bushke wondered as he studied her now.

It was impossible to know, however. She couldn't read him. His appearance gave the impression of softness, but just beneath it lay steel. She couldn't see past it.

Unsettled, she waited for his answer. Finally, he said, "Send him out slowly. We'll have to bind him until we can verify what you say about the ammunition is true."

If it was her, Yasmeen wasn't certain she could have allowed them to do that. But when she glanced at Longcock, he seemed unperturbed. With a nod, he started down the plank. They used ropes rather than chains. At least there was that. Once tied, two new guards began a long search of his individual weapons. The placement of one pistol required him to drop his trousers.

After a moment of silence on the deck, Vashon looked to Yasmeen. "So his name *is* accurate."

Apparently.

Archimedes went next. A guard moved in, ordered him to remove his jacket and boots. Yasmeen tensed as those gloved hands ran the length of Archimedes' legs, but the guard didn't use any undue force. He cupped Archimedes' groin, then slipped under his waistcoat and shirt.

She looked to the rest of the crew. "Take off your boots and carry them down. Mrs. Fortescue, you're next."

They searched under her skirts. Goddammit. They didn't find anything; Mrs. Fortescue had only been the test. Yasmeen glanced at the other women aboard, and there was a soft clatter as more weapons were unstrapped and dropped to the deck.

She glanced at Maria Barriga de Lata. The scullery woman's face was pale, but determined.

"Go on," Yasmeen said.

All went as before until the guard's hands found the tin can of her belly. Maria began to panic, pleading for help in babbling Portuguese, holding the latch over her breastbone.

"Mr. Bushke!" When the man looked at her, Yasmeen said. "My scullery woman's guts are barely contained by that thing. Please take care."

Bushke nodded to the guard. Sobbing, Maria let her hands be drawn away from the latch. The guard began to draw down the door.

Yasmeen hadn't known exactly what Cook, Tom Blacksmith, and Maria had concocted between them, but the guard suddenly gagged and turned his face away. The loop of an intestine slid out. A few of Yasmeen's crew bent over, retching. The others watched in horror.

Bushke spoke softly—the guard's name. Visibly steeling himself, the guard removed one glove and gingerly reached in. For the space of three seconds, he poked around, then backed away. Maria's hysterical weeping as she stuffed the intestine back in and closed the latch had a wild note of laughter.

Mrs. Fortescue wept in earnest and put her arm around the woman when the search was over. The navigator hadn't known the truth. Most of the crew didn't. Bilson frowned a bit, but didn't give anything away.

The rest proceeded smoothly. When they were all gathered below, Bushke addressed them, spreading his arms.

"I welcome you to New Eden. No doubt you have questions, but the hour is late, and we have time to address them in the following days. Tonight, you only have to know that you are free here." His gaze settled on Yasmeen. "You are all equal. We have no captains here, no cabin boys—we are all citizens of paradise."

He paused, perhaps looking for a response, or to make a stronger impression on them. After a moment, he continued, "We have quarters set up for you to take your rest. I apologize for the austerity, and for the bars. It is only a temporary measure and created for the protection of our citizens. We are a simple people, and our survival dependent upon shared labor and belief. As soon as you have learned the rules that govern this city, you will be allowed to roam freely."

It was a short distance, a walk through a grove bursting with plump oranges and carpeted by thick grasses. The low bleating of a lamb carried across the terrace, underscored by the thrum of the engines below. The sweet fragrance of jasmine mingled with the lush coconut of the pinkball flower.

An old cargo hold formed their quarters, the hull covered with long green calabash. Here she saw the source of the perfume; jasmine wound through the melon vines and around the iron bars that had replaced the loading doors. Inside, bunks formed rows within the hold, which looked out over the central gardens.

The doors clanged shut behind them. The lock clicked home; a glance at the mechanism told Yasmeen that it would pose no difficulty when the time came to open it. She watched the guards leave, then faced the crew, who were milling between the bunks. A few had already claimed theirs. "Sleep, if you can," she told them. "We'll have a better look in the morning."

Beside her, Archimedes plucked a sprig of jasmine and tucked the stem above his ear. "And I will wear this as an adornment, since I can't hold you tonight. Will you sleep?"

No. "I'll keep watch."

"If you agree to rest, I'll cover your bunk with flowers." He glanced at the single privy in the corner. "I have to admit this is clever. After a few days in here, staring out at all of that incredible beauty . . . Who wouldn't agree to behave just to escape this little prison?"

Who wouldn't, indeed? At the bars, Yasmeen broke off a bloom of jasmine—her namesake. She crushed the delicate

star-shaped petals with her thumb, releasing a burst of perfume. "Paradise," she murmured.

Archimedes nodded, and looked out over the moonlit gardens. "And there's no doubt who the snake is."

To Archimedes' relief, she rested after a while—in a
fashion. He dragged a thin pallet off one of the bunks and over
to the bars, and they sat together, watching the dawn come.

With it, the city woke. In droves they came to the gardens,
all of them dressed in the homespun tunics and trousers. They
carried with them spades and hoes, and sang as they worked.
His father had never allowed singing, but Archimedes still
recognized the hymn.

Children played, many of them laughing and running
through the terrace paths. A few approached the bars, curi-
ously peering at *Lady Nergüi*'s crew, their faces fresh and
clean, their clothes well-worn and well-scrubbed. Now and
again a shout from the adults warned them not to play too near
the rubbish holes—an order which they seemed to gleefully
disregard.

Two men arrived not long after the sun had risen—the
civilian guards, Archimedes guessed. One of them was a
familiar face.

Bilson leapt toward the doors. "Joseph!"

There was no mistaking the genuine joy on Bilson's face,
or the shock on his brother's. Laughing, the two men
embraced, arms awkward through the bars. Joseph's companion watched the reunion, grinning, and near enough that
Archimedes could have reached through, grabbed his shirt,
and smashed him unconscious against the iron bars.

Obviously, these guards were just for show. Their only
weapons were light clubs attached to a woven belt. Bushke
apparently had no real fear that anyone might escape—or
prove to be a threat if they did.

Joseph's gaze lit on Archimedes then. His jaw dropped.
"Gunther-Baptiste?" He laughed again. "I'm astonished I
didn't recognize you first! That waistcoat outshines the sun."

"It's my handsome face that blinds you, not the clothes."

He clasped the man's hand, told him quietly, "Your brother has mounted a rescue. Do you see how well it has gone?"

"A rescue?" Joseph's grin faded a bit. His gaze darted to Bilson's. "Why?"

"Why?" Bilson frowned. "You have to ask?"

"No, but . . . You shouldn't have." He stepped back from the doors. "I'm not going to leave."

"If you're afraid, Joseph, then know that we can—"

"Stop." The younger man interrupted whatever assurances Bilson was about to make. "Stop talking, Miles. Listen. I understand that you think I've been abducted, forced to work, desirous of nothing but escape. And when those flyers came, I was terrified. But this is the truth, brother: Now that I'm here, *I don't want to leave.*"

Beside Archimedes, Yasmeen began quietly laughing. "Oh, fuck me," she said.

Joseph glanced at her, paused, then stared. Fear slipped into his eyes. Slowly, his gaze lifted to Archimedes'. "You two hired *her*? She killed your father."

A controlling man, who never hesitated to kill someone who didn't fall into line with his plans. "That made her the obvious choice," he said dryly.

"Well, I appreciate it, I do. But, Miles, you shouldn't have come. I'm married. I'm *content*, as I never have been before. This is my home."

His face reddening, Bilson shook his head. "You're only saying this because you feel that you have to. Bushke has persuaded you—"

"Bushke is the only reason I would *ever* consider going," Joseph stopped him again. "Because you're wrong. You're *wrong*. And you shouldn't have come. God knows if you'll be able to get away. I'll help you, but I won't go with you."

Apparently family could fluster Bilson, when nothing Archimedes had seen before ever had. He stalked away from the bars, sitting down hard on his bunk, and leveling a stare at his brother, as if a flounce and a pout might convince him when words couldn't.

Joseph sighed and looked to Archimedes. "I'm sorry. I truly am. I understand why you came—if I'd heard that Miles had been taken, I'd have tried to rescue him, too. But this place is . . ." He turned to look out over the gardens, seeming to struggle with the words. "I've never been a part of anything like this. No one lacks for anything. We share all that we sow. I feel at home here, and I never want to go. And I know it's difficult to believe, but there are many of us who don't want to leave."

This might not be a wasted trip, then. "But there are those who do?"

"Of course. It doesn't suit everyone." A shadow crept over his face. He glanced to his companion, who was nodding. "Some of them, like Doyle here, they quietly ask and they wait. I've been with them when they've spoken with Bushke. But he's determined. This is a war for him—a battle against the corruption of the outside world."

Considering the manner in which he waged his war, that made no sense. "They why bring outsiders in?"

"So he can save them. He's a bit of the Good Works sort, but without the hellfire and damnation. He doesn't need that; he has the guards."

Yasmeen's green eyes narrowed dangerously. "And those who don't ask quietly?"

"They're sent down to the furnace to stoke. I haven't been here long enough, but others tell me that no one who goes down comes back up."

"Not since I've been," Doyle spoke up. "And going on seven years now."

"It's Bushke, I know. When we talk to him about releasing those who want to leave, there's *no* argument that he doesn't seem to turn about. Not even shooting down those airships who won't come. He justifies it every time, that if he let them go, they'd be a threat. That it just takes one one balloon exploding here to kill two thousand of us, so the flyers are the city's greatest defenders, not murderers. Within a few days, he'll justify ripping that man's guns off of him."

He gestured toward Longcock, sitting on a nearby bunk. The first mate looked up, his expression bemused.

"I'm tempted to wait and see them try."

"Resist temptation, my friend," Archimedes said. "Especially in Eden."

"Especially here," Joseph said more seriously, and met Archimedes' eyes again. "I thought of you often since coming here. You and the brotherhood, and those handbills we used to write. The way you could always point to a book that would help us find the right thing to say. I wish now that I'd paid more attention, and maybe I could find the words that made a difference."

Flattering, but it probably wouldn't have helped. "Some men, the words aren't there, because they aren't interested in the argument. They're only interested in being right—*their* interpretation of right—and no argument will shake them from that." Archimedes had learned this lesson well; he'd spent a good portion of his life trying to prove his father wrong. "In the end, you realize that the only thing to do is to get away from them, if you can. And if you can't, to kill them."

With a slight smile, Yasmeen looked up at him. "Or just be thankful when someone does it for you."

And then fall madly in love with her.

"That won't make *me* right," Joseph said.

"It wouldn't," Archimedes said. "But when he decides that even the ones who quietly ask are a threat, you aren't as likely to be sent down to the stoker's quarters."

With a sigh, he nodded. He looked over at his companion when Doyle gestured beyond their quarters, then glanced that way. His expression tightened. "Well, they've come already."

A pair of gloved guards, their aviator goggles down around their necks. Had they been the ones to shoot down the *Canary*? Archimedes couldn't be certain. And by tonight it wouldn't matter.

"Captain," the one on the right said. Though slightly bulkier than his companion, taller and darker, they shared the same lack of expression. "We've begun our inventory. Please accompany us to Father Bushke's quarters. He will have questions regarding your crew and ledgers."

"I will." Yasmeen nodded coolly. "I suppose it's to the city's advantage if I tell him exactly which task each of my men and women are best suited for, and how much coal I'll be adding to your bunkers."

"Yes, ma'am."

And this was exactly what they'd hoped for. Yasmeen

could scout the route to Bushke's quarters and their layout. Still, Archimedes couldn't stop the dread that filled his chest. He wouldn't be at her side.

While the guards unlocked the door, she slanted a look at him from beneath her lashes. "I'll be all right."

Of course she would. He still worried. "I'd be less concerned if you had a weapon," he said softly.

"I do." Lightly, she traced a claw down his forearm. "And if I need another one, I'll just take the guards'."

Grinning, he watched her go. The door clanged closed again. A path led across the garden terraces, branching off here and there, leading to different stairs that apparently each descended into the living quarters of an airship. He'd never seen her amid such greenery. Her long easy stride was beautiful to behold anywhere, but here the feline grace seemed especially pronounced, almost a prowl. Perhaps because she walked past so many people who had no idea the sort of woman who'd been caged in their presence. Perhaps because the scouting mission brought her hunting instincts to the fore. Perhaps because he simply preferred to see her free.

Not that she hadn't been already free, in a manner of speaking. She'd only remained caged because she'd chosen to stay there.

Whatever the reason, he could easily have spent all day, simply watching her walk—except that after a few minutes passed, he happened to glance at Joseph and Doyle. They watched her, too, but without the same awe. Frustration, pity, and helplessness marked their faces, instead.

Archimedes gripped the iron bars, his heart suddenly racing. "Joseph?"

Fists clenched, the man shook his head. "There's nothing you can do for her."

"What? What are you saying?"

Doyle answered. "A decade ago, perhaps a bit more . . . rumor is, a couple of men managed to escape. Since then, others have tried. Most failed, but they *tried*, leading the others who'd come with them."

"All of them had been the masters of their ships, someone who was already in a position to lead them," Joseph said. "So

Bushke began to eliminate the problem within the first few days."

Eliminating it? Christ. Archimedes swung around, saw that Longcock had already risen to his feet and was heading for Maria Barriga de Lata.

Hurry. But Archimedes slowed, forced himself to learn more. He couldn't run into this situation blindly. "How?"

"On the main deck of his quarters. He meets with her, as they said. He'll discover what he needs—strongbox combinations and the like. Then . . . they make it quick."

Yasmeen was quick, too. But though she would be wary, he knew she wasn't expecting this. *"How?"*

Doyle exchanged a glance with Joseph, then sighed. "From what I've seen, it's a shot to the back of the head."

God. Even Yasmeen couldn't outrun that. "Open the doors."

"You can't do anything—"

"She's my *wife*!"

Joseph stilled. With wide eyes, he looked to the others inside the cage. Whatever confirmation he was seeking, he must have found it.

"I'm sorry. I'm so sorry. We don't have the key."

No. Archimedes didn't waste time with the denial. It would slow him down, but he could pick the lock—if only he had a goddamn pick. Mrs. Fortescue rushed up, yanking a long pin from her hair.

With a saucy wink, she said, "We don't need a key, sir."

She went to work. Crouching beside him, Longcock opened a leather pouch streaked with drying offal. "Gun?"

"A revolver, my grappling, and the red-handled daggers." He tore off his jacket, shrugged the grappling apparatus over his shoulders like a harness. He tucked the pistol beneath the leather band around his back, then pulled off his boots. "Joseph, take off your tunic."

"What?"

"Now."

The man drew off his top, shoved it through the bars. Archimedes pulled it on. Without needing to be asked, Joseph shucked his trousers, then looked doubtfully at the orange breeches Archimedes tossed him in return. A moment later, Mrs. Fortescue opened the door with a flourish.

Archimedes hauled up the homespun. "I will kiss you later, you wonderful woman."

"I'll settle for another look at your backside."

"I'll give you both. Mademoiselle Vashon, I expect that there will soon be a commotion coming from Bushke's quarters. Wait until most of the guards have run in that direction, then please free *Lady Nergüi* from her tether."

"She told me that we would carry that exercise out tonight, sir."

"We're doing it now."

"Yes, sir."

"Did she point out the rapid-fire guns to you?"

"Yes. We've got those covered, sir."

He looked to Longcock, who was sliding bullets into the ammunition chambers in his arms. A blissful smile carved the first mate's face as he thrust each cartridge home. "You'll take the hangar shed?"

"I will."

Then Doyle, last. "You know others who want to escape?"

"Yes."

"Then spread the word and tell them to get ready. I expect hell to break loose in about ten minutes." He held the other man's eyes. "You'll have to fight with us. Use your hoes, if you have to. We need to take out the guards and flyers. Everyone else, we're happy to leave alone as long as they don't step into our way."

With a glance at Joseph, who nodded, Doyle took off at a run. Archimedes stepped through the door, closed it behind him. If any guards happened to come this way, there was no reason to give them advance notice of their impending escape.

He tore off a sprig of jasmine and tucked it near his heart, then started off across the gardens.

Bushke had brought too many good people to New Eden. By the time Yasmeen was halfway across the gardens, she'd seen her impending death in the slump of their shoulders as she passed, in the angry stares they directed toward the guards leading her to Bushke's quarters, in the closed eyes and prayers whispered on behalf of her soul.

Would they shoot her while she walked out here in the open? *No*, she thought. Fear could keep people complaisant, but terror often pushed them to action. Bushke could have made examples of any of the dissenters he'd sent below the city, but instead they'd quietly disappeared.

Once they reached his quarters, she'd probably be taken below, too, using his access through the hangar—or her throat slit while they spoke, and her body disposed of over the side.

A flash of reflected light caught her eye. Across the gardens, a guard stood on the bow of an old cloud trawler with a spyglass in one hand; he used a mirror to signal the two in front of her. Her escorts stopped, facing the direction from which they'd just come, their gazes focused beyond her.

Yasmeen turned. She scanned the gardens, the path—
Archimedes?

His gaze had fixed on her. That look told her what she'd already guessed: Bushke had meant to kill her. He must have learned it from Joseph or his companion, and come to warn her.

No, not just warn her. He'd have set the rest of their plan in motion, as well. And perhaps if he hadn't been so damn handsome, perhaps if—even wearing the same tunic and trousers—he didn't hold himself so differently from everyone else in New Eden, he might have followed her without attracting attention.

But since he had, she'd protect him now, too. "He's my husband," she said to the guards. And if Bushke wanted to speak to the *Lady Nergüi*'s captain, she'd give him a reason to bring them both in. "He's co-captain of my ship."

Another flash came from the opposite side of the garden, repeated twice. Another guard, another spyglass. The signal repeated again.

Twenty yards away, Archimedes abruptly stopped, eyes widening. His gaze snapped to hers. Behind her, she heard a familiar click: a gun, the hammer cocked.

By the lady. "Archimedes! Down!"

The roar of a blunderbuss drowned out her scream. Red bloomed in his shoulder. He spun, then staggered to the side.

"Archimedes!" She sprinted toward him, heart bursting in her chest. A shoulder shot wasn't so bad. It wasn't so bad—

He fell.

Vanished.

Her cry caught in her throat. She threw herself after him. Thick soil cushioned her knees. A hole opened in the ground before her.

Access to the level below? If so, the guards wouldn't have an angle for another shot. Now she would look down, and he would be on the platform below, grinning up at her. Almost laughing now, she braced her hands, glanced over.

Nothing. Just water, far below.

That couldn't be.

He'd be hanging on the framework, then—

He wasn't.

This couldn't be right. Her vision was blurring, and she just wasn't seeing properly. Closing her eyes, Yasmeen shook her head, looked again.

He would be there.

But there was only water. Only the dissipating smoke trail from a flyer. Only gulls, cawing. And a woman crying that she needed to wake up now, needed to wake up, because she couldn't lose him.

Then pain exploded in the back of her head, and she was swept into darkness, instead.

Chapter 8

He truly was the luckiest man alive—and now, *still* alive.

And he'd finally, finally proved his father wrong: God *did* love men who wore adornments. He must, because there was no other reason for the Almighty to send a steam-powered flyer streaking beneath a floating city at the very instant that Archimedes Fox fell through a rubbish hole.

The pilot was a bit less lucky—or just too foolish to have strapped himself to the flyer's body. The jolt of Archimedes' landing bucked the man straight off. With a whoop, Archimedes scooted into his place. He didn't know how to pilot the damned thing, but he just needed to steady it a bit while he tore off the god-awful homespun tunic—bloodied now. The wind whipped it away. His shoulder hurt like hell, but he'd had worse.

He'd have much worse if he didn't get off this machine before he flew it into a steel beam or rode it into the water. There were the turbines passing overhead—he shifted his weight, and the flyer banked toward the bow of the ship. He had no idea how to land it in the hangar, and didn't want to kill himself trying.

Thank God for sending the flyer—and for pneumatic-launched grappling hooks.

He was losing altitude. Now or never.

The launcher's recoil shrieked through his shoulder. The grappling whipped around a railing on the suspended walkway. The cable drew taut and yanked him off the flyer. The harness saved his arms from being ripped from their sockets—climbing a cable after being shot by a blunderbuss was painful enough.

He was almost to the railing when a group of men started across the steel walkway. Stokers, by the look of them—each one of them covered in coal dust. They suddenly quieted when Archimedes pulled himself over the rail and tumbled to the steel grating.

They gaped as if they'd never seen a ridiculously handsome bleeding man in a turquoise waistcoat fall through a rubbish hole and then save himself with a grappling hook before. What *did* they do for fun in New Eden?

But he had no time to ask. He had a wife to save.

He reached for his revolver. "How do I find William Bushke? I have a message to deliver."

With a bullet. Except, goddammit—the revolver wasn't in his harness. Falling onto the flyer or being yanked around by the cable must have shaken it loose.

No matter. He'd make do.

One of the men pointed to another suspended walkway. Archimedes nodded his thank-you, then added, "If you'd like to leave this damn city, I'm a madman with an airship and a plan. Just follow along, maybe throw a punch or two if one of the guards makes it past me, and we'll get the hell out of here."

With that, he started down the walkway. No time to wait for their answer.

Not while Yasmeen waited for him to return to her side.

She didn't know which one had pummeled her head with his steel glove. She didn't know which one had shot Archimedes. It didn't matter. She would kill them all.

Not yet, though. Not yet. Not when she couldn't even draw breath.

Her tears dripped in a steady stream, splashing against the polished deck between her knees. She'd opened her eyes in William Bushke's quarters, but she hadn't yet made it to her feet.

She *would* get up. She would.

Not yet.

Archimedes could survive the fall to the water. Even though he bled and the ocean teemed with sharks, Archimedes would return to her side.

He had to. Or she would die with him.

"I am sorry for this tragedy, Mrs. Gunther-Baptiste. Truly I am." The kindly faced tyrant crouched in front of her. "But my guards believed he carried a weapon beneath his tunic—and that he was en route to my quarters. They were only protecting the safety of our citizens."

She would kill him, too. It would be easy. This old wardroom had been transformed into a library. Six guards stood in the cabin with them. None of them had their guns ready. She would leap for the nearest guard, rip his throat out with her claws and take his weapon. The second would fall just as the others finally began to react. The third's body would serve as a shield, and she'd use the guns she'd collected while ripping out throats to shoot the remaining three guards. Bushke would be last, the slowest.

But she couldn't yet. Taking that revenge meant admitting there was something to take revenge *for*. And he wasn't dead.

Another reason, perhaps. Even over the sounds of her tears and the screaming of her heart she heard the faint sounds of gunfire echoing up through the companionway outside the wardroom. The others hadn't heard heard it yet, but she knew the sound: George Longcock was in the hangar shed.

She would have to be careful not to slip on her tears—they were as slippery as blood.

With a sigh, Bushke rose and made his way back toward his desk. "I can see that you are overwhelmed, but there are matters which must be attended to, and . . ."

He paused, head tilted, and moved toward the passageway to listen at the open library door. Yasmeen listened, too, but there was no more gunfire. Longcock had finished.

She would need to get started.

But not yet. Not until her heart beat again.

Shaking his head, Bushke faced her. He sent a quick glance at one of the guards, who began to move around behind Yasmeen.

Bushke picked up where he'd left off. "And so, Mrs. Gunther-Baptiste, I thought we might have a little chat about—"

His eyes widened suddenly, his body stiffening. His left arm rose. Blood bubbled from his mouth. He fell forward, facedown and flat on the floor.

A red-handled dagger jutted up from his back.

Archimedes.

The wonderful, incredible man. Joy rushed through her, fierce and sweet. Her laugh burst, easing the pain around her lungs, lifting the weight from her heart.

The guards shouted, heading for the door, guns drawn. Heading for Archimedes.

She caught the guard who rushed past her; he didn't have time to scream. The next guard's neck snapped like a twig. She took down the third, and the other guards hadn't even recognized the fury coming from behind. Another one fell, and finally, another guard noticed. He had time to widen his eyes.

The last one she left for Archimedes. He didn't disappoint. The matching dagger flew through the doorway, embedded in the guard's throat.

Her husband came through next. He paused for a moment, staring at her before crossing the room, catching her face in his gentle hands. His thumbs swept over her cheeks. "Not these, Yasmeen. Not for me."

"I won't," she said. But her eyes filled again. She touched his hair, his jaw, his mouth. Solid, real. Her voice trembled. "You came back to me."

His smile all but wrecked her again. "I promised I would. And I had to save you."

He had saved her, more than he could know. Then his mouth was on hers, bringing her heart into the space between them, restarting it with the sweetest kiss.

When he lifted his head, she followed him up. She *would* stop kissing him.

But not yet.

Brighton, England
December 3

Miss Zenobia Fox,

> *I have reconsidered my position regarding Lady Lynx and her heart of steel. Perhaps a love interest would not be unacceptable—particularly if you put him*

in danger, and let the villainous bastards reap the consequences.

The first story will open with a call for help from a duplicitous bastard. In the end, Lady Lynx and her suitor will have so many passengers desperate to escape a floating city, that there simply isn't room for the bastard on the return trip. But they'll promise to send a rescue . . . eventually.

Yours,
Yasmeen Fox

P.S. You ought to call it Lady Lynx and Her Fifty Percent Royalties. *Then perhaps I'll finally tell you why I have tufts at the tips of my ears.*

Keep reading for a special look at
Meljean Brook's next Iron Seas novel

Riveted

Coming soon from Berkley Sensation!

Before Annika had begun her journey, her mother had assured her that the people in the New World weren't all that different from the women in their village of Hannasvik. Her mother reminded her of how the peoples of Africa and Europe had sailed across the Atlantic four hundred years ago, fleeing from the Mongol Horde that had ridden from the east on the backs of their conquering war machines—just as, a century before, Hanna and the Englishwomen had escaped the New World slavers and had made their home in Iceland. She'd spoken of the enormous mechanical warriors that the New Worlders had built on their coastlines, sentinels that served a warning to the Horde, should that great empire ever develop a navy and follow them across the sea—just as Hannasvik's trolls protected their village and intimidated any enemies who might attempt to drive them from their home.

The Horde never followed the New Worlders, however. The sentinels stood for centuries, staring out over the open sea while wars over territory and trade routes were fought behind their backs, and they were slowly stripped of their armaments and engines.

And they were slowly falling apart. Annika glanced up through the drizzling rain and eyed the immense Castilian warrior guarding the gates to the port city of Navarra. In the three years since she'd left Hannasvik and joined *Phatéon*'s crew, Annika had come to accept the truth of her mother's words: Individually, the people of the New World weren't that different from those in her village.

The governments and rulers, however, must have been.

No elder in Hannasvik would have allowed Annika or any of the other engineers to neglect their trolls, not when lives depended upon their maintenance. The same obviously wasn't true in the New World, and Castile's sentinel was the worst. Aboard *Phatéon*, Annika had seen every machine still standing along the Atlantic coastline—from Johannesland's colossus in the north to the Far Maghreb's twin warriors, three thousand miles south of the equator—and the warrior in Navarra was by far the most decrepit. Rust ate away at its plate armor and crested helmet; corrosion pitted the iron around every bolt and rivet. Sand had drifted into the crevices, forming a solid mass at every joint, topped by grassy nests. Gray seagull dung crusted the spiked shoulders and gauntlets.

Once a marvelous and deadly machine, now it was simply dangerous. Even if the sentinel had still possessed the engines that allowed it to walk, the great hinged knees would have buckled after a single step. Struts buttressed its lower half now, a framework of steel supporting the towering legs that served as Navarra's port gates.

What a horrible waste. If the Horde *had* come to the New World, they likely wouldn't have been intimidated by such useless machines . . . unless the New Worlders' defensive strategy was to crush any invaders beneath a rusted ruin. More likely, however, visitors to the city would be killed by the falling pieces.

Visitors like Annika. Only an hour earlier, she had walked the north port road through the gate and into the Castilian city without being crushed—but while she'd been at the printer's office, purchasing another season of personal advertisements, an icy breeze had begun to blow in from the ocean, carrying rain and sand that stung her cheeks. A strong gust might rip away the sentinel's giant hand or armored shoulder and throw it to the ground, squashing Annika in the street.

If a steamcoach didn't squash her first.

A horn blasted near her right ear. Two tons of rolling iron sped by, the front wheel whipping her skirts forward. With a yelp, Annika yanked the red silk tight to her leg before the rear wheel could catch the fabric and rip it away—or drag her along the sandy road behind it. That damned idiot driver. Only a blind man wouldn't have seen her walking along in a brilliant crimson skirt and canary yellow coat.

Though the coach was already lost from her sight beyond

its dense trail of smoke and steam, she yelled after him, "You rotting rabbitchaser!"

Pointless, but satisfying—until she sucked in a lungful of the acrid smoke. Coughing, she pounded her fist over her chest, then glanced over her shoulder just in time to avoid the three-wheeled cart that rattled around a horse-drawn wagon and attempted to squeeze between the plodding beast and her leg. Her fierce scowl went unnoticed by the driver.

Well, hang them all. It was true that the row of shops that separated the north and south roads made narrow corridors of each street, leaving little room to maneuver—but they were headed in the same direction, and the port gates were only a hundred yards away. Was running her down to gain a few seconds truly necessary? Given the manner that some of them handled their vehicles, she suspected they were *aiming* for her.

Perhaps they were. Perhaps she'd broken some unspoken Castilian rule that no one aboard *Phatéon* had thought to warn her about. Perhaps she was unintentionally giving a message: *Please crush me to a bleating pulp alongside this road.*

And now that the thought had entered her mind, it wouldn't leave. She looked over her shoulder again. No vehicles were bearing down on her . . . yet.

Oh, and her mother would have been shaking her head now, telling Annika that her dread was only a product of her imagination. That might have been true, once. Growing up, Annika's tendency to woolgather had been a source of consternation and amusement for the women in the village. Her imagination had continually gotten the best of her—and was why she currently served as second engineer aboard an airship, flying from port to port, rather than eating supper every night in her mother's cozy earthen home. She'd often fancied dangers that weren't there and daydreamed when she should have been wary.

No longer, though. Within a few months of joining *Phatéon*'s crew, Annika had discovered that port cities in the New World each came with a unique set of dangers, and she'd learned to be wary until she was familiar with them. Manhattan City's entry inspectors didn't just examine the documents proving her origin and certifying that she wasn't infected by the Horde's nanoagents. They groped her legs and arms to make certain she wasn't hiding a mechanical apparatus beneath her clothing—and swinging a fist at an officer who groped too fervently would land her in a cell until her airship's captain bailed her out. Inside the city, a curse spoken within hearing distance of a constable resulted in a hefty fine; exposing a bare ankle or elbow earned a rebuke and a trip in a paddy wagon back to the port's gates, where her salacious behavior was reported to Captain Vashon and the airship threatened with docking sanctions.

In Oyapock, however, Annika could have walked naked down the paved streets without garnering a second look—and given the number of light-fingered war orphans who swarmed visitors entering Liberé's capital city, it was only by virtue of her trouser buckles that her pants weren't stolen off her bottom while she wore them. On her first visit to Oyapock, Annika might have considered nudity a blessing, however. The city sat at the mouth of the Orinoco River; accustomed to colder climes, even Annika's lightest clothing had seemed to suffocate her. But the urchins hadn't left her nude on that trip—they'd taken her money and her hair, instead. She hadn't felt them lift the purse from her waist. A slight tug at the back of her head had been the only warning before her thick braid had disappeared and her curls sprang into a dark halo. With her hand in her newly shorn hair, she'd stared in openmouthed shock as they'd scampered away. She'd learned, though. Now she kept her hair short, and only carried as much money as she needed into Oyapock, leaving the bulk on the airship.

Annika took her valuables with her in Port-au-Prince. Though a Vashon airship was welcome at any of the French islands in the Caribbean, *Phatéon* wasn't exempt from arbitrary searches by the king's men looking for treasonous nobles or cargo left unaccounted for on the tariff sheets. When Annika had reported her money missing from her berth after a search, *Phatéon*'s old goat of a quartermaster had laughed before informing Annika that she'd paid *"le fou de l'impôt."* She hadn't known enough French to understand him then, but his meaning had been clear: only a fool left her money onboard when the king's men came—but Annika preferred to take it with her, anyway. Though many of the French cities seemed to be sinking into an elegant ruin, all trading routes led through the Caribbean, and the islands were ripe with spices and fruits unlike any she'd ever had in Iceland. The fish seemed flakier and the mutton lighter when eaten in a French market, and the stalls were filled with lustrous fabrics that she couldn't resist purchasing. King's men or no, Annika always left the islands with an empty purse.

Now, Annika knew each city's quirks well enough that she rarely felt trepidation passing through the port gates. Navarra was no exception—and in many ways, was pleasant to visit. Entering the city was painless, the inspection process consisting of a glance at her papers and a wave through the gates. No orphans waited to steal her money. The drapers sold cloth that matched the French markets in quality, if not quantity; the food was bold and tangy, and the people she spoke with no more rude or friendly than in any other city, even when she stammered along in her butchered Spanish.

But she knew not to enter the city if any part of it was burning. She knew that if a crowd began forming in the streets, she needed to return to *Phatéon* as quickly as possible. The queen's guard wouldn't care whether she was actually participating in the bread riots—simply being in the area was enough to justify arrest, and Annika had never heard of any crew member of any airship returning from a Castilian gaol.

Since leaving home, she'd been as wary as her sense and instincts dictated. And if her imagination suggested a danger that didn't exist, no harm was done . . . except to her nerves.

A shout came from another vehicle, the words barely audible over the huffing engine—but she didn't understand much Spanish, anyway. Shoulders stiff in expectation of being run down, she glanced round. A cab driver gestured and shouted from two feet away, probably telling her to use the wooden walkway that ran along the front of the shops.

She would have used it, if there'd been room. But a church must have been distributing food nearby—men, women, and children with sunken cheeks and tired eyes stood in lines on the weathered boards, shuffling forward now and again, everyone quiet and orderly.

The fried sweetbread Annika had purchased near the printer's office suddenly weighed like a rock in her stomach. In many ways, the New World was *nothing* like Hannasvik. There was hunger in her village—oh, she'd known it many times, when the winters had been long and the nets empty, when the flocks had been thinned by the wild dogs, when even the rabbits seemed scarce—but if one person lacked food, then everyone in the village did. Yet here, she dared not even give any of the people the few coins left in her purse. If seen, she'd be arrested for inciting disorder.

And though she could imagine many ways to secretly pass the money to someone, she could also imagine the gaol too well if she were caught.

What a strange land, where giving a small bit of help might put a noose around her neck.

Oh, but she missed home. Longing gripped her chest—to see her mother, to feel the heat of a troll's belly as she stoked its furnace, to smell the sea and the smoking fish and the sheep. But she couldn't return, not yet. Not until she found her sister, Källa.

Until then, she was fortunate that *Phatéon* had become something of a home, too—and it was not far away now. She was almost to the port gates. Prudently, she opened her canvas umbrella to shield her from the seagulls' rain that fell from the buttresses. Ahead, directly beneath the center of the sentinel, port officers watched the south road from a wooden guard-house, making certain that no one attempted to avoid the inspections on the north road and enter Navarra via the southern gate. Beyond the guardhouse, the sand-strewn cobblestone road widened to accommodate the shops and pubhouses serving the aviators and passengers who weren't allowed into the city. Steamcoaches idled in front of the inns, the liveried porters loading and unloading luggage.

A strong gust blew more sand into her face. Around her, above her, the sentinel and the supporting framework seemed to shudder. With the sound of droppings splattering against the taut canvas, Annika didn't dare look up—and she resisted the urge to break into a run. Sense reminded her that the sentinel had weathered the hurricanes that roared up the coast every summer; surely it could survive a bit more wind.

On the other hand, how many times had she heard the story of the shepherdess who killed a giant with a single stone . . . ?

Annika quickened her step. Over the docks, the airships swayed and bobbed in the wind, pulling against their tethers like fat haddock fighting on fishing lines. A large cargo carrier, *Phatéon* didn't appear to move as much as the smaller airships, but Annika knew the mooring anchors groaned under the strain and the cables vibrated with tension.

Far ahead, dark clouds crowded the eastern horizon. If that storm moved in before *Phatéon* had been fully loaded, the night promised to be a rough one. They'd be jostled in their bunks and stumbling around the decks until the tether was unhooked.

Not so terrible, except that the second mate—who slept in the bunk above Annika's—tended to become portsick on such nights.

Another shout sounded, but this one from her left. Annika paid it no mind. If the person wasn't set to run her down, their business was none of hers, and the noise simply added to the cacophony on the road. Someone was always shouting near port gates; only the language changed. She thought that had been either Spanish or Portuguese, but was only certain that it had been male.

Even that had become familiar. Since leaving Iceland to search for Källa, she'd become accustomed to new cities, a new life—and to seeing men everywhere. They were exactly as Annika's mother had described them: much like women, but hairier. And, when part of a group, stupider.

The shout came again, closer and louder. Annika slowed, paying more attention now. A uniformed port officer had left the guardhouse and strode in her direction, his thick mustache shadowing his frown. Annika glanced to the side. No one stood nearby. The guard's gaze had fixed on . . . Annika.

Her heart clenched, then began racing. *Oh, no.* But he was only one man, and not in a group. Surely, whatever it was, she'd be able to reason with him.

A gray dropping splattered against his hat brim. The officer didn't seem to notice. He spoke again, and *she* felt stupid. She didn't understand a single word. Most likely it was Spanish, but so quickly said that she couldn't make it out. Stopping a short distance away, he held out his hand, impatiently flicking his fingers.

He wanted something from her. But what?

Annika glanced down at herself, looking for the answer.

She didn't carry anything but her umbrella, and didn't know how to ask him what the problem was. Her knowledge of the language didn't extend far beyond *No estoy infectada* and *¿Cuánto cuesta?*

Her fingers tightened on the umbrella stem. Her imagination didn't help her now. She could only picture the worst. Sudden nerves made her words loud and shrill. "*Parlez-vous français?*"

Annika had been forced to learn French when she'd joined *Phatéon*'s crew, and not just because Captain Vashon hailed from the Caribbean islands. French was the trader's language—and this was a port city. Surely he understood a little.

Dismay slid through her when his mouth firmed. Slowly, he said, "*Muéstrame . . . sus . . . cartas.*"

His voice sharpened on *cartas*. Annika wracked her brain. Had she been blocking a cart or another vehicle? Was it something else? Not the identifying papers she had tucked away in her purse; she knew the word they used for that: *documentos*.

But they only asked for those when she was passing the inspection point on the sentinel's north side. Why stop her while she was leaving?

Once, she'd been briefly detained in Manhattan City when a constable had asked where she'd acquired her clothing. Even though he'd spoken English—an odd version of it, to be certain, even odder than she'd heard spoken in London—it had still taken Annika several minutes to realize that he suspected her of *stealing* the clothing, because the expensive fabric lay beyond a stoker's means. And despite her explanation that she'd purchased the silk on the cheap at the French markets and sewed the pieces herself, he hadn't seemed to believe her until a nearby group of women had come to her aid. Laughing at the constable, they'd assured him that Annika couldn't have stolen the clothes, because no woman of quality would own anything so ridiculous as a white skirt over indigo trousers, pairing it with a lavender-blue bodice.

No lady would ever be seen in a costume resembling a Liberé flag.

Today, Annika wore red and yellow. Perhaps the colors had marked her in some way—and she supposed that she *did* resemble a Lusitanian flag. But what of it? They weren't at war with Castile.

But there were no women to save her now. She scanned the faces of the people nearby, and though several had turned to watch the encounter, she didn't recognize anyone from *Phatéon*'s crew.

And what stranger would dare help? Not here, not in Castile.

Panic fluttered wildly in her chest. She faced the guard again. "Do you speak English?" As he had, she spoke slowly, trying to make herself understood. "Please tell me, what is the matter?"

With another sharp word and gesture, he shook his head. His hand shot out, seizing her wrist. He turned toward the guardhouse.

"No, please! Wait!" She dragged her heels, trying to slow him without openly resisting. Her heart pounded. Only with great effort did she stop herself from smashing her umbrella over his head and sprinting to the docks and *Phatéon*. Desperate, she tried again. *"Norse? Mælt kann norse?"*

"He's demanding to see your letters of entry."

The answer came from behind her, a male voice. She barely had a moment to feel her relief when the newcomer spoke again, but not in English—and not directed at her.

The guard looked around and stiffened, as if in alarm. He let Annika go, his hand dropping to the short club at his belt. *"¡Retírese, señor!"*

Whoever he was, the stranger apparently posed more of a threat than Annika did. She opened the purse tucked within her skirts, stealing a glance back. Beneath a wide-brimmed hat, the man wore a faint smile—not exactly an expression of amusement, she thought, but as if he'd heard an old, worn-out joke. A gleaming monocle concealed his left eye. Focused on the guard, he lifted his hands as if to show the officer that he wasn't armed.

Oh, but he *was*. Annika's fingers froze around her folded papers, and she took another, longer look.

His right hand resembled every other person's—large, perhaps, with broad palm and long fingers, but proportional to his height. His left hand and wrist were of the same size, yet they were human only in shape; the skeletal limb had been constructed of steel. The fluid movement as he spread his mechanical fingers was indistinguishable from the same movement in his right hand, and spoke to the intricacy of the design—the contraption wasn't stiff, but responsive . . . and probably incredibly strong.

No, he didn't carry any weapons. But from the guard's perspective, the man's hand *was* a weapon—and the man himself a danger to Castile.

Prosthetic limbs were common enough in the New World; if not used by soldiers injured at war, then laborers who'd suffered accidents in the factories and fields. Those replacement limbs were often stiff and clunky, however—a hook for a hand, a wooden leg strapped into a boot—and only if replacements were used at all.

But there was nothing clunky about this man's elegant hand, which meant that it hadn't just been contoured around his arm or strapped on, but *grafted* on so that the steel contraption had become a working part of his body. Only the Horde's nanoagents could graft a mechanical apparatus to human flesh, making it as maneuverable as a natural arm. This man had to be infected with those tiny machines—the same machines that the Horde had used to forcibly graft tools onto their laborers. Most of those tools hadn't been designed to function or appear as human as this man's did, but Annika knew that it wasn't the hand itself that alarmed the guard. It was the nanoagent infection.

Although an infected person was stronger and could heal faster, the nanoagents had also allowed the Horde to control the populations in the occupied territories of England and North Africa, using radio signals from tall broadcasting towers. A few of the towers had been destroyed, freeing the people in England and Morocco—but many in the New World thought the revolutions were only a temporary setback in the Horde's inevitable advance across the ocean. Others in the New World feared that the nanoagents would reanimate their corpses after death and transform them into hungry, savage monsters, like the zombies that roamed much of Europe and Africa, leaving it uninhabitable. Others were revolted by the idea of tiny machines crawling around inside their bodies like bugs.

Annika knew too many of the infected to share the same fears, but the port officer obviously did not—or he knew many infected people, and still feared that the nanoagents might spread.

Brandishing his club, the officer gestured toward the nearest inn. Annika didn't need to understand his sharp commands to know that he was ordering the stranger to turn back, away from the gates.

The stranger didn't move. He looked to Annika, instead, and the turn of his head offered a better impression of the features between his hat brim and gray wool scarf. He possessed a clean-shaven jaw, perhaps in the native style—or simply because a beard would never grow in evenly. Pale scars mottled the left side of his face, with several wide, ragged stripes running diagonally from his forehead to his cheek. Oh! And that was not a monocle at all, but some sort of optical contraption that had been embedded into his temple and shielded his left eye with a dark, reflective lens.

Utterly marvelous. What could he see through that?

"A noble was poisoned last week." He spoke clearly, the tones deep. She couldn't place his accent, but had no trouble understanding him. "Rumor is that the assassin was a Liberé woman carrying Lusitanian papers."

So she *had* been marked, not just by the colors of her dress, but also by the darkness of her skin. Truly, if Annika were the assassin, she wouldn't have announced it so boldly. With a sigh, she unfolded her documents and presented them to the guard.

"Norway," she said, and because the officer seemed reluctant to look away from the stranger long enough to verify her origin, Annika helpfully pointed to the proper line. "Born in Bergen."

His gaze darted to the papers. Apparently not the least bit concerned about an assassin now, he waved her on. For a moment, she stared at him in disbelief. He could have so easily disrupted—no, *destroyed*—her life, as if she were nothing. Now he set her free as if she were nothing. It did not engender grateful thoughts, yet she still managed a "*Gracias, señor.*"

It did not come out as genuinely as she intended, but he didn't seem to note the bitter anger lacing her reply—and Annika was not a fool to wait around long enough for him to recognize it. She turned and set a brisk pace, her heart still hammering. The stranger waited a long second, as if making certain that she wouldn't be further disturbed, before falling into step beside her, his hands clasped behind his back.

Since coming to the New World, she'd often been told that her manners were coarse, but Annika had never thought that the application of genuine gratitude could be found lacking.

"Thank you, sir. I can't express how much I appreciate your interference."

He nodded. She thought that would be the end of it, that now he would return to the two men waiting in front of a nearby inn, and who were obviously his companions. Dressed in the same style of wool overcoat that buckled asymmetrically across the chest, long trousers, and sturdy boots, the men watched them pass. The younger man seemed to make a remark; the older shook his head and laughed, his breath puffing in the cold air. Beside them, porters loaded crates onto a lorry. They must have been standing there when the port officer had shouted for her to stop, she realized. Her rescuer had heard her desperation and come to her aid.

She glanced up at the stranger again. He walked to the left of her, his eye contraption only visible as a glint of metal beyond the bridge of his aquiline nose. His hair was as black as hers, though without a hint of curl. The straight ends touched his shoulders, the forward strands drawn away from his face and contained by four steel beads tucked behind his ears.

Did he intend to accompany her all the way to *Phatéon*? Surely that wasn't necessary. "I believe I am out of danger now, if you wish to return to your people."

"My people?" His brow rose, and he glanced toward the men. "Ah. They'll manage well without me."

And she wouldn't? She ought not to say that, however, not after he'd rendered such an incredible service to her.

She ought not say it, and so of course she did. "But *I* can't manage without you?"

His sudden grin was nothing like his earlier smile, which had seemed a weary response to an old jest. This appeared to burst through him as if he knew laughter was the only reply he could give.

Annika had to smile in return, and then laugh when he asked, "I trust you were *not* hired to kill a Castilian noble?"

"Perhaps I was," she said. "If I were a clever assassin, I'd carry fraudulent papers that claim I was born in Norway, not Lusitania."

"Are they fraudulent, then?"

Yes. Not for the purpose of assassination, however, but for the purpose of mobility. This exchange had become unexpectedly fun, however, and so she played along. "Oh, of course."

"And what would your true origin be?"

A hidden village on Iceland's western shore. But even as a joke, she could not risk exposing her people, and chose the farthest location away from them. "A smuggler's haven in Australia."

That seemed to disappoint him. His grin had already faded to a pleasant, amused expression, but now she detected a hint of frustration in the tightness of his mouth and the intensity of his gaze. He was truly looking for an answer, Annika realized. This was not simply polite conversation to pass the time; he wanted to know where she was from.

Or was that just her imagination? She had guarded the truth of her origin for three years. Perhaps the constant vigilance made her suspect everyone of trying to discern it.

Annika couldn't be certain if her wariness stemmed from instinct or fancy, but when he didn't respond to that lie, she covered her unease with a dramatic sigh. "In truth," she said. "Australia would be far more exciting, but alas, Norway it was—and is where I am bound again."

"You're flying out immediately?"

Perhaps Annika imagined the sudden tension in his voice, but she couldn't mistake the way his gaze moved over her face, as if searching for the answer—or hoping for a specific reply. "The airship departs early tomorrow morning," she confirmed.

The stranger's lips tightened before resolve seemed to firm his expression. He nodded. "En route to Bergen?"

Eventually. *Phatéon* was scheduled to fly to the Norwegian port within a month, but it would not be a direct flight.

"Yes," she said, her unease deepening. Why did he ask so specifically? Perhaps he was only making small talk, but she wasn't comfortable with the direction he'd taken. Best to change the subject.

And if this truly *was* conversation, it was time that she held up her part and made intrusive inquiries of her own. "Will you also be departing soon? Or do you make a habit of waiting near port gates and running to a stranger's aid?"

"No. Typically, I'm running after erupting volcanoes."

"To study them?" Annika guessed. She couldn't think of any other reason to do such a thing—and only if it paid well. "That is your profession?"

When he nodded, she studied *him* more closely. What sort of person made a living from such a thing? She had witnessed an eruption in Iceland before, and would have said that only a reckless fool would go chasing after one. This man didn't appear foolish, however, and his manner seemed too contained to be reckless. Something else must be driving him to pursue such a dangerous occupation, something that he didn't readily show.

Asking him to reveal that reason, however, would require Annika to venture beyond the boundaries of *intrusive* and into *unforgivably rude*. Even she couldn't cross that line. She settled for, "I didn't realize volcanoes were so fast that one had to run after them."

His amusement returned. "I suppose it's more accurate that I'm often running *away* from them."

She arched her brows and glanced at his mechanical hand, still clasped behind his back. "Not always fast enough?"

"No, that was another sort of explosion." His gaze narrowed slightly. "You've spent time in England."

"In England? Well—Yes?" Confusion tripped her up. What an odd response. She *had* spent a little time in that country when *Phatéon*'s route took her there. But why would such a statement follow hers . . . *Oh*.

Fierce heat bloomed in her cheeks. Prosthetics and mechanical apparatuses were so common in England as to be unremarkable. But in the New World, such topics were handled with more delicacy, if not outright avoided. Her insensitive comment must have been distressing to him, though he hid it well. Perhaps that was an indication of his fine manners; he didn't point out her lack of them, though he had every reason to.

She had long come to terms with her failings, but Annika hated knowing that she might have hurt someone with them.

"I am so sorry. How horrid of me to make light of injuries that must have been extremely painful."

He shrugged. "And long ago."

Was he dismissing the topic, or her apology? He didn't seem distressed, but rather uninterested in discussing himself—and examining her features as if interested in *her*. Well, if he wanted to know what sort of woman she was, he was soon to learn that she had difficulty letting anything go without proper resolution.

"Whenever it happened, I am sorry for my words now," she said. "I'm often told that I don't possess any proper sensibilities, but that doesn't excuse—"

"Who tells you this?"

"Everyone," she said ruefully, and the stranger laughed before subjecting her to a considering look.

"If you're truly sorry," he said, "have supper with me tonight."

That was *not* an offer she expected to come from someone with manners. Not offended, but incredibly surprised, she shook her head. "Pardon? I believe I misheard."

"Share a meal with me at the inn," he said unmistakably, before softening his expression with a smile. "I wouldn't usually take advantage of a woman's obligation to me, but I have no choice. If you leave tomorrow, I'll have no other opportunity to enjoy your company, and I want to know you better."

The intensity of his gaze deepened as he spoke, as if the entirety of his being had focused on gaining her consent. Annika stared up at him, uncertain how to respond. She'd have liked to spend more time with him, too. She wanted to know why he chased volcanoes, and what had possessed him to come to her aid—and there was nothing that forbade her from sharing a meal with someone. But her instincts were ringing, and she couldn't ignore the alarm they raised. She had been propositioned before. She'd been flirted with before. This was . . . different. Though she couldn't have articulated why she felt the need to be wary, Annika was certain that this man wanted something from her—but not company, not courting, not even to share a bed.

"I'm sorry," she said, feeling very stiff. "The captain has

asked that we all return to the airship early, so that we're aboard before the storm hits."

He nodded, but she saw the clench of his jaw, the frustration that suddenly shadowed his expression. Annika continued her brisk pace. The stranger remained at her side, but as they crossed from the cobblestones onto the wooden docks, the rumble of lorry engines and the shouts of the stevedores made further conversation impossible. Annika walked in silence, her thoughts in tumult. Perhaps she'd been mistaken? Perhaps she was only wary because his offer had been so unexpected. Perhaps she had just insulted him again.

If so, there was nothing to be done now. It was with some relief that she reached *Phatéon*'s mooring station. The cargo lift had been raised against the side of the airship, but the ladder hung down to the docking boards.

She stopped and folded her umbrella before turning to the stranger, who had tilted his head back to look up at the airship. "Thank you again."

His gaze lowered. Though his smile had not returned, she thought he seemed pleased. Satisfied, perhaps. "You're traveling aboard *Phatéon*? I've heard that she is a fine ship."

"Yes." She caught the rope ladder, steadied it. "Very fine."

He nodded. "I will leave you, then. I wish you a safe journey, miss."

"I wish the same for you."

Politely, he touched his hat—and stood, waiting . . . for her to climb safely aboard, she realized, and felt silly of a sudden. All this way, he had only been helpful. It had been kind of him to stay with her until he'd made certain that she'd arrived at her destination unharmed. It had been kind of him to offer a meal.

Still, Annika sensed his gaze on her as she climbed the ladder—and could not shake the feeling that the stranger hadn't gotten what he wanted, and that he wasn't done with her. That she would see him again, that he would be waiting for her in Bergen . . . or somewhere else.

But perhaps that was only her imagination.